SKINNERS

BOOK 1

Blood Blade

MARCUS PELEGRIMAS

An Imprint of HarperCollins*Publishers*

EOS
An Imprint of HarperCollins*Publishers*
10 East 53rd Street
New York, New York 10022-5299

Copyright © 2009 by Marcus Pelegrimas
Teaser to *Howling Legion* copyright © 2009 by Marcus Pelegrimas
Cover art by Larry Rostant
ISBN 978-0-06-146305-1
www.eosbooks.com

First Eos paperback printing: February 2009

Printed in the U.S.A.

10 9 8 7 6 5 4 3 2

This one's for Megan, who kept me going.
For Mom & Bob, who always believed.
And for Cherry, who put me on the right track.

SKINNERS

Blood Blade

Prologue

A steely wind howled. Like a colony of orange-vested ants swarming a freshly stomped hill, workers navigated the mess behind the mansion. The old house sagged and was collapsing in places that were cordoned off by bright yellow tape and sheets of clear plastic. At the back of the mansion, floodlights illuminated a massive heap of rubble separated from the dilapidated structure by no more than twenty yards.

As night had fallen, the land beneath the workers' feet had grown hard and cold. Clouds filled the sky, smearing away whatever light might have been cast by the stars and the milky half-moon peering down upon the site. Scattered among different spots on the property, workers took measurements or huddled around small heaters that chugged next to portable generators connected to the mansion by thick cables. Beyond the reach of those lights, the workers farthest from the house walked on the fringes of shadow. One such worker stood motionless at the top of the heap, with one hand wrapped around a thin metal post and the other shoved deep into the pocket of his dirty coat.

The worker shifted from one foot to the other, doing his best to keep his balance on top of what was essentially a giant pile of dirt, bricks, and cracked wooden beams. Removing the hand from his coat pocket, he brought a walkie-talkie to his mouth and asked, "Did you hear that?"

A colleague near the western corner of the mansion pressed his eye against a small telescope mounted onto a tripod. When the walkie-talkie on his belt crackled to life, he lifted it to his ear and replied, "You say something, Brian?"

"Yeah," the worker on the pile replied. "I asked if you heard that."

"Heard what?"

"Some kind of rumbling."

The man at the telescope chuckled. "The owner of this place said he heard screams a few times. You didn't hear screams, did you?"

Picking up on the sarcasm coming through the radio, Brian said, "No. It was rumbling. Like . . . under my feet."

"Just hold still so I can get these measurements." Squinting through the telescope, he struggled to take advantage of the pathetic light and scribble his notations into a notebook strapped to his wrist.

"Can you even see me out here?" Brian asked.

"Barely, but I want to get this done so we can get the hell out of here. It's bad enough we've got to do a topographical study of an old pile of garbage, but the deadline they gave us is complete—"

The view through the man's telescope turned black, making him think his eyes had finally been strained past their limit. When the man looked up, he saw that someone had stepped directly in front of him to gaze out at the heap of rubble.

"Hey," the worker said from behind his tripod. "Are you supposed to be here?"

The figure blocking the telescope wore a black coat that hung well past his waist. It might have been leather, but it had a slicker, shinier quality, as if it had been dipped in oil. He was a tall, bald man with black marks on his neck that stretched all the way up the back of his head. Before the worker behind the tripod could get a better look at the meandering tattoo, the stranger turned around and stared intently at him.

"Scott?" Brian asked through the radio. "Who is that guy?"

Stepping out from behind his instrument, Scott replied, "I'm about to find out." He lowered the radio and raised his voice to the level that usually caused his subordinates to rethink whatever they'd been about to mess up. "What the hell are you doing out here? Don't you know this is private property?"

The tone wasn't working on the bald man. His eyes remained fixed and he whispered, "Stay," as if commanding an overanxious dog.

"What?" Scott grunted. "All right. Whatever you're doing, I don't got time for it."

Just then the ground rumbled and shook beneath Brian's feet. He tightened his grip upon the post he'd been holding for Scott to see but was unable to keep from falling as the heap beneath him caved in.

Unable to hear the rumbling, Scott couldn't miss the screams that followed.

The other ten workers, too busy to notice the man in the black jacket, now all looked to the heap where Brian had been. Those who hadn't seen him fall were drawn to his pained cries. Scott tried to rush past the stranger in the black jacket to see what had happened to his partner but was knocked off his feet by what felt like a cement post slamming against his chest.

The bald man stood with his arm effortlessly outstretched after hitting Scott, as if working a kink out of his shoulder. As the other workers hurried to the top of the heap, the stranger crouched over Scott's crumpled body and grabbed him by the hair. The surveyor wheezed and fought to refill his lungs as his head was yanked upward and pointed toward the heap. When he tried to pull away from the bald man's grasp, Scott was driven to the ground by an elbow that pounded directly between his shoulder blades. There was a sharp, burning pain at the small of his back, followed by something sharp that ripped away the side of Scott's neck.

"I told you to stay," the bald man hissed.

The screams from the collapsed heap became louder as more and more workers added their voices to the mix. Some of the workers disappeared as if swallowed up by the heap itself. Others ran panicked from the mound, wanting only to get away. Just . . . away.

Scott could hear long, controlled gasps coming from the man pinning him down. Fighting back proved to be useless. All he could do was watch helplessly as part of the heap rose up, stretched out, and swung at one of the fleeing workers.

Come.

Scott couldn't tell if the word was a statement or a question. He didn't know if it was meant for him or someone else. He couldn't even tell if he'd heard it or thought it.

The figure emerging from the heap was just a lump at first. It moved and swayed and flailed its arms, but it didn't seem able to lift its own head. As it kept moving, more of the dirt was shaken off. Once enough of it fell away, the rough outline of shoulders and arms could be seen. Long legs, thick with muscle, held the figure upright. Its arms were uneven, yet powerful enough to knock one worker off his feet and send another to the ground amid the crunch of breaking bone. And still its head swayed back and forth like a disconnected pendulum.

Some of the workers managed to get away from the thing, but they didn't make it far before the beast leapt up high enough to close the distance between them. It clipped one worker's head as it landed, and rolled for a few feet before scrambling back to its feet to slam a fist into another worker's chest and tear away a chunk of flesh.

"Get them all, Henry," the man in the black jacket whispered. *"Gather every last one."*

Scott knew he had to get away from there or end up like Brian and the others. He had to move and call for help, but the crazy bald asshole was pinning him down. As much as he wanted to run, as badly as he wanted to fight, his body would not comply. When he realized he couldn't feel his legs or arms, Scott knew he was done. The ground was warm and wet with blood that had come from his own veins, explaining the cold dizziness filling his mind.

The crazy man knelt beside him. Blood dripped from the man's mouth and coated his hands in a slick crimson paste. Every so often he glanced down at Scott, but most of his attention was fixed upon the filthy thing that recklessly jumped from one worker to another, snapping legs and clubbing heads with thick, flailing limbs.

"Leave some alive," the crazy man whispered.

Then Scott heard a groaning wail that was too powerful to have come from any of the workers. The sound aspired to be human, but fell noticeably short of the mark. As the cry drifted through the air, the monstrous shape near the heap of rubble turned toward Scott and rocked back and forth. Despite his condition, Scott could still see that figure standing there, looking back at him. It held onto Brian's face with one gnarled hand, leaving the rest of the worker's body to dangle limply like a broken doll. The thing was almost twice as big as Brian, but cowered as if afraid of something.

"I know you're hungry," the bald man whispered. *"Gather them up and then you can feed."*

"Wh-Why . . . ?" Scott moaned.

The bald man quickly glanced down, as if he'd forgotten Scott was there. Scowling in a way that revealed the bloody fangs extending over his human teeth, he grabbed a handful of Scott's hair, lifted his head off the ground and then slammed it upon a partially buried rock.

As Scott drifted away, he heard the bald man softly whisper, *"Of course you know me, Henry. I am God, and I have come to show you the new world."*

Chapter 1

"What the hell is that thing supposed to be?"

Cole Warnecki squinted and leaned forward as he tried to come up with words to describe what he was seeing on the monitor. Drawing a complete blank, he shook his head and replied, "I don't know. Some sort of monster?"

The man next to Cole didn't take his eyes from the thing that had caught his attention. He shook his head, but not in the vaguely bewildered way that Cole had a second ago. "A monster or maybe some kind of alien?"

Cole snapped his fingers. "A demon! That's what it is."

"What kind of demon?"

"The kind that . . . wait a second . . . maybe it's some sort of guardian spirit."

Jason Sorrenson shifted his eyes away from the thirty-two-inch screen, swiveled in his chair so he could face Cole, then reached for a pair of glasses. He slid the dated wire frames into the grooves they'd worn over both ears and onto the bridge of his nose before asking, "Isn't this your game, Cole? Shouldn't you know exactly what every one of these things are?"

Cole kept looking at the monitor and the image frozen on it. In his hands he held a controller that was connected to a black video-game console on a table beside Jason's desk. Finally, Cole set the controller down and pressed his fingertips against his closed eyes. "Shit, you're right. You know how crazy things get when we're this close to going gold."

"Going gold? We're barely through play testing and you think we're ready to start manufacturing disks?"

Letting out a breath, Cole flinched as if someone had just blown pepper up his nose. "A Cerberus! That's what it is!"

"What?"

"You know, like one of those demon dogs from Greek mythology. But it's different than those other ones that showed up in—"

"Save it, Cole." Jason was in his mid-forties, but carried himself as if he had sixty years of grief on his back. Leaning back, he sunk into the expensive padding of his chair, clasped his hands behind his balding head and stared at Cole through the dated wire frame glasses. His office matched the chair in comfort and had enough windows to fill it with whatever light the gray Seattle skies could offer. In comparison, the rest of the offices in the building seemed like dungeons. Outside, a stiff breeze blew in from Puget Sound; all the bare branches in the nearby park swayed in a slow rhythm. Winter hadn't arrived quite yet, but the city looked plenty cold already. "What's going on with you lately?" Jason asked with more concern than might be expected from someone so high on the corporate ladder.

Cole was about ten years younger than his boss, but he let out a sigh as if he was the older of the two. Working his way through the ranks of Digital Dreamers Inc. had been a labor of love, but times like this didn't feel so romantic. "I don't know," he said before his pause became uncomfortable.

"Do you want to abandon *Hammer Strike*?"

Glancing back to the monitor, Cole looked at the pause screen displaying the game's title and options. "I've been working on *Hammer* for over two years. Giving it up now would just be . . ."

"Lazy?"

"I was going to say stupid, but I guess both are pretty close."

Jason got up and sat on the edge of his marble desktop. "I'd hate to lose you, Cole," he said while picking up his own controller and hitting a button to put the game back into motion. "You're anything but lazy, but you do seem sort of distracted."

"That's putting it nicely. It feels more like I've had my head jammed up my ass."

Chuckling under his breath like a preteen boy too nervous to follow up his friend's swearing with a bad word of his own, Jason let his fingers drift effortlessly over the game controller. He moved his muscle-bound, onscreen avatar to one of the Cerberus-type creatures and used the titular hammer to pound it into a mess of pixilated gore.

Cole pinched his chin between a thumb and forefinger while watching Jason maneuver through the game. "Do that combo I showed you."

"The killing move?"

•"Yeah."

Jason's fingers flew through the prescribed set of motions, causing the digitized character to perform a jerky dance. "It's not working," he said while shaking his head.

Cole took the controller from Jason's hands and went through the same motions, only a bit faster. After a few more attempts, he bounced the controller off the floor and turned his back to the screen. "God dammit!"

"Maybe you need to take a vacation. You know . . . relax a little?"

"I can't take a vacation this close to the release date."

"So we'll push the date back. It wouldn't be the first time."

Letting out a breath, Cole straightened up and turned around to face his boss again. He knew he might not have been in the best shape of his life, but with his natural athleticism, he held up better than most guys his age. Considering how much time he spent in front of a computer screen, his lack of a gut was even more impressive. He chuckled at his own expense and dropped back into his chair. "I don't think a vacation is what I need, Jason."

"I'm not letting you quit." Lighting up like the power

button on his game console, Jason said, "I know! What about Nora?"

"I haven't seen her for a while."

"She works one door away from the programmers' lounge. You must see her every day."

"I mean I haven't seen her . . . like that. Not for a while."

Jason nodded slowly. "Why not?"

"Not just a boss, but a relationship counselor too? I think you should prescribe me some painkillers. You know, the good ones that put you to sleep for a while?"

"I just thought it would do you some good to get your mind off of work, and Nora seems a lot more qualified than me to do that trick."

Cole laughed and scooped the controller up from the floor. He only meant to test that it wasn't broken, but quickly found himself entering back into the digital fray. "Maybe I will give her another call. She's nice."

"And fine as hell."

"Don't let H.R. hear you say that, but yeah, she's hot."

"All right, then. Take a week off. Rest up and then come back to work so you can tell me about what Nora wore on your date. Feel free to be as graphic as you'd like." Looking around as if he truly feared an H.R. bug on the wall, Jason added, "But that's just a friend talking."

Cole knew it was true, that Jason was speaking as more than just a boss trying to put an employee at ease. Jason had always been a good friend. In fact, he was the sort of guy who couldn't be a prick if his life depended on it. That was a great quality for a person, but not for the head of a growing company. Fortunately, Digital Dreamers had more than enough professional pricks to make up for Jason's good nature.

"Since I'm being forced away from here," Cole said, "maybe I could do more than just sit around my apartment and try to get my hands under Nora's blouse."

"What more do you need? What more would anyone need?"

"I don't know."

"Sure you do," Jason replied as he picked up a controller for himself. "Otherwise you wouldn't have said anything."

"Maybe I can get away and do something exciting. After putting together so many games, I've been thinking I could do an even better job if I had something real to draw from."

Jason glanced at Cole just long enough for his character to get blindsided by a hulking swordsman wearing glowing armor. "You mean something more than those trips to the firing range or those ninja classes? Were those even real, or just semiclever ways to get some research money?"

"I still go to the firing range," Cole replied, "and those classes were real." After inputting a specific sequence of button presses, his avatar reached over his shoulder and drew a new, impossibly big, weapon from an undersized holster. The weapon was a spear with a grip that wrapped around both of the warrior's fists. The upper end narrowed into a gleaming point, while the lower end forked open, which came in handy to block an incoming blow from one of the game's demons. "I just put that weapon in. Pretty cool, huh?"

Jason didn't reply. He was too busy glaring intently at Cole.

Finally, Cole buckled. "All right. I went to two of those ninja classes before I quit. Too much jumping. I only paid for a month of lessons anyway."

"Consider it my contribution for this vacation you need so badly. Although I don't think you'll find a getaway advertised anywhere that'd put you close to the sorts of things you put in your games."

"Not even on the Internet?"

Without taking his eyes from the screen, Jason shook his head. "Not even on the Internet."

"What about one of those extreme vacations?"

"Jesus, Cole. Didn't they stop doing that kind of crap ten years ago? If you want to snowboard, just do it."

"Not snowboarding. Something better than that. Like a hunting trip."

"Hunting? When have you ever hunted?"

"Never."

"Then what made you think of it?"

Cole paused so he could skewer the last enemy on the screen with a flourishing combination. He then walked his character over to Jason's guy and stabbed him in the gut.

"You're fired," Jason replied in a monotone. "Clean out your desk."

Ignoring his boss, Cole said, "I got an e-mail a while ago about some kind of hunting trip in Canada. It'd be pushing it, but I should be able to get a seat on that plane before they're all booked up. Firing some rifles and crawling around outside would be great research for when I start in on *Sniper Ranger 4* next month."

Jason shook his head and let out a breath. "Seems more like a lame attempt to get Digital Dreamers to pay for your vacation."

"Was it that lame?"

"Yeah."

"Whatever. That hunting trip in Canada is short a man. It's so cheap it's almost free, and I've even got my own gun."

That caught Jason's attention. "Should I be worried by that?"

Cole did his best to scowl, but didn't need a mirror to know he wasn't pulling it off. Aborting his attempt at intimidation, he said, "My dad took me out a few times and left a rifle at my place last winter. I don't know what kind it is, but it should be all right for hunting."

"You really don't know how to hunt, do you?"

"Sort of. Well . . ."

Chuckling even harder, Jason set down his controller and leaned back into his chair. "Personally, I just wish I could be there to see you on a trip with a bunch of gun freaks."

"Hunters, Jason. They're hunters."

"It sounds like a good deal. Just promise me to take plenty of pictures and some video when you shoot yourself in the foot. I want to post it on our website."

Rather than try to stick up for himself, Cole said, "The plane leaves the day after tomorrow."

"Isn't that short notice?"

"That's why the tickets are so cheap, moron."

Rather than trade any more insults with Cole, Jason said, "Take your vacation. Since you decided to pick up and leave this close to deadline, you get to apologize to all the websites and gaming magazines for the delays."

Cole got up and tossed his controller onto the chair he'd just vacated. "Or I could refrain from telling H.R. about how much you admire Nora's—"

"Go!"

Cole's apartment was on the fourth floor of a beige, stucco building on Yale Avenue. He didn't think it was quite worth as much as he paid to live there, but the owners were doing their best to give the place a better image. Mostly, that consisted of spending money to print newsletters convincing tenants that the chipped paint was stylish, rather than just repainting the damn walls.

The apartment had acquired an even more rumpled appearance once he put his own things into it. A new couch and recliner sat amid a coffee table and lamps that had been with him since high school. His bed was fairly new, but the dining room table and chairs had come along with him after he moved out of his parents' home in Yakima. Of course, like anyone else in his line of work, the television and entertainment center were top of the line and got upgraded whenever he received a bonus, or simply couldn't control himself while walking through one of the many electronics stores he frequented.

For the most part, Cole could relax in his apartment. At the moment, however, the main thing on his mind was getting out from within those walls, even if he had to scrape and claw to do so.

"This is a nice place, Cole," Nora said as she wandered through the one-bedroom dwelling. "Kind of a mess, though." She was a nice person and a good friend. Any man with functioning senses would readily admit that she was appealing to every last one of them. Her voice was soft. Her hair and skin were smooth. Her touch was gentle. Her curves were nicely proportioned. She even liked to play video games, which was a bonus if not absolutely necessary. All in all, Nora should have been everything he was looking for in a woman. The real mystery was why having her in his apartment made him want to bolt for the street.

Cole looked up from the bag he was packing just long enough to glance around. The apartment wasn't in the best shape, but it had sure looked worse. "Messy? What do you mean?"

But Nora wasn't biting. She lowered her chin and looked at him over the top of her glasses in a way that had made nearly every man in the Digital Dreamers offices melt at one time or another. "Where should I start?" she asked. "How about the fact that you invited me over just so I could watch you throw clothes into that old duffel bag?" Suddenly, her eyes widened and she clapped her hands together. "Are we going somewhere for the weekend?"

"Actually, I'm the one that's going away. Just me."

The disappointment in her eyes wasn't obvious, but it was there for anyone looking closely enough to see it. "Oh."

"I asked you over as a way to . . . wrap things up."

"Oh," she said in a more somber tone.

Cole tossed the last pair of socks into his bag and walked over to her. Nora was almost as tall as him, which put her well above an average woman's height. Straight, dark blond hair hung past her shoulders, and perfectly even bangs made a straight line over her eyes. Her glasses had quirky plastic frames and lenses that were too thick to be mistaken for a fashionable attempt to look smarter. She always wore skirts to accentuate her shapely legs, but never wore tight blouses or sweaters.

The moment Cole stepped up to her, he could feel Nora moving closer to him. He placed his hands on her hips, and in response she reached up and slipped her hands around the back of his neck.

Doing his best to ignore the instincts raging inside of him, Cole said, "Maybe it's not such a good idea for you to be here."

"Why?"

"Because I don't want to give you the wrong impression."

Her muscles tensed and the softness in her expression faded a bit. "Does this mean you're breaking up with me?"

"Come on, Nora. We really haven't been together for long."

"I know," she said while letting out a breath and taking a step back. "It's just that I was afraid this might happen from the first moment I thought about approaching you."

"You were going to approach me?"

She nodded with a hint of embarrassment. "I hung back because we work together and that can always get weird. But, we don't really get out and meet people anywhere else. At least, I don't."

"I don't either," Cole quickly added.

"Then why break up?"

"Because I'm going on this trip to clear my head. The way things have been going, I'd like to wipe everything away and start over."

"Reboot the ol' system, huh?"

It was just that sort of geek-talk that had captured his heart. That, and how good she looked in her short skirts and button-down blouses while playing the newest build of *Zombie House 6*.

"You could put it that way," Cole said. "I didn't think it would be fair for me to string you along, take off to reboot and then expect you to wait for me like some dutiful wife from an old war movie."

Nora smiled and closed some of the distance she'd created with the backward step she'd taken. "One, you're not going to war. And two, there isn't a man alive who could turn me into a stereotype. Most guys would catch hell just for lump-ing me into that category, and technically, I should hurt you for including me with everything else that's just supposed to be wiped away."

"Sorry about that. I just—"

"You just talk a few steps ahead of your brain, Cole. I know that. You're also not most men." She pressed herself against him and whispered into his ear, "I think it's cute that you brought me over here to get one more bit of lovin' before you take off on your manly Canadian guy-fest." Smirking at the bit of surprise she saw in his face, Nora added, "But you're right. We're not hitched, and there'll be time to see where we stand when you get back. For now, why don't I send you off in style, soldier?"

Cole nodded and kissed her. Nora's lips tasted like strawberries, and the skin under her sweater was even smoother than it looked.

Chapter 2

Two days later
1,000 feet over Kunaklini Glacier
British Columbia

The twin engine prop plane rattled around Cole's body as another wave of turbulence struck it like an invisible boot. High winds blew in from Silverthrone Mountain, raking along the desolate, snow-covered expanse to beat against the aircraft's hull like a set of iron claws. The sounds echoed within the metal tube, which only had exposed bolts and rusted brackets where seats should have been. Fortunately, he was wrapped up in enough thick layers of wool, down, and other winter gear that he could barely feel the jagged points sticking up from the floor.

Although blue skies could be seen through the frosted, oval porthole windows, it was difficult to say where the plane was in relation to the ground. The barren fields of ragged white could just as easily have been fifty or fifteen hundred feet below. Cole winced and quickly rubbed his hands together; playing off his reaction as if it had been caused by the cold, and not to the ever-present fear of plummeting to his death.

He looked toward the front of the plane, expecting to find the pilot fighting with the controls. The skinny man behind the wheel seemed more concerned with adjusting his headphones, which didn't make Cole feel any better about his prospects for surviving the trip. The other five passengers didn't have much else to offer him either. At the back of the plane were a pair of young guys from UCLA who'd spent the choppiest sections of the flight going through the motions of convincing each other they'd been through a lot worse. While they might have been fooling each other, they were obviously petrified, and that made Cole feel better. Misery might love company, but it sure as hell didn't love being the biggest loser in the pack.

Just then a voice fought to be heard above the roar of the propellers. "Hey, man. You all right?"

"I'm just freaking great," Cole screamed to the guy directly across from him. "How about you?"

"Not too bad. You fly much?" Like Cole, he was sitting on a rough patch of steel floor where a seat had once been.

"Sure I do, but this is more like being inside a tin can with wings." The plane trembled then, causing every screw in the fuselage to cry for mercy. Cole gritted his teeth, forced a smile and added, "This thing does still have wings, doesn't it?"

The other man looked through a plate-sized window and nodded. "We're still good. My name's Brad, by the way." He was a skinny guy with sunken features and wire-rimmed glasses held in place by an elastic strap looping around the back of his head. Thick, curly, dark brown hair poked out from a dark blue stocking cap. His smile wasn't affected by the turbulence or anything else around him, and it never seemed forced.

Cole extended a hand wrapped up in an old pair of skiing gloves. "I'm Cole."

After peeling off his own glove, Brad shook his hand. There was strength in Brad's grip, which was more than a little surprising, considering it came from a man who seemed to be outweighed by the winter gear he wore. Cole couldn't help but notice the fresh scars on the palms of Brad's hands. "What're you doing out here, Cole?"

"I signed up for one of those extreme vacations."

Cole's voice carried farther than he'd thought because those last two words elicited a round of shouts and fist pumps from the college kids at the back of the plane.

Brad nodded to the frat boys and then rolled his eyes to Cole. "Please tell me you're not with them."

"I might be. Actually, they're probably why my tickets were so cheap. What happened to your hands?"

Twisting his hand so he could look at his palm, Brad glanced at the scars for an instant before pulling on his glove. "Burned it while fixing my motorcycle."

The college kids were either motorcycle owners themselves or just generally enthusiastic, because they let out another round of noise.

Brad ignored the hollers from the back of the plane, lowered his voice and said, "Look at it this way, Cole. Those jocks back there will probably wind up passed out in a snowbank twenty minutes after we land."

"They'll probably wind up dead," grumbled an older man sitting next to Brad.

Cole had noticed the grizzled man before but had almost forgotten about him. He wore less gear than Brad, but his clothing and equipment had obviously seen far more use. The lining in his jacket was shredded, and his black stocking cap was frayed all the way around its edge. His gloves looked as though they'd been stitched together from pieces of an old catcher's mitt, and his feet were covered by thick, well-worn moccasins.

"Don't mind him," Brad said. "He's not one for the silver lining."

Cole extended his hand to the older man anyway. "Cole Warnecki."

The older man looked at Cole's hand as if he thought it might be diseased. Eventually, he looked into Cole's eyes and shifted his jaw back and forth beneath a thick layer of silver whiskers. "Gerald Keeler," he said while shaking Cole's hand.

Where Brad's grip had been surprisingly strong, Gerald's was just strong enough. In fact, the muscles in his arm and hand barely even tensed, making the old man seem like a bow that had only been halfway drawn.

"I know why he's here," Gerald said while hooking a thumb toward the large man who sat closest to the pilot and hadn't said a word since Cole boarded the plane at Anchorage. "What about you?"

"Extreme vacation," Brad said.

More whoops from the back.

Cole nodded and put his back to the cheering section.

After sizing him up, Gerald shrugged and looked away. He didn't seem to believe what he'd heard, but he wasn't interested enough to dispute it. Crossing his arms over his folded knees, Gerald rested his forehead on them. Snores rumbled from the older man moments later.

The plane shook again. This time the motors sputtered and the sensation of dropping through empty air swept through Cole's stomach like bad Mexican food on its return trip toward the top of his throat. Despite the fact that it was already close to freezing inside the plane, a cold sweat broke out beneath his gear.

"That's normal," Brad said in response to the question Cole didn't need to ask. "We're almost there."

"Whether we land or crash, I'll just be glad to get the hell off this thing."

"Try closing your eyes for a few minutes and picture something else. That helped me the first few times I flew in a crate like this."

Cole's first instinct was to picture the most recent night he'd spent with Nora. That didn't do him any good. Just the thought of being undressed made the cold seep that much deeper beneath his skin. A few seconds later he latched onto something that brought a faint smile to his face.

"What'd you come up with?" Brad asked. "Hawaii?"

"No."

"A warm fire?"

"You know how, when someone travels in the movies, they show a red line going from one dot to another dot on a map?"

"Yeah."

"That's all I got. At least there's no turbulence on that line."

Brad laughed and looked through the closest window. The portals were set at the height someone's eyes would be if their backside were in a seat. In his current situation, however, Brad had to raise himself up and then try to find a spot where the glass wasn't too cracked or iced over.

As the plane's nose tilted toward the ground, the frat boys at the back of the cabin put on their best tough-guy faces.

The quiet man behind the pilot's seat stared, his eyes burning holes through the fuselage.

Gerald kept snoring.

The red line in Cole's head lost its appeal before too long, so he went back to his first thought. Mainly, he kept replaying the moment when Nora let her hair hang freely over her shoulders like she was posing for a photo shoot. Even after she'd stripped down that night, she left her glasses on. Cole didn't know why she did that or why he'd gotten such a kick out of it, but it was one hell of a memory to ponder while trying not to think about the plane going down.

When the plane made its final approach, Cole didn't open his eyes. He didn't even glance out a window as the airborne bucket rose and dropped a few more times amid the constant groaning of the frame and wings. He couldn't help wondering what it would feel like if the plane cracked open and dumped him onto the rocky, snow-covered ground below.

Finally, the wheels hit the landing strip, slamming him roughly against the steel beneath him. Before the plane could roll to a complete stop, the squat pilot waddled from the cockpit and scratched beneath the three grimy flannel layers covering his belly. He kicked open the door and then climbed out as if he was late for an appointment to crash another plane. Youthful enthusiasm brought the frat boys out next, and survival instinct forced Cole to follow.

Outside, it was cold enough to freeze the snot in his nose, but the crunch of actual earth beneath his feet brightened his spirits. After that, a waving attendant wrapped in a parka, along with a few well-placed signs, directed him to a bench where he sat with his duffel bag.

Cole steadied his breathing while staring at a rectangle of bright yellow paint marking the pavement in front of him. Beyond that, there wasn't much. The airport had one landing strip and a pair of large shacks to one side. He thought he could see a road leading away from the smaller of the two shacks, but his eyeballs seemed to be freezing within his sockets and preventing him from studying anything too closely. All the other passengers were huddled nearby, some of whom looked out into the white nothingness at distant spots of more white. Cole tried to see what they were seeing but only got an ache behind his temples for his trouble.

The frat boys were loaded up with equipment that still smelled like the inside of a sporting goods store. Brad and Gerald carried bags that appeared to have been trampled by every form of transportation known to man. The quiet guy was last. He had the most stuff to haul, and wouldn't allow anyone else touch it.

Still feeling the joy of being alive, Cole tapped Gerald's shoulder and asked, "What's that guy's story?"

Gerald looked over to the quiet man and then back to Cole before shrugging. "How should I know?"

"You said you knew why he was here."

"Hunting trip."

"Oh. Did you talk to him?"

Gerald shook his head and fixed his eyes upon some of the quiet man's gear.

Following the older man's line of sight, Cole spotted the rifle stocks protruding from a black vinyl bag held shut by zippers and metal clamps. "Probably after moose or a polar bear or something like that, huh?"

"Sure after more than what you could drop with that popgun you're packing," Gerald replied.

Cole looked down at the rifle he'd packed and couldn't help but feel more than a little inadequate.

Brad sipped from a flask he'd been carrying inside his jacket. Stepping up to Cole, he offered him the flask and said, "We're a little too far south for polar bear. Are you sure you're ready to be out here?"

"I'm not ready for it at all," Cole said as he gratefully took the flask. Despite being completely unprepared for the harsh mix of whiskey and gasoline that Brad was drinking, he did his best to hold onto his last dignity and kept the liquor down. "That's why there's a perfectly qualified guide that's supposed to be meeting me," he croaked.

"Good. At least that way you should have a better than average chance of making it out of here alive."

"Slightly better than average," Gerald chuckled, before taking the flask from Brad's hand.

"What brings you out here, Brad?" Cole asked. "I'm guessing you're too smart to sign up for the same trip as me and the party boys over there."

"He brought me out here," Brad replied while nodding toward Gerald. "We're meeting a friend who owns a cabin a ways out from here."

Cole spotted a truck rolling toward the spot that had been cleared in front of the bench. Recognizing the name on the side of the canvas canopy as the one from his tickets, he stood up. "Maybe we'll cross paths again," he said to Brad and Gerald. "This is my ride."

"Take a look around," Gerald said. "It's all of our rides."

When he glanced from side to side, Cole saw everybody from the plane standing up and looking at the approaching truck. Sure enough, there were more than half a dozen emblems painted onto it, ranging from hotel logos to the gleaming "extreme" maple leaf on top of Cole's ticket. The quiet man flipped up his jacket collar and heaved the largest of his bags over one shoulder. The frat boys nodded like toys stuck to a dashboard and slapped each other's hands, which caused the ends of their jester style stocking caps to dance against their necks.

Before the truck came to a stop, the passenger door swung open and a burly man with a thick beard looked out and said, "Looks like all of ya are here. My name's Sam and this is my chariot. Hop on in the back."

Cole waited for the others to load their gear into the truck before climbing up after them. By now he barely even felt the weight of his duffel bag as he lugged it behind him. On the other hand, he couldn't feel his toes either.

"Are you sure I'm in the right place?" he asked as he dug his ticket from inside his jacket and held it out for Sam to see.

Sam nodded without giving more than a passing glance. "Yep. This is the place."

"I thought this was a bigger group."

"The four of you will be meeting up with the rest of the group about sixty or seventy miles from here. From there, you'll all head out together."

"The four of us?" Cole asked as two possibilities drifted through his mind.

"Yeah. Them other two with the funny hats and that guy with all the firepower are headed for the same place. All of us need to make it to Yorktown Lodge, and it gets real hard to find our way in the dark, so let's not burn any more daylight."

Cole looked into the cab of the truck and took a quick inventory of all the radios, transponders, and GPS trackers bolted on or beneath the dashboard. "Isn't that what all that's for?"

Having burned through all of his friendliness, Sam snapped, "Just get in, all right? This ain't exactly LAX, and there ain't a row of cabs lined up to take you to the spa. This is a little airport that's about to close. You're all headed to the same camp, and we're not going to let you get lost. If you want to go home, run back into that building over there before the owner of this airport heads out for his dinner."

For a moment Cole considered following Sam's advice. When he looked back at the airport, he was quickly reminded that it wasn't much more than a four-room shack. The plane that had brought him this far was rolling to the opposite end of the runway and gunning its engines amid a geyser of smoke and a roar that was nearly lost in the cold wind that whipped over the flat stretch of land.

Thankfully, his stomach was no longer churning and the fresh air was doing him more good than the strongest brew from the coffee shop across the street from his office. Leaning forward, he asked, "Could I at least get you to dump those schoolboys into a snowdrift somewhere along the way?"

Sam grinned and patted him on the shoulder as he climbed back into his seat. "I'll see what I can do, buddy."

By the time Cole walked around to the back of the truck, Brad was jumping down to greet him.

"I thought you'd gotten lost," Brad said. "You need some help with that bag?"

"Nah, it's all right. I've carried it this far, so I can carry it into a truck."

"Actually, you'll need to carry it up to the top of the truck. The Great White Hunter's taken up almost every bit of space inside."

Cole squinted through the glare of the snow on the ground and tried to make out the shapes huddled in the darkness beneath the truck's tarp. He could see the quiet man sitting with his back against the farthest end of the cab, his bags gathered around him like a fort. The frat boys didn't seem to mind sitting in each other's laps, and Gerald had staked out a spot for himself. That left just enough room for Brad and himself. Unless he wanted to balance his duffel bag on top of his head, Cole knew it had to go somewhere else besides the back.

"God damn it," he muttered.

Brad let out a sympathetic laugh. "Come on. I'll climb up and you can hand it to me."

"Don't bother. I can haul myself up." But before Cole was even finished saying that, Brad had already taken hold of the tarp's frame and pulled himself onto the steel arch.

Cole's duffel bag was quickly brought up and strapped onto the truck using a length of rope provided by Sam. He then barely managed to wedge himself in between Brad and the cold, rusty tailgate before the truck lurched forward.

Once the exhaust thinned out a bit, Cole was treated to a view that constantly shifted between brilliantly clear skies to rolling plains of snow. Scents from the truck mingled with the crisp taste of uncivilized air. He had smelled trees and seen snow plenty of times before, but this was something else. To compare this to the stuff back home would have been like comparing Mom's homemade cookies to the sweetened disks that came along with a fast food value meal.

For the first few hours of the drive, there was nothing but miles of flat, white ground in all directions. As the sun worked its way across the sky, the truck rumbled past trees and frozen lakes. Cole even glimpsed mountains here and there. He wasn't sure which mountains they were or if they were just big hills that he'd mistaken for mountains, but that didn't make them any less breathtaking. He spotted a few animals running freely along the side of the road. One of them was some sort of bear, loping through the snow faster than a creature its size had any right to go.

The frat boys never stopped talking.

The quiet man stayed quiet.

Brad and Gerald swapped a few words now and then, but Cole couldn't take his eyes from the view.

The longer he gazed outside, the more he wanted to see. Before he could give his eyes a rest, the sun dipped beneath the horizon and the breath was taken from his lungs all over again. Brilliant hues of orange and red became even crisper after being reflected off the pristine snow. Another bear sat a ways from the road, watching the truck pass with mild interest. Only after the shadows overpowered the light did Cole shift his focus back to the inside of the truck.

There was no change in the quiet man, but the frat boys had finally shut the hell up. Cole couldn't have asked for anything more.

"We should be there before too much longer," Brad said. "How'd you sleep?"

"I didn't," Cole replied.

"You haven't moved for hours."

"I know. It's been great."

"For Christ's sake, leave him be," Gerald grumbled. "You talk any more and you'll wake up them two little shits with the stupid hats."

Chapter 3

"We're here," Sam said cheerily. "Get your stuff and head for the lodge."

When he lifted his head, every muscle in Cole's neck creaked like a bunch of gears that were trying to turn after being frozen in place. He, along with the rest of the men, jumped out and made their way outside amid a cavalcade of grunts and groans. The night was darker than anything he had ever seen. Even though the stars glittered overhead like diamonds on a jeweler's cloth, that wasn't nearly enough to put a dent in the inky blackness that had settled over the world. When he looked up, Cole thought he could see into eternity. When he looked back down, he could barely see the duffel bag that had been tossed to the ground near his feet.

"There'll be food in the lodge," Sam said.

Cole looked to where some of the others were headed and saw a large shack with smoke drifting up from the roof.

"That's the lodge?" he asked.

"Yeah," Brad said as he walked by. "Cozy, isn't it?"

"Not exactly how I would describe it."

Gerald was the next to walk by. He carried one pack

over his shoulder and used a worn stick to keep his footing. "There's food in there," he said. "I can smell it."

The quiet man was last. He didn't seem to mind the cold as he lugged his bags slowly through the snow while looking carefully in every direction. When his eyes settled upon Cole, he stared him down until Cole looked away. Only then did the quiet man resume his shuffling journey toward the lodge.

"Jesus," Cole muttered to himself. "This'll teach me to buy a vacation without a real travel agent to yell at once I get back."

The lodge turned out to be much better on the inside. A large fireplace took up a huge section of the wall opposite the front door. That way, the breeze from the door fanned its flames while providing immediate comfort from the cold. There was also a kitchen supplying food to three large tables set up in the main room. Seated at one of the tables was a woman with shoulder-length blond hair and a thick sweater that hugged her figure like a second skin. Another man stood next to the coatrack, bundling himself up before heading back into the cold. The two of them glanced at the front door and halfheartedly waved at the new arrivals.

"Beds are in there," Sam said to everyone who walked into the lodge. He pointed to the only other room, which was to the right of the entrance.

Having served time in summer camp in his youth, Cole instinctively went into the other room to stake his claim on one of the beds. There were only six to choose from, and the frat boys had already picked theirs out. Cole dropped his duffel onto the bed at the opposite end of the room from the younger men and headed back toward the smell of food.

Brad made himself comfortable at the blonde's table. Her legs were curled up beneath her, so she leaned one elbow on the table and used her free hand to play with some of the curls dangling from under Brad's cap.

The cook was a burly man with a bald head and full beard. At the moment, he was setting up a row of wooden bowls in front of him. After the neat row was completed, he used a dented ladle to fill them. The smell drifting through the air told Cole that whatever was in those bowls was hot and tasty.

The quiet guy headed for the other room and stayed there.

"Come and get it while it's hot," the cook said.

Cole didn't have to be asked twice, so he walked over to claim a bowl for himself. "What is it?" he asked.

The burly man replied, "Just beef and potato stew. It's from my ma's recipe, so if you got complaints, keep 'em to yerself."

After taking a bite, Cole looked up and replied, "No complaints here. I just hope there's more."

The cook slapped Cole on the shoulder and walked back to the stove. "I got enough to feed a pack of wild animals in here."

Cole went to a table and didn't look up until he'd devoured half of his second helping. When he glanced around, he saw everyone scattered among the tables eating their meals. Naturally, the bros with the funny hats settled in at his table to regale him with stories of how many different ways they could drain a bottle and then fall down afterward. Looking around for a beam to hang himself, Cole realized that not everyone from the truck was there after all. Brad was still making good time with the blonde, but Gerald was nowhere to be seen. Cole pushed away from the table before his new buddies could start in on tales from spring break. After dropping his bowl off at the kitchen, he stepped out through the front door.

Gerald was outside, sitting beside an oil drum that contained a crackling fire. His hood was pulled up and cinched tightly around his face to protect him from a cold wind that cut like sharpened steel. In defiance of the fierce elements, Gerald remained focused upon a task that monopolized every bit of his attention. No matter how hard the wind howled, the older man kept his hands moving and his head low.

As far as Cole could tell, he was carving something into his walking stick. It had to be the same walking stick that Gerald had before, but Cole only now noticed the groves worn into the wood. Flickering light from the fire played across the intricate carvings along the thinnest section of the staff.

"It's a lot warmer inside," Cole said.

Gerald didn't look up, but he did nod.

Cole took a few steps closer until he was able to reach out and warm his hands by the fire. "This fresh air is doing wonders for my sinuses. I'm from Seattle, so it practically takes a miracle to clear out the smell of coffee grounds from my clothes." Laughing reflexively at his own joke, he noticed that his was the only voice drifting through the air. "That one usually goes over a little better."

"Not with someone who was born in Seattle, I bet," Gerald said sternly.

"Oh. Were you born there?"

Gerald kept his eyes fixed firmly upon the small knife in his hands as he smirked and replied, "Nah. Just keeping you on your toes."

"Heh. Good one."

Gerald ran coarse fingertips along the wooden staff that lay across his lap. Despite the beefiness of his fingers, he handled the jackknife the way a surgeon used a scalpel. While rolling the staff along the upper portion of his knees, he carved into the wooden surface in a constant flow of motion. Considering how thin the wood was on top and how hard he was working, it was a wonder to Cole that he didn't slice the staff into bits.

After a few seconds of working quietly, Gerald asked, "You saw it, didn't you?"

Cole kept his arms stretched toward the fire and looked around. "Saw what?" he asked.

"During the ride on the truck. You saw that thing that was following us."

"I did?"

Gerald nodded and flipped the staff around so the clean end was closer to his jackknife. Probably because of the flickering firelight, that end now looked thinner than the one with all the carvings. "I saw you watching it. You were probably wondering how a thing that big could move so damn fast."

Just as he was getting uncomfortable with the conversation, Cole made a connection in his head. "Oh! You mean those bears?"

Gerald nodded.

"There's probably bears all over the place around here,"

Cole said. "Good thing we've got that nut job with all the guns staying here with us."

"I guess."

"There aren't any bears . . . you know . . . like, right around here, are there?" Cole asked.

"I don't know. Why don't you see for yourself?"

Cole looked up again and took some more time to study his surroundings. His eyes drifted toward the trees that encroached upon the cabin from the north. They grew there in a thick wall of large trunks that seemed to be as solid as the black shadows between them; infused with some ominous presence or possibly keeping one at bay. For a second, light from the fire seemed to catch a figure within one of those distant shadows. Cole rubbed his eyes and took another look just to be certain.

The figure was gone. Looking up, he noticed something in the darkness that could only have been reflections from the glittering array of stars over his head. "Looks safe to me."

"Good," Gerald said as he reached down and brushed away some snow to reveal a kit that was made from a few sheets of leather stitched together and unrolled into a mat. Various tools were kept in pockets specially made for them, ranging from picks and knives to things Cole hadn't seen since his leather-working unit in shop class. Gerald was using the rag in his hand, stained by some sort of rust-colored polish, to smooth out some of the rough edges on the staff's fresher carvings. The rag left behind a wet smear, which he wiped away until the polish had been worked into the grain of the wood.

"Where are you headed from here?" Cole asked. "Bear hunting?"

Looking up to the exact spot where Cole had seen those reflections, Gerald replied, "Ain't no bears stupid enough to go where I need to be."

Suddenly, the cold air and stilted conversation took their toll. Cole looked over his shoulder and saw the fire beckoning through the lodge's front window. "All right, then. Good luck with that," he said to Gerald. "I think I smell hot cocoa, so I'll just leave you out here to polish your stick."

As he turned and started walking toward the lodge, he heard Gerald getting up. It sounded as if the older man was having some trouble, or possibly losing his balance, which would account for the quick, heavy scraping. Heavy breathing drifted through the air, followed by the smell of turned soil and freshly cut timber. Even though he knew the older man would probably refuse any help, Cole turned around to offer it anyway.

"Go inside," Gerald snapped before Cole had turned far enough to get a look at him. "Now!"

Cole turned away, but at the continued scuffling sounds, turned back to see a beast charging across the snow toward Gerald like a runaway tanker truck. It flew over the ground so quickly that its claws barely seemed to push all the way through the snow. Steam poured from its flared nostrils and spewed from a mouth filled with row upon row of jagged teeth, overwhelming his senses. The beast came to a stop a few yards from Gerald, its massive torso blotting out the moon and most of the stars.

"Holy shit!" Cole screamed as he leapt out of the creature's path. His feet flew out from under him and he hit the ground with a solid thump. Breath rushed from his lungs, adding to the panic that had already washed over him.

Watching the scene as if somehow detached from it, he couldn't decide just what the hell the thing was. It had the bulk of a bear, but with larger hind legs and longer front paws. Daggerlike claws curled from the ends of thick, gnarled fingers. It had a squat head with a long snout. None of its teeth extended at the same angle, and some had even ripped through the beast's cheek as it opened its mouth to let out a rumbling, unearthly roar.

Whatever the thing was, it didn't seem to be interested in him. After craning its neck to find Gerald, it charged straight toward the older man. Its upper body reared up and stretched outward at the same time in a constant flow of frenzied muscle. The left forepaw slammed down to grab hold of the earth while the right was pulled back toward its long, pointed ear. The older man was eclipsed by the enormous creature, turning his back to it while struggling to retrieve something from his kit.

Despite his better judgment, Cole opened his mouth and hoped something intelligible would come out. "Gerald! Look out!!"

The beast put its upper body muscles behind a mighty swipe of its front paw and lashed out, but Gerald was fast enough to roll away, so the thing only managed to kick up a spray of earthy snow. Letting out a thundering growl, it dug its claws into the ground as if to punish the spirits that had forged it and propped up the front half of its body with both front paws. Turning like a muscle-bound cougar, the beast shifted its weight to look at Cole.

A chill shot through Cole's body as he wondered if he could gouge out one of the creature's eyes before he was ripped into several pieces.

Then the beast opened its mouth and let out a roar that was even louder than the first. Saliva poured from the corners of its mouth and flew through the air as it lifted its head to the sky. Its roar then turned into a howl.

Cole scuttled toward the cabin like a crab before flipping himself over and jumping to his feet. When he turned around again, he caught a glimpse of Gerald rushing directly toward the creature, to drive the sharpened end of his walking stick into the meat behind its right shoulder.

The beast turned then, and took another swipe at Gerald with its left paw, but the older man managed to duck and roll out of its range. Now, Cole could see that Gerald wasn't holding the walking stick he'd had before. The weapon in the old man's hands looked like a longbow with a spearhead on one end.

As the creature swiped at him again, Gerald was quick enough to block the incoming paw with his weapon. Even more surprising than the old man's speed was the fact that the wooden staff held up to the beast's attack without exploding into a shower of splinters. His fists remained closed around the weapon as blood began to trickle from under his palms. Cole saw three tips protruding from the upper end of the staff. With this wooden trident in hand, Gerald gritted his teeth and drove all three points into the creature's side.

Cole yelled for help. Footsteps pounded against the snow and he turned to get a look at who was coming.

Brad rushed outside, holding a short machete in one hand. "Get behind me!" he said.

Cole was breathing so quickly that he was getting dizzy. "I'll bring help," he wheezed.

"No! Just get inside the lodge and stay there. Tell the others to do the same." With that, Brad charged the creature.

Massive paws thumped against the frozen ground and a savage growl gave voice to a hunger that was older than the dirt. Without knowing what else to do, Cole turned toward the lodge and ran for the doorway.

"What the hell's going on out there?" the young guy in the jester cap asked. "What the fuck is that thing?"

"I don't know what it is. Just—" When he saw Jester Cap's eyes open wide and the color drain from his face, Cole quickly looked over his shoulder and saw the creature rushing toward the cabin with a feral spark gleaming in its eyes.

Cole shoved the kid aside and slammed the door. Unfortunately, the creature didn't need a door. It tore through door frame and walls alike as if the eleven-inch-thick logs had been made out of cardboard. From there, it planted its front paws against the floor and tore up several planks before its eight-foot-long body came to a stop.

The quiet man emerged from the next room as if this was the moment he'd been waiting for. In one hand, he held a sawed-off shotgun, and in the other a large-caliber pistol that reminded Cole of something he might give to one of the characters from his games.

"Come and get it, motherfucker," were the first words Cole heard from him since the beginning of the trip. Then the formerly quiet man pulled both triggers, filling the room with the roar of gunfire and the stench of burned cordite.

The creature grunted as bullets met its body. Although it lowered its head and winced, it barely seemed to acknowledge the ordnance that was being thrown its way. What started as a grunt turned into more of a sniffle as the smoke from the gun barrels drifted into its nostrils. Letting out a low, rumbling growl, the beast stalked deeper into the cabin.

From the corner of one eye, Cole could see a flicker of movement as the blond woman who had been talking to Brad emerged from beneath the front table and crawled to another table, away from the action. He rushed over to her, keeping his head down.

"What's going on?" the blonde cried. "Where did that come from?"

"I don't know." Cole winced and pulled her closer to the floor as more gunshots blasted through the lodge. His ears were ringing, but he went through the motions of rubbing the woman's shoulders and covering her with his own body. "It's going to be all right," he lied. "Everything will be all right."

She didn't take much comfort from his words, but didn't seem overly panicked either. With all the growling and the gunshots, he realized that she might not have even heard him. They both kept their heads down, wincing at the sounds of the creature stomping so close to them. As much as Cole wanted to run, there was nowhere for him to go. The beast's snarls seemed to come from every direction. Its steps rattled the floor of the entire structure.

Then the possibility of staying low and waiting out the storm was abruptly flung aside as the heavy wooden table was knocked off the ground and tossed across the room by a paw that swung through the air like the arm of a catapult. Claws reduced the table to splinters in midair, followed by a second set that sliced over Cole's head, missing it by a scant few inches.

"Run!" he shouted.

The blonde's face was drained of all color as she looked at him with the blank expression of a lamb that had already resigned itself to being slaughtered. Cole locked eyes with her and shouted once more.

"Run!"

She nodded quickly and started to move.

There was nowhere for him to hide, so he stood and chased the woman he'd just sent away. No more than four feet behind him the gun nut was shouting and firing round after round into the creature's chest. Somewhere along the line, he had swapped out his first two guns for an automatic rifle of questionable legality.

The creature was on all fours now, tearing up chunks of the floor as its thick, shaggy limbs carried it forward despite the hot lead being thrown its way. Now that he was closer to the thing, Cole could see the taut layers of muscle heaped onto its shoulder blades. Judging by the damage done to the fur along its chest and ribs, those were the gun nut's primary targets. The lower half of the creature's body looked trimmer now. Its hind legs were planted firmly against the floor and it stretched its neck forward with jaws wide open, exposing glistening, crooked teeth. With one, snapping bite it turned its head sideways and clamped down on the gun nut's chest.

Cole could only watch in horror. Hanging like a toy from the creature's mouth, his eyes impossibly wide and his jaw strained open well past its normal limits, the man was unable to utter more than a strained, wet gasp. Still, he managed to slam the butt of his rifle against the creature's head. It loosened its grip on him for an instant and then lunged forward again to sink its teeth into the man's neck and shoulder. The automatic rifle let out a prolonged burst. Pieces of the creature's coat smoldered and caught fire, but not one drop of blood was spilled. Finally, the beast shook its head from side to side until the body in its jaws simply fell apart.

Blood and flesh hung from its teeth as the creature reared up on its hind legs and clawed at the cabin's roof, letting out a deafening howl. Then it dropped back down so it could nip at the fires on its back.

"We've got to leave," Cole rasped into the blonde's ear. "We've got to leave, and it has to be right now."

Although she was close to hyperventilating, the blonde replied, "Back door . . . in the next room."

"Let's get outside and get to the woods," Cole demanded. "Maybe we can lose that thing or get some help once we're far enough away."

That was all the blonde needed to hear. Keeping her head down, she gave the creature as wide a berth as possible as she rushed around it and headed for the door to the smaller room.

Cole followed her into the bedroom. When he caught sight of the two frat boys huddled in the corner, he snarled, "What the hell are you two still doing here?"

There was a roar from the main room followed by heavy steps as the creature stomped through a pile of wet human remains. The young snowboarders nodded as if their heads were coming loose and got to their feet. They had barely moved toward the smaller door that led outside when the light from the other room was blocked by the massive creature's shaggy frame.

Crystalline, blue-gray eyes glittered in the shadow of the creature's brow. A few persistent flames crackled from the fur on its back, but the monster let them burn while calmly assessing the contents of the smaller room. Those brilliant eyes fixed upon the college kids for a moment, causing Cole to step forward and shout as if trying to scare a stray dog off his porch.

The creature glanced at him only a second before baring its teeth and once more fixing its gaze possessively upon the fresh meat in the funny hats. A growl churned at the back of its throat before exploding into a blast of hot, fetid breath seemingly pulled from the bowels of hell.

The two boys jumped over the beds and raced for the back door. The creature reached into the room with one paw and tore through the spine of the one wearing the jester hat with one swipe. Before the creature could take another step into the room, it buckled and let out a high-pitched yelp. When it raised its head again, there was a fire in its eyes that made its previous rage pale in comparison.

Putting its back to Cole, it hunkered down and let out a growl that sounded like an approaching freight train. Cole shoved the blonde toward the back door but was reluctant to follow her. The second frat boy was already outside and running through the snow.

"Come on," she whispered urgently. "This may be our only chance."

He waved her off while backing into a shadowy corner. "Go ahead. There's other people still in here."

"They're already dead or gone and there's nothing you can do against that thing!"

"Gerald and Brad were doing something!" Cole barked. "Maybe I can too!"

The blonde wasn't about to waste any more of her breath on him. With tears pouring from her eyes, she bolted through the back door and ran away.

The creature was standing with its back to the bedroom, but was close enough for Cole to feel heat from the fire that still sputtered in its fur. Then it shook like a dog coming in from the rain and extinguished the flames. It kept shaking until several small, dark objects fell from its thick layers of fur and clattered to the floor.

One of them rattled against the floorboards and rolled to within a few inches of Cole's grasp. He snatched the object up, saw that it was a small chunk of warm metal that appeared to have melted. Then he realized the metal hadn't melted, but had been squashed. Holding the object closer to his eye, he saw the distinctive shape of the back end of a bullet, along with the gnarled remains of a caliber marking. More of the flattened slugs rained down from the creature's coat then, pelting the floor like hail. Since there wasn't any blood on the floor or on any of the bullets, it seemed that the earlier gunfire had been wasted.

"Jesus," Cole whispered.

The creature had stepped away from the door. The beast's hulking, battle-scarred form filled up most of the room, but Brad and Gerald had taken up positions to fight it. The triple points of Gerald's staff had been broken off into a single jagged tip. Cole could also make out spiked protrusions along the handle of the staff.

Gritting his teeth, Gerald tightened his grip around the weapon, thorns and all, and jabbed the spear into the creature's side. Brad still wielded his blade, which Cole could now see resembled an elongated spike forged from dirty steel. Although Gerald was carefully picking his targets and taking clean shots, Brad swung the blade erratically. Oddly enough, the creature seemed more concerned with that blade than the spear, which continued to gouge into its flesh. Bloodied and barely standing, the men did their best to coordinate another attack.

If the blood hadn't been rushing through his head with such force, Cole would have been able to make out more than a few words.

"Remember what I taught you," Gerald said.

Brad nodded, gripped his weapon by the blade and flung it through the air. It rotated during its flight and landed solidly in the beast's chest. As the creature howled with pain, Brad drew an identical blade from a scabbard at his hip.

The creature reflexively turned away from Brad, allowing Cole to see a trickle of blood from the spot where the blade had hit.

Finally seeing a chance to do something other than run or hide, Cole rushed forward, reaching out with both hands.

A chill spiked through his blood the moment the creature looked in his direction.

After another step, his legs no longer wanted to work and he had to rely on his own momentum to carry him forward. His left hand snagged the creature's coat, which felt like a coarse, matted tangle of bare wires and nylon cords. His right hand found the blade in the creature's chest and twisted it.

Gerald appeared then, next to the creature, and jabbed it with his wooden spear. He screamed something to Cole, but it was lost amid the slamming of Cole's heart in his chest.

Letting out another thunderous cry, the creature wheeled around and dragged Cole along for the ride. Brad was cut down by a single swipe from the creature's claws, and Cole was close enough to hear the last sound the other man would make. As he felt the creature turning toward Gerald, Cole tried to steer him away by twisting the knife again.

Despite the knife in its torso, the creature still knocked Gerald through the air with a powerful backhand. The old man's back slammed against a nearby table and the wet crunch of breaking bones filled the lodge.

There were more voices and more gunshots, but Cole couldn't make out any details. He was dragged a few more feet as more shots were fired. A bullet shredded through the creature's fur and thumped against what might as well have been a slab of solid rock.

More gunshots followed, and Cole recognized Sam's voice through the chaos. Something hit his shoulder then and sent him skidding across the floor. His back and head knocked against a wall, and afterward he couldn't move a muscle. But he could still feel his fist wrapped around the knife that he'd pulled from the creature's body.

Sam shouted something and the cook shouted back. Their voices were soon engulfed by a deafening howl as the creature leapt toward the kitchen.

Then consciousness slipped from Cole's grasp.

He didn't expect to wake up.

Chapter 4

Cole woke up, but wished he hadn't.

Just lifting his eyelids hurt more than the worst hangover of his life. He was slumped over and jammed against a wall. His lungs burned with every breath and his ribs felt like they were about to rip through his torso. If he hadn't been wrapped up in so much bulky winter gear, he knew he'd have several broken bones to add to his list of complaints.

Gritting his teeth, Cole pushed himself up and got to his feet. Whenever he thought he couldn't make it any further, memories of the creature got him moving again. For a moment he suspected he might have taken a knock to the head and dreamt the rest. That theory was squashed as soon as he realized he was still holding the weapon that Brad had thrown into the monster's chest.

It was heavier than he'd expected. Although it didn't seem right to call the thing a knife, the weapon wasn't quite long enough to be a machete. He guessed that some of the guys who'd worked on the line of Digital Dreamers fantasy games would know more about swords and blades like this one. As far as he was concerned, a knife was a knife. This knife, however, had intricate carvings etched into the blade. Upon closer inspection, the steel didn't just seem dirty. It was smeared with something, but the streaks were on the inside. It looked like it should be slippery, but it wasn't.

Cole held the blade up for a closer look at the markings. They weren't any sort of writing he recognized, but that didn't mean much. If it wasn't English or programming code, he wouldn't know it. Unfortunately, he didn't have the time to stand there and ponder the mysteries of that blade. The scent of blood was so thick in the air that it coated the back of his throat.

The cabin had been completely destroyed, every table reduced to wood chips that stuck to the gore drying on nearly every surface. On top of that, he had no idea how long he'd been out, and his only real hint was the daylight streaming through a nearby window. Pushing his questions aside for now, he braced himself to get out of the cabin no matter how much it hurt to move.

Nothing vital seemed to be broken, but that didn't help ease the pain that wrapped him up tighter than his winter gear. Looking to the spot where he'd landed, he noticed he'd missed hitting a wooden beam by about a foot and a half, and had slammed against a relatively smooth section of wall. Compared to the others laying nearby, his landing had been more than lucky.

He recognized the jacket Sam had been wearing on a bloody torso that lay upside down in a corner. Brad was still nearby, but had been torn into unrecognizable pulp. He knew the mess against the wall next to the bedroom door had once been the gun nut. Cole picked up the rifle laying within a few feet of the body and started to clean it off. Then, remembering how much good the rifle had done for its owner, he let it slide out of his hands. The cook was laying against the stove. His eyes were wide open and clouded over, but Cole knew dead when he saw it. Nothing with any life in it would have been as still as the cook or any of the others inside that cabin.

As he worked his way to the front of the cabin, he felt like a passenger inside his own body. His thoughts weren't exactly incomprehensible, but they came quickly enough to overwhelm him. He took a few breaths, accidentally filled his lungs with the stench of death and ran outside.

The contents of his stomach hit the snow, where they were

almost immediately buried. Cole pulled in some of the crisp morning air and felt a little better. As his pulse slowed to a pace just shy of frantic, he spotted movement a few yards away. His hands balled into fists and he suddenly wished he hadn't left the rifle behind. Squinting through the brilliant daylight, he spotted something shifting beneath a layer of freshly fallen, freshly bloodied, snow. Taking a few tentative steps forward, he asked, "Who's there?"

No response came.

"Hey. You all right over there?"

"Is . . . it . . . is it gone?" the shape asked.

Recognizing the strained voice, Cole rushed over and knelt down beside the shape. "Gerald?" After dusting off some of the snow, he spotted the older man's face beneath a mask of frozen, crusted blood. "Jesus, it is you! I thought you were dead."

Gerald was regaining consciousness quickly, and he sat up as if to take a swing at him. When his fist bounced off of Cole's shoulder, the older man let out a pained grunt. "I . . . was dead," he said through clenched teeth as he opened his fist to let several pieces of broken glass fall out.

"Almost," Cole said. "So was I."

Although some smaller shards of glass were wedged into Gerald's fingers, only one large rounded piece had managed to puncture his palm. Now that Cole could look at the older man's hands up close, he noticed the thick tangle of scar tissue coating most of Gerald's palms. Although they looked like burns, there were several rounded patches smaller than the size of a dime that stuck out from the rest. Compared to the condition of Gerald's face, neck, and chest, however, the glass wedged into his palm looked like a paper cut.

Cole's hands hovered above the older man uselessly. As much as he wanted to stop the bleeding, close up the wounds, or do anything at all to help, he simply didn't know how to do any of those things. "Try to relax," he said in the most comforting voice he could manage. "I'll . . . uhh . . . I'll get some help."

Lurching toward Cole, Gerald grabbed hold of him with enough strength to knock him off balance. "No," he snarled.

"Listen to me!" Somehow, the older man managed to sit up and collect himself; more wounds revealed themselves as freshly fallen snow fell away from his body. Gashes in his torso and legs seemed to go all the way down to the bone.

"Holy shit," Cole said. "You need to lay back down!"

"Shut the hell up and listen to me! Brad had two knives. That thing got one of 'em. Do you think you can find the other?"

"Yeah," he said as he held up the machete for Gerald to see. "I grabbed one of them before I was knocked out."

"Good. There's a card in the lining of my coat . . . near the collar. Call the number on the card and tell them what happened. Tell them you need to talk to Paige in Chicago. They'll arrange for you to see her."

"What? We're going to freeze to death or bleed out before—"

"Stop talking!" Gerald's voice had a hint of the ferocity that shook Cole all the way down to the frozen tips of his toes. "Paige needs to know what happened and that Brad and I won't be coming back. More importantly . . . she needs that knife! We didn't go through all this to lose both of the damned things."

Suddenly, the nightmare from the previous night rushed back to clamp its jaws around Cole's mind. "I thought I could help," he said. "I wanted to do more."

Oddly enough, Gerald's voice became steadier as Cole's broke up. "You did a hell of a lot more than most anyone else," he said. "When you talk to Paige, she'll know you did plenty. Be sure to tell her that it took a goddamn Full Blood to put Brad down."

"A what?"

"Just tell her that. Can you remember?"

Cole nodded, knowing it would take a hell of a lot more than time or even another knock on the head before he'd ever forget those words.

"That blade . . . the one Brad carried," Gerald said. "You need to bring it to her. Make sure Paige gets it. Do you understand me?"

"I think so, but—"

Gerald seized the front of Cole's jacket with almost enough force to pull Cole down on top of him. "You'll take that blade to her! You got to. After what you saw . . . after what you did . . . you ain't got another choice! She'll know what to do!"

Cole could think of plenty of other choices. He could push that crazy old man away and do his best to get back to civilization before he froze to death. He could lie to Gerald and tell him he'd do whatever he wanted just to shut him up. Actually, he didn't think that would work on the old man. Gerald's eyes were too clear for him to be fooled by such a pathetic smoke screen. Finally, Cole settled upon his only real choice, the responsibility of carrying out a man's dying wish settling upon his shoulders.

Patting the scarred hand gripping his jacket, Cole said, "All right. But I don't know who Paige is, and we need to get to some police or a medical team or something before anything else."

Gerald was starting to fade. "If you drag the cops into this, it'll just get them killed when that thing comes back. You know just as well as I do that Mounties will be scouring this area for a good long while trying to figure out what happened. That Full Blood's got your scent as well as the scents of everyone else in that cabin. It's hurt now, but—"

"That thing can smell me?" Cole snapped. "Is that what you're saying?"

Gerald nodded. "It knew we were here. It came here for a reason. It'll be coming back even if the only thing left here is bodies. When the Mounties show up, they'll just bring their popguns like that asshole who got ripped apart in there." In a cool, level voice, Gerald asked, "When it does come back, whether there are cops here or not, do you think there's a damn thing you or anyone else can do to keep that monster from finishing what it started?"

Cole didn't have to think very long before replying, "No."

"Then do what I ask, Cole. Brad got himself killed pulling that Full Blood away from you before it could finish you off, and I don't have enough in me to keep convincing you that you need to get the hell away from this place and leave me behind."

"All right," Cole said with a single determined nod. "But you can come with me."

Shaking his head, Gerald replied, "Take the card from my collar. It has a number for you to reach someone, and they can get you in touch with Paige." The words were spilling out of Gerald like the blood that had reddened the snow around him. "Just mention me and Brad and tell her what happened here. She'll help you get to where you need to go. You'll have to travel, but you need to get that Blood Blade to her."

Cole nodded and reached for Gerald's collar. "Where's the card?"

Rather than explain, Gerald knocked Cole's hand away and tore open his jacket collar as if it was made out of tissue paper. His fingers fumbled through the stuffing and emerged with a laminated business card. "It's right here," he snarled as he slapped the card into Cole's hand. "I got a phone in my bag that works damn near anywhere. Get it and call the damn number. That Full Blood could come back any time. Once it's close enough to smell two more living souls here, it'll all be over."

Cole examined the card. It had two numbers on it, one of which was an 888 number, the other a bit shorter than a Social Security number. Other than that, the only other thing printed there was the name: MEG BR 40. Cole guessed that it was a business name or e-mail address, but didn't take the time to think it through more than that.

Looking up from the card, he noticed that the flow of blood from the wounds on Gerald's arms and chest had stopped. In fact, those wounds were already dried and scabbed over. As the older man shifted upon the ground, the flesh beneath his tattered clothes actually held together. "Don't try to move," Cole said. "You probably shouldn't be sitting up."

Anyone with eyes could tell that Gerald shouldn't even be breathing.

Gerald nodded as his scowl faded. He was sitting up straight, blinking slowly and absently rubbing his stomach as if he had indigestion rather than gaping wounds. The older man must have shifted within his shredded clothes, because the flesh that was visible through those rips was only scratched and smeared with blood.

Cole found his cell phone right where it should be. The cold piece of plastic felt like a little slice of home, and he merely had to snap it open to get that comforting bit of technology to come to life. Although the phone's screen showed the picture he'd downloaded brightly and clearly, it also showed him two disheartening words: NO SIGNAL. He didn't like leaving Gerald there, but he suddenly had a lot to do. He thought about where he might find a medical kit, some clean blankets, or even any survivors who'd escaped during the attack. Then again, he also realized that if any other survivors had somehow escaped the creature, they weren't about to be tracked down by a panicked game designer from Seattle. Focusing on what he actually could do, he headed back to the cabin

The inside of the lodge didn't look any better now than the last time he'd been there. He stepped over human remains without actually paying attention to what was in front of him. When the smells got too strong to bear, Cole opened his mouth and breathed that way.

"Bad idea," he groaned as soon as the smells were translated into tastes and reached down to his stomach.

The cabin hadn't grown in the last few minutes, so he spotted the bags scattered near the entrance fairly quickly. After spending so many hours packed into that truck, he didn't have any trouble picking out which of those bags had been wedged between Gerald's feet throughout the ride.

"I got it!" Cole yelled as he hurried outside while holding up the bag as if he expected to get a prize.

Grateful to fill his lungs with fresh air, he walked about three more steps before he grunted, "Damn. I was going to get a medical kit while I was in there, but I got distracted." He stopped a few yards shy of where Gerald was laying and set the bag down. "Actually, distracted isn't the word. Disgusted is more like it. In fact," Cole said as he swallowed a bit of bile that gurgled to the top of his throat, "how about we talk about something else? Or . . . since you weren't talking about it . . . why don't I stop talking about it?" He laughed nervously, but cut himself short as soon as he saw that Gerald wasn't laughing. In fact, he wasn't reacting at all.

He wasn't even moving.

"Gerald?"

He had to be certain that Gerald was dead before he would leave him there to freeze. As soon as he reached out to feel for Gerald's pulse, he was introduced to something even worse than the stillness he'd been expecting.

Beneath the collar of Gerald's coat, dark gray marks stained his neck as if dozens of threadlike tendrils were creeping beneath his flesh. The lines also snaked along Gerald's arm from beneath his sleeves. For a second Cole swore he saw those lines shake like shadows being cast by a flickering light. A small syringe still protruded from the middle of the dark marking on Gerald's wrist.

"Oh my God," Cole muttered as he reached out with one hand to touch the vein in the side of Gerald's neck. What he felt instead of a pulse was the last, desperate twitch of another dark tendril wriggling somewhere between the meat of Gerald's flesh and the outermost layer of his skin. Those dark gray filaments stretched and strained as if doing their best to reach Gerald's throat from the inside.

Cole snapped his arm back with so much force that he nearly sprained his own elbow. A flurry of obscenities poured out of him as he jumped to his feet and backpedaled from Gerald's body until the back of his heel knocked against the bag he'd brought from the cabin and his backside thumped against the snow. The sight of Gerald's contorted face was repulsive, but also mesmerizing. The gray threads kept sliding beneath Gerald's flesh, wriggling like frantic tadpoles.

"He's dead," Cole said to himself. "He's dead. That's all I need to know."

Snatching up a flannel shirt from inside Gerald's bag, he ran toward the road so he could signal for any vehicle that might pass by. He made it about seven paces before remembering what the old man had told him and the plan of action they'd agreed upon. He felt like an idiot for agreeing to any of those orders.

Then he heard a howl in the distance.

It wasn't like anything in the movies or nature shows he'd seen on TV. It was powerful and pained at the same time. It could have drifted through the air from miles away or it could have originated from the closest row of trees.

Cole laughed to himself and shook his head. "I gotta be out of my damned mind."

Turning toward the cabin, he took another few steps and heard the howl again. It came from that direction.

He didn't know if there were survivors, where they would have gone or how long ago they'd started running. What he did know for certain was that the only thing he could do if he found that creature was make it sick by clogging its stomach with his own body.

Hefting the bag over his shoulder, Cole turned from the cabin and ran.

Chapter 5

Cole ran until his legs could no longer carry him. Surrounded by tall trees and with the cabin nowhere in sight, he felt safe. Then he realized the creature was probably more at home in those trees than it had been inside the cabin. Dropping Gerald's bag, he leaned against the nearest tree and slid down the trunk until he was seated with his legs splayed out in front of him.

"What the hell do I do now, Gerald?" he asked aloud as he laughed and leaned his head back against the tree. "Come on! You wanna guide me? Show up and guide me! What's the matter? There are monsters, but no ghosts? Of course there aren't any ghosts! A ghost would be too fucking helpful right now, so heaven forbid one might actually show up to make my life easier!"

Cole was suddenly very conscious of the fact that sweat was freezing onto his forehead. When he tried to touch his brow, he cracked the handle of Brad's knife against his head. Having forgotten he was even carrying the knife, he set it down so he could open the bag and sift through it. Some of Gerald's clothes were in there, along with a shaving kit, books, a pair of glasses, and then all the way at the bottom he came upon an object that made him smile.

Recognizing the brand of the satellite phone in his hand, Cole fought the urge to kiss it. "Screw it," he muttered as he placed his lips upon the plastic cover and gave it some love. He almost gave it some more when he flipped open the cover and saw one bar of signal strength showing up on the display. Sure enough, the phone was connected to a satellite service that had always been too expensive for him to use. He took Gerald's laminated card from his pocket and read it over so he could be sure to dial the correct number. The last thing he wanted to do was waste battery life on stupid mistakes. After checking the number once more, he pressed the Send button and held the phone up to his ear.

There were a few clicks, followed by a series of beeps. Then, like a song from an angel, there came a ring tone. Finally, someone answered.

"Hello, this is MEG Branch 40," said the voice on the other end of the connection. It wasn't an angel and it sure as hell didn't sound like someone who would be named Meg.

"Uh, hello?" Cole replied.

"This is MEG Branch 40. How can I help you?" The voice on the other end sounded like a man at least ten years his junior, and more than a little perturbed. After sighing heavily, the man asked, "Are you looking for anyone in particular or do you have an instance to report?"

"An instance?" Cole chuckled to himself and let out a breath. "I sure do have an instance, but I don't think you'd believe it enough to write it down in a report."

"Try me."

Using a cell phone and speaking to an annoyed operator had given Cole a small dose of normality. He'd also settled down enough to remember why he'd dialed the number in the first place.

"I need to speak to Paige," he said.

"Paige who?"

And, with that one simple question, Cole realized an important question he'd forgotten to ask Gerald. "Uhhh, the one in Chicago."

"Look, I understand you may be a bit confused right now," the operator said in a surprisingly calm and supportive tone. "If you have someone you need to speak to, I can try to get you in touch with them. We don't have a Paige who works here, though. You said you had an incident to report. Why don't you start with that?"

Lowering his voice as if he was afraid a nearby beaver might be eavesdropping, Cole said, "I'm a friend of Gerald's and he had this phone on him."

"Gerald, huh? Is this a prank?"

"No. You've got to listen."

The annoyance was back in force within the young man's tone. When he spoke again, Cole had no trouble picturing one of the skinny little code crunchers from Digital Dreamers rolling his eyes and doodling on whatever paper was in front of him.

"You got some story you want to tell?" the young operator asked. "Then go ahead and tell it. Just make it real funny or real dirty, otherwise I'm sure I've heard better from some of the other comedians that call us."

"There's a man named Gerald—" Cole started.

"Cool. I've never had someone call with a limerick before."

"Just shut up and let me finish." Sensing he'd just bought himself no more than a few seconds of the operator's attention, Cole went for the jugular. "Gerald's dead."

Without much of a pause, the operator said, "All right. Have you been seeing this Gerald person or do you just hear his voice? Are you certain the man you're talking about is Gerald and not some other manifestation?"

Cole stared down at the snow and then at the phone in his hand. Although he wasn't convinced he was insane just yet, he was getting awfully close. "What in the hell are you talking about? Who are you?"

"This is MEG Branch 40, sir. You dialed us, remember?"

Looking at the same words as they were printed upon Gerald's card, Cole asked, "Does MEG stand for something?"

"Of course. We're the Midwestern Ectological Group. Branch 40. Did you need another branch?"

"An ecological group?"

"Ectological," the operator clarified. "As in spirits and other nonphysical entities."

"Is 'ectological' even a word?" Cole asked.

"If you want to report a manifestation, get to it. The only reason I haven't hung up on you is because you're calling from one of our satellite lines. Come to think of it, whose phone is this? Did Walter put you up to this? Goddamn it, he did, didn't he? Or did you steal this phone? Oh man, you'd be wise to drop it and run right now."

Still looking at the card, Cole said, "I have a number to give you."

"Go ahead."

He rattled off the digits that were printed on the card beneath the phone number. At first he could hear the operator grumbling something about sending Walter a scathing e-mail. But before Cole was halfway through the numbers, the operator was scrambling frantically enough to knock something over on his end of the connection.

"Holy crap," he said. "That's a . . . you're . . ."

Hearing the panic and frustration in his voice did Cole a bit of good. It seemed misery truly did love company. "Do you need me to repeat that number?" he asked.

"Hold on a second."

A series of clicks was followed by a few short bursts of static. Meanwhile, Cole felt his stomach flop again as he thought he'd been disconnected. When the operator's voice came back, it wasn't as clear as it had been before, but there was more than enough intensity in it to make up the difference.

"I'm really sorry about all of that before," he said. "I had to secure the line. Could you give me that number one more time?"

Cole repeated the digits. This time he even included the dashes that were written between a few of them. When he was done, he could hear the unmistakable clacking of fingers on a keyboard.

"Are you still there?" Cole asked.

"Yeah, yeah. Just looking up your ident code."

"Ident code?"

"Yeah," the operator replied. "It's short for identity code."

"Clever. Who are you?"

Unlike the last time he'd asked questions, the operator responded as if he actually had some interest in helping, rather than just tolerating him. "We're the Midwest Ectological Group. We cover reports of paranormal activity throughout the U.S. and Canada. Maybe you heard of us?"

"Nope."

"We've been on television a few times. Well, cable television. Are you one of those . . . you know?"

Guessing it was easier to lie than try to figure out the proper response, Cole said, "Yeah. I'm one of those," and hoped for the best.

"Perfect! This is great! I've never actually caught one of these calls before. According to this code, this phone belongs to Gerald Keeler? Oh . . . you said . . ."

"Yeah. Gerald's dead."

The silence on the other end of the connection was almost thick enough to seep through the device in Cole's hand. The words that broke it were meek and genuinely regretful. "Right. You mentioned that. What about . . . Brad Books?"

"Brad too," Cole replied somberly.

"Jeez, I'm really sorry to hear that," the operator replied.

Despite the awkward situation, Cole was grateful just to hear someone else's voice. "What's your name?" he asked.

Judging by the silence on the phone, the operator wasn't used to hearing that question. "I'm Stu."

"Hey, Stu. My name's Cole Warnecki."

"Oh . . . uh . . . you're not supposed to use last names on these calls."

"Really? Why?" Cole asked.

"I don't know. That's one of the rules you guys use."

"Fine. Gerald gave me this phone and this number so I could get in touch with a woman named Paige. She's supposed to be in Chicago."

There were more clicks and clacks as Stu's fingers flew over his keyboard. "That would be Paige . . . well . . . yeah. I've got a Paige listed in Gerald's file and she's in Chicago."

"I need to talk to her. Actually, I need to see her. The only problem is I'm kind of a long ways from an airport or anything."

"I know. The phone has a GPS in it and I've got your rough position on my screen right now."

"Nice," Cole said as he closed his eyes and pictured himself as a brightly colored dot on the display screen of the global positioning system that had recently been installed in Jason's company car. As much as Cole got lost, he still hadn't gotten high enough on the Digital Dreamers ladder to warrant such a fancy expense. "You guys have any way to get me out of here before I get ripped to pieces?"

"Oh sweet! You mean you're on site with one of those creatures?"

"Sure. Maybe I can snap a few pictures for you before I get eaten," Cole growled. "Why don't you just tell me what the hell I'm supposed to do to get out of here? Gerald was pretty adamant that I don't wait for the cops."

"Yeah, that would be way too messy," Stu chimed in. "There's someone in the area that should be able to meet you somewhere within a mile or two of your location. Up for a walk?"

Cole didn't answer right away because he was distracted by the sound of what might or might not have been distant thunder. When the sound died away, he whispered, "I'm up for a run. Just tell me where I need to go."

"I've already sent word to one of Gerald's contacts in that area. Head due south until you meet up with a paved highway that's running from northeast to southwest."

"Hold on a second. I'm a city boy. We don't come equipped with compasses."

"You don't have a compass on you?" Stu asked.

"Just a minute." Without waiting for confirmation, Cole set the phone down and started rooting through Gerald's bag. Sure enough, he found a survival knife complete with a compass in the handle. Just what every boy wanted for Christmas. Picking up the phone, he announced, "Found one."

"Good. Head south until you hit that highway. It shouldn't be more than two or three miles."

"Two or three miles?"

"Yeah," Stu replied. "Maybe four. No more than five, though. I can't get an exact fix on your position."

"Never mind. I'm on my way."

"Do you need them to bring anything?"

"A division of Marines and a tank would be nice," Cole replied.

Stu chuckled and capped it off with a snort. "I mean like a medical kit or food or anything."

Checking the phone's screen, Cole saw that there was still plenty of life in the batteries. Apparently, Gerald was one of those rare, mythical breeds of men who had a thousand dollar phone and didn't have it surgically connected to his ear long enough to wear the charge down.

"What's the matter?" Stu asked intently. "You sound hurt."

"Not hurt," Cole gasped as he zipped up the bag, then hefted it over his shoulder and started running. "Just moving faster than I have for months. I really need to start going back to the gym again."

"You're pretty high up and it must be cold there. Let's see . . . yep. I just checked the weather in your area."

"And?"

"It's cold," Stu reported.

Now it was Cole's turn to laugh. With his legs churning through the snow and his feet already tingling within his boots, he didn't exactly have breath to spare. It did, however, feel good to take action rather than just try and piece together what was going on. "What about Paige?" Cole asked. "I still need to get ahold of her."

"I can try to connect you if you don't mind holding."

"I've got nothing else to do right now. If it sounds like I'm dying, just ignore it."

As Stu clicked away at his keyboard, he said, "You gotta tell me more about that creature sometime, dude. I'll bet it was awesome."

Now that he'd cleared the trees, Cole was dashing through a wide-open field of snow. He could still hear the occasional roar in the distance, but it sounded like it was getting farther away rather than closer. When he thought he heard another animal's growl mixed in with the first, he put some more steam into his strides and kept running. The compass in the knife handle rattled noisily within its plastic casing, but indicated that he was more or less southward bound.

"Awesome isn't really . . . the word . . . that comes to mind," Cole wheezed.

Gerald's bag was strapped across his back, and the knife stuck out from one of his jacket pockets like a mutated pen. Having seen a few models similar to the old man's satellite phone, Cole quickly found the earpiece in one of the carrying case's little pockets. Once the piece was plugged into the phone and his ear, Cole gasped, "Hello? Can you hear me?"

"Yeah," Stu replied instantly. "What's wrong?"

"Just checking the equipment."

"You sound a little rough, but I can hear you."

"That's not surprising," Cole said. "If my legs don't freeze, they may just fall off in protest. Not to mention . . . the very distinct . . . possibility of a heart attack."

"Eh, don't be so hard on yourself. So is something chasing you? What is it?"

Before Cole was forced to make up a story that didn't end with him being slapped around and tossed aside, Stu interrupted.

"Just a sec, Cole. I've got Paige ready to join in. Here she is."

The next voice that filled Cole's ear was sharp and concise. Compared to Stu's easy rambling, this woman sounded more like something stabbing him through the eardrum.

"Who is this?" she snapped.

"My name's Cole. I'm a friend of Gerald."

"Never heard of you. How'd you get this phone number?"

"Gerald gave it to me." He had to stop so he could catch his breath. Thankfully, the terrain was kind enough to slope downward and give him a few tall trees on either side for cover, so he wasn't charging like a dark dot in the middle of a white field. The cold air must have been doing him some good, because his breath was coming easier and his limbs weren't killing him. Either that or his body was just numb enough to keep working through the agony that he'd earned from years of sitting on his ass with a video-game controller in his hand.

"Gerald is . . . he's . . ." Wincing even though he didn't know this woman, Cole forced himself to spit out the truth before he was cut off by any number of flukes that could interrupt a phone signal from the middle of nowhere. "He's dead."

Instead of crying or expressing the shock he'd been expecting, the woman asked, "Was there anyone else with him?"

"Yes. Brad was there."

"Is he dead too?"

Cole felt a bit of relief since he didn't have to spell it all out. "Afraid so."

When she spoke again, Paige's voice was considerably less severe. "And who are you, Cole?"

"I met Brad and Gerald on a hunting trip. Gerald told me to tell you what happened before you heard it from anyone else. I know you may not believe this but . . . he told me to tell you that it took a . . . it was . . ." Gritting his teeth, Cole struggled to cut through everything else that had happened so he could focus upon one particular moment. Finally, he remembered the exact words Gerald had used. "He said to tell you . . . only a Full Blood could take Brad down. I don't know what that means. I may have gotten it wrong, but—"

"You didn't get it wrong," Paige said with a touch of sadness in her voice. "So they're both really dead."

Now that he picked up on the sorrow he'd been expecting from the woman, Cole felt like an ass for wanting to hear it. "Yeah," he said as he slowed to a stop and pulled in a few more breaths. "We were attacked by some sort of animal. I think it's still chasing me."

"You saw it?" Paige asked. "You saw the Full Blood?"

"If a Full Blood is a big, ugly monster that can tear through a room full of hunters and shake off automatic fire, then I saw it."

"Are you the only one who survived?"

"I think so," Cole replied as he looked around. There was a surprising amount of distance already between him and the cabin. Other than a few trees, he didn't see much else. "A few others made it out, but I've been hearing that thing prowling around. It might be after them."

"Have the MEG guys arranged for someone to pick you up?"

"Yeah. I'm headed there now."

"Good. I'll find out who's picking you up and get in touch with them. This is very important, Cole. Did Gerald or Brad give you anything to take back?"

"Yes. I've got a knife. Or maybe it's a sword."

"Perfect. Does it have anything on it?"

"There's some blood and some markings." Chuckling, Cole added, "Honestly, I don't know what I'm looking for."

"That's perfect. Keep the knife the way it is, blood and all."

"Seriously?"

"Yes," Paige said. "Wrap it up and bring it with you. It's very important. Have the police or anyone found the bodies yet?"

"I don't think so. Gerald told me not to call the police, and we're kind of out in the boonies here."

"Good. Keep running and get to that pickup spot. I'll arrange to have you flown straight here as soon as possible."

"Flown?" Cole gasped. "I need to get in touch with my job or my friends." The notion of calling his mom didn't sound unappealing, but he wasn't about to make that known to a complete stranger. "After all that's happened, I may not be able to get onto a plane. I sure as hell won't be able to get this sword thing through security."

"Don't worry about that. Just get to the pickup and we'll take care of the rest. And don't call anyone else. Understand that? Nobody."

"We? Who's we? Come to think of it, who are you? Why can't I call anyone?"

"Do you really want to drag any of your friends or family into this?"

"No," Cole said without hesitation.

Paige laughed once under her breath. "Believe me, this all may seem a bit strange, but I'm your best chance for making it out of there alive. Just do what I say and try to keep your head down."

Cole noticed that she didn't exactly guarantee that he was home free just yet, but he wouldn't have believed such a claim anyway. It did him a lot of good just to hear someone admit that things were a hell of a long ways from normal. "What's a Full Blood?" he asked.

There was no reply.

"Are you some sort of scientist?" Cole asked. "Is that why you want that thing's blood?"

"You sound like you're out of breath," Paige finally said. "Just do me a favor, save whatever you've got left and keep moving. You've already come this far, so don't mess it up now."

Cole nodded reflexively, even though there was nobody around. As far as he could tell, there was still nothing close enough to hurt him, but he started jogging, and then broke into a run just to be safe.

"Can you still hear me?" Paige asked.

"Yeah. Just . . . taking your advice."

"Good. I'll see you when you get to Chicago."

"Chicago? I need to go all the way to Chicago?"

The only thing he heard in response to his frantic questions was the crackle of static from his earpiece. Cole wanted to yell at someone, but didn't have enough breath. He checked the phone and saw there was still some battery life and a bit of signal strength, but the connection had been broken. Whoever Paige was, she'd hung up on him.

He went to pull the earpiece out and winced when it didn't come loose. It seemed to have frozen into his ear, but came free after a bit of painful coercion. Without breaking stride, he shut the phone off, wrapped the earpiece's wire around it and stuffed the whole thing into his pocket. That left him with nothing but the wind and the snow to keep him company.

The last time he had been forced to run more than half a block, he was at the mercy of a gym teacher who had a whistle stuck between his teeth and a rod shoved up his ass. Even then, he could at least slow down when the overaged jock wasn't looking. This time, he had to keep moving. It wasn't a question of if he was in good enough shape or had enough breath in his lungs. It was a simple matter of survival. If he wanted to live, he had to keep moving.

Every so often Cole would stop just long enough to catch his breath and check the compass in Gerald's knife. He thought he saw spots drifting through his line of sight, but ignored them. He thought his legs were straining to the point of ripping muscle from bone, but he ignored that as well. All in all, he was amazed at how much he could ignore when he had a real monster tracking him down.

The highway wasn't much more than a strip of iced-over gray in the distance. If not for a few crooked light posts, Cole might have overlooked it completely. By the time he caught sight of it, the thought of getting killed by the creature didn't seem so bad. At least that would have been quicker than slowly fading within a shell of his own frozen sweat.

It took the better part of an hour before he was close enough to actually feel cement under his boots. When he did, his aching knees were the only things preventing him from dropping down and kissing that dirty stretch of road. Cole's joy lasted all of three minutes before he realized he was still alone. There was no truck in sight. There were no cars. There wasn't even a nice, well-lit gas station advertising good eats and walnut bowls.

"What I wouldn't give for some good eats right now," he grumbled. "Hell, I'd even take a nut bowl. What the hell are those things, anyway? Am I saying this out loud? Can anyone hear me? Am I already dead? Why can't I stop talking?"

Cole stumbled along the side of the road without knowing where he was headed. Since he might not be able to get moving again if he stopped, he just kept stumbling along as he dug into his pocket for Gerald's phone. Before he could mash his deadened fingertips against the keypad, he heard the distinctive crunch of something heavy against the snow. He closed his eyes and prayed for the sound of an engine rather than a growl.

For the first time since he got a look up Katie Fenner's skirt in his junior year of high school, his prayers were answered.

The truck looked like something from one of the hundred or so World War II games he'd worked on over the years. It rumbled up to him, and the window was lowered so a gnarled man wearing an orange stocking cap could lean over and ask, "You Cole?"

"Yeah. I . . . sure am."

"You wanna get in?"

"Oh yeah."

"It's open," the driver said. "Hop inside."

And Cole did need to hop because the driver wasn't about to hit the brakes. The moment his backside hit the seat, he leaned back and let out a breath he might have been holding since he'd left the cabin. At the tail end of that same breath he started laughing. Oddly enough, the driver laughed along with him.

"Feel good to be sittin' down, eh?" the man asked in an accent that had an equal chance of being Canadian as it had of being a bad impression of a Canadian.

"It sure does."

"Who sent ya?"

Cole had peeled his gloves off and was rubbing his hands in front of the closest vent. He was concentrating so hard on thawing out his fingers that he let that question slip right past him. He sure didn't have any trouble hearing what came next.

The pistol was a .44 revolver, and it seemed to have materialized in the driver's hand. When he pointed the gun at Cole's head and thumbed back the hammer, the click seemed to echo through the entire cab.

"I asked you a question," the driver snarled.

"Gerald," Cole spat. "He . . . no wait! His name was Stu. He was on the phone and told me to come here." When he saw that his words weren't changing the driver's foul mood, he added, "And Paige too. She told me to meet up with you. In fact, I think she said she might have called you about bringing me something for the ride to the airport."

The driver lowered his pistol before Cole had his fourth nervous breakdown that day. Glancing toward an expensive radio setup bolted to his dash, the driver grunted, "Just bein' careful. Never know who might be wandering along the road, eh?"

"Yeah."

"I got some hot coffee and candy if you want. Paige said you might be hungry."

"I'll pass."

The rest of the ride was spent in silence. By the time they reached the airport, the sun was long gone and the stars were out. Cole got some rest and was only forced back into consciousness when the truck rattled to a stop. It was the first time he'd been still the entire day.

"No need to open both eyes," the driver said. "Once you're in the plane, you can go right back to sleep."

"We're at the airport?" Cole asked as he absently wiped at his eyes.

"Yep. Sounds like she's all ready to go."

Cole pushed open the truck door and was greeted by the rush of icy wind that carried the louder roar of a plane's engines. Although he couldn't be certain about the airport, he had a sneaking suspicion he'd seen that plane before. As if on cue, a man wearing the same three flannel shirts layered on top of each other waddled around the plane and waved toward the truck.

"That's Andy," the driver said. "He'll be takin' you all the way into Chicago."

"I know who he is. He's the same guy that flew me here."

"Really? Then you should feel right at home."

While he might not have felt right at home, he was already feeling the plummets and barrel rolls that had brought up everything in his stomach on the way into Canada. "Can't we just fly on a jet?" he asked. "It'd be faster. And . . . uh . . . wouldn't kill me."

"Oh sure," the driver replied as he pulled Gerald's bag from behind the seat. "You got anything in there that you'd like to check through customs?"

"Point taken. I suppose that pilot knows how to fly into the States without hitting customs? Does he have smuggling compartments under the seats?"

Chuckling, the driver replied, "You watch a lot of movies, don't you? We ain't terrorists. Andy goes through customs like anyone else. Private planes get a little more slack on personal property, is all. You ain't carrying any drugs or nothin', are you?"

"No."

"All right then. Wouldn't want you making me look bad."

Cole managed to catch the bag that was tossed at him before it knocked him in the teeth. After checking to make sure he had everything, he asked, "Does the pilot need a password to refrain from shoving a gun in my face?"

"Keep up that smart mouth and I'm sure he'll think of something you'll like even more. You have a good flight, now."

Even though the driver settled behind his wheel and gunned his engine, Cole didn't close his door right away. Instead, he extended a hand across the passenger seat and said, "I don't think I thanked you for picking me up."

"No. You didn't."

"Well . . . thanks. It's been kind of a rough day."

Smirking, the driver shook his hand with almost enough strength to snap it off. "Comes with the territory."

Releasing his grip on Cole's hand, the driver eased up on his brake just enough for the truck to roll slowly forward. Once the door had cleared Cole's shoulder, it was pulled shut and locked with a few quick swats of the driver's hand. Even after the truck picked up some speed and rumbled away from the airport, Cole was still standing in the spot where he'd been left. Slowly, he allowed some steam to drift from his mouth and straightened himself up. Since there was nowhere else to go, he hauled his things toward the plane.

"This extreme enough for you, dumbass?" he asked himself. As he got close to the plane and started tossing his things on board, he put on a smile and shouted to be heard over the propellers. "Any chance I could get you to swing past Seattle?"

The pilot grinned and replied, "Nope. But do me a favor and look around for some parachutes. The safety inspectors have really been busting my ass about that."

Chapter 6

Approximately 30 miles southeast of Madison, Wisconsin

It was a cold day. Rain threatened to fall from gray clouds that rolled across a harsh autumn sky. A single, navy blue van moved along a dirt road and pulled off onto a trail that wasn't much more than a set of crooked ruts in rocky soil. As soon as the van was far enough along the road for the driver to spot the collapsed remains of the old mansion, he sped up, the wheels spinning faster, kicking up a gritty mix of dust, gravel, and dead leaves. On the back of the van was the lettering MEG BRANCH 25.

Steve sat in the passenger seat and was tall enough for the top of his balding head to scrape the roof. His rounded face had yet to display anything less than a smile as he told more than enough jokes to fill the drive from Madison. "That's the place," he said. "Park anywhere you like."

The driver was in his mid-thirties, but had enough youthful energy in his eyes to make him look at least five years younger. His dark brown hair was buzzed close to the scalp and his face was clean-shaven. Finding a parking spot wasn't difficult, and the driver pulled to a stop just off the faded old road that led the rest of the way to the mansion. "You say this place is haunted?" he asked.

Steve nodded. "I sure do, Jarvis," he replied, using the driver's name in a way that seemed well-intentioned but obviously didn't set well with the driver. "I could tell you plenty of stories from several other people, or I could tell you a few of my own."

Jarvis leaned over the steering wheel to get a better look at the rubble in front of him. No matter how much squinting or straining he did, he could still only see the sagging remains of a three-story mansion. The roof was full of gaping holes. One half of the building had fallen down altogether. Even the fence surrounding the place was rusted and broken in several spots. "What's anyone even doing out here?" Jarvis asked. "The place looks pretty run-down."

"Oh, it is. The property is still held by the original family, and they've been thinking about restoring the entire mansion. It's a big undertaking, so a lot of consultants have been coming and going to get a look for themselves. Some members of the family just want the land cleared off and sold, so it's become sort of a tug-of-war."

Nodding as he removed the keys from the ignition and pushed his door open, Jarvis said, "Okay, let's have a look around."

"Don't you want to take any equipment with you?"

"This is just a walk-through," Jarvis said. "Our closest tech crew is in Minneapolis. I'm going out to Milwaukee on other business, so I thought I'd take a look at the place rather than stick you at the back of a six month waiting period."

"Oh. All right. Do you still want to hear the stories?"

"Just tell me about your own personal experiences," Jarvis replied.

That was enough to get Steve going. He excitedly recounted stories ranging from feeling like he was being watched when poking around in dirty old rooms to sightings of glowing orbs in hallways. He capped it off by describing a shadowy figure lurking in a particular section of the house. When he tried to get a closer look, he heard screams coming from the basement.

For a seasoned member of the Midwestern Ectological Group, it was all pretty standard stuff. Jarvis nodded and reacted accordingly when Steve got worked up about something, but he didn't share the other man's enthusiasm. All too often, old run-down houses were thought to be haunted when they were simply old and run-down. Rotting beams creaked. Animals nested in basements and attics. Old pipes moaned under proper weather conditions. For those reasons, all MEG branches sent scouts to potential sites rather than waste the time and money it took to dispatch an entire team and its equipment for a full investigation. In fact, Jarvis had some business in Milwaukee, so he was forced to take the job that would normally be handed off to one of the MEG rookies. So far, he was confident that he wouldn't be there too long.

"All right," he said as he got to the front of the mansion, "show me the spots with the most activity."

That brightened Steve's face and he immediately launched into another story about screams and other sounds that came from under the floor. By the time he was through with the basics of that story, both men had their hard hats on and were walking through the sturdy, imposing front doorway.

As he listened, Jarvis examined the old mansion with the help of a flashlight that could have easily doubled for a nightstick. It looked as if a few cleaning crews had been there recently to gather up the rubble that had fallen when the main staircase collapsed. Dirt was thick upon the tiled floor, and broken furniture lay strewn along almost every wall. The upper portion of the staircase was propped up by wooden supports that were too squared and clean to be anything more than a month or two old. Most of the flooring at the top of the staircase was gone, leaving a wide balcony overhead instead of a proper second level.

"You said a family lived here?" Jarvis asked. "Did anyone die here?"

"Plenty of people died here," Steve replied with a quick nod. "Sometime in the late 1880s this whole property was turned into an asylum by a man named Jonah Lancroft. Depending on which of Lancroft's decedents you ask, he was anything from a misguided, poorly trained doctor to an overpaid prison warden. Other members of the family say he was a philanthropist who tried to run a reformatory for the surrounding communities. You can guess which sides want the place knocked down and which want it restored."

"Which side of the fence do you land on?"

"Oh, I'd love to see this place restored! I'm the one who thought about getting it officially declared as haunted, so there'd be some reason to keep it from being demolished. There's already been plenty of interest from some of the Lancroft family in coming back here to see if they might recognize something of Jonah Lancroft himself."

Jarvis nodded and immediately regretted asking the question. From this point on he couldn't allow himself to believe any of Steve's stories. "So you heard scraping sounds?"

"Yep. They came from the floor."

"You're sure there's not just some animals scraping under the floor?"

"The sounds come from the places where workers have heard the screaming."

"And you're sure there's no animals? I mean, there were a lot of farmhouses and woods around here," Jarvis explained. "It could be damn near anything."

Rather than put any more of his own claims to the test, Steve nodded and said, "That's why we called MEG. There are plenty of animals around here, but they don't seem to come too close to the place. In fact, we haven't seen so much as a squirrel for weeks. We called you guys because nobody else will check up on all the other claims."

"Like the voices, huh?"

"Exactly."

Jarvis swung the flashlight toward the back of the foyer. Sunlight streamed through the holes in the roof, contrasting with thick patches of shadow. There was more than enough dust in the air to turn the light into a gritty fog. Because of all the years of construction work Jarvis had done before he could work full-time at MEG, it was easy enough for him to guess that the upper half of the mansion was a long way from being close to code.

"Most of the voices and scraping came from the back of the house and the structure that used to be there," Steve said. "Should I show you?"

"Sounds good."

"What if you hear anything? Shouldn't you bring some of your equipment?"

Although their appearances on cable TV had done wonders for getting exposure and some funding for MEG, it also made people like Steve expect a whole lot from scouting trips like this one. Just to put those expectations to rest and keep on good terms with potential clients, all scouts carried the bare minimum wherever they went. Jarvis took a handheld digital camera and audio recorder from his inner jacket pockets and showed them to Steve. That was enough to make Steve nod anxiously and hurry toward the back of the house.

"Only a few rooms on the upper floor were actually used by the Lancroft family," Steve said as he slipped into a voice that would have been perfectly at home on a tour bus. "The ground level was for staff and visitors, while the basement levels were used to house the more docile patients. The main points of interest are in the old East Wing."

Ducking beneath some half-assembled scaffolding, Jarvis said, "This place doesn't look like much of a reformatory."

"There weren't a lot of patients, really. Not by our standards. Maybe only a couple dozen or so were here at any given time, and they probably never saw this house after they were initially brought here. After that," Steve said as he made it to the end of the cramped hallway, "they spent their time in the East Wing."

Once out of the hallway, Jarvis was led into what had once been a kitchen. Cracked counters were blanketed in layers of dust and nailed to walls or merely propped up where they'd once been. An iron stove, a table, and a few chairs were still in recognizable shape, but the rest of the room was completely trashed. A few sections of new drywall had been stacked nearby, but weren't nearly enough to fix the gaping section of wall that had crumbled off the back of the mansion. The hole was covered in the same plastic that sectioned off many other rooms of the house, and it flapped with every passing breeze. The tattered bottom edge of the plastic scraped against a floor that could very well have been on the wrong end of a bombing run.

Jarvis stepped forward and made sure it was all right to walk through one of the many rips in the plastic sheet that formed the back wall. Once he got a nod from Steve, he walked through the plastic and into the backyard. To be fair, it was more of a back field. "What've you got back here?" Jarvis asked. "Four, five acres?"

"Three and a half, actually," Steve replied. "But the East Wing only took up one."

However bad the mansion looked, the East Wing looked worse. At least the mansion still had the general shape of a building. All that remained of the East Wing was several large piles of rubble that formed a barn-sized heap. Some sections of the heap were so covered by dirt and overgrowth that they looked as if they'd been reclaimed by the nearby hills.

"I've heard scraping and voices from over there," Steve said as he pointed toward the heap. "Since there's supposed to be at least two levels of basement under all that, the surveyors told us to stay away until they were certain there wasn't going to be a cave-in. That was enough for me to keep from getting any closer than this."

"That and the scraping, huh?" Jarvis asked with a smirk.

For once, Steve didn't return a smile. "That's right," he said with a single nod.

There was enough loose dirt to give the air a gritty texture that caught in Jarvis's nose and formed a crunchy layer between his teeth. "Where did you hear those sounds?" he asked.

"I was walking around the rubble, looking for anything that could be salvaged. According to the records we found, the East Wing was demolished somewhere between 1910 and 1915. It was a very modern scientific facility for its time, but all the equipment was said to have been left behind. Some of the rooms had ceilings that opened up to let in the sunlight. Those rooms were supposedly buried and a few patients were left down there when the structure fell. Ever since then, there's always been stories of ghosts."

"I'll bet. Can I get a closer look?"

"We should stick to the perimeter. The surveying crew started in on this spot a few months ago, but we haven't gotten any results. There's a lot to dig up."

Jarvis nodded as he continued walking forward. "I was a contractor for thirteen years before taking this job, so I know my way around messes like this one."

Even though Steve didn't seem comfortable with Jarvis continuing to walk onto the rubble, he wasn't about to rush forward to stop him.

After all the dark corners Jarvis had looked into, the feeling of being near something truly supernatural was unmistakable. It wasn't anything as simple as a chill or hairs standing up on the back of his neck. It was something deeper and more primal. Perhaps it was the same thing that made deer snap their heads up as danger approached or that caused every cricket within earshot to stop their chirping at · the same exact instant.

Like most people who lived or worked so close to such things, Steve had also gotten familiar with that sensation. "Creepy, isn't it?"

"Yeah. What's that hole over there?"

Steve kept his hands clasped casually behind him and leaned forward. Making a face, he shrugged and replied, "Don't know. I haven't stepped foot out here since the surveyors told us to stay away."

"And how long ago was that?"

"A month or so. Too bad you couldn't get here sooner. We could've crawled all over there if you'd arrived before the surveyors came. They must be on vacation or waiting for supplies, because I haven't heard from them for a while."

"Sorry about the delay," Jarvis said. "We get a lot of different calls." He kept walking toward the hole, which was a black pit just big enough for a refrigerator to be lowered through it. The entrance to the pit was tucked at the bottom of one of the slopes made up of cracked bricks and powdery mortar. Everything from beams to copper pipes stuck up from the debris, making the East Wing look as if it had been crushed beneath the heel of God rather than knocked over by mere mortals. "Is it all right if I get a look inside?"

Steve winced. "It may not be safe and we may be liable for any accidents. Speaking of which, I really should have you sign something just so—"

"I think I hear something."

"Really?"

Jarvis scrambled to climb the closest pile of rubble before his guide could expand upon the legal ramifications of doing so. Although the footing was shaky here and there, he felt a solid base under his boots. Before he got to the edge of the pit, Jarvis hunkered down and steadied himself with one hand while using his other to aim the flashlight into the hole.

"What do you hear?" Steve asked. "Is it voices?"

When he leaned far enough for his front foot to slide, Jarvis crouched down to regain his balance. The motion loosened some of the rocks as well as a clump of dirt from the edge of the pit, which dropped down into the darkness to make an echoing clatter. The sound also triggered a few restless, snorting breaths.

"Are you all right?" Steve shouted.

Jarvis swung his hand back toward the other man, which was enough to quiet Steve down. He then aimed his flashlight toward a spot at the bottom of the pit where he'd heard those noises. The first thing to catch the glare of his flashlight was the reflective tape on the edge of a bright yellow vest. Next, Jarvis's eyes were drawn to a series of quick flicking motions coming from one section of the hole. Laying there, curled up on its side, was a twisted abomination of a living thing.

Although it wore the shredded waistband and one leg of a pair of jeans, along with a few shreds of an oversized sweater, the thing inside those clothes was far from human. In worse light and through a dense fog, it might have been mistaken for a large hound or wolf. Most of its body was covered in skin that looked like a coagulation of fluid that had sprouted irregular patches of coarse hair. One of its knees had the reversed bend of an animal's hind leg, while the other was still human enough to keep its work boot in place. The longer Jarvis shined his light onto its face, the more the thing twitched and snorted its way out of a fretful sleep.

Jarvis hoped to avert a disaster by moving the light away from the thing, but only managed to find two more of them laying on a thick bed of leaves and garbage a few yards from the first one. One of those things looked partially human, but the other was gnarled beyond recognition. That one was larger than the other two, and lay without any shreds of clothing on its body. Lighter hairs sprouted to form a tangled shell over a bony frame. Its muscles looked as if they'd been tied into knots beneath its flesh, and at least three of the ribs pressing against its leathery flesh were clearly broken. The longer Jarvis looked at the things down in that pit, the more he wanted to figure out what the hell they were. And then, not long after he noticed the dark glistening puddles on the pit's floor, the scent of blood hit his nose.

Suddenly, the fretful breathing from the pit caught in the back of a gnarled throat. Dirt scraped against rock as one of the things shifted in the darkness.

Jarvis could feel those things' eyes pivoting toward him without needing to see them. Natural reflex got him rolling away from the edge of the pit before one of the things caught sight of him looking down at them. The moment his back hit the pile of rubble, he froze. The sound he'd made echoed through his ears like an explosion, but it quickly faded; only followed by more shifting and a choking snore.

Doing his best to collect himself, Jarvis got to his feet and hurried away from the pit as quickly and quietly as he could.

"Find anything?" Steve asked anxiously.

"No, I just slipped a little. There's . . . a hole. That hole over there. See it? Stay away from there. In fact, don't let anyone near it."

"Is it about to collapse?"

Relieved to have such a good excuse handed to him, Jarvis nodded and said, "Yep. It's pretty dangerous."

"What about your investigation? Will you be coming back with a team?"

Now that he couldn't smell the blood and couldn't see those twisted, half-animal wretches, Jarvis was able to think a lot clearer. "Yeah. I'll be coming back with a team, but I need you to do me a favor."

"What?" Steve asked as his eyes lit up with anticipation.

"It's very important that this site isn't disturbed any further. Spirits get agitated when their homes are messed with, and if there's any activity, we want to be here to record it." Sensing the gears turning within the other man's head, he added, "When they're agitated, they just might disperse, so we may only get one chance at recording some real good activity."

Steve kept nodding passionately. "All right. The renovations are already on hold, but I'll leave a note for the caretakers to take some time off. Just let me know when you're coming back."

"Will do. Are there any records or plans for this place, because I'd sure like to see them."

"They're in my office. I'll be right back." With that, Steve jogged back toward the remains of the mansion and headed for the quarter of the structure that had actually been rebuilt enough to stand on its own.

Once Steve was safely out of sight, Jarvis reached for his phone and flipped it open. The expensive piece of equipment snagged a few bars of signal strength right away and made its connection as soon as he hit the speed dial button.

"MEG Branch 25," droned the voice at the other end of the connection.

"Hey Will, it's Jarvis. I'm at the Lancroft Reformatory. Look up Prophet's number, will ya?"

"Why don't you have it? Aren't you supposed to be meeting him soon?"

"He's one of those guys. You know the ones."

"Oh. Give me a minute." The sound of fingers clacking against a keyboard drifted through the phone as Will asked, "You find anything at Lancroft?"

"Yeah. It's something Prophet might know what to do with. There's not enough time to explain it to you right now and I wish I could forget I'd even seen it."

"One of those cases, huh? Sweet."

Chapter 7

Cole was no stranger to flying. In the first few weeks after he was hired by Digital Dreamers, he'd been forced to fly more than a southbound duck as he made the move from Modesto and got everything squared away. And once his job began, he was saddled with the chauffeur hat dozens of times to pick up visiting executives when they arrived at Seattle-Tacoma International. He'd even been to O'Hare a few times.

Now, landing at O'Hare in a sorry excuse for a prop plane was like ambling along the Los Angeles freeways in an old pickup that couldn't do more than forty miles per hour. By the time the landing gear bounced on the tarmac, he was longing for the sweet touch of the customs officers who'd sifted through the plane and other things at a smaller airport in Montana.

While he'd been probed in Montana almost as much as the plane itself, his luggage was logged and the bloody knife stashed in a compartment above the landing gear. The officer performing the inspection went through the motions, but wasn't about to hold the plane up any longer than it took for the proper forms to be filled out. Cole thought he saw some scars on the officer's palms that vaguely reminded him of

Gerald's, but before he could decide if that was important or not, the plane was on its way to its next refueling spot. He was more than happy to distance himself from what had happened up there.

The old plane had taken its sweet time getting to Chicago, which made it easier for him to focus on more immediate things, like sleeping, being sick, or praying. Landing at O'Hare took place in much the same way: rough, yet successful. Even though he winced at the sound of all those bigger jets in the vicinity, Andy touched down and taxied to his spot without a hitch. After they rolled up to one of the smaller terminals, the engines were cut and Andy pushed open the door.

"This is where we part ways, Squid," he said, using the affectionate nickname he'd given to Cole after watching him squirm during some of the rougher landings along the way.

Cole staggered down the bent metal steps leading from the plane. Almost as soon as he'd stepped onto terra firma, he was catching Gerald's luggage as it was tossed from the cargo hatch.

Hunching down beside the musty compartment, Andy asked, "You got anything else?"

"Yeah," Cole replied as he hefted Gerald's bag over his shoulder, "but it's all back in Canada."

"I don't think you'll want to go back to that cabin anytime soon. I heard some Mounties found the whole bloody mess."

"What day is it?" Cole asked.

Andy looked at his watch. "Thursday. Looks like I made good time getting here."

"Good time? I could've driven here quicker."

"So I had some stops to make. It ain't like you had to pay for your damn ticket. Besides, we had to kill some time before our boy at the Montana customs office was on duty. At least you won't have to visit customs here. They got real fat fingers and know just where to stick 'em."

Cole didn't want to argue, and he sure didn't want to take this conversation any further. Instead, he wanted to find a nice, overpriced airport lounge where he could buy an obscenely expensive drink and let nature take its course. Then again, the thought of those fat fingers was a difficult one to shake, and there were plenty of other places to drop too much on a drink.

"You'll want to go through there as quick as you can," Andy said, pointing to a small building at the perimeter of the commercial terminals. "Anyone asks any questions about yer bags, just show 'em the ticket you got in Great Falls. Don't linger, though. Wouldn't be wise to push yer luck. Think you can find yer way from here, Squid?"

"Yeah. There might be a sign or two pointing to the front doors."

The pilot waved at Cole as if sending back an order of undercooked chicken. "It's been a real . . . well . . . it's been real."

Walking through the smaller building with almost as many knots in his stomach as he'd had when running away from the rampaging animal back in Canada, Cole nodded at a pair of disinterested customs officers while showing them the slip he'd gotten in Montana. After navigating the crowded metallic mess of walkways, magazine shops, and overpriced fast food booths, he stepped outside of O'Hare's main terminal. Now he just needed to make his way to the rows of cabs, buses, shuttles, and other vehicles lined up outside the place.

Gazing longingly at the vehicles, Cole reached into his pocket for his phone. It had a strong enough signal, but none of the phone numbers he needed. He flipped the phone shut and replaced it with the satellite device he'd taken from Gerald. After pushing a few buttons and waiting through a few ring tones, he finally heard some familiar words.

"Hello. This is MEG Branch 40. What can I do for you?"

"My name is Cole and—"

"Hey Cole," the operator replied. "This is Stu again."

"Don't they ever give you a day off?" Cole asked.

"Hell no. Ahh. I see you're in Chi Town. You need to hook up with Paige?"

"Just meeting her would do fine."

Stu chuckled and clacked through a few more keystrokes. "Actually, I was about to call you. She wanted to know as soon as you landed. I'll patch you through."

Before Cole could say another word to Stu, another voice came along to replace his.

"That you, Cole?" Paige asked.

"Yeah. I'm at O'Hare."

"Great. Here's the address to meet me. Grab a cab and tell them to step on it. I'll pay for whatever you can't cover."

"All right."

Paige rattled off an address and Cole repeated it back to her. She then asked, "You feeling all right?"

"I think so," he replied with a grateful breath. "That plane ride was brutal. Maybe we could get something to eat."

"Sounds good."

"You like pizza?" After a few quiet seconds passed, Cole asked, "Would you rather have burgers? Hello?"

The line was dead. Even though the silence of empty air was unmistakable, Cole held the phone down so he could get a good look at the screen. "She hung up on me," he muttered. Rather than try to convince himself the state-of-the-art satellite connection had failed, he put the phone in his pocket and looked for a ride.

The cab at the front of the line was driven by a bald man in his early fifties chomping on a pen cap. "Help ya with that bag?" he grunted as he jumped from the sputtering car.

"As if your tip depended on it," Cole replied.

The cabbie took that comment as it was intended and started laughing. "What's in there? A bomb?"

Cole chuckled. "No. Just some—"

"It goes in the trunk."

The cabbie squinted at the security tags stuck to the bag and shut the trunk tightly.

He lightened up a bit once he was back behind the wheel with his backside pressed securely against his beaded seat cover. "Where you headed?" he asked.

Cole leaned forward and grunted as some of the pain from his ribs and back seeped through his body. After reciting the address he'd been given, he added, "There's a big tip in store if you get me there real qui—"

The cab lurched forward and squealed away from the front of the line with enough force to push Cole into the trunk.

The springs beneath him felt poised to snap through a thin layer of upholstery that felt more like wadded newspapers. Horns blared from his left and the whistle of the cop directing the cabs sounded to his right. Braking and slamming on the gas a few more times amid a flurry of obscenities, the cabbie finally made it to smoother waters.

Glancing into the rearview mirror, he asked, "That address is in Cicero, ain't it?"

"Sure," Cole replied, even though he had no clue.

"Your lucky day, my friend. I grew up not too far from there."

It did Cole plenty of good just to get some concrete under his feet and see some familiar buildings around him. He might not have been able to rattle off business names and addresses, but the city had a feel to it that was just . . . Chicago. Every time he visited the place, he'd sworn to come back when he had more time to look around. During one of the Digital Dreamers gaming tournaments that were held in Aurora, he'd gone to Chicago and had a hot dog that made him want to pack his things and move there. Right now, the simple fact that Chicago wasn't Canada was more than enough to give the city a few stars in his personal rating.

Cole leaned back and pulled in a lungful of air that was saturated with too much freshener and a hint of burnt exhaust from the heater. Chicago rolled past his window in an endless stream of lights, dirty buildings, and illuminated billboards. The sun had been setting when his plane was landing, so it was completely dark by now. A commercial for an upcoming festival by Lake Michigan sounded through the cab's speakers, and the cabbie kept right on chatting throughout the entire duration of the ride.

"You live here or you just visiting?" the cabbie asked as he tapped the brakes.

"Visiting."

"Well, you should have a great time while you're in town." With that, he brought the cab to a stop and pressed a button on his meter. "You want help with that luggage?"

"We're here already?"

"I told ya I'd get you here fast, didn't I?"

"I guess I was just enjoying the ride." Cole got out as the cabbie walked around to the trunk. Although he didn't know what to expect, he hadn't been expecting to be taken to a restaurant that was already closed up for the night. "You sure this is the right place?"

Abruptly, the cabbie lost his smirk and rushed over to his side. "That's the address you gave me!" He closed his eyes, moved his lips as he grumbled to himself, and finally let out a breath. "This is the place," he said defensively.

Cole looked at what was painted on the white walls near a set of thick, wooden front doors. There had once been a name written over the door, but all that was left was enough lettering to spell out RASA HILL. Even though the numbers beside the door matched the ones in his head, he dug in his pocket for his phone anyway. "Stay here," he said to the cabbie. "Let me just double-check something."

He flipped open the satellite phone and started to dial MEG's number. Before he could finish, the screech of rusted hinges caught his ear. He turned toward that sound and saw the front door of the restaurant being opened by a short brunette.

"No need to waste your minutes," she said while holding the heavy door open. Her faded jeans, black shirt, and old tennis shoes were obviously more comfortable than fashionable, but didn't take away from the her trim, athletic figure. The hair pulled behind her head had a tussled look about it even though most of it was corralled by a couple of elastic ties. Despite the downward curve of her lips, her face retained an undeniable attractiveness. Her nose was slightly crooked, as if it had been broken once or twice in the past, but even that didn't take anything away from her. She looked at him and the cabbie with an air of authority that rolled off her like smoke.

"You must be Cole," she said.

He nodded a bit too much in a weak attempt to mask the fact that he'd been staring at her. The cabbie, on the other hand, made no such attempt.

"I'm Cole, all right." Looking to the cabbie, he added, "This must be the right place after all."

"It sure the hell is," the cab driver said. "I was just about to ask if I could stay myself."

"That won't be necessary," the brunette said as she stepped forward to hand the cabbie some money. Despite the fact that she was several inches shorter than the older man, she dismissed him as if he was a schoolboy. "Here you go."

"Thanks a lot, ma'am. I'll unload this bag and carry it inside for ya."

"I think we can manage just fine."

"I lugged this stuff all over the airport. Another few feet won't hurt," Cole said as he grabbed his duffel bag from the open trunk and sucked in a pained breath. "Actually, it may hurt just a little."

The brunette gave him a quick smile, took the duffel in one hand and walked into the restaurant. Cole looked toward the cabbie just in time to see the driver's door close and the cab drive away.

The brunette waited at the door for him and held it open so Cole could walk inside. "I'm Paige Strobel, by the way. But I guess you already figured that out by now."

"Hello, Paige. I'm the guy with bruised ribs who dragged his ass across the continent to pay you a visit as a courtesy to your friends."

Without moving from her spot by the door, Paige added, "And I'm the woman with the dead friends who arranged to have you brought all the way out here."

"Ouch. Guess I had that coming. Sorry about the attitude. It's been a long trip."

"Don't feel too bad," she said as she shut and locked the door once he was inside. "I know you've been through a lot. I've been just settling in here, so there's a lot on my plate too. Make yourself comfortable, and you'll just have to excuse the mess."

The place was a restaurant, but looked as if it had been condemned for a year or more. Some of the tables were in place and most of the lights worked, but there was a layer of dust on just about everything. When he looked a little closer at the floor, Cole could see a path through the dust that led from the front door to the kitchen.

Seeing Paige was about to disappear through the kitchen door, he realized he was being brushed aside just like the cabbie had been a minute ago. More than that, he felt like an idiot for going through so much bullshit to make such a tedious trip in the first place. He rushed to catch up to her, but before he could, the door was slammed almost directly into his face. "Hey!" he shouted as he pushed it open the door and stomped into the next room. "I've come a long way and I think I deserve some explanations! Who the hell are you?"

Paige stood with her back to him in a large, clean kitchen. She was behind a counter, so he could only see her from the waist up. When she turned around, she looked at him with sharp eyes that weren't exactly cold, but were a long way from warm. In her hand was a small syringe. "Were you hurt in the attack?" she asked.

The concern in her voice was genuine, which shifted Cole's focus away from his anger. He reflexively reached for his ribs and took a shallow breath, but only got a slight pinch in return. "It could have been worse. I was wearing a lot of layers when I got knocked around. Brad and Gerald drew that thing away from me before it could . . ." That night at the cabin screamed back into his thoughts, and he did his best to shove those memories back into the spot they'd been hiding.

"So you're feeling all right?"

"Yeah. More or less. I mean, I might have broken something, but it's better now."

Paige nodded and raised an eyebrow to put the icing upon a cute, sympathetic frown. "Or maybe you weren't hurt as badly as it seemed at the time."

"No. I *was* hurt. I was slammed up against a freakin' wall!"

Keeping her eyes locked upon him, Paige walked around the counter. Until that moment, Cole could say that he'd rarely ever seen a woman saunter. There was no mistaking it this time, however. Whether she meant to do it or not, Paige's walk was most definitely a saunter. Considering the slow shifting of her hips and the grip her eyes had upon him, he discovered he liked sauntering very much.

Once she got within arm's reach of him, she snapped out one hand to flick her fingers against his ribs.

"What the hell?" he said as he was abruptly pulled from his happy place.

"If your ribs were broken, you'd be in tears right now. Or close to it, anyway. Seems like you're just bruised up. If you're still hurting, though," she added while holding up the syringe, "I can help."

"You can help, huh? Oh no. I'm not letting you give me any drugs."

Paige held out the syringe to show that it was only slightly bigger than the pencils handed out at miniature golf courses. "If you must know, it's a vitamin serum," she explained. "It'll make it a whole lot easier to breathe and it might even give you a bit more energy after all the traveling you've done."

"You sound like you're talking from experience."

"I am. Are you going to let me give you this or not? I promise you'll feel better." When she saw the uncertainty in his eyes, she added, "It's the least I can do for everything you've done so far."

Cole placed his hands on the cool metallic surface of the countertop and let his head hang down. "If I can have some ice water, that would be just fine."

The moment those words were out of his mouth, Paige leaned forward and slapped her hand down on top of his. She moved so quickly that he couldn't even think about reacting before she dropped her other hand and stuck the needle into his arm.

"Fuck!" he said reflexively.

She pushed down on the little plunger and then removed the syringe. "Don't be such a baby. It's already over."

"I'm not being a baby."

"Yes you are. These are the same needles I use to give insulin to my diabetic cat, and you're pitching a bigger fit than he ever did."

Cole stared her dead in the eyes and lowered his voice to an intense growl. "What did you put in me?"

Rather than reply, she placed the needle on the counter, showed him her empty hands, then jabbed him in the ribs.

Cole tensed and let out the first half of a pained scream. The second half didn't come out because no pain followed the punch. Looking down at himself, he patted his chest and tentatively pressed down on what had so recently been the sore spots. "What in the hell?" he asked while patting his torso harder and harder. "What the *hell*?"

"You swear a lot, you know that?"

"Yeah? Well here's some more for ya. What the fuck is going on here?"

Paige looked at him with the slightest trace of sympathy in her eyes. "Would you like something other than water to drink?" she asked through her laughter.

"I could use a beer."

"How about some whiskey?"

"Even better."

Walking farther into the kitchen, she made her way to a large cabinet. It wasn't the saunter she'd used before, but her body naturally moved well enough to hold Cole's attention. She reached inside the cabinet and came out with a bottle in one hand and two shot glasses in the other. After setting the bottle down on the middle of the counter next to the empty syringe, she placed one glass in front of her and the other in front of him.

"If you'd like to sit down at one of the tables in the next room, we can talk like civilized people," she said.

"I just hope you don't spike my drink or force me to fly to another part of the country in some milk crate of an airplane."

"Or," Paige added in a cool, level tone, "you could always leave."

"Just walk out of here and try to buy a cheap ticket to Seattle with whatever's left in my wallet, huh? I don't even have my own luggage. I've been wearing your friend's clothes since I bolted from that cabin." Suddenly he winced, and added, "I'm sorry. I just meant that . . ."

"I know what you're saying," Paige said with a sigh. "I could arrange for another plane ticket."

Cole nodded while she filled his glass with whiskey. As much as he wanted to down the liquor, he waited for her to sip from her own glass first. Only then did he allow himself to drink. He wasn't normally a whiskey sort of guy, but the stuff did a hell of a good job loosening the knot that had been tied in his chest.

"You're dying to ask questions. Where do you want to start?" Paige asked.

"What did you inject me with?"

"Vitamins . . . mostly. Also," she added, "it was an immunization. After getting into a fight with the thing in that cabin, there was a chance of you . . . catching something."

Cole's eyes widened and he straightened up. "Like a disease?"

"Sort of."

"How will I know if I have it or not?"

"Since you haven't keeled over yet, I'd say you should be fine. Apparently, that thing didn't tear you up too badly or draw too much blood."

"I could've told you that much," he grumbled.

Paige shrugged and topped off their drinks. "Better safe than sorry. Do you have another question?"

"Who are you?"

"My name is Paige Strobel, just like I told you before. Gerald and I worked together for a while. In fact, he was supposed to be the one moving into this place instead of me."

"What kind of work do you do?"

Paige kept her eyes down. She reached for the whiskey, but didn't pick it up. "That's a little harder to explain."

"What about Brad? Was he in the same line of work?"

She nodded. "All three of us work for the same cause."

"Oh Lord," Cole moaned, "Is this a religious thing? I was going to guess a drug ring, with all the syringes and smuggling contacts, but . . . I honestly don't know which would be worse at this point."

"It's not either of those. Why don't I approach this another way?" Paige placed her hands flat on the counter, straightened her arms and then shook her head as if silently agreeing to an unpopular decision. Finally, she asked, "Why did you come here?"

The scowl on Cole's face dissolved the moment he heard that question. He let out a breath and then looked up to watch Paige's face as he said, "Gerald's dead. So is Brad. Gerald wanted me to come here and tell you about what happened

personally, before you got the news from . . . well . . . I guess
you may have already talked to the cops since it took so
damn long for me to get here."

After a brief pause, Paige said, "Go on."

He recounted what had brought him to Canada, and Paige
listened to every word. When he got to the part of his story
involving that night at the cabin, he reflexively picked up his
shot glass.

"I don't know what it was," he said. "At first I thought it
was a bear, then I thought it was a wolf. But it wasn't any
of those things. It was huge. I've never even heard of anything like it. One guy shot it, but that didn't do anything.
Gerald and Brad tried to kill it. They lasted longer than most
anyone, but I guess that thing finally got to them too."

"You guess?"

"I was knocked around pretty good," he sighed. "I woke
up the next morning. There was blood everywhere. Brad was
dead, but Gerald was outside. He was hurt really bad."

He paused to see if he needed to give her a moment before
continuing. Paige was listening intently, so he went on.

"Gerald told me to call you. He said that I should come to
see you in person to tell you what happened. He also told me
to tell you that Brad was killed fighting a Full Blood. Does
that mean anything to you?"

Paige kept staring straight at him, then finally looked
away and nodded.

"He gave me a card and I called the number using his
phone. You must know the rest."

"How was he in the end?" she asked.

Cole felt as if his words were anchored down so heavily
that it took extra effort to pull them up. "I don't think he was
in much pain. It was so cold—"

"That's not what I mean," she snapped. "Did he seem
strange? Did he look strange?"

"Strange?"

Paige scraped at the base of her throat and said, "Black
marks here. Maybe they looked like ink?"

"Yes," Cole replied as the image was suddenly brought
into sharp focus. "Yes, he did have marks like that!"

"Was he holding anything that looked like this?" With a quick flourish of her hand, Paige removed a small vial from her pocket. It was the size of a stick of lip balm, but was actually one glass tube inside another. The inner capsule was filled with dark liquid and there was a layer of cloudy water separating it from the outer tube. Two small bumps extended from one side that tapered down to a pair of small, clear pins connecting the outside of the vial to the inner capsule.

"He had something in his hand, but it was broken," Cole said without taking his eyes from the peculiar object resting in Paige's grasp. Just then, he noticed the scarring on her palm. It wasn't quite as bad as what had been on Gerald's hands, but was very similar. "I guess it could have been something like that. Some of the broken glass stuck in his hand did look like those two things on the side of that tube."

"And he got better," Paige said more to herself than to him.

"Yeah. He did."

"What happened after that?"

"Gerald died before I left. I don't know for sure, but it looked like he injected himself with something." This time, Cole didn't need to watch closely to see a reaction.

"Thank God," she said while letting out a breath and lowering her head.

"I mentioned he was dead, right?" Cole asked. "He looked better, but he was dead by the time I left."

"I know." Looking up, Paige showed him a relieved if somewhat tired smile. "At least he'll stay that way. This," she said, showing him the glass tube in her hand, "is called a Resurrection Vial. It's used to give someone a bit more time if they think that . . . well . . . if things get bad. The only problem is that the stuff in this vial may cause some pretty bad side effects. Once someone's done what they needed to do with their extra time, they inject themselves with the antidote and nature takes its course."

"You mean they kill themselves?"

Paige shook her head. Although she seemed a bit frustrated, there was plenty of relief to dull the edge that had been in her voice before. "If they're using the vial, they're already going to die. If they don't use the antidote, they'll be turned into something else that will kill them off and turn them into something else."

Cole stayed still for a moment as he tried to think about what he should do next. Although he'd come to Chicago to put what had happened in Canada to rest, the whole thing just kept growing into something more. Talking to Paige hadn't helped. In fact, meeting her had only presented even more information that he couldn't sort out. Instead of trying to make sense of anything else, he decided to stay confused. "All right," he said. "That's it. I'm leaving. Thanks for the plane tickets and whatever you shot me up with, but I'll just find my own way home."

Paige got to her feet and moved around the counter to stand between him and the front door. "Don't leave, Cole. Please."

"I've seen more than enough to keep me up at night, and I did what I promised to do for Gerald. I'll leave your bloody knife here and then I'm through. So long. Have a nice life."

"A Full Blood can track a scent for thousands of miles," she said abruptly. "And you wouldn't have agreed to come this far if you weren't just a little curious about what attacked you."

Cole let out a tired breath. "Curiosity is one thing. The stuff that's going on here . . . I may not understand it, but I know when I'm over my head."

"Taking what's in the Resurrection Vial wasn't easy. There was a lot more risk involved for Gerald than if he'd just let himself fade away. He did that for a reason, and only part of it was the job he asked you to do. Considering how much trouble you've already gone through, the least I can do is keep you alive until we can figure out what attacked that cabin. If it wasn't a Full Blood, it still might be able to hunt you down. Wouldn't you like to do something to keep that thing or others like it from running around and tearing people apart whenever they damn well feel like it?"

"Sure, but . . . if I'm doing all of that, I want to know everything else you haven't told me."

Paige smiled like a poker player who'd gotten someone to go all in when there wasn't a card in the deck that could save them. "Better yet, why don't we take a field trip? Bring that knife."

Chapter 8

Cole knew he should have followed his first instinct and gone home.

He also should have been feeling pain in his battered body, but that wasn't acting like it was supposed to either. Sitting in the passenger seat of Paige's used two-door Chevy Cavalier, he poked and prodded his sides and actually hoped to feel a sting. He felt something that shook him more than pain. He felt his fingers pressing against his ribs, and that meant he wasn't just numbed by whatever Paige had given him. His ribs were better. In fact, they felt stronger than before.

"You said there was a danger of some kind of infection," he reminded her. "What was that about?"

Paige nodded but kept her eyes on the road. "It'll all go down a lot easier once you see some things firsthand. Besides, the man I'm taking you to see can explain it a lot better than I can."

Looking out the window, Cole asked, "All right, then. Where are you taking me?"

"We're headed to The Levee."

Cole thought for a moment and asked, "You mean like in that Led Zeppelin song? The Levee that breaks?"

"Sort of."

"Isn't that the old Red Light District?"

"That's the original Levee. This is sort of an homage,"

Paige said, while letting the last word roll off her tongue in a way that put a little grin on her face. "It's a nice little stretch of road just south of the Loop. If you're looking for some exercise for your lower back now that you're in better shape, I'm sure we can rent you a partner for the night."

Cole studied her for a second. Judging by the grin on Paige's face, her mind was in the same gutter as his. "You're talking about hookers."

"Pretty much."

He let out a sigh and shook his head. Even though the streets outside the car's windows still looked vaguely familiar, they weren't nearly as comforting as the ones he'd seen from the cab. "I must be crazy to go along with this."

"You probably are a little crazy," Paige agreed. "But you must also be something else to have made it this far. Gerald wouldn't have sent you to me unless he saw some spark in you."

"I barely even knew the guy."

"Exactly! You barely even knew him, but you still made a promise to him and you kept it. Plenty of people do the first part, but not many bother with the rest. Let me ask you something," Paige said as she turned off of I–290. "What did the rest of those people do when that thing attacked?"

"And that's another thing! What the hell is a Full Blood?"

"We'll get to that later. Just answer the question."

"They screamed," Cole replied. "They ran. They died. There was a whole lot of the last one going around."

Paige nodded and ran the tip of her tongue along her upper lip. "And what did you do?"

"Not much. I tried to get some of those people out of there. I tried to help Gerald or find Brad, but I wound up getting my ass knocked against a wall."

"You tried to fight," she said emphatically. Pointing a finger at him, she added, "You tried to fight even though you had no clue what you were up against and you had no weapon to use against it. You tried to help those people, and when it was all over, you made a promise to a dying man and went through a whole lot of craziness to see it through. That's extraordinary, Cole."

Although he'd been ready to fire back with something else, he didn't quite know how to respond when she looked at him with genuine admiration. "Uh . . . thanks?"

"What did Brad and Gerald do when the thing attacked?"

"I don't even know. All I do know is that they were the only ones to even scratch it. They saved my life."

"That's right," she said while patting the bundle resting on Cole's knee. "And because you brought this knife back, we'll be able to make that sacrifice worthwhile."

No matter how many gruesome images filled Cole's mind, he couldn't be diverted from the fact that Paige's hand was in his lap. Sure, there might have been some steel wrapped in a plastic bag and cotton rags separating her from the rest of him, but he could feel the warmth of her touch all the way through those things. Looking up at her, he raised his eyebrows and smirked.

"Good Lord," Paige grumbled as she took her hand back. "I thought you were supposed to be traumatized."

"I am, but I'm not dead."

Paige shook her hand while weaving between two cars that had the nerve to uphold the speed limit and replied, "I can fix that real quick."

"So tell me about the Full Blood," Cole said, as a way to steer the conversation out of the weeds. "Was Gerald after that thing?"

"We don't know for certain it was a Full Blood yet," Paige declared. "But they sure as hell weren't in Canada for that. Full Bloods are smart, though, and somehow this one must have found them before they could prepare for it."

Cole looked out the window to watch as more of Chicago flew by. He pulled in a deep breath and let it out through his nose.

"You seem to be taking all of this pretty well," Paige said. "Better than Brad did, anyway."

"Let me guess. You were all chasing ghosts together or maybe trying to snap a picture of Bigfoot?"

"What?" Paige said as a scowl settled upon her face.

"That phone number," Cole said. "You know . . . Stu? MEG Branch 40?"

Paige nodded and her scowl disappeared. "Oh! The MEG guys. We just use those guys for communications and the occasional high-tech thingie."

"High-tech thingie? You keep talking like that and you'll ruin that tough exterior you're trying to maintain."

Paige glanced over at him with a cute smirk that made her nose crinkle. By now some more of her hair had slipped from where it was tied in the back so it could dangle on either side of her face. In the glow from the cars and street-lights that rushed past the window, a light brown hue could be seen amid the strands of black. "It's a long story, but the MEG guys investigate hauntings and demons and other crap like that all over the country."

"Ghosts don't rank as high as monsters, huh?" Cole chuckled.

Shrugging impassively, Paige continued. "The ectological group crossed our paths a few times after one of the founders nearly got killed by a Half Breed in western Nebraska."

"A Half Breed?"

"More about that later," she said while quickly waving away the questions Cole was about to ask. "Anyway, MEG's already got an international system set up to communicate with all their members and branches. Since they spend most of their time videotaping haunted houses or trying to talk to static, nobody really watches them too closely in any official way."

"And anyone who might listen in on their networks wouldn't be too surprised to hear talk about a monster attack?" Cole asked.

"Bingo," Paige replied with a snap of her fingers. "They're really nice, but they get a bit too anxious sometimes. Whenever we run across something that's not too dangerous, we hand it over to MEG and they put it on a T-shirt or sell it to some kook on eBay. We get our own little section of their network and help with the technical stuff, and they get exclusives that no other paranormal club or tabloid would ever dream of. Everybody's happy."

"Yeah," Cole grumbled as he looked out the window at scenery that appeared to be worsening with every block.

"Everybody's real happy. I understand Gerald wasn't your husband, but you don't seem too broken up about him or Brad dying."

"Dying sure beats the alternative."

"What's that supposed to mean?"

"It means that the thing you saw in Canada wasn't the only thing out there."

Cole gripped the door with one hand and the dash with the other. "Holy shit! There's one of those things out here? We're heading toward it?"

"No," she said impatiently. "There are all kinds of different shapeshifters, just like there are all kinds of other supernatural things out roaming around."

"Like what?" he asked uneasily.

Twisting her mouth in a shape that drifted from a frown to a wince and back again, she replied, "It's actually easier for you to see for yourself. I'm taking you to meet someone who will answer some questions I have. Get a good look at him. Ask him anything you like. He's a doctor, so he likes explaining things, but also look and tell me if you saw anyone else like him up in that cabin."

"How will I know if anyone looked like him?"

"You'll need a comparison. That's why you're with me now." Glancing over to his side of the car, Paige added, "You're quick."

Watching the city roll past his window, Cole waited for more of an explanation. When he didn't get it, he gritted his teeth and let out an exasperated sigh. The more he stewed, the more Paige seemed to enjoy it. Finally, he snapped. "So what else are we talking about? Zombies? Vampires? Trolls? Hit me with it."

Paige raised an eyebrow. "Two out of three ain't bad, but you only get to see one tonight."

"What?"

Ignoring his question, she turned onto a dirty street that was populated with dirty men and women dressed in next to nothing. Junkies twitched in the alleys and car stereos thumped their bass lines into the cool breezes blowing in from Lake Michigan. "We're here," she said. "Stay quiet and follow my lead. If anything happens to me, you get behind this wheel and . . . oh, what the hell is this?"

Before Cole could say another word, Paige stopped the car. She rolled down the window and within a few seconds a woman with smooth skin the color of lightly creamed coffee approached her. She was a thin, wiry Latina wearing a tattered denim miniskirt and a bright red halter top beneath a jacket that looked as if it had been made from a very unfortunate poodle. When she bent down to lean against Paige's window, the Latina pressed her pert breasts together in a move that had been honed to perfection.

"Hola, chica," Paige said with a warm smile and a voice that sounded closer to a purr.

The Latina returned Paige's smile and upped the ante with a slow lick of her lips. "You like what you see?"

"I don't know. Are you a cop?"

Cole listened to the exchange as he spotted a blonde kneeling over a scraggly looking guy with pasty skin in a nearby alley. Even from his spot in the car he couldn't help noticing that the blonde's overly generous breasts were about to explode from her white blouse. Turning as if she could feel his eyes on her, the blonde stood up and approached the car.

"Sure, I'm a cop," the Latina said as she straightened up and lifted the front of her skirt to reveal a little patch of pubic hair trimmed into the shape of a heart. "See my badge?"

"What's your name, sexy?" Paige asked, staring at the dark veins on the Latina's thighs rather than the little heart between them.

"Racquel."

"What about your blond friend over there?"

The Latina kept her eyes locked on Paige as if her legs were already entangled around her. "That's Wendy. She likes to party too, but it'll be extra."

"And why's Wendy feeding out in the open like that, Racquel?"

As soon as she heard that, Racquel narrowed her eyes and curled her upper lip to reveal a single set of fangs protruding from her upper jaw. Lowering her skirt, she growled, "Why don't you and your friend keep driving before you get hurt?"

"You know the deal, *chica*," Paige said with a slow shake of her head. "You keep your feeding in private without doing any real damage. That way, me and mine won't have to come down hard on you and yours the way we cleaned out that bunch over on Lake Shore Drive."

Wendy was still strutting toward the car. Her shirt was cropped short on the top and bottom to show a belly that was just shy of being flabby. The pasty man was now slumped over so his upper body and one arm flopped onto the sidewalk. Blood spilled from a large wound in his neck to pool on the cement.

"Uh, Paige," Cole muttered. "We might want to get out of here now."

Paige glanced quickly toward the sidewalk, spotted Wendy and the bleeding man, then slammed the car into Park. Before Cole could do anything to stop her, she was out of the car and pushing past the Latina. "In public *and* drinking someone dry?" Paige growled as she moved toward the blonde. "That's a death sentence!"

"Hey, go fuck yourself, shorty!" Wendy shouted as she spat some of the dead man's blood through the air.

Cole didn't need to see Paige's face to know that her fuse had already burned right down to the chewy, explosive center. The shift of her hips and the snap of her head as she flipped open her denim jacket to reveal the holster strapped under her left arm said more than enough.

Paige suddenly took a quick backward hop that bounced her against the mix of rust and flaking white paint covering the Chevy's exterior. Less than a second later Cole heard a loud thump. He wasn't quite sure what had dropped onto the street, but it had to have been big. He swiveled in his seat just in time to notice a large, gnarled figure behind the car, standing amid a cloud of exhaust fumes. Its head swung like a loose pendulum at the end of its neck.

When he spotted Wendy again, Cole saw another man standing beside her. He had a shaved head and eyes that were narrowed by a wide smile. His skin was chalky and peeling from what might have been a horrifically bad sunburn. Beneath the flaking layers were black markings that were

a lot thicker than the ones on the Latina's neck and thigh.
While hers resembled veins that had been traced in black,
his were more like tentacles that flowed up from his neck,
wrapped all the way around small, rounded ears, and slid up
along his skull. The tentacles met at the back of his head to
form subtle ridges where they writhed against the nape of
his neck. His mid-length, brown leather jacket barely even
rustled as he raked his fingers down the front of Wendy's
chest, ripped away the flimsy material of her shirt, and then
grabbed her roughly by one breast. Before she could react or
even protest, he sank his teeth into the spot where her neck
met her shoulder. Less than a second later blood began to
spill from her shredded jugular.

"Paige!" Cole shouted. "We need to get out of here!"

But Paige had problems of her own. She and Racquel had
put their differences aside for the moment so they could take
in the sight of the gnarled, drooling figure loping toward the
Chevy. As the thing walked, it also seemed to grow until it
was almost double the size of a normal man. After taking a
few more steps, it leaned forward and used one hand against
the cement to support his upper body. Its head remained low
and hung to one side. When it tried to get a better look at
the car in front of him, the lopsided thing winced and let
out a pained groan. Putrid rags hung off its body as if they'd
grown there and partially rotted away. Matted hair sprouting
from patches of his skin was almost long enough to cover
him where his tattered clothes couldn't reach.

"Henry!" the bald man shouted. "Catch!" With that, he
lifted Wendy's limp body off the ground and tossed it to the
thing the way he might toss scraps to a dog.

Thick, jagged fingernails scraped against the pavement as
Henry loped toward the body. His bare feet slapped against
the street inches from Wendy's half-naked body and he
began clawing at her chest. "Golden hair," he grunted. "And
the other. Dark hair. Want you both." Fluid sprayed from
Wendy's ravaged chest cavity as Henry kept tearing her
open. The stuff was a mix of dark red and oily black.

Paige drew a .45 pistol from the holster under her jacket,
and the Latina beside her drew a smaller gun from a little

pouch strapped around her waist. Both women pulled their triggers at the same time, sending their rounds into Henry's thick, dirty hide.

Cole wanted to help, but programming video games hadn't exactly put him into the habit of walking around with a gun strapped beneath his arm. Hoping that he might find another weapon somewhere in the car, he reached for the first possible hiding spot he could think of. As his fingers were fumbling with the latch of the glove compartment, another set of thin, bony fingers tapped on the window a few inches from his face. The bald man stared at him with a set of dark green eyes that showed the slightest hint of black threads wrapping around them from the inside of their sockets. He smiled widely to show just how much of Wendy's blood was smeared upon his lips and teeth.

"You want to come out now, Skinner?" the man on the other side of Cole's window asked. "Or should I come in there after you?"

Feeling every muscle in his body tense, Cole leaned toward the open driver's door and shouted, "Paige! Let's go!"

Paige had already emptied her clip into Henry and was replacing it with a fresh one. She fired another two rounds into Henry's shoulder and side, only to see a few shreds of Henry's clothing and the upper layers of skin disintegrate on impact. She might as well have been shooting at a side of thoroughly frozen beef.

If Henry even felt the bullets hitting him, he gave no sign. He flailed and convulsed on top of Wendy in a perverse set of motions, but wasn't invading her in the most obvious way. Rather than commit such a recognizable sin, he was scraping at her chest with his jagged fingernails. His hands, slick with the blackened fluid of her blood, moved quickly enough to send a gory spray through the air. Henry was digging into the woman's chest the way a dog would dig into the earth.

After Wendy's ribs had been pulled apart, he struggled to widen the terrible breach. The deeper his hands scraped within her, the faster Henry's arms flailed. As she lost the strength to hold her head up, Wendy let out a gasp and allowed her eyes to wander amid the stars above her.

"Get in the car," Paige said to Racquel.

Once Henry had ripped away the last layer separating him from his prize, he stopped and gazed down into the hole he'd made, tears welling at the corners of his eyes. Although his face was vaguely human, the way it swayed loosely at the end of his neck made the sight completely alien. It only got worse when he reached into the savaged chest cavity and pulled out something that looked like a black eel. Dozens of thin black tendrils reached desperately into the blond woman, causing her to twitch and squirm as they fought to pull the rest of its slimy black mass into her. Unable to extract the black eel thing completely, Henry leaned down and sank his teeth into the biggest section. As soon as they punctured the filmy skin, a greasy liquid rushed down his chin and into his mouth.

Although she'd been ready to fight Paige a little while ago, Racquel accepted her invitation now by jumping into the backseat of the car.

As soon Racquel's backside hit the upholstery, Paige jumped behind the wheel and slammed the door shut. "Watch yourself, Cole," she said as she gunned the engine.

Cole looked through his window to find the bald man reaching out for him with hands that were like skeletal claws wrapped in smooth, pale leather gloves. When the car sped away, the man leaned forward and allowed his nails to scrape noisily against the glass. Straining to get one more look, Cole was able to see the figure casually wave back at him. "What in the *hell* was that?" he hollered.

"That's Misonyk!" Racquel shouted as she stabbed her finger toward Cole's window. "That's him. Oh my God, get out of here!"

"Who the *hell* is Misonyk?" Cole asked.

"Meeshonyick," Racquel corrected. When she pronounced the name, it wrapped around her tongue and made her voice drop to an intimate purr.

"I don't care who he is or how you say it!" Paige shouted. Hooking her thumb toward Henry, she snapped, "What was *that*?"

But Racquel wasn't able to answer any of the questions.

Her face had lost its color, which made the black lines beneath her skin stand out even more. As if reacting to the chaos around her, the lines retracted beneath the part of her that was covered by her shirt.

Paige gripped the steering wheel in one hand and took a corner almost fast enough to put the rusted Cavalier onto two wheels. Ignoring Racquel's swearing and Cole's involuntary, somewhat girlish yelp, she handed her pistol to him and said, "There's fresh clips in the glove compartment, Cole. Can you reload this?"

Desperate to rebuild the dignity he'd just lost, he grabbed the gun and flipped open the glove compartment. "Yeah. I can do that, no problem."

"Good, because that thing with the appetite is coming after us."

Both Cole and Racquel twisted around to look out the back window. Sure enough, Henry was bounding down the street behind them, closing his distance from the car several yards at a time.

"Start talking, Racquel," Paige snapped. "What is that thing?"

Sitting upright and straightening her top and skirt, Racquel slid back into her street persona. She showed Paige a bratty scowl and asked, "Why should I tell you anything? Just who the hell are *you*?"

"I'm the one taking over Gerald's territory, and your friend should've known better than to feed in public. If that blond bitch hadn't already been torn apart, you know damn well I'd be putting her down myself!"

Although Cole was completely lost in the conversation, he wasn't about to turn his back on Racquel for long. Looking up every couple of seconds from what he was doing, he could see the Latina twitch at the sound of a solid impact behind the car. Racquel didn't even look behind her to see what had hit the cement in the Chevy's wake. As soon as Henry landed close enough for Cole to make out the slick black ooze hanging from his chin, the Chevy was thrown into a sharp turn and the engine roared toward the upper limit of its performance.

"That thing's Henry," Racquel said.

Struggling to get control after the maneuver she'd just performed, Paige asked, "What the hell is Henry?"

Racquel sank down into her seat. "I don't know what he is, but most of us didn't even think he was real. Wendy used to talk about him. She said . . ." As much as she tried to fight it, Racquel couldn't keep herself from wincing before her words stuck in the back of her throat. She swung her hand toward the back window and then pulled it back again when Henry landed behind the speeding car and took a swipe at the Chevy's bumper. Calcified nails screeched against rusted metal before the car was once again out of his reach.

Cole held the gun out toward Paige and said, "Here you go. I think it's ready."

"Good," Paige replied as she twisted the wheel to take another corner, scattering the group of kids who had been standing there. "Now do me a favor and shoot that thing."

Cole rolled down the window and stuck his arm out before pulling it back in again. He shifted in his seat and started to aim out the window but caught a very surprised glance from a bar they were driving past. He tried shifting again, nearly dropped the gun, then fell back into his seat with a frustrated grunt. As much as he wanted to lean out the window and fire away, he grudgingly had to admit it looked a hell of a lot easier in the movies.

"So, what about Wendy?" Paige asked as she looked at Racquel in the rearview mirror.

Racquel pulled in a breath to steady herself. "She's been listening to Misonyk and preaching all his bullshit to me and anyone else who'd listen."

"Okay, tell me about this Misonyk," Paige said.

"Gerald knew about him," Racquel replied. Didn't he tell you?"

"No. What's Misonyk been spreading around? And will you shoot already, Cole? That thing already took my bumper off!"

"I'm trying! I don't do this every day, you know!"

"Fine," Paige snarled. "Both of you hold on." With that, she blew past an expensive looking SUV and gunned her engine down a long stretch of road. She had to blaze through a few red lights along the way, but it was late enough at night and in a bad enough neighborhood for there to be a minimum of other cars around. The only police car Cole spotted was parked outside a Jack in the Box four blocks ago.

Paige stared at the road intently, pulled the wheel to the left and slammed on her brakes. She only needed to watch the rearview mirror for a few more seconds before Henry landed on the street with a loud thump and began slamming his hands against the trunk. Throwing the car into Reverse, she stepped on the gas and drove the Chevy right into Henry's gut. She kept the car moving until she pinned him against a telephone pole. "There," she said as she looked over to Cole. "Easy enough target for ya?"

Twisting around to lean out the window, he gripped the gun with both hands and took aim. Henry's lower body was crushed between the pole and the back end of the Cavalier, but he was still squirming and slapping his hands against the trunk as if he wasn't so much hurt by the impact as confused that he couldn't move. Cole fired and missed his first few rounds. Cars screeched to a stop somewhere nearby and sirens wailed in the distance. There wasn't a lot of time before more people would be dragged into this mess, and he knew it would be better for the cops to find a bizarre corpse than a live, heart-eating freak. He let a few more bullets fly and saw them hit their mark amid a fine spray of dirty hair and a hint of blood.

Gritting his teeth as he pulled the trigger again, Cole shook his head and fired his last few rounds. "This isn't doing much," he said. "I don't even think I'm hurting it."

The moment his gun was empty, Paige drove the Chevy forward a few feet, slammed it into Reverse and backed into Henry again. The impact rocked everyone inside. Henry moaned and wailed, but wasn't losing steam.

Paige shook her head, threw the car into Drive and sped away. Looking into the rearview mirror, she nodded quickly and said, "I think that shook him up a bit."

Cole dropped back into his seat beside her and opened the glove compartment angrily. "Next time, tell me before you do that! I was still hanging out the goddamn window!"

"Next time try aiming for the head!" she replied. "I thought you were the big video-game freak. Isn't that rule number one when shooting at something?"

As much as Cole wanted to shout back at her, he didn't have much to say. Paige was right about rule number one. He reloaded the pistol, while shifting his focus between several different spots. Racquel was curled up in the backseat with her arms over her head. Paige was speeding toward a ramp that would take her onto I–94. And most important, Henry was still shaking off the gunshots and impacts from the Chevy when Cole lost sight of him.

"Keep talking, Racquel," Paige said in a miraculously calm voice. "What's Misonyk been spreading around and what the hell is that Henry thing?"

Racquel sat up again, but didn't even try to regain her composure. Instead, she rubbed her face with trembling hands and replied, "I need a drink, but nowhere around here."

"Where should I go?"

"Try Oak Lawn. The only Nymar out there keeps to himself and won't have anything to do with Misonyk or anyone who'd listen to him. Plus, he runs a pizza place and it's open all night."

"Thank God," Cole said. "I thought it'd be forever until we got some food."

Paige smirked at him and dug her phone from her pocket. "I still want to meet up with Daniels, but he should be able to meet us for pizza. What's the address, Racquel?"

"Are you talkin' about that little guy from Schaumburg?" Racquel asked.

Paige looked at her in the rearview mirror. "Yeah."

"He used to be one of Wendy's regulars, but he ain't been in town for weeks. A lot of Nymar left after Misonyk showed up, so he's probably one of them."

As if on cue, Paige received a disconnect message from the number she'd dialed. "Great," she muttered as she snapped her phone shut. "That's just great."

Cole looked at her with concern etched deeply into his face. "We're still going for pizza, though, right?"

Chapter 9

The place was called DiGuido's, and it was a little family-style restaurant on a quiet street amid several drugstores and a few funeral parlors. Cole didn't pay complete attention to where they were going, since he'd been more concerned with being chased by the twisted abomination that they left plastered against a post. When Paige pulled to a stop in front of the pizza place, he was hesitant to leave the car. Once scents from the nearby kitchen drifted into his nose, however, he couldn't get into DiGuido's fast enough.

Although DiGuido's didn't appear to be open for business, the front door offered no resistance, and the unusual party of three made their way to a booth against a wall of fake wine bottles. The lighting was dim. The tables were just a bit dirty, and the music sounded as if it never strayed from the Rat Pack's greatest hits. Paige and Cole slid into one side of the booth, while Racquel slid into the other.

A perturbed man with a greasy shirt and an even greasier apron around his waist walked up to the booth. The moment he got a look at the black markings on Racquel's neck and wrists, he lightened up a bit and asked, "What do youse guys want?"

Since Racquel waved her hand to pass, and Paige seemed slow on the draw, Cole jumped in and replied, "How about a large sausage and mushroom?"

"No fungus," Paige said.

"Fine," Cole said. "Sausage and pepperoni. And black olives! How about black olives, too?"

The guy in the greasy apron nodded and turned his back to the booth. Cole was about to shout a request for garlic bread but was distracted by the sight of the black markings crawling up the back of the guy's neck. But feeling better just knowing food was on the way, he asked, "All right, so who's going to start?"

"I can't stay long," Racquel said. "Henry is supposed to be able to sniff out a Nymar from miles away."

"What's a—" Cole started to ask, but was cut short when Paige's raised a hand.

"Who's Misonyk and what's he been telling you?" she asked.

Racquel sighed like a teenage girl cornered into a sex talk with her mother. Rolling her eyes, she muttered, "Misonyk's been in town for a few months. He laid low for a while, but then word spread about how he's been preaching to everyone how they could gain power from drinking souls."

"Drinking souls?" Paige asked.

"Yeah. Draining people dry instead of doing things the normal way. I don't mean just killing them, either. I mean drinking them *dry*. He's all about controlling minds, and says we can all hear each other's thoughts if we juice up by killing as many humans as we can. And before you ask, he knows about Skinners, too. He just don't give a rat's ass about your rules. Some Nymar think he's loco and just trying to get big in Chicago. Others think he's God or some shit."

"What do you think?" Paige asked. She had to wait to get her answer, because Greasy Apron came back to set a pitcher of cola on the table along with three red plastic cups. He'd never asked about a drink order and didn't seem to care about one, since he turned and walked away.

Racquel took one of the cups and poured some cola from the pitcher. "I know he's loco, but I also know he's not just all about ruling Chicago. He ain't even from here."

"How do you know that?"

"Wendy told me. She's been hangin' with Misonyk for a while and told me he comes and goes from somewhere up in Wisconsin. What the hell a guy like that would want in Wisconsin, I do not know."

"You're sure about that?"

"Yeah," Racquel said with an offended snap of her head. "She told me he dragged her ass all the way up to some old house up there so he could infeed offa her along the way. I told her she wouldn't come back from there, but she went along anyway. She always liked that kind of stuff."

"So how can someone like that just walk in and start doing whatever he wants?" Cole asked. When he'd started to ask that question, he could feel Paige bristle beside him. Once she heard it, however, she seemed more interested in the answer.

Cocking her head, Racquel looked at Cole with a sneer that bordered on disgust. "Is this guy one of yours? He sure don't act like one."

"Just answer the question," Paige said sternly.

For the first time since they'd lost sight of Henry, Racquel seemed truly afraid. "All right, whatever. Misonyk's been telling everyone he's got a way to control more than just Henry. He says he can call down all the shapeshifters that're sneaking around and will use them to sniff out anyone he wants, including all you Skinners, and make you pay for what you did."

"Chicago's been one of the quieter cities as far as things go between us and the Nymar," Paige said. "What's got Misonyk so upset?"

"I don't know! I'm just telling you what he said. Personally, I think he's blowin' smoke, but a lot of other Nymar out there think he's on to something. Mostly, they'll sign up with anyone who's got a chance at cleaning out Skinners for good. No offense or nothin'."

"None taken," Paige said cheerfully.

"Anyways," Racquel continued after drinking the rest of her soda, "Misonyk's been talking a lot of shit about killing Skinners, but he's been killing more of us than anything else. Some folks said he was feeding Nymar to some fucked up pet or somethin', but nobody really believed it. I believe the hell out of it now, though."

"That'd be Henry?" Cole asked.

"Yeah," Racquel told him. "Wendy said they went to pick up Henry that time they drove out of town. They picked up a few other Nymar along the way, some freshly seeded locals, I think, and he fed them to Henry. Wendy was on drugs even before she got seeded herself, so I didn't know how much to believe about that either. Seems like it was all true. And if Henry's really real, maybe that stuff about the shapeshifters is too."

"Is there anything else you can tell us?" Paige asked. "Anything to help us catch Henry or Misonyk? If he's encouraging murder, he's breaking the truce and you know we'll go after him."

"I wish you would go after him. Some friends of mine woulda done it, but Misonyk's old," Racquel said. "I don't know how old, but he can do things like get into your mind and stuff. It ain't a new trick, but he's real good at it. Better than anyone I ever seen. And Henry . . . he follows Misonyk like a puppy. I may just get the hell out of Chicago, like your friend Daniels."

"Is Henry a . . . is he . . . ?" Cole started to ask before he ran out of words.

Paige picked up his slack and asked, "Is Henry a Nymar?"

"You really are new," Racquel snipped. She shook her head and then looked at Paige as if she was the only other one in the room. "Have you ever seen a Nymar like that?" she asked.

Paige shook her head.

"He could be one of them other weird shapeshifters, but I never seen one of them either." Furrowing her brow, Racquel asked, "They don't even come into the cities, do they?"

"No," Paige said thoughtfully. "They don't."

Racquel suddenly became even more anxious, and started sliding out of the booth. "That's all I know, and I ain't staying here anymore. If what they say about Henry is true, he can smell Nymar from miles away and track us down like dogs. I already knew Misonyk is loco, and it sure as hell ain't safe to be around no Skinners with him around."

"We appreciate the help, Racquel," Paige said. "Do you need a ride somewhere?"

"Not with you," she replied with that familiar disgusted look on her face as she began moving away. Tossing a wave to Greasy Apron on her way out, she pushed open the front door and was already taking a cell phone from her skirt before the door closed behind her.

"Jesus, Cole," Paige muttered.

Cole laughed and poured himself a drink. "I know. I didn't even realize she had pockets in that skirt."

Paige smacked him with the back of her hand and said, "This isn't funny. In fact, this could be really bad."

Savoring the genuine bliss that came along with ignorance, Cole shrugged. "Since I don't know much of anything that you two were talking about, it doesn't seem so bad to me. And since we're here and nothing's trying to kill us at the moment, would you mind giving me some of those answers you promised?"

Turning in her seat so she could face him, Paige grabbed the pitcher with one hand and filled a cup. She was small enough to maneuver between the back of the booth and the table, so she managed to get one foot propped up and tucked in close to her hip. "I was honestly hoping to have Daniels explain some of this to you," she replied with a tired but friendly grin. "What's on your mind?"

"First of all, what's a Nymar?"

"That's just the fancy name the vampires call themselves. Kind of a technical term."

Cole laughed uneasily. "Everyone's got to have a fancy name for themselves."

"I know, right?"

"So they drink blood and all that?"

Paige nodded and shifted again. "A Nymar is actually a growth on someone's heart. Kind of like a tumor, but a whole lot worse. As far as we've been able to figure out, this tumor—they call it a spore—attaches to a heart and uses blood to keep it going as it pumps something else to take the blood's place. The spore grows and spreads until you can see it under a Nymar's skin where you'd normally see someone's veins."

"Those black marks?" Cole asked.

Paige nodded and pointed toward him. "Very good. Gold star for you."

Cole smiled as the air was flooded with a wonderful smell. Greasy Apron walked up to the table and set down a large pizza that looked like a heavily loaded cardboard disk slathered in cheese, thick slices of pepperoni, nuggets of sausage, and black olives. Scattered about the top of the pizza were small pools of grease. Ignoring the steam and heat rising from the pizza, Cole pulled off a large square piece for himself. Fortunately, the big guy who'd brought the ambrosia was quick enough to set a plate down before Cole dropped anything on the table.

"Here's yer bill," Greasy Apron said. "You don't got no escort anymore, so get out as soon as you can. In fact, pay up now."

Cole handed over some money. Instead of change, he got a grunt and a curt, upward nod from the other man. Even though the pizza was about to melt his fingers together, Cole paused and asked, "Should I . . . uh . . . eat this?"

"Are you a vegetarian?" Paige asked.

"No, but considering who or . . . what the cook is . . ."

"It's fine," she said as she picked up a piece for herself. "Gerald actually recommended this place to me when I first got to Chicago. He said it was the best pizza in town."

Cole smiled gratefully and took a bite. The greasy pizza burnt his tongue something terrible, but he kept smiling all the same. "Good Lordy, that's fantastic."

"This," Paige said as she carefully took a bite for herself, "is real Chicago style pizza. That thick pan crust you see everywhere else is for the tourists. Anyway, as I was saying, the Nymar feed on humans to replace the blood needed to keep the spore alive, but they can get what they need without killing. If they do get overly zealous, we come in to show them why that's not such a good idea."

"You hunt them?" Cole asked.

She responded with a shrug. "It's not as bad as it sounds. Mostly, they keep themselves in line and we make a pretty good example of the ones who cross that line."

"So you're like cops?" Before he got an answer, Cole tensed and added, "Speaking of cops, weren't there cops chasing us before?"

"Yep, but I'd say they're pretty busy examining those bodies and taking statements about Henry jumping down the street."

"You're not worried about them finding you?"

"Not really. If there were witnesses, they'd be distracted by all the blood, the shooting, and that freak. Considering everything else we're hiding from, the cops are the least of our worries. If the police are able to figure out where we are, something a lot worse would have already wiped us out. Just to be safe, though, remind me to swap the plates on my car before we leave."

"Okay, but who's 'us'? Did Racquel call you Skinner?"

"We're called Skinners, Cole," Paige replied calmly. "Gerald was one. Brad was training to be one. I'm one."

"What's a Skinner?"

"We track down things that most people won't even believe are out there. Shapeshifters are the worst. They always have been. They're good at sneaking or blending in, so most of the world doesn't know they exist. They're also good at running and fighting, so the people who do stumble on them don't live long enough to tell about it. I don't know all the history and I doubt anyone does, but Skinners teach each other how to kill these things so we can try to take back our spot at the top of the food chain."

Cole laughed under his breath and asked, "You mean we're not in the top slot now?"

"You saw that thing that killed Gerald. You've met Henry. You tell me." Paige leaned forward so she could stare intently at Cole. The passion in her voice made him feel as if they were the only two people in the world. "Gerald saw something in you, Cole. I've only known you for a few hours or so and I can already see it."

"See what? In case you haven't noticed, I've been one jolt away from pissing myself."

She shook her head and took another bite of pizza. "You've got good instincts and common sense," she said in a way that was as heartfelt as possible, considering all the food in her mouth. "That's not something anyone can learn. You're either born with it or you're not."

Cole chuckled and kept eating. Now that his pizza had cooled a bit, the square slice melted into cheesy perfection on his tongue. "Common sense, huh? That's why I'm using words like 'monster' and 'vampire' in a real conversation?"

"You gotta trust your eyes and ears. Believe me, most people would much rather believe what they're told to believe instead of face the insanity that's really around them. You looked into that Full Blood's eyes and stood your ground when the other survivors had already run away or gotten themselves killed."

Hearing her say that brought the memory of the creature's eyes into sharp focus. For a moment the coppery scent of blood drifted through his nose to mix with the inviting smells of sausage and perfectly burnt crust.

"Why did you come along with me this far?" Paige asked.

"Because I thought you were crazy and would try to kill me if I left?"

"You're curious," she said with a knowing grin. "And, deep down inside, there's a part of you that wants to know what the hell is happening and what the hell else is out there."

"How do you know all this?" he asked.

"Because that's the sort of thing every Skinner thinks. It's what we all feel. Gerald sent you to me because that's how we pass on what we know. We have to look for that spark in other people and hope we live long enough to make sure there's always a few more Skinners out there to keep fighting. That Full Blood wasn't just a wild monster. It's smart and it's powerful. Some say it can live forever. There's not a lot of ways it can be killed, but Skinners have found a few tricks that actually work. Without us, things like shapeshifters and all the others out there could do whatever they like to humans as if we didn't even matter. We may not be the top of the food chain, but that doesn't mean we should just have to line up for the slaughter."

As much as Cole wanted to dismiss her words, the picture she painted actually made sense to him. In a way, that bothered him more than the rest.

"So what's a Full Blood?" he asked.

"They're shapeshifters. Compared to Nymar, shapeshift-ers are pretty rare. Full Bloods are the rarest of them all. They're the only ones that are born what they are. They're not bitten by another shapeshifter, under any sort of curse, or affected by any number of things that can cause someone to change. They just . . . are."

"Is Henry a Full Blood?"

Paige winced as if the question simply didn't taste very good. She fixed that problem by inhaling a square of pizza and washing it down with some pop. "Honestly? I don't know what Henry is. I've seen a Full Blood, plenty of Half Breeds, even a few Mongrels, but nothing like Henry. I've never even heard of anything that tore up and ate a Nymar like what we saw tonight." Still contemplating that gruesome sight, Paige shook her head and picked up a prime piece of sausage that had fallen onto the dented metal serving dish that held the rest of the pizza. Suddenly, the dim lights in the place flicked on and off. "I think we're being kicked out of here," she said.

"You got that right," the owner said as he stepped up to the booth with a cardboard box in his hands. "Unless you want to start working for me, I don't want you in my place. Bad for business."

Cole slid out of the booth, but Paige took her time before moving. Although she did inch her way to the edge of the seat, she stopped with her legs dangling over the edge. Look-ing up at him, she showed Greasy Apron one of her tired yet cute smirks. "We won't be working for you," she said, "but we could arrange to do some favors now and then if you wouldn't mind helping us out. What's your name?"

After a heavy pause, Greasy Apron muttered, "Just call me Manny. What kind of favors you talkin' about?"

"You know a Nymar called Daniels?"

"Short guy with long hair and glasses?"

"That's the one."

Manny nodded. "Yeah. He's the only one who orders the vegetarian special."

"Daniels has a real good palette, and I was hoping to get his opinion on something tonight. When Gerald told me about this place, he mentioned the cook might have an even better palette."

"That'd be me. What's it matter to ya?" Manny asked with a sigh that reflected almost as much impatience as the recent flickering of the lights.

She dug out the bundle from the inner pocket of her jacket and unwrapped it. Handing it forward, she asked, "Think you can tell me what kind of blood that is?"

Manny took the knife from her, swiped his finger along the mostly dried, partially sticky streaks of blood along the blade, then placed his finger on his tongue as if sampling a new tomato sauce. "Shapeshifter," he said. "Ain't Half Breed. Too pure for Mongrel. Could be Full Blood."

"You're sure?"

"You asked me and I told ya," Manny replied. "Now get out."

Paige shrugged and took the knife back from him. "Good enough for me," she said to Cole. "Let's go."

Once he and Paige were outside, Cole asked, "*That's* why that knife needed to be hauled all the way back here?"

She shook her head without even trying to hide her excitement. "Nope. That just tells me what it is and what it can do. Since that knife actually cut a Full Blood, it can kill a Full Blood. Only Blood Blades can kill Full Bloods. And since these little babies only get stronger as they soak up more shapeshifter blood, this one's ready to do some real damage. Plus, I've got a project of my own that's been at a standstill until right about now."

Cole sighed and decided to let go of the next batch of questions that filled his mind. Instead, he asked, "Weren't you supposed to swap a license plate before we left?"

"Already on it," Paige replied as she unlocked the trunk and searched inside. When she walked back around the car, she was holding a screwdriver and two dented Illinois license plates that were different from the ones already on the Cavalier. "This should keep any overeager cops from getting lucky and stumbling on us. Feel better now?"

"Oh yeah," Cole droned. "This makes everything just wonderful."

Chapter 10

The drive back to Rasa Hill went by fairly quickly. As Paige talked on her cell phone, Cole looked out the window at the scenery and thought about what the hell had happened to him since he'd left Seattle.

He'd seen men die. He'd seen monsters of several shapes and sizes. Some of them had sharp teeth. Some had big breasts. Some had both. His head spun and his stomach clenched as he realized there was still a job waiting for him back home. There were still reports to be filed and levels to test. *Hammer Strike* had plenty of bugs in it, and he had forgotten to submit them all before packing up and heading into Canada. He gritted his teeth until the car pulled to a stop behind the deserted restaurant. A dull ache began to fill his head.

Paige strode toward the building's back door in a quick, bouncy stride. She paused before going inside and turned to glance back at him. "You coming, Cole?"

"Yeah. I just need to check my messages."

Although he had expected some sort of warning about keeping what he'd seen and heard a secret, all he got was a shrug from her. "Just let me know if you still want to go home. I can scrounge up some money for a plane ticket." She then held her own phone up to her ear and entered the restaurant.

Cole removed his phone from his pocket and was grateful to see the lights on the scratched plastic surface telling him he had coverage. It looked as if he might not have enough battery life to check the forty-six voice mails and sixty-seven text messages he'd missed. "Good God," he muttered as he looked at those numbers again. "Are you kidding me?"

With a snap of his thumb, he moved the cover of his phone aside to reveal a small keyboard and a screen that looked complicated enough to enter trajectory data for a barrage of missiles. Since he didn't even know what most of those blinking lights meant, he ignored them and sifted through his text messages. The first few were of the "How's your vacation?" variety, and then they drifted toward the "Where the hell are you?" end of the spectrum. Rather than start punching out replies, he swiveled the cover shut and dialed his voice mail.

The recordings were about the same as the text messages. After listening to the first five or six all the way through, Cole started deleting them once he'd listened long enough to get the general flow of the message. After that, he deleted them after hearing the tone in the caller's voice. Finally, he pressed and held down the button that was the speed dial for Jason's private line.

After a few rings the connection was made.

"Jason Sorrenson," droned the voice on the other end.

"That's so pretentious when you answer that way," Cole said. "Can't you say hello like a normal human being?"

"Cole?"

"That's me."

"Jesus, man, we were starting to think you'd gotten lost or weren't coming home," Jason exclaimed.

Cole chuckled and ran his fingers over his eyes. "Afraid I'd get addicted to maple syrup?"

"That or hockey. What have you been doing? Are you still in Canada?"

"No. Actually, I'm back in the States."

"You need a ride from the airport?"

"Not that state," Cole added. "I'm in Chicago."

After a slight pause, Jason said, "That's not a state, moron."

Cole laughed a bit too hard at the snide comment, but couldn't help himself.

"So why haven't you come home?" Jason asked. "A pool just got started around here that you shot yourself through some part of your body and were too embarrassed to call from the hospital."

"What did you have your money on?"

"The right shin. A grazing shot through the right shin. I know it sounds a little obscure, but it's a better payoff."

"Asshole," Cole muttered.

"Hey! You don't even want to know where Nora put her money."

"Is she upset?"

"She misses you." Cole had no trouble picturing the cruel grin on Jason's face as he added, "Kind of like a pet."

Before Jason asked about it again, Cole told him, "There was . . . an incident in Canada."

"That doesn't sound good. Are you all right?"

"Yeah. It was messy, but I'm okay. Have you heard anything on the news about . . ."

Once a few seconds had ticked by, Jason asked, "About what?"

Cole realized then that he couldn't explain anything to him. He knew better than to try and lay out the facts that he'd been attacked by some sort of monster and was now in the care of a Skinner. Jason wouldn't believe it. Nobody in their right mind would believe it. He, on the other hand, had no choice but to believe. Even if he might somehow manage to convince Jason, it seemed a cruel thing to do; kind of like dragging a preschooler off the playground so you could explain topics like rape and war. Unless there was a good reason, it was just mean to tell so much to someone who was so unprepared for it.

"Come on, Cole," Jason prodded. "About what?"

"About some stupid American shooting himself in the right shin."

"Yes! I just won enough to pay off my new home theater."

"Glad I could be of service," Cole replied.

After the laughter died down, Jason asked, "When are

you coming home? A lot of us were really worried when we couldn't get ahold of you. I might have been worried too, if I didn't already know that piece of crap phone you insist on carrying couldn't get a signal beneath an antenna."

"Leave my phone out of this. It wasn't her fault. Things have . . . changed."

"Now that really doesn't sound good."

Although there was nobody to see the wince on his face, Cole knew his voice would reflect it. "There's a lot going on, but I should tell you I probably won't be back for a while."

"Aw, damn it. Are you sure?" Jason moaned.

"Yeah. If you want, I can sign into the system from here and—"

"We're too far along now to start sending stuff out of our own system. All we need is one asshole kid to get hold of one of those screen shots or some of those character models and it'll be all over the Internet."

"Free publicity," Cole pointed out. "It's never a bad thing."

"Sorry, Cole. You've earned the time off, but this is a hell of a bad time to take so much of it."

"Yeah, I know. I wouldn't even ask if it wasn't something really big."

"Big enough to maybe give you some ideas for the next pitch meeting?"

Cole chuckled and let out a breath. "Hell yes."

"Then do what you gotta do. I know you wouldn't put me in this spot unless you had a good reason."

"Thanks, Jason."

"Can you at least e-mail me those bugs from *Hammer Strike* tomorrow?"

Cole nodded, then reminded himself yet again that he was alone and said, "No problem."

"How long are you gonna be gone?" Jason asked.

That was the question he'd been dreading since he dialed Jason's number. "Honestly, I don't know. It may be a while."

A heavy sigh drifted through the earpiece. "As your boss, I've got to tell you this may cause some bigger problems than just *Hammer Strike*."

"I know," Cole replied.

"As your friend, I just want to make sure there's nothing else I should be worried about."

Anything he should be worried about.

That one made Cole smile.

Once again resisting the urge to drop the bomb that vampires and flesh-eating monsters actually existed, he said, "No. I'll check in before too long."

"I'm going to get back to sleep now, since some of us need to go to work in the morning."

"All right, Jason. Take care."

The connection was cut after a short beep and a snap of static. Cole looked at the screen, but didn't know what he expected to see. After putting the phone in his pocket, he dug out Gerald's satellite model. He went through the motions of choosing one of the few numbers in the phone's memory and hit the button to get the call rolling. It was answered after one ring.

"MEG Branch 40."

"Stu?"

"Yeah," the voice on the other end replied. "Is this Cole?"

"Yes it is. Doesn't anyone else answer that phone?"

There was a tired chuckle and the familiar clack of fingers on a keyboard. "I practically live here. Besides, this place has one hell of a computer setup."

"Really?" Cole asked. "What've you got?"

"More than enough to keep tabs on lunatics like you. Also, I can play in three different *Sniper Ranger 2* matches at the same time."

"*Sniper Ranger 2*? What about *Sniper Ranger 3*?"

That question caused Stu's voice to slip into a more relaxed tone that hovered somewhere between a whine and a yawn. "*Three*'s not bad, but it's got a crappy single player component. *Two*'s got a lot more variety in multiplayer. Do you play?"

"Yeah. I worked on the teams that developed both of those games."

Cole couldn't be certain, but he thought he heard the sound of a desk being rattled as Stu sat up at attention. "What? You work at Digital Dreamers?"

"Yeah. At least, I hope I'll still be able to work there when I decide to go back."

"Why would you ever leave a job like that?" Stu asked with genuine bewilderment.

"Things just sort of happen, you know?"

"Oh . . . yeah. I suppose I do know. Still . . . awesome job! What did you do over at Dreamers?"

Chuckling while looking up at the clear night sky, Cole replied, "I worked on the single player campaign for *Sniper Ranger 3*."

"Of . . . course you did," Stu groaned. "I'm such a tool."

"But you've got good taste in games. Besides, you'll forget all about *Two* and *Three* once you get your hands on *Four*."

"There's a *Sniper Ranger 4* coming out? *When*?"

"That's classified . . . but it might come out sooner if I decide to go home and get back to work. You think I should do that, Stu?"

There was a heavy pause as Stu caught his breath and truly thought about the question. It wasn't long before he said, "That's your call, dude. Sounds like you've got one hell of a job waiting for you, but me and everyone else over here at MEG are always wishing we could work our way into partnering up with one of you guys."

"What do you know about . . . about these guys?" Cole asked.

"We're not told a lot, but we are given the occasional lead every now and then."

"What sort of lead?"

"Every so often we'll get a reliable tip about where we can find someplace that's crawling with spectral activity. There were a few demon hauntings that still give one of our founders nightmares, and we wouldn't have known about those if not for you guys. Personally, I got to study a real Chubacabra that one of Paige's buddies across the border ran into."

"A what?"

"Chubacabra," Stu repeated. "You know. A Goat Sucker. They're in all the tabloids, but they're real enough. I saw it myself. None of the zoologists believe me, but that doesn't matter. None of us are here to get published in a scientific journal. I'd bet the magazine we put out on the Web gets read more than those Ivy League rags anyway."

Cole shook his head and laughed. "There's a lot going on that I never knew about."

"Yeah," Stu sighed. "Ain't it great?"

"Sort of."

"Whether anyone knows about it or not, you guys do a hell of a lot of good. Especially now with all that's been going on."

"What's been going on?"

Stu clammed up so hard that Cole could almost hear his lips slapping together over the satellite connection. In a guarded voice he eventually said, "Let's just say one of our guys down at Branch 25 called in about some bunch of messed-up animals in a hole somewhere. Far as I know, you guys were already told about it, so I probably shouldn't say anything else. I'm sure Paige will fill you in. If I step out of line, she might just pull me through this phone and slap the hell out of me. She sounds cute, but . . ."

"Don't worry," Cole said as Stu fought for his next words. "I know what you mean, and you're right."

"I got some more calls coming in," Stu said. "All I can tell you is to take a look around and think about what you might be able to accomplish with Paige and whoever else is there. I knew Gerald and Brad. They were great guys who helped a lot of people. You could do a lot worse for yourself than by joining up with the likes of them. Hope that helps."

"Actually, it does."

"Cool. Don't be a stranger. Maybe we can run through a few rounds of *Sniper Ranger* sometime. I'd love to school another guy from Digital Dreamers."

"Another one, huh? Fine. I'll defend the company honor later."

"Talk to ya." With that, Stu broke the connection.

Cole held the satellite phone in his hand and ran his thumb along the chipped plastic casing. He wondered where that phone had been and what sort of impossible things it had seen. As he let his thoughts wander, he reminded himself about Gerald's face and the urgency that had been in his voice.

A cold breeze got him moving back to the restaurant. He walked in through the door and found himself staring down the barrel of a shotgun.

"Holy shit," he gasped.

Paige glanced at him over the shotgun and then lowered it. She held her phone up to her ear with her free hand and nodded casually to Cole before getting back to her conversation. "Yeah, go on," she said into the phone. "What did the MEG guys find?"

Holding up his hands, Cole said, "No problem. Honest mistake. Don't worry about me."

Paige smiled and nodded. "Good. Thanks." It wasn't clear whether she was talking to him or to whoever was on the phone.

As she turned her back to him, Cole couldn't help but notice that she'd changed into a pair of black sweatpants and a matching halter top. Although her attire was less provocative than a few outfits he'd seen at the gym, Paige's curves were even more impressive now that they weren't hidden by jeans and a jacket. When she walked toward the kitchen, her hips twitched more than enough to take his eyes away from the shotgun she so casually slung over her shoulder.

Suddenly, Paige turned around. The motion was so fast that it was almost painful for him to pull his eyes up to a more appropriate level. "I need to go to Wisconsin. Are you coming with me or not?"

Having just noticed the freckles sprinkled along the smooth, tanned skin just above the slope of her breasts, Cole had to use a completely different section of his brain to form a reply. "Huh? Are you talking to me?"

"I've got one of our trackers on the phone," she explained as she took the phone away from her ear. "He's found something that may be linked to Misonyk and this Henry thing. It's a small road trip, but we can see if anything's hunting you by moving around. If nothing follows us, you should be clear . . . more or less. You in?"

"Yes," he said before he had a chance to think better of it.

Lifting the phone again, she said, "Yeah, there'll be two of us. Where are we meeting?" After a pause, she rolled her eyes and groaned. "Are you serious? Why? . . . Fine, we'll see you there." After hanging up, she tossed the phone onto a nearby counter as if afraid of catching something from it. Then she turned to him and asked, "Did any of those Nymar touch you?"

"Pardon me?"

"Not on your clothes, but on your skin. Even something like this."

As she said that, Paige reached out to brush her hand along his arm. She was at least a foot shorter than him, but seemed even smaller now that she was in her bare feet. When she looked up at him, her easy smile was framed by a tussled mess of dark hair. She couldn't have looked better than if she'd spent the day in a spa.

He tensed the muscles in his jaw and forced a breath out through his nose to keep from reaching out and doing some touching of his own. Her fingers lingered upon his wrist and sent a chill straight through him. "I don't remember," he admitted. "So much happened that it's all running together."

"This may sound weird, but did any of them . . . spit on you?"

Wincing, Cole replied, "No. I would've remembered that. Why?"

"Just to be safe, give me your wrist."

"Which wrist? This one?"

Cole extended his right arm. Paige gently took hold of him and brushed her fingertips against his skin. The longer she touched him, the more Cole was worried he might slip and say something he couldn't easily explain. Finally, she encircled his wrist with her fingers and ran her other hand along his arm so she could push up his sleeve. Every inch of the way was a test of his resolve.

After a quick look at the veins on his wrist, Paige smiled at him even wider. She didn't take her hands away just yet. "There would have been some black showing up on you by now if any of them tried to infect you, so you should be all right. Just so you know, Nymar can produce venom like a snake. They'll spit it at you, and if it gets in your eyes, well, that's really bad."

"It is, huh?"

She nodded slowly and kept her eyes locked upon his. "You did really well tonight," she said as she patted his wrist and allowed his hand to slip free. "You didn't panic and you kept me covered."

"I didn't panic? You must not have been watching me very closely."

Paige laughed, but then pulled away and turned her head. He might have been overly tired or overly optimistic, but he thought there was some color flushing into her cheeks. Before she pulled even farther away, he reached out and closed his hand around her wrist. Before he could unleash the smooth talking he'd planned in his mind, Paige lifted his wrist straight up, to effectively and painfully lock the joint.

"Sorry," she whispered as she loosened the hold. "Reflex."

Now he was the one to back off. "It's all right. My fault."

The way she looked at him now, Paige might as well have been staring at him through a microscope. Slowly, her eyes wandered down along his body and then worked their way up again. "It may get rough around here, but I'd really like it if you stayed. I can keep an eye on you better that way."

"Well," Cole replied in the coolest tone he could manage, "maybe I should come along to keep you covered."

Paige smiled and patted his cheek with her free hand. As she turned around, she put just enough muscle into her final pat to make it something close to a smack. "You're cute," she said. She picked up the shotgun and angled the barrel to keep it from scraping against the floor as she walked away.

Even after some distance had been put between them, Cole could still smell the scent of her hair and feel the bit of sweat that had been on her scarred, yet soft hands.

"I'm going to jump in the shower," she said. "You're welcome to stay here tonight if you want. There's a cot in the freezer. It's a walk-in and the refrigeration unit doesn't work, so I was going to use it for a safe room since it's got the thickest door in the place."

"Sounds too good to be true," Cole groaned. "By the way, what are the odds of that thing really tracking me all the way from Canada to Chicago? I mean, aren't there enough smells in this city to cover mine up?"

Paige stopped and cocked her head to one side while keeping her back to him. Her hips shifted, drawing his eyes and holding them for the duration. "I once had a shapeshifter follow me for three months and across twelve states, but that was different. I wanted it to follow me. I'd say there's about a ten to fifteen percent chance of that Full Blood losing interest in you. If you wanted to be safe, I could always teach you how to handle one of those things if they did find you."

"You mean like train me in the ways of the Skinner?" Cole asked in a voice ripped from every cheesy movie trailer he'd ever heard.

Paige walked toward a door at the back of the kitchen that led farther into the restaurant. Since she still wasn't looking back, he allowed himself to fully savor the way the sweatpants hugged her tight, rounded backside.

"I don't need a partner," she told him as she came to a stop near one of the back rooms, "but having one would make things a whole lot easier."

"I think you're forgetting something. I program video games for a living."

"That was before, Cole. There's too much out there for a man like you to just turn his back on it. If you're waiting for a sign or a prophecy or any of that sort of crap to let you know what to do, you'll be waiting a long time. I think you've already seen enough to know what you want to do."

"You got any advice?"

"Sure," she said as she sauntered from the kitchen. "Don't gawk at a woman's ass when she's carrying a shotgun."

Chapter 11

Cole still couldn't shake Paige's scent even after she'd left the room. He could still feel her fingers roaming over his wrists and could imagine every strand of hair as it curled around her face. Her movements ran beneath everything in his head like a current of energy. He could feel the heat from her body no matter how many rooms separated them within that old restaurant.

Not that the cot in Paige's freezer didn't sound appealing. In fact, he looked inside the metallic room to find a surprisingly comfortable living space. There was a television and, for a bit of irony, a mini fridge. When he had just about convinced himself that he might be able to make it through the night without ripping through his jeans, he'd seen Paige walk by with her hair dripping wet and a thick, navy blue terry-cloth robe wrapped around her. She'd been showing more skin when she was in her sweats, but the thought that she was wet and naked beneath that single garment was enough to drive him out of his skull.

Since he still had his doubts about making the leap from video-game designer to monster killer, he put temptation behind him and called for a cab. Paige had asked him to stay, but didn't take any drastic steps to keep him there. He needed some time to consider her proposition, and he couldn't do that when his mind was preoccupied. At least, that was the most polite term for what he was feeling.

The Afton Inn was just off I–55 and could have easily been mistaken for a thousand other hotels across this and probably many other countries. Cole wasn't interested in ambience or uniqueness. All he wanted was a clean bed, a place to shower, and a free breakfast in the morning. No matter how many monsters were out there, it just didn't make sense to stay in a hotel that didn't at least serve breakfast.

The hotel's shower was great. Water trickled out like it was being spit from the nozzle, and it took half an hour to warm up, but he was able to stand under it for as long as he wanted without anyone else vying for his attention. For the first time since he'd left Seattle, he wasn't packed into a cab, plane, car, or room with anyone else. As he stepped out of the bathroom with a thin, overly bleached towel wrapped around his waist, he didn't care about the fact that he didn't have any clean clothes to replace the ones in a heap on the bathroom floor. He didn't bother sucking in the gut that had showed up in the days following his thirtieth birthday. He just turned on the television and nodded as the screen glowed with an infomercial about college girls and all the glorious ways they could disgrace themselves for a free T-shirt.

"Oh yeah," Cole sighed. "That's the good stuff."

After he'd sat through the first run of the infomercial, he heard a breeze rustling outside. He got up, walked over to the window and pulled back the cheap curtain just enough to take in a scenic view of the parking lot. He could even count the dents on the roof of a dirty RV parked there. Shaking his head, he wondered why the hell people bought RVs, only to park them at hotels. Then again, he'd never understood the whole camping mentality anyway.

When Cole looked down a bit more, he caught sight of a latch at the bottom of the window. It was rare that hotels even allowed their windows to be opened, but he tried this one anyway. The latch popped free of the window frame, allowing the window to swing open a good one or two inches before it was stopped by a bracket. There was more than enough breeze to get through the narrow opening, so he pulled in a deep breath. The air wasn't as crisp and clean as the stuff he'd sampled in Canada, but it was cool and it put a smile on his face. As far as he was concerned, savoring cheap thrills was the key to a truly happy life. All he needed now was some of that leftover pizza. Unfortunately, he hadn't thought far enough ahead to take the DiGuido's box along with him.

Cole gazed out to the nearby street on the off chance that he might catch sight of a twenty-four-hour coffee shop. Just as he was about to give up and pull the curtain shut, he noticed a large cat peeking from the shadows at the edge of the parking lot. It might have been a dog, but its eyes reflected the hotel's security light with a feline glimmer. Then the thing darted out of sight.

Someone slammed a door in the hall, and he looked reflexively in that direction. A few heavy footsteps stomped outside his room, making it seem very possible that he would be getting inconsiderate yetis as his neighbors. All he needed now was a screaming baby added to the mix, and the Afton Inn truly would be just like any other hotel in the known universe.

Cole sighed and looked out the window as if he could actually watch his peace and quiet drift away. A window rattled one floor beneath him, just as a lean, gray paw reached up to get a hold upon his windowsill. Long claws dug into the sill, allowing a creature with black and gray fur to scale the outside of the hotel and climb up to his room.

Until that moment, Cole wasn't aware that he could cover so much distance by simply jumping backward. He cleared the floor and flew back far enough to knock his legs against the bed and land on the starched, pale gold comforter. Losing his towel somewhere along the way, he rolled over the bed until he dropped off the mattress and hit the floor on the other side.

Though he didn't have any weapons and didn't know what he was up against, he put his back to the wall and stood up. He was sick and tired of running.

After opening the window with just enough force to snap the bracket holding it in place, the animal took its time crawling into Cole's room. Its body was long and lean. As it slowly crept over the windowsill and dropped onto the floor, the light in the room played off its wiry fur, shifting between hues of gray and black. Sometimes the black patches seemed to overpower the gray. At other times, the gray nearly swallowed up the black. Long front arms stretched out to bury claws into the stained carpeting near the television stand. Shorter, more muscular legs curled up behind the thing's narrow rump like a freakish cat getting ready to pounce.

Cole met the cat's glare but found it difficult to hold it for long. Its eyes were clouded over from the inside, but stared back at him as if they could see all the way through to the wall behind him. Thin, pointed ears twitched against the animal's head and then flicked straight up again. Its mouth remained open just enough to show upper and lower sets of needle-thin teeth that fit perfectly between one another.

"All right, shit bag," Cole said as he planted his feet and grabbed the lamp from the bedside table. "I've already seen much worse than you. Show me what you got or get out of my room."

The animal slunk around the bed, its fur glistening in the light from the television. It was nearly as long as he was, but Cole had trouble distinguishing where the animal's body ended and the carpet began. He chalked that up to the fact that a good portion of the room's light had been snuffed out when he'd yanked the lamp's cord from the wall.

Lowering its chest to the floor, the gray cat raised its head and opened its jaws wide. Its hissing exhalation and the scrape of its claws against the floor were nearly drowned by the sounds coming from the television, but Cole didn't need to hear anything to know what was coming. He tightened his grip on the lamp and then threw it at the creature's head before it could lunge.

The animal pushed off with its powerful rear legs and sprung forward with both front arms extended. Cole jumped away from the bed and heard the muted thump of its body hitting the wall behind him. Reaching for the first weapon he could get, he grabbed a luggage rack that was made of two bent metal bars joined by a pair of screws. It was a weapon better suited for a professional wrestler, but it would have to do. He raised the rack over his head and brought it down on the animal's shoulder.

Now that he was closer to the thing, Cole could tell there wasn't a lot of meat beneath that shadowy fur. He raised the rack for another swing but only caught empty air when he brought it down again. The cat hunkered low to the floor and scurried into the corner formed by the bed and the edge of the room. Now that the animal's back was to him, he was about to make his move when it whipped around to snap at his face.

Cole backed away while bringing the rack down to block the incoming mass of needle-shaped teeth. As the cat's mouth scraped against bent steel, he grabbed onto the other end of the rack to keep it at arm's length. He pushed the rack away while the cat-thing chewed on the cheap metal like it was gnawing on bone.

The room was arranged like any other hotel room, with the bed against a wall shared by the bathroom. Gritting his teeth and twisting both arms, Cole knocked the animal's head against the wall beside the bathroom's door frame. It wasn't an earth-shattering impact, but it was enough to rattle the gangly creature. It shook its head and spat the rack from its mouth. After backing toward the same window it had used to enter the room, it let out a barely audible growl.

"Too late to cry now," Cole snarled as he closed both hands around one end of the rack. Not caring where he hit the thing, he lifted the rack over his head and brought it down in a vicious blow that pounded against the floor and nothing else. He hopped backward while scanning the room.

The cat was difficult to spot. Its shape could barely be picked out against the floor or wall as it paced the room, making it seem as if it had been partially erased from sight. It kept its head low until the last second, but the light from the television eventually glinted off its fur. By the time Cole spotted that, the creature was leaping straight at him with claws bared. He stumbled away from the bed as claws scraped against his shoulder. But before the creature could do any real damage, he hit it with the luggage rack.

The oversized cat let out a hissing snarl and tore up the mattress as it jumped onto the bed. The moment it had Cole in its sights, it bounded forward and bared every tooth and fang in its arsenal before catching another glancing blow from the rack.

Cole turned away from another incoming set of claws while swinging the rack to bat away a paw. That gave him enough time to trip over the chair next to the open window. As he watched, the animal faded into clarity. Black and gray fur shimmered until the cat looked more as it had when it crawled through his window. Its eyes remained on him as it hopped down from where it had been balancing between the bed and dresser. Hitting the floor with casual grace and no sound whatsoever, the creature paced toward the window and faded completely from sight.

Holding the rack in front of him, Cole circled away from the window until he wound up with his legs once more scraping against the bed. A few seconds later he picked out a blurry spot in the air that definitely wasn't caused by the irregular light from the television. As he watched, that blur dissolved to reveal a creature roughly the same size as the big cat but without fur. In fact, its skin was smooth and flowed like milk as it contracted into a much more familiar shape.

Claws retracted and were covered up by distinctly human fingers. Paws shrank down and flattened into feet and hands. A tail flowed up into a spot at the base of a human spine and just above a very feminine backside. As hind legs became too awkward to crouch upon, the thing straightened them and stood upright. By then the front legs had become slender arms and the feline facial features smoothed out into those of a woman. She locked eyes with Cole and smiled enticingly as blond hair flowed from her scalp to unfurl until it hit her shoulders. Even though she stood naked before him without making a move to cover herself, he was too distracted by her face to notice much of anything else.

"You?" Cole gasped. "The last time I saw you . . . you were . . ."

She nodded and finished his sentence for him. "I was running away from a Full Blood in Canada."

"I thought you—"

When the phone rang, Cole nearly jumped out of his skin.

Right about then he realized he was just as naked as she was.

Every time the phone rang, the woman's ears twitched. "Aren't you going to answer that?" she asked.

He kept his eyes on her as he walked around the bed and gathered some sheets to hold in front of him. The only move she made was to back away, so he reached for the phone and picked up the receiver. At least he still had something in his hand that he could use as a weapon. "Hello?" he grunted.

"This is the front desk, sir. Is there a problem in your room? I've been getting noise complaints."

"Uh . . ." As he tried to think of what he should do, Cole watched the naked shapeshifter casually cross her arms. Sure she'd been a cat a few moments ago, but he couldn't think of anything the guy at the front desk of an Afton Inn could do about that. "Everything's fine now," he finally said. "Sorry about the noise."

"Well, if there are more complaints, I'll have to take action."

"I know. Sorry again." With that, he hung up and reached for the luggage rack.

"This is kind of funny," the blonde said. "Last time I saw you, we were on the same side."

"And the last time I saw you, you were human, not some kind of . . . thing!"

If the blonde still had her fur, it would have bristled. "I'm not a thing. I have a name, you know. It's Jackie. And you don't have to take that tone with me. After the way you attacked me, you're damn lucky to be alive."

"I attacked *you*?"

Nodding slowly, Jackie said, "From the moment I came in. I thought you'd be startled, but you really hit the ground running."

"And you nearly ripped me into pieces."

"You hit me in the head with a lamp," she retorted.

Still feeling the adrenaline rushing through him, Cole tightened his grip on the phone receiver. "I've got a door in this room," he snarled. "It came with the rest of the room. You could have used it instead of the freaking window."

"If you give me a moment, I can explain." Her features softened in a way that had nothing to do with her shifting abilities; at least, not as far as he knew. "I need to talk to you. If I got rough before, it was just because you threw the first punch."

Cole reflexively started to say something in his own defense, but cut himself short when he took a moment to think about what had happened. "I guess you've got a point there. Did I hurt you?"

"No, but it looks like I hurt you."

Cole glanced down at his shoulder. There was a long row of scratches, but only a slight trickle of blood. "I'm not worried about that. I am worried you might have just changed to look like that woman from Canada. For all I know, you can change to look like anything you want."

"It was really me," she replied. "Although," she added while opening her arms, "I was wearing a bit more at the time."

Jackie's body was smooth and trim, but not perfect. Her breasts were pert and a bit small, while her hips were just a bit too muscular for his tastes. Even so, she was doing a hell of a job of making him rethink those tastes. "Why were you in Canada?" he asked as a way to test the identity she was claiming.

"I was at that cabin to meet with Brad," she told him. "Do you remember him sitting and talking with me over dinner?"

"Yes."

"I don't know if that Full Blood was after me or Gerald, but you've got to believe I didn't know that was going to happen the way it did."

All he had to do was think back to the panic in her eyes the night of that attack for him to believe what she was saying.

"I did my best to make sure that other college kid got away," she insisted. "When I came back to check on you, I caught the scent of that Full Blood nearby. I tried to lead it away long enough for you to get away. You've got to believe me."

Nodding, Cole told her, "I heard growling and sounds like that the whole time I was running."

She nodded as well, but with a lot more desperation. "That's right! I wasn't able to hurt it, but I could outrun it once it followed me."

"So why go through all the trouble of coming here?" Narrowing his eyes, he added, "I still don't think you could have followed me all the way here from Canada. Even if you had my scent or whatever, I spent a hell of a lot of time locked up in a plane over a thousand feet in the air."

Obviously impressed with herself, Jackie replied, "You were on the phone most of the time before you got to that truck. Chicago was mentioned quite a bit."

"And you heard all that while hopping onto that plane without anyone noticing?"

She shook her head. "I went to an airport and bought a ticket to Chicago just like anyone else. I had to have beaten you here by at least a day, and I caught your scent about an hour ago. Believe me now?"

Before admitting defeat, Cole asked, "So why the Spider-Man entrance tonight?"

"Your new friend Misonyk has a way of keeping tabs on my kind no matter what form we take. The window was the quickest way in and will be the quickest way out."

Jackie walked to the television and turned it up. She seemed to enjoy sauntering naked in the cool breeze that drifted in from the window. Cole had definitely acquired an eye for sauntering. After making her way back to him, she spoke just loudly enough to be heard above the television. "I doubt they've got your room bugged, but Misonyk and his followers could be listening from the hall or somewhere close."

"What do you know about Misonyk?" he asked.

"I contacted Brad about that maniac and the abomination that follows him around, but Gerald wouldn't listen. He didn't trust me or any of my kind."

"What kind is that?" Cole asked.

"If anything, you'd know us by what the Skinners and Full Bloods call us: Mongrels."

Cole nodded and did his best to appear as if he'd heard more than a brief mention of that word from Paige. "Why would Gerald and Brad have to meet up with you in Canada?"

Jackie blinked and lowered her head a bit. She stood close enough to him that her hair fell over one shoulder to brush against her chest as well as his. As it turned out, she was merely waiting for the infomercial to kick back into another loud cycle. It wasn't long before the steel drums and giggling coeds were at it again.

"Before I left, Misonyk was spreading a lot of wild ideas. But he wasn't much more than another crazy Nymar until he had Henry enforcing his word as if it was law. Henry may like feeding on Nymar, but he can easily become a threat to my kind. I've been holding onto the Blood Blade so it could be used against a threat like that. If not for Brad, I would have kept it even though it's a Skinner weapon. I should have just kept it."

She broke into her reserves of strength to keep the tears from eyes that subtly became feline before shifting back again. "If the rest of my kind found out I played a part in trying to harm a shapeshifter, I'd be considered a traitor and . . . I don't even want to think about how they'll make an example of me. I have a niece that lives up in Canada, and it was as far away as I could get from here. Brad was the only Skinner willing to trust me and come such a long way at the request of a Mongrel. I don't know how that Full Blood knew we were there or if it just happened to catch our scent, but no Skinner will ever trust me again."

"Gerald and Brad were the only two Skinners there," Cole said. "At least, I think they were."

"It doesn't matter," Jackie said solemnly. "The others will know. Everyone always finds out everything. I'm so sick of it all."

"Where did Henry come from?"

"Someplace called Lancroft. It's up in Wisconsin, but I don't know any more than that."

Cole shook his head as the sensation of drowning once again swirled through his head. "Maybe you should tell this to Paige. She'll know more about—"

"No," Jackie cut in. She leaned against him so her breasts touched the front of his body. "The only reason I came all the way back here is to honor my deal with Brad. He . . .

let's just say I owe him a favor, and telling all I know about Henry and Misonyk was going to be my way of paying him back. After what happened to him and Gerald, I know he would've wanted someone else to hear this. I don't know if you're a Skinner or not, but I do know you can pass this along so it can do some good."

"All right, then. What do you know about Misonyk?" Cole asked.

"He's crazy and powerful, but that happens to a lot of the older Nymar. He talks about slaughtering humans to drink their souls and nailing Skinners to the floors of dark rooms. He's insane. That's why most Nymar don't pay any attention to him. At least, they didn't before Henry came along.

"Henry is one of them," she continued, "but he's also one of us. I've never seen one just like him, but his scent is close to a Full Blood's. When Henry was just a rumor among the Nymar, Brad was the one who wanted to take action. The old man was content to let anything go as long as it only killed Nymar, but I knew there was more to it than that. I could hear it."

"You could hear it?"

Jackie nodded and tapped the side of her head just above her ear. "It was a whisper at first. I thought I was hearing things or maybe . . . maybe going crazy. But it wasn't just me that heard. Every Mongrel I know heard it. Maybe every shapeshifter in the state could hear it."

"What did they hear?"

"Crazy thoughts at first," Jackie explained, as if just the memory was enough to make her uncomfortable. "Words that were strung together without a space or a breath in between them. Conversations with God. Most of it didn't make any sense. When I got close enough to Henry to pick up his true scent, I knew those whispers were his thoughts. He screamed them from his mind. Stuck in there amid all the babble and all Misonyk's teachings was something else. It was one of the few coherent things in all those thoughts, and it was a gift that could only be given to us by that twisted piece of filth."

Not knowing whether she was talking about Henry or

Misonyk, Cole tried to push her through whatever had caused her eyes to wander and her voice to trail off. "I'm listening."

Her head flinched so she could look straight at him again. The ends of her hair tickled his skin. "After spending so much time around the Nymar, Henry discovered the lie that we've all been told, and he shouted it into the minds of every shapeshifter for hundreds of miles in every direction. By now all of them may know."

"What lie?"

Her eyes narrowed as if she was looking at him in a new way. "My kind should thank Henry for what he's told us. We should all just pray that no Full Bloods were around to hear it." Turning away from him, Jackie headed for the window. "There's a lot of Nymar in Henry's scent, so maybe that part of him will overpower the rest."

Feeling his urgency growing now that Jackie had already made it to the window, Cole snapped, "What lie? You want to tell me these things, then start making sense!"

"I've told you plenty. Bring this to one of your partners and they'll know what it means. Even if Misonyk was using some sort of mental link to control Henry, those thoughts are being screamed out to the rest of us. We know what Henry's capable of. Sooner or later he'll break free. When that happens . . ." She pulled the window open with a hand that had already begun to grow claws. "All I wanted to do was let the Skinners know what they're up against. You're the ones who do the fighting, so use the weapon I gave you. I have to go. Henry will be able to smell me long before I can smell him, and that wouldn't be good for either of us."

Jackie turned her back to him and lifted one leg through the open window. Cole started to follow her and said, "Maybe you should tell Paige about this. I may not remember all of it."

"You'd better remember," Jackie replied. "'Cause I'm done. I owed Brad a big favor, but I've done more than enough to see it through. Best of luck to you, Cole. Maybe I'll look in on you again." Lowering her line of sight below his waist, she added, "You've definitely got some promise."

Cole adjusted the sheet in his hand to cover himself up. Before he could say or do anything else, Jackie had shifted into her black and gray animal form. Her body simply flowed from one shape to another as if she had smoke for flesh and water for bones. With one effortless leap, she jumped out the window and was gone.

He didn't bother looking outside to see where she went. He started losing sight of Jackie the moment her fur had fully sprouted. He lunged for one of his phones and dialed the number for Rasa Hill. Paige picked up on the third ring, and he explained what had happened as she yawned on the other end. When he was done, Cole expected something drastic from Paige. What he got were a few simple words.

"Get some sleep," she told him.

"Isn't this important?"

"Yes, but we both need a few hours sleep. Besides, I'm waiting to hear from a couple different sources and we're not going anywhere until I do. Just come back here early in the morning."

"What about my wound?"

"It's just a scratch?" she asked.

"Yeah."

"Sleep it off."

"These things are tracking me, Paige," Cole snarled. "Gerald was right. At least one of 'em's got my scent, and I don't like it."

"Yeah, that's never fun," Paige yawned.

"I won't be able to shake them, will I?"

After a bit of a pause she told him, "There's a few options, but nothing's guaranteed."

"What's this lie Jackie mentioned? Is that something you know about?"

"All Nymar lie," she replied simply. "We can sift through it all later. Stop talking so much and get some rest."

Cole ran his fingers along the scratches on his shoulder and felt his stomach clench. A while ago getting back to a normal life seemed possible. He could always settle back in and try to forget about the weirdness he'd seen. Now, the weirdness hadn't just beaten him up a few times, but had followed him across national borders and shared a fairly intimate moment with him. There was no easy way to forget about that.

"I want in, Paige," he said. "Since this shit is just going to follow me around, I might as well do something more than wait for it to find me. It's either become a Skinner or spend the next bunch of years looking over my shoulder waiting for the next thing to track me down."

Paige's voice was still tired, but it was also soft and comforting. "You really need to sleep on it, Cole. We'll talk about it more tomorrow. Are you all right where you're at?"

"Sure," he replied as he looked over at the window that was still hanging from its broken bracket. "I think I can kiss my deposit good-bye, though. Do you think they'll come after me again?"

"Sounds to me like she could've killed you already if she wanted. You're welcome to stay here, you know."

Cole looked around at the shredded mattress and messy room. "I'll think of something. See you in the morning, Paige."

Since Jackie had tracked him all the way from Canada, going to another hotel didn't seem like it would do much good. He also didn't want to head back to Rasa Hill. After all the shapely female bodies he'd seen that night, he needed some quiet time.

Chapter 12

The sun was making its first appearance for the day when Cole left the hotel. Rather than try to get comfortable on a bed that had been ripped apart, he'd wrapped himself in the comforter and fallen asleep in a chair. After a quick and very cold shower, he climbed down a set of stairs so he didn't have to walk past the front desk on his way outside. He simply didn't want his free breakfast enough to take the chance of being forced to make up a reason for all the noise that had come from his room the night before. After circling the building, he walked down the street and found a cab parked in front of a little drive-through coffee place.

Cole bought a large Colombian blend and a bagel, hopped into the cab and gave the address for Rasa Hill. When the cab pulled up to the abandoned restaurant, he spotted another car parked just outside the front door. The early morning sun was obscured by a thick patch of clouds, making it difficult for him to see much of the car's details. Ditching the rest of his bagel and swigging the remaining coffee, he bolted from the cab and rushed toward the restaurant.

The cabbie was quick to grab a chipped baseball bat from under his seat and take off after him. He ran a few paces before letting out a hacking cough that had been fermenting in his lungs since he'd first started smoking nonfiltered cigarettes and shouted, "Get yer ass back here! You owe me money, goddammit!"

Cole approached the front of the restaurant, pulled on the front door and found it locked. Without so much as glancing back at the angry cabbie, he circled around to the side of the building.

"Hey!" the cabbie yelled. "I'll kick yer ass!"

The cabbie ran as fast as his legs would carry him, keeping his bat cocked near his head and ready to swing as he approached the restaurant. When he cleared the front, he could see Cole around the next corner farther along the building. Then, from the shadows surrounding a stack of empty crates, a pale redhead stepped up and placed her hand around the cabbie's throat.

The redhead wasn't much shorter than the cabbie, but she looked to be at least fifty pounds lighter. Her arms and legs were covered in black nylon. Whatever curves were present on her skinny figure were accentuated by a dark purple mini-skirt and matching tube top. Darkly painted lips curled into a smile as she tightened her grip upon the cabbie's throat and absorbed a blow from the bat without so much as a flinch.

"What's the matter, cutie?" the redhead asked as she smiled to reveal one set of short, thin fangs that curled down to brush against the side of her tongue. "You'd get a lot more action if you didn't swing your little bat around like that."

As Cole rushed around the building, he looked for anything he could use as a weapon. The first thing he grabbed was a stick. He replaced that with a rock a few seconds later. By the time he got within sight of the restaurant's back door, he threw the rock away and replaced it with a piece of lumber from a broken pallet. There was a bunch of trash cans next to the back door, but he didn't take one of those. He did grab something else that seemed useful and then pulled at the door before he had enough time to think better of it.

The door opened into a dark and quiet storeroom. He stomped in to try and draw as much attention as he could. "Paige!" he shouted. "Are you in here?"

There was a rustling to his left. When he turned, he

tightened both hands around the makeshift weapons he'd collected and prepared to put them to use. A man stepped through the door that led to the kitchen and took a moment to look him up and down. He was around Cole's height, had a similar build, and a rusty hue to his skin. Stringy black hair was combed over to one side, but the other side of his head was buzzed almost down to the scalp.

The man took one step forward, squinted into the darkness and parted his lips to show one set were extended canines and the others, growing beside them, were thinner and curved.

"Where's Paige?" Cole snarled as he planted his feet and squared his shoulders.

"She's here," the man replied in a smooth, casual voice.

"I want to see her. If you've hurt her—"

"Take it easy, slick."

"Fuck easy!" Cole snapped. "Anything that's happened to her, I'll make sure it happens to you twice as bad."

Taking another few steps forward, the man said, "I don't know who you are, but you got your signals crossed."

"I'll decide that once I see Paige."

The man had both hands open and out to his sides. Lifting his chin a bit, he looked over Cole's shoulder and asked, "How did this guy get past you, Steph?"

Cole grinned and shook his head. Before he could say anything about not being tricked to look away, he felt the gentle touch of fingernails against his shoulder.

"I had to take care of the cab driver," replied the redhead in the nylon body stocking and tube top.

The sound of that voice and the brush of those nails caused Cole to twist around and take a swing with the piece of lumber he was carrying. There was some power behind it, but his arm was batted away with just as much effort as the redhead had used to tickle his shoulder. Steph kept walking and then flicked her fingernails against Cole's chin. Winking, she licked the edge of the slender fangs she had on display. Her skin was the color of fresh milk, giving a sharp contrast to the black lines running along her neck and making her hair look just a bit brighter than freshly spilled blood.

"Where's Paige?" Cole demanded. "You can bring out all

the helpers you want, but if she's dead, you'll all get piled up in the same corner!"

Steph stood in front of Cole with her hip cocked in one direction and her head cocked in the other. Running her hand up between her breasts, she kept it going until she could slide her tongue out between her fangs and lick her fingertips. "If that short broad with the dark hair told me you were coming, I would've worn a little less." Her eyes slowly moved down until she got a look at what Cole was holding. Then her smile widened and she started laughing in a way that was anything but seductive. "I knew you Skinners were low-tech, but come on!"

This time Cole couldn't help but follow the vampire's gaze. He was holding his lumber in one hand like a sword, and a trash can lid in the other like a shield. All he needed to finish his outfit was a hat made out of folded newspaper.

When Steph laughed at him even harder, Cole swung his left arm out to catch her with a backhanded blow. The trash can lid banged against her torso, forcing her to take a couple stumbling steps to the side. He moved around and built up some momentum so he could push her toward the back door and into the breaking dawn.

Steph was still laughing, but she was also trying to sink her nails into Cole's arm. Just as she was about to reach around his bargain bin shield, she was knocked through the doorway with enough force to separate a man's shoulder. Wincing while still moving backward, she didn't truly look angry until her shoes scraped against the ground and one of her heels snapped off beneath her weight.

Lowering his shoulder, Cole gave one more push so the vampire was completely clear of the building. He could feel the warmth of daylight in the air, but the sun wasn't quite high enough to clear the top of the building across the street. Raising his shield once more, he charged at Steph again. When he hit her, it was like pounding against a brick wall. Even so, he swung his piece of lumber and connected with her upraised arm. He followed up by driving the end of the lumber into Steph's belly and pushing her beyond the shadow cast by the restaurant.

She hobbled upon one broken heel and spun away from him. When she whipped back around to face him, her face was illuminated by the rising sun.

"How do you like that, bitch?" Cole asked victoriously.

Steph stood there with her snarl in place. She looked up and squinted into the dull glow of the dawn, then looking back at Cole, straightened and lowered her chin to display a well-practiced pout. "Oh help me," she droned. "I am burning."

Cole's brow furrowed as he looked up to double-check that the sun was shining on her. It was a long cry from high noon, but that bright ball in the sky was pretty distinctive.

Now, Steph was laughing so hard she could barely form a sentence. Lifting one arm to place it dramatically along her forehead, she tossed her head back and let out a sob that could have been plucked from any daytime soap opera. "I am burning! Oh, curse you pure rays of the sun. You have cast me out and now I will surely perish in a storm of ash."

Letting out a sigh, Cole grumbled, "I get it. You can cut the act."

"You have slain me, valiant knight," she wailed. "Your shield and magic helmet were too much for me."

"I get it!" Cole shouted.

Since Steph was having too much fun carrying on and not burning in the sunlight, he went back inside, to find her companion waiting for him. This time, however, the man was not alone.

"Cole?" Paige said as she walked in from the kitchen. "When did you get here?"

Cole dropped his trash can lid and rushed to hold Paige at arm's distance. "I thought you were in trouble," he said while looking her over.

"That," the man next to Cole said, "remains to be decided."

Ignoring the other man, Paige asked, "What happened to you, Cole? Did Steph try to hurt you?"

"No, but . . . the cab driver! He's right outside and he might have—"

"I told you I took care of him," Steph replied as she stepped back inside.

"What did you do?" Cole snarled.

Her lower lip drooping in a mischievous pout, Steph replied, "I paid him. He said you promised triple the tip. You cost me everything I had on me, naughty boy."

Cole pulled away from Paige and stood next to her so he was facing both Nymar with his back to the wall. "All right. Someone—and I don't care who—just tell me what's going on here."

Paige patted his back to let him know she was nearby. "I invited Ace and Stephanie here. We were just about to talk business. Isn't that right, Ace?"

Now that he was closer to the other man, Cole could see the symbol shaved into the buzzed half of the Nymar's scalp. It was a single, three leaf clover straight off the ace of clubs.

"You bet your ass that's right," Ace said. "And I wouldn't get too comfortable thinking this is a friendly visit. Considering how your boy treated Steph, I should start skinning some Skinners right here and now!"

Leaning over to whisper into Cole's ear, Paige told him, "They represent some of Chicago's finest working girls, including Racquel."

Cole shook his head and let out a tired laugh. "You guys are undead and the best way to spend your time is running hookers?"

"Working girls, cutie," Steph said. "And boys. Hookers are humans who give themselves up to strangers. We cater to your kind who pay us to be fed upon. They like the biting and all the rest, so we make sure it's worth the price. Maybe you should try it."

"Well, we saved your working girl's life," Cole said. "I don't think we should be catching any grief for that. As for the other thing . . . I'll pass."

"Racquel told us what happened," Steph said. "That's why we haven't killed you yet. Things ran a whole lot smoother when Gerald was here. When can we talk to him?"

"Never," Paige said coldly. "You'll talk to me."

Keeping her sights set upon Paige, Steph walked across the room as if trying to kick holes into the floor. "Fine. I'll say this to you. Chicago is under Nymar control! We're the ones who tolerate Skinners being here, and that's only because you're good for keeping the assholes in line."

"Which assholes are we talking about?" Paige asked with a grin.

"You're new around here, girlie," she shouted as she poked a garishly painted finger at Paige. "You don't get to strut around like you own this place. Not even Gerald got to do that! If you want to strut in this town, you're gonna have to pay your dues. Otherwise, I'll gather up a few of my bitches and burn you out of here." Steph's eyes darted back and forth between Paige and Cole. Up close, those eyes looked green with a violet tint. "How many of us do you think you could get before we killed you?" Steph asked. "Two? Three?"

"Maybe I could just get one," Paige said. "But it would be you. And when I got through, not even the kids at the goth store in the mall where you got those shitty clothes would recognize you."

Before Steph could respond to that, Ace stepped in to pull her back.

"We took Racquel away from those lunatics and let her go safe and sound," Paige continued. "As for your girl Wendy, she killed a man right out on the street for everyone to see. You know damn well that Gerald or any other Skinner on this planet would have killed her after that, but neither one of us even laid a finger on her. Some freak ripped her chest open and ate the spore attached to her heart. When the hell have you ever heard of a Skinner doing that?"

Although Steph needed a few seconds to simmer down, the anger in her eyes faded away. She nodded to Ace and ran her tongue along her lower lip before admitting, "You're right. Still, you should've waited until we could introduce you around a bit before you started playing up the new sheriff in town thing. We have a certain standing in the Nymar community. Gerald must have told you."

Paige nodded, but she didn't look impressed. "Yeah, he told me some things. Can we move on?"

Steph and Ace looked at each other and then settled the matter with a silent nod.

"Wendy drifted over to Misonyk and lost touch with us," Ace said. "The way she talked about him, it seemed the last thing he would do is hurt her. We heard about how she died, but lately just about every death's been blamed on that freak. We wanted to look in your eyes when we asked about her just to be safe." Glancing sideways at Steph, he added, "The ones who pointed the finger at you were in Misonyk's pocket anyway."

Rolling her eyes, Steph asked, "Have you heard of Misonyk?"

"Yeah," Cole replied, so he could be something more than a casual amusement in the room. "We've heard of Henry too."

"Good. What you need to know is that most Nymar don't give a shit about what Misonyk has to say. He's got the support of one coven at the very least, which comes to a dozen or so Nymar scattered through the city who buy into all of his bullshit about drinking souls. They're the ones breaking the rules by killing humans and feeding in public. That sort of shit just cuts into our profits."

"What's he say about drinking souls?" Paige asked.

Ace leaned against a wall and ran his fingers along the symbol shaved into his scalp. "He says that if you drink someone to death, you get their soul. When you get enough souls, you get to tap into the Spirit World. When you tap into the Spirit World, you can project your own spirit into someone else and then tap it for even more power."

"Nothing but a psychic pyramid scheme," Steph said.

As bad as his first impression of the redhead had been, Cole couldn't help but laugh at that one.

Paige wasn't as amused. "Does any of this spirit drinking actually work?" she asked.

"Yeah," Ace replied. "His followers have gotten into a few heads, but most of 'em have been human. He's the only one that's been gettin' into Nymar brains. I wouldn't have believed it until he pulled it on me. He tried getting me to tell all my employees to sign up with him. I almost did it too, if it hadn't been for Steph."

The redhead smiled proudly and stood up straight, as if

she'd just gotten a perfect score on her report card. "He tried whispering into my brain when Ace kicked him out of his," she announced. "I'd rather take my chances giving Henry a ride before I'd tell any of my girls to follow some infeeding asshole like Misonyk."

"Nymar are feeding on each other?" Paige asked.

Both Ace and Steph nodded. "It always happens every now and then," Ace said, "but Misonyk is really pushing it. Normally, the covens would do something about it themselves, but Henry's torn apart anyone who's made a move against him."

"I know," Cole replied. "We've seen it."

"And that's what I wanted to tell you," Steph said as she stepped forward and slid her fingers down Cole's chest. "If there's one thing you Skinners can do, it's kill freaks. You kill Henry, and there's a reward in it for you. All the covens have pitched enough money into the kitty for you to set yourselves up somewhere nicer than this dump. You might even be able to buy a neat new stick and trash can lid." Smirking at Cole's glare, Steph turned away from him like he no longer existed. "Don't look at me like that, stud. My kitty doesn't have the money in it, but I could do a little somethin' somethin' if you take care of Henry."

"You'll owe us plenty," Paige said. "But money's not all we had in mind."

Ace grinned and tapped Steph's shoulder to send her back a few steps. "Henry's head is worth the money and plenty of favors down the stretch. Don't worry about that. Just be quick, because Misonyk is doing damage every day, and it ain't just here."

"Where else does he go?" Paige asked.

Steph tagged herself back in. "He drives up north. Sometimes he goes into Indiana, but mostly he's a cheddar head. Misonyk covers his tracks pretty well, but Henry don't exactly fit in a car. He runs and jumps like a . . ."

As Steph searched for an appropriate analogy, Cole asked, "Like a Full Blood?"

Paige got ready to smooth over Cole's comment, but was surprised when she saw Steph nod and smile.

"This one here is sharp," Ace said while looking at Cole. "A bit loose in the head, but I like him."

"Loose, huh?" Cole asked. "Am I the pot or the kettle here?"

"I've never seen a Full Blood," Steph admitted, "but everything I heard about the big doggies say they can run fast enough and jump high enough to go from one end of the state to the other in record time. You may be on to something . . . what was your name?"

"Cole," Ace said.

Steph smiled as if she'd become absorbed in the act of rolling his name along the back of her throat.

"So how much reward money are we talking about?" Cole asked.

Before either of the two Nymar could answer, Paige overruled his question with one of her own. "Where can we find Misonyk?"

"There's a meeting between Misonyk and one of the Milwaukee covens taking place at a diner right off the highway," Ace replied. "Wendy was feeding us some information to keep in our good graces, but it looks like Misonyk found out about that and sicced Henry on her. I can give you directions to the place."

"Is there anything else you can do on your end?" Paige asked. "Any way you could possibly get us any more information about Henry? He may have shapeshifter blood, but he's no Full Blood."

Steph shifted her eyes over to Paige and said, "I guess a Skinner would know that better than anybody."

"Are there any more informants we should know about?"

"I wouldn't count on anyone else in Misonyk's little group to be of any help after what happened to Wendy," Ace replied. "Once he's gone, the rest should fall back into line. The rest of us don't have time to spy. We're either leaving Chicago for somewhere outside of Misonyk's stomping grounds or trying to keep an eye out for Henry."

"You guys always know when to hide, huh?" Paige asked.

There was an angry flash in Steph's eye, but she couldn't exactly refute the accusation. "Here's the place where that meeting's being held," she snapped as she produced a small folded piece of paper from her skirt pocket. "That's all we've got for ya, girlie." With that, she raised her arm until Ace walked up and put himself beneath it. As they stepped outside, both of them let out overly dramatic cries of pain about the rising sun. Even as the door swung shut, Steph's laughter could be heard echoing throughout the restaurant.

"All right," Cole said as he whipped around to look at Paige. "Why didn't you tell me vampires aren't afraid of sunlight?"

"Who ever said that sunlight bullshit was real anyway? In fact, even in the movies, why *would* sunlight work on them?"

"I don't know. It's just . . . *supposed* to work!"

"Well, now that your training can officially start, I'll fill you in on one thing." Paige lowered her voice to a whisper and said, "Sunlight doesn't bother vampires. If it did, they'd all explode on their own sooner or later and we wouldn't have to put up with crap like that from assholes with clovers shaved into their heads."

After letting out a sigh, Cole walked through the restaurant until he could take a look through the front window. Not only was the parked car no longer there, but the cab was gone as well. Since there wasn't a dead cabbie in sight, he guessed Steph really had just paid the guy and sent him away. "Is there a handbook or something I'm supposed to get?" he asked as he let the shades fall back to cover the window. "Because all my years of researching monsters through comic books and TV haven't done me any good."

Paige laughed from the kitchen doorway. "Myths, legend, and folklore have been rotting kids' brains way before television was invented, so don't feel too bad. Come on in here and let me get a look at you. Last night, didn't you say you were scratched?"

Cole followed her into the kitchen, and Paige began rooting through one of the many sets of cabinets. "Yeah, but it's not bad."

"Well, tell me what happened again while I get a look for myself."

While he repeated everything about what Jackie had told him in his hotel room, Paige dabbed away the flecks of dried blood from his shoulder and examined the scratches. They weren't even deep enough to need a bandage.

Upon reaching the end of his story, Cole asked, "So what's a Mongrel?"

"I'll tell you more about them later," Paige replied. "Are you sure all you two did in that room was talk?"

There was no mistaking the intent in Paige's eyes as she waited for Cole's answer. The expression she wore was encouraging, but also a bit scary. Cole knew he wasn't nearly a good enough liar to get one past her when she was looking at him like that. Fortunately, he didn't have to lie when he told her, "That's all we did, Paige. Although, it seemed like there could have been more if I was on my game. What is it with these things all being so damn horny?"

She shook her head and laughed under her breath as she put away the medical kit. "You know how everyone always talks about the oldest trick in the book? Well," she said with an irresistible wrinkle of her nose, "when a woman is dealing with a guy like you, that's it."

"Oh," Cole grumbled. "You don't even sound surprised that Jackie tracked me down like that."

"It's not as miraculous as it sounds." She walked to another bedroom that Cole hadn't seen before. Even though there was only a cot and a few piles of clothes, the room had a distinctly feminine feel. Paige didn't seem to mind those feminine things being on display as she sifted through them and selected some to be thrown into an old gym bag. "Once they track you to civilization, they just shift into their human forms and follow you the old-fashioned way. After she got here, she could let you get a bit farther away and still be able to sniff you out just fine. They're all real good at that"

"How far away can they get and still keep tabs on me?" he asked.

Paige shrugged, sniffed a black halter top for freshness and said, "Maybe five or six miles. Some of them can get as far as ten or twelve without too much problem. It sort of depends on what they shift into. That's why Mongrels are so tricky. Don't be so hard on yourself, Cole. You've held up pretty well so far. Charging in here the way you did was very . . ." Pausing, she looked at him and smiled. "It was very noble."

"I thought you were going to tell me it was stupid."

"No. The thing with the trash can lid was stupid. And the part where you shoved Steph into the sunlight . . . well, that was cute."

"Looks like you're packing for a trip. I take it we're headed into dairy country for a while?"

Paige zipped up the gym bag. "You got it. Things may get a little rough, so if you're serious about joining up, you could start your training somewhere safer and learn another specialty. There's tracking, research, investigations . . ."

"Refrigeration, veterinary medicine, gun repair," Cole added. "I've seen the commercials. So what's your specialty?"

"I like to get my hands dirty."

"And if I leave for somewhere safer?"

"I'll send you a postcard from Wisconsin," Paige replied. "One of our own trackers spotted something that could be connected to Henry, so between that and the thing at the diner the asshole with the clover-shaped hair mentioned, I don't know how long I'll be gone."

Cole took a moment to think about the choices in front of him. On one hand, there was the very real possibility that Paige was a lunatic who carried a weapon everywhere she went. On the other hand, there were other things out there that were a whole lot worse than guns.

"If you need to think it over . . ." Paige offered.

"No," he replied. "I've already done stuff that I never thought I'd be doing without using a controller or watching it on a monitor. These things know about me. They've got my scent. I'm on their radar. However you want to say it, I don't like the thought of running or hiding for the rest of my life. If I'm gonna give skinning a try, I'd like to stick with you."

"You're sure?" Paige asked. "Once I take you past a certain point, there really is no turning back. These things gossip and chatter worse than a group of old ladies at a bake sale. If you leave now, I might be able to help you stay hidden, and they'll probably lose interest in a while. If you're seen with me or others like me much longer, you'll be tagged as one of us and nobody will believe any different."

"I kind of figured as much. This isn't exactly what I imagined I'd do with my life, but I got to admit . . . it's pretty cool."

Paige grinned. "I was hoping you'd see it that way."

The gym bag hit Cole square in the chest like a kick from a mule.

"Put that in the car while I get a few more things," she said. "Then you need to show me the hotel room where you were attacked."

"That's okay. There's not much of anything left in there."

"Very wrong, young one," Paige said as she took on the tone of a kung fu master from a late night movie. "Your opponent leaves more than words in her wake."

"Huh?"

"Just get moving!"

Chapter 13

It took a few trips back and forth from the car and the restaurant to get all of Paige's things loaded up and ready to go. Apart from the gym bag, there were pots and pans, some funky cooking utensils, and some black plastic cases that just looked like bad news. Before Cole could ask what was in them, Paige started the car and revved the engine as if she was going to fly away from there without him. He barely managed to get into the car with all his limbs intact.

"You said you were at the Afton Inn, right?" she asked.

"That's the place. Are there guns in some of those cases?"

"A few."

Cole let it drop at that.

The sun was out in full force, but didn't shine down with enough heat to burn through the early morning chill. Considering it was autumn in Chicago, that situation wasn't bound to get much better. Morning rush hour was growing into a living, sprawling behemoth, so Cole let Paige drive without any more distractions. Before too long he was busy hanging onto whatever he could as she wove between other vehicles without the fear of a mortal being. Doing his best to let go of his love for life, he tried to focus on something more relaxing . . . like the plane ride into Canada.

He still hadn't drawn a full breath by the time they'd parked at the Afton Inn and headed upstairs to the second floor. Normally, the cool, sterilized air of a vaguely nice hotel was enough to soothe his nerves. Places like that smelled like vacations or, at the very least, business trips where marginal food was put on the company's bill. This time, even the faint odor of chlorine didn't make him smile. Instead of thinking about whirlpools and saunas, he could only think about hissing blondes with sharp claws and greasy fur.

"Which room is yours?" Paige asked.

Cole pulled in a breath and dug the key card from his pocket. Walking to his door, he paused and asked, "What if it's in there?"

"You think that thing attacked you so it could use your room?"

"No . . . but . . . what if another one came back? I don't have a weapon."

"Wait right here," Paige said. "I think I saw a luggage rack by the elevator."

Plugging his key card into the reader on the door, Cole grumbled, "Smartass."

When the light on the card reader turned green, he turned the knob and opened the door. Before he could take a step inside, however, Paige walked past him and surveyed the room.

"You made a real mess in here," she said.

"Yeah."

"That thing came in through the window?"

Cole walked into the bathroom, flicked on the light and gathered up some of the things he'd left in there. "Yep. In through the window, onto the bed, and back to the window."

"I've heard of worse ways to spend a night," Paige said as she ran her hand along the carpet in front of the TV. She rubbed her fingers together and shook her head. The expression on her face brightened considerably when she saw the window, mostly shut against its splintered frame. "You said it came and left through here?"

"I said it twice. Jesus, my credit card's gonna take a hit for this damage."

Running her hand along the window, Paige grinned as if she'd just looked under the bed to find a wad of cash the previous guests had left behind. "Bring me a towel, Cole. There's some good stuff here."

He grabbed a handful of towels from the segmented steel rack above the toilet and brought them out to her. "What sort of good stuff are you talking about?"

"How about this?" Paige asked as she brought her hand around for him to see. At first glance it seemed there was nothing but waves of heat coming up from her sleeve. With a flip of her wrist, the back of her hand became visible. She repeated the trick by flipping her hand around a few more times. Now you see it, now you don't.

"Wow," he whispered. "That's cool." After squinting and adjusting his eyes a bit, he could make out the vague shape of Paige's hand when she twisted it around again.

Grabbing one of the smaller towels Cole had brought her, she wiped off her hand and examined it to make sure all her fingers were visible and accounted for. "Now I know why Gerald was willing to go all the way to Canada to meet this Mongrel. I bet he intended on getting some of this invisible stuff after Brad was done talking to her."

"He never told you for certain?"

"He mentioned her a few times when he was arranging for me to come to Chicago," she said while holding up her hand to display a finger that had a hazy, mostly invisible tip, "but he hadn't been able to track her too well. Gerald said she could secrete some sort of oil to coat her fur so she could . . . I don't know how to explain it . . ."

"Bend light?"

Paige nodded as if Cole had guessed the number she'd been thinking of. "More or less. You got that from a movie, right?"

"About a hundred of them, and a dozen or so video games," Cole added. "I was going to steal that one for one of my own."

"Real original."

"Thanks."

"Anyway," she continued, "Gerald told me this Mongrel

was a hell of a spy thanks to this trick with disappearing or bending light or whatever. She claimed to have some information, but Gerald didn't trust her."

"Why not?"

"Because she's a hell of a spy and he couldn't track her. Let's just say she was lucky Brad was so new at all this or she wouldn't have made it out of Chicago. Gerald was traditional and it's not Skinner tradition to sit down and chat with shapeshifters. The only reason Gerald agreed to the meeting at all was because the Mongrel had escaped and it was the only way to pick up her trail again. This stuff goes a long way to recoup some of our losses. We'll have to do a little fiddling, but there's going to be plenty of uses for this."

"Fiddling. Real technical term, there. Do you think . . . she might have had anything to do with killing Gerald and Brad? If she can change shape, maybe she could've changed into that other thing."

Paige shook her head at that. "That's not how it works. I don't know any breed of shapeshifters that can change into totally different animals. Full Bloods can change a few different ways, but even their fur stays roughly the same color and you'd never mistake one for a cat. Besides, her story about almost getting killed along with you holds up. Full Bloods and Mongrels hate each other, and that's not just colorful language. We're talking *hate*. Come to think of it, her being there might have kept you alive just by distracting that Full Blood long enough. And if she had anything to do with what happened to Gerald and Brad, she wouldn't be stupid enough to come all the way back here so I could pick up her trail again."

"A lot of what she said fits with what Ace and Steph told us," Cole pointed out.

"Yep, and since there's no way in hell a Mongrel would work with Nymar like them just to put together a good story, it seems both sources hold up pretty well. Give me some more towels." Once Cole handed them to her, she carefully wiped up the greasy residue Jackie had left on the walls and bedside tables.

"So Full Bloods hate Mongrels," he said. "That's good to know, I guess. Now, these things are full-blooded . . . what?"

Going over another patch of residue that was on the dresser, Paige said, "They're werewolves, Cole. Nothing much can harm them, but whatever wounds they do get tend to heal up real quick unless they were put there by charmed weapons like that Blood Blade. Those things are hard to make, and only a few Gypsy families know how to make them. That's why we've got to protect whatever blades we get our hands on."

"A werewolf?" Cole asked. "A real werewolf?" He let out a breath and ran his fingers over his head. "Does it howl at the moon?" he asked, and chuckled.

Paige nodded. "Yep. They do like to howl. They can change whenever they like, and as far as we know, they can live for over a hundred years."

"Yowza."

"Sorry, Cole. Usually we don't just spool it all out like this, but you're kind of getting the crash course since you've already seen some of these things firsthand. To be honest, most of us don't get to see a Full Blood for years. Living through it is even more rare."

"What was the first you ever saw?" he asked.

Reluctantly, she said, "A Half Breed. It was a bad situation, so just leave it at that."

"And they're not as bad as Full Bloods?"

She winced, and after a moment replied, "They're different. They can't change whenever they want and they're wilder. They also . . . well . . . it's kind of hard to explain."

"Do they live a hundred years?"

"Oh, no," she quickly said. "They're mean, strong, and very fast, but they can be put down like any other big, ugly animal. When they change all the way, it takes a lot more. Big enough guns can do the trick, but there are other methods that work a whole lot better."

"I wouldn't mind putting a few of those things out of their misery," Cole said. "After seeing what happened in that cabin, it would do me some good to stand up to them."

Paige bundled up a towel soaked with the residue. Slipping back into her kung fu voice, she said, "Now is the time for my disciple to settle a score of another sort." Seeing the eager look on Cole's face, she added, "The hotel bill. Take this." She slapped a wad of money into his hand. "Pay the bill, pay for the damages, make sure nothing's charged to your card, and then leave."

After picking up his few remaining personal things, Cole headed for the door, but stopped short before opening it. "I just realized I've been wearing the same clothes so long that they're sticking to me."

Unable to keep a straight face, Paige said, "That's probably how that Mongrel tracked you all the way from Canada. If you need new clothes, we can get some on the way out of town."

At the desk, Cole spoke to a perky little man with bad skin, a worse toupee, and a surprisingly genuine smile. When he told him he was checking out, the clerk asked if everything was okay and then offered him a complimentary muffin. The clerk threw a mild fit when he got the phone call from the maid he'd sent to check on the room, but quickly calmed down after Cole handed over enough cash to settle the entire account. On his way out, Cole took his complimentary muffin, then ducked back inside to snag a second one.

Twenty minutes later he and Paige were headed north on I–94. Paige was doing the driving while munching happily on the treat Cole had brought her. She looked so happy that, if her mouth wasn't stuffed full at the moment, she might have been ready to sing.

"Wha ki id di?"

"Did you actually form words just now or was that some sort of code?" Cole asked.

Chewing up the rest of the muffin and wiping the crumbs from her chin, she said, "What kind is this? The muffin?"

"Oh, uh, I don't know. One of the dark, healthy looking ones."

"Damn, that was good." Reaching for the coffee she'd bought at a gas station, Paige sipped from the foam cup, blew on it, and then sipped again.

As he watched her, Cole couldn't help but smile. "You're a morning person. Strike one."

"Not a morning person, but I do like breakfast," she amended.

"Now that you're done stuffing your face, how about we pull over to get me some clothes? I think these are about to start walking on their own."

She shook her head while taking another pull from her coffee, which resulted in dripping enough to produce a nice, dark stain on her shirt. "Not yet. There's an outlet mall near the state line," she said while swiping at the spilled brew. "We'll stop there."

"Like you're so strapped for cash. What about that bundle you showed me at the hotel?"

"Those are funds to be used when necessary," she said, as if quoting from a manual. "And before you ask, they come from a pool made by other Skinners and any number of fine people who feel they owe it to us to keep us properly outfitted."

"So, you save someone's ass from a werewolf and they chip in for the cause?"

"Pretty much."

"I guess that makes sense. So, what's a Mongrel?"

"They're shapeshifters," Paige explained. "But not werewolves. Werewolves turn into wolves, or something along those lines. Mongrels turn into everything else."

"Like what?"

Paige shrugged, and rolled down the window to let a breeze rush through the car that felt just as capable of separating flesh from bone as the subject of the conversation. "I've seen some cats and foxes," she said casually. "One or two bears. Those are very tough, by the way. Snakes, lizards . . ."

Cole started laughing, and wrapped his hands around his foam coffee cup. "It was a real question, Paige. No need for the bullshit."

"I'm serious!" Holding up her hand to tick off her fingers, she added, "Leopards, tigers . . . but I haven't seen all of these myself. Lions, coyotes . . ."

"Such crap," he muttered.

Paige stopped, but only to take a sip of coffee. Although

there was still some good humor in her eyes, there wasn't enough there to make Cole certain she'd been kidding. Finally, she said, "All shapeshifters are tricky and dangerous. They don't need to feed on people, which means they don't need to expose themselves like the Nymar. They're territorial, so they fight for turf and kill to keep it. One Skinner from way back said he found evidence that shapeshifters used to try and live away from humans so they could just do their own thing. According to him, the more humans pushed into the wilderness, the more the shapeshifters pushed back."

"Sounds like an environmentalist's worse case scenario," Cole grunted.

"It may go a bit further back than that."

"The sixties?" Cole offered.

"Eighteen sixties, maybe."

"Seriously?"

Paige laughed and let her foot off the gas so she could slide past a cop while doing something close to the speed limit. "Don't sound so impressed. They're common legends and most are recorded in devices called books. You know, those things where words are written down on paper and not on a computer screen?" Seeing the dry look on Cole's face, she eased up a bit. "Skinners don't live forever," she said. "Considering our line of work, we barely get to live as long as Gerald. We mostly pass on what we know one on one, but there's a lot to be learned from history and folklore."

"Do the vam—I mean Nymar, get to live forever?"

"I don't think so. There are legends, but those could just be about one man living in the same castle, passing his disease down to his servants or cousins or something. The legends about the Mongrels and other shapeshifters have been proven, though. You open up a mythology book from just about anywhere in the world and you'll find werewolves, wereleopards, weretigers, you name it. We've documented enough actual sightings to verify them and a lot more."

"Yeah," Cole said. "So have I."

"There you go. Start keeping a journal. That's not a request either. We can't afford to open a school, so we need to make sure to pass it along before we . . ." The casual, easygoing smile on Paige's face dimmed for the first time in a while. Focusing on the road and hanging one arm out the window, she said, "When we die. Everything we've picked up builds on what everyone else has learned. Hopefully, someday we'll know enough to take back our spot at the top of the food chain. Until then, we're just another bunch of sheep hoping the wolves don't get hungry."

"I like the learning idea better," Cole said.

"So do I."

After a deep breath, he asked, "Are all Mongrels invisible?"

Paige settled right back into her comfort zone. "They all have their own abilities. Some breeds don't do much, but others can surprise you. There's always something behind it that explains how they do their tricks. Once we figure out some of those tricks, we can use them for ourselves."

"That's why you collected that grease from the hotel?" he asked.

"Yep. With all the Skinners in the world, there's bound to be someone who can figure out a good way to use the weird stuff we find."

"You don't know how great it is to hear you say that," he said.

"Say what?"

"That something's weird."

Paige laughed at him and said, "You haven't seen the worst of it yet, my friend. You've been real lucky to make it this far. Just stay close to me and do what I say. When we reach that diner, let me do the talking. When we meet Prophet, you listen and watch."

"Prophet," Cole repeated. "Is he psychic?"

"More or less. He claims to have dreams about the future that are accurate enough for him to be in the right place at the right time to catch certain people or track certain things. He mostly works as a bounty hunter, but does some tracking for us when he can. Charges an arm and a leg, but it's usually worth it."

"Must be awfully nice to have a psychic on your side."

She groaned and slowly shook her head. "He's a great tracker, but a lot of that's pure talent. The dreams he has are . . . I don't know. At least he's a great tracker."

Cole nodded and resisted the urge to chuckle. "How'd you find this guy?"

"Actually, he found one of us. A Skinner named Rico was doing work in St. Louis when he ran into this guy who claimed to have a psychic vision or something that told him where to find a nest of monsters. The psychic stuff sounded iffy, but he led us to a den of Half Breeds, so we put him on the payroll."

"And his name's Prophet?" Cole snorted. "Maybe his mother was psychic too. Can't wait to meet him."

"His name's Walter, and I'm sure you two will get along just fine."

"Sure! All of us Skinners got to stick together, right?"

"He's not a Skinner," Paige said with a laugh. "Although we've tried to recruit him more than once."

"Aw, come on. All you'd need to do is go in there and bat those pretty eyelashes at him and I bet he'd cave."

"Not every man's as easy to work as you," she said.

Cole pulled in a sharp breath and hissed, "That one stung."

Chapter 14

There was time to kill before the meeting at the diner Ace and Steph had mentioned. Paige wanted to get there early, which still left them with an hour or two to hit the outlet mall. Cole picked up some new clothes and they were out the door before he could try on his half-priced jeans.

The diner was supposed to be west of Milwaukee off of I–94. Somewhere along the way, Cole dozed off until he was awakened by a smack on his arm. The second smack wasn't so subtle and nearly cracked his head against the window. "What the hell?" he grunted as he sat up and immediately felt every kink in his neck and shoulders.

"Get up," Paige snapped. "There's a revolver in the glove compartment. Take it."

"Is it time for the meeting already?" he asked as he fumbled for the gun.

"No, but there's plenty of Nymar there already."

"How can you tell?"

Paige flexed her hand and steered the car off the next exit. "You might want to stay in the car," she told him. "If things get ugly—"

"If things get ugly, I doubt a locked car door will do me any good," he interrupted.

She brought the Cavalier to a stop and left her keys in the ignition. "Then get ready to drive away," she said. "If you have to, just drive away and call MEG." With that, she pushed open her door and jumped out of the car, with Cole not too far behind.

They were parked in front of a diner that could have easily passed for an empty shell off the side of the road. The next lot over was filled with rows of broken gas pumps and a smaller building that was completely hollowed out. Judging by the layers of filth on the pumps and the boards in the windows of the neighboring building, the gas station hadn't been open for a long while.

Seeing no movement through the diner's window, Cole tucked the revolver under his waistband and pulled his shirt over it. "What's wrong?" he asked while running to catch up to Paige.

She kept flexing her hands and shaking them every now and then, as if working out a bad cramp in her wrists and fingers. Her eyes were fixed upon the diner and only darted to him for a second. "Where's that gun?"

"I've got it. We shouldn't just—"

"Keep it ready," she cut in. "You might need it."

He drew the gun and checked it over. He wasn't an expert marksman, but he'd been to the firing range enough times to know how to flick a safety off. Reflexively lowering his voice, he asked, "What's the matter?"

"Something's here," she replied.

That was enough to make Cole nervous. The parking lot had a few other cars in it, but even they had an eerie emptiness to them. Since Paige was approaching the front door, he stayed beside her. The closer they got, the more suspicious he became. The air felt heavier, and as they got closer to the diner, he could see some kind of dark liquid staining a few of the windows.

After a few more steps, a putrid mix of rusty copper and rotten meat hit Cole's nostrils.

"Jesus," he groaned as he pressed a hand to his nose and mouth.

Paige shot an intent glare over her shoulder and shushed him, then held up her open hand in the universal gesture used by crossing guards around the world.

Apart from telling Cole to stop, she also gave him a good look at the scars on her palm, which now looked like a fresh case of poison ivy. Before he could get a closer look, he heard something crash inside the diner. That was followed by a familiar half groan and half scream.

"If you have to shoot," she warned, "aim for the head or heart. Follow my lead and make sure you have a good target before wasting a shot."

"And what if I need more than this gun?"

"There's more weapons in the trunk," she replied.

The rancid smell was thicker now that they'd taken a few more steps toward the diner. Every time Cole pulled in a breath, he swore he was coating the back of his throat with blood.

"There's a lot of them," Paige said. "It looks like this wasn't a very friendly meeting."

"Is it the Nymar?"

She shook her head. "I don't know for sure. Could be Nymar. Could be shapeshifters. Could be both."

Paige stepped up to the front door and pulled it open. They could now hear crashes and pounding from inside the place, but the main dining room was deathly still. Propping open the door with one foot, she bent at the knees and reached for one of her moderately fashionable, black leather cowboy boots. They came equipped with sensible heels and a club concealed in a sleeve that ran along the inside of each calf. She removed a club from her left boot while pushing the front door all the way open. The blunt weapon, made out of polished wood, was just a bit shorter than her forearm. She winced as she tightened her grip on the handle and took another step forward.

There was another scream from within the diner, followed by the crashing of plaster and wooden beams as a body exploded through the narrow window where orders were placed and picked up. Chunks were knocked from the wall around the opening, leaving only the metal shelf beneath the window intact.

Cole was so distracted by the sight that he didn't notice the rest of the bodies strewn on the floor until the airborne figure landed on a few of them. He followed in Paige's footsteps as she moved away from the door and took up a position next to a booth made for four. It currently held two diners who were facedown and bleeding on a mess of spilled nachos.

Now that Cole was inside, he was nearly overpowered by the stench of raw death filling the diner. There were close to a dozen corpses laying at the tables or on the floor. Blood collected in pools thick enough to ripple when another body flew through the opening in the wall and landed on the counter next to a clunky cash register. Unlike the first body, the second one didn't flop to the floor like a broken doll. He was coated in drywall dust and paint chips, but Cole still recognized him as the man with the shaved head who'd tapped on his window while Paige and Racquel had tried to deal with Henry.

"Don't move!" Cole said as he raised his gun and took a hurried step toward the counter. He was stopped by Paige's hand, which slapped against his chest like an iron paddle. She pointed at the gaping hole in the wall behind the counter.

Another face peeked out from the kitchen. Long, stringy hair hung from Henry's scalp like a mane, and his drooping head wobbled as if only connected to his neck by a vein or two. Henry gripped the edge of the hole in the wall with thick fingers capped by long cracked nails. As he looked at them, he pulled himself toward the hole so he could launch himself through the wall at Paige. All she could do to defend herself was raise her single wooden club.

Cole let his instincts take over and leapt toward Paige. Somehow getting to her before Henry, he wrapped an arm around her waist so he could knock her to the floor. Henry flew over their heads and crashed into a booth, breaking the table and crushing the dead people sitting there under his feet.

"Get off of me!" Paige snarled as she shoved her way out from under Cole and turned toward Henry.

Then Cole felt a steely hand grab his shoulder and haul him up to his feet. Twisting around to see who'd grabbed him, he found himself staring into Misonyk's clouded green eyes. He didn't waste a second before jamming the barrel of his gun into the Nymar's chest and pulling the trigger.

Misonyk staggered back, but only a few steps. He wore a casual gray suit and a starched white shirt that were now coated in everything from blood and drywall dust to the oily black substance that coursed through Nymar veins. His head hung forward, showing Cole the thick black lines that writhed slowly, as if caressing the top of his skull beneath his scalp.

"I'm glad you came," Misonyk said in a voice that was steady and calm despite the escalating war going on behind him. "Now you can see what happens to those who defy me. You can hear the symphony of their cries. Are you ready to sing for me?"

Cole pointed his gun at the Nymar's chest and pulled his trigger again.

Each shot made a wet impact and sent a spray of oily black through the air. Before Cole could fire another shot, Misonyk snapped his hand out to grab hold of his wrist. The Nymar tightened his grip and twisted until Cole was gritting his teeth and hoping his arm would just hurry up and break so some of the pain could ease up. Meanwhile, he got a good look at the freshly made bullet holes in Misonyk's chest, which opened to reveal strips of waxy muscle stretched over a solid plate of bone.

"Better than you have tried to kill me," Misonyk said in a rasping voice. "Since I know you Skinners enjoy your experiments, I'll try one of my own."

Cole struggled to free his arm, but it might as well have been caught in a steel trap. He tried to point the gun at Misonyk, but his hand was quickly twisted painfully back in the other direction. When he tried to kick the Nymar, his feet slammed against solid, unforgiving muscle. As Cole tried to think of something else he could do, Misonyk peeled back his lips and opened his mouth to show a second set of fangs that slid from his gums and curled down beside the straighter fangs. From the bottom jaw, a third pair of shorter, thicker teeth sprung up like a set of stalagmites. Those worried Cole the most, since he knew there was no way in hell he'd be able to shake free if they sank into him. As Misonyk leaned his head back, a substance resembling spoiled milk dripped from the snakelike set of upper fangs.

Cole pushed against Misonyk to put as much distance as possible between them. He thought about pulling his trigger, but knew that would only waste a bullet. And then, just as he started to brace for the inevitable, his hand slipped free. Staggering back against an upended table, he brought his gun around and looked for a target. Unfortunately, that meant both of his eyes were wide-open to catch the spray of venom Misonyk spat into his face.

Pain burned through his head. It was so intense that he crouched down and pressed both hands against his face. Even though the pistol grip was knocking against his head, he kept pushing, as if shoving his eyeballs all the way in to the back of his skull was the only option left open to him. "Son of a bitch!" he screamed.

As the pain soaked into him, it lessened enough for Cole to open his eyes. The good news was that he could still see. The bad news was that Misonyk had already walked past Henry and was entering the kitchen through a swinging door.

Cole tried to rush after Misonyk, but his feet skidded on the slick surface of the floor. He felt the tendons in his knees and groin beg for mercy, but managed to shift his weight and keep his legs beneath him. Just when he thought he'd be able to stand up straight, he felt the impact of Henry's fists against the floor. The thump was enough to loosen one of Cole's heels and knock that leg out from under him. His ass hit the bloody tiles and he reflexively reached back to brace himself. As his left hand slapped against the floor, he raised his right and fired a round at Misonyk. The shot punched a hole through the door, which didn't prevent Misonyk from disappearing into the kitchen.

By now Paige had climbed onto Henry's back and wrapped one arm around his neck. She raised her other arm to lift something that most definitely wasn't the club she'd drawn from her boot. This weapon might have been made from the same material, but it was almost twice as long and had a handle that wrapped around her wrists like petrified vines. The end was sharpened to a point, and Paige drove it straight down into the back of Henry's neck.

Henry let out a howl as he reared back and threw both arms

straight out. When he ran out of breath, he stretched his ropy limbs to reach around and grab hold of Paige. Any other set of arms wouldn't have been able to do much more than scratch or swat at her, but Henry's joints popped and cracked in every direction. When he angrily punched the floor again, Henry made a big enough impact to keep Cole off balance. Rather than continue to struggle after Misonyk, Cole turned his attention to the fight going on in front of him.

Henry's gnarled arms and dangling head all twitched with a collective set of muscle spasms. His upper body swelled outward until the top of his head almost brushed the ceiling, and then he contracted in what seemed to be a deep exhalation until he was only slightly taller than seven feet. This allowed Paige to cinch her grip around his neck and wrap one leg around his shoulder. Every time she drove the pointed weapon into Henry's body, the wound puckered up and closed on its own. Pasty fluid dripped from Henry's mouth and dribbled from his chin. It looked like poorly mixed paint, mostly black but with traces of dark red. Henry finally managed to grab hold of Paige's jacket and used it to throw her to the floor. She extended both arms and landed with a solid thump, but broke her fall well enough to work her way back to her feet.

Henry looked around with glazed eyes to survey the grisly mess within the diner, and his loud panting caused his entire frame to rock back and forth.

"They were loud. God . . . God *told me to kill them*!" he shouted, using a voice that was dredged up from the belly of a prehistoric beast. "You won't lock me *up again*!" With that, his chest swelled and his arms flailed up over his head. Henry's fists were only loosely balled, but they still took out chunks from the counter as they knocked against it.

Seeing that Paige had put some distance between herself and the flailing creature, Cole fired his remaining bullets into Henry's chest. The impacts caused the gnarled tangle of humanity to take a few steps back, which bought enough time for Paige to draw the second club from her boot. Smoke from the gun along with everything else must have affected his eyes, Cole realized, because the club now looked like a sickle, complete with long, curving blade and a handle that wrapped around her knuckles.

"What do you want me to do?" he shouted.

Before Paige could answer, a glancing blow from one of Henry's arms knocked the wind out of her. She slashed at Henry's stomach with the sickle, stabbed him with the first pointed weapon, then ducked out of Cole's sight to avoid a powerful swing from Henry's forearm.

"Paige!" he shouted.

" . . . help . . . me . . ."

Those words hadn't come from Paige. They were weak little mumblings coming from the counter in front of the shattered section of wall where the order window used to be. Looking in that direction, Cole found the first man who'd been tossed into the dining room.

"Please," the man creaked. "Help."

For the moment, Paige didn't need any help. She was cracking the handles of both weapons against Henry's head to make it looser than ever at the end of his neck. Henry wheeled around to face her, which placed him between Cole and Paige. Once Henry stepped aside, Cole could see that Paige was now carrying a sickle in each hand. Although the curved blades looked more suited for cutting wheat, they sliced Henry just fine. Paige bared her teeth in a half snarl and half grin as she continued to swing.

"I can handle him while you reload," she said to Cole. "If I don't make a dent after a few more tries, aim for his head. Not anywhere else, you hear me? Just the head." Without waiting for so much as a nod from Cole, she swung her right weapon toward Henry's ribs. Henry turned and batted her away with ease.

"Reload," Cole grumbled. "Reload with what?"

As he tried to decide if he should run back to the car and look for more bullets, he felt something grab his shirt. He looked down to find the man who had been begging for help a few moments ago.

Deciding to kill two birds with one stone, Cole reached down to support the man under one arm. "All right," he said. "We're going outside. You gotta be quick, though."

At first it looked as if the man was agreeing with him by nodding weakly. After letting his head fall back, however, he revealed the fangs on his upper and lower jaws. There was no mistaking the hunger in the Nymar's eyes as he set his sights upon Cole's neck and lunged for it.

Throwing the wounded Nymar away from him, Cole nearly tripped over a few of the closest bodies. Chunks of their necks had been torn out as if flesh had simply been scooped away from bone. That sight only confirmed what he had already guessed as to the grip of those lower fangs.

The Nymar's teeth clamped shut, but only after his back had hit the floor. Having missed Cole without so much as scratching him along the way, the Nymar arched his back and let out an anguished moan.

Henry snapped his head toward Cole so quickly that it looked as if it might come off. When he caught sight of the Nymar at Cole's feet, he cocked his head to one side until it was almost level. His gaze was knocked off-kilter once again as Paige dropped the handle of her weapon onto his temple and followed up with a kick that snapped his chin straight toward the ceiling.

Wheeling around in a crazed flurry of arms and fists, Henry knocked over tables and chairs with one wild swing after another. He hunkered down until he was closer to the size of a normal man, but the shape of his body was more gnarled and contorted than ever. His left fist sailed toward Paige, but she was able to hop away. Henry's knuckles sent a chair flying, but his next attack was quicker.

Even though Paige was able to raise one of her weapons as a shield, there was more than enough force to send her skidding across the slippery floor. She grabbed onto a table and pulled it down with her so it could shield her from Henry's next swing. A meaty fist cracked the thick plastic tabletop. Paige waited for the next blow, but it didn't arrive. Instead, Henry loped over to the Nymar on the floor.

Cole circled around Henry and reached for Paige's arm to help her up, but almost got one of her weapons jammed down his throat. "Easy," he hissed. "That thing's distracted."

Paige blinked furiously and gathered herself up so she

was crouched behind the table and ready to spring. "What's distracting it?" she asked.

"Looks like our friends with the fangs are good for something after all."

Taking a quick glance over the table, Paige watched as Henry stood in front of the Nymar and lowered his head. He then wrapped both arms around himself as if hugging his own stomach. The Nymar tried to scoot away, but Henry flew at him before he could get far. Shouting incoherently, Henry swatted at the floor and sent tiles through the air. With the same reckless abandon, he swiped at the Nymar's chest and ripped away several layers of flesh and bone. "You!" Henry grunted. "Justliketheothers! Justliketheothers!"

The Nymar grabbed onto Henry's wrist and had just enough strength to keep the gnarled fingers from reaching into his exposed rib cage. Once Henry's hand came free, the Nymar flipped over and got to his hands and knees. Dropping his face to the floor, he lapped up some of the blood that had pooled there and then sent his leg straight back to pound against Henry's midsection.

Henry skidded backward and crashed against the counter. His head lolled crazily as he stood up and swelled to something even bigger than when Paige had been on his back. He howled something that could have been words but were wrapped up in too much snarling to make any sense. Gripping the back of the Nymar's head, Henry slammed the guy's face against the floor, his other hand sinking wrist-deep into the middle of the Nymar's back. He pressed down even harder against the Nymar's head and pulled his other hand up to send several chunks of vertebrae through the air amid a spray of oily, blackened blood.

"You seen anything like that before?" Cole gasped.

For once Paige was speechless. She shook her head as Henry stuffed his face into the breach he'd created and started gnawing.

Come.

The word rolled through the air, causing Cole and Henry to snap their heads up and look toward the kitchen. Henry's mouth was covered in Nymar blood, and rubbery chunks of the spore dangled from his teeth. Without a moment's hesitation Henry stood up and leapt for the order window. His second jump took him out of sight completely.

"Come on!" Paige shouted as she hurdled the overturned table.

Cole was moving before she'd given the order.

The kitchen was a smaller area than the dining room, but was in an equally messy state. Pots and pans were scattered everywhere. Blackened hockey pucks that had once been burger patties sizzled on the grill, and a man in a white apron and T-shirt lay on the floor with his neck torn open. Cole led the way through a hole in the wall that might have been a doorway before Henry had shoved through it.

The back of the diner was a gravel-covered lot with several cars parked in a row. There were a few more parked off to one side, but they weren't arranged as neatly as the first bunch. Pushing past Cole to emerge from the diner, Paige held her arms up with her weapons flipped over her forearms to protect her face. But there was no attack coming and nobody was there to ambush them. Cole's attention was drawn to a dark, late model four-door speeding away from the diner. Henry bounded alongside that car like an obedient dog, then got in front of it with his next leap. The car left the diner behind amid a spray of loose gravel that wasn't quite loud enough to drown out Paige's fierce swearing.

"We can still catch it!" Cole said. "Let's go!"

"This place is right off the interstate. They'll be in the fast lane before we get the car started."

Cole wanted to argue and drag Paige to the car, but after running around the side of the building, he saw she was right. The highway was less than a hundred yards away, and Misonyk's car was already pulling onto it. "So we just let them go?" he asked.

Paige let out the breath she'd been holding and nodded. "There's a survivor inside. I saw her at one of the tables."

"And what if the survivor isn't human?" he asked.

Holding up the weapon in her right hand to show Cole that it was the straight, sharpened stake, she replied, "One more body in there won't make much difference."

Chapter 15

The survivor was a woman with rounded features and wire-framed glasses. Her reddened face was streaked with tears, and her black, curly hair hung like a curtain over her eyes. Her arms were tightly folded on top of the table and her head lay sideways upon them as if she was either playing dead or being punished for talking during story time.

"There's a medical kit under the passenger's seat in my car," Paige said as she crouched down beside the woman's table. "Go get it."

As Cole headed for the front door, he watched Paige gently examine the woman's neck and wrists. He ran for the car, waiting for police to skid to a stop in front of the place or news helicopters to gather overhead. But there was none of that. It seemed everyone was perfectly content to drive by and listen to their radios. Finding what he was after, he rushed back while trying to decide if he was grateful for or disgusted by the absence of his fellow man.

Paige's medical kit was something that might have confused an army field medic. Opening like a tackle box, the kit contained everything from mundane bandages to syringes filled with stuff that he didn't even want to think about. After cleaning off the short-haired woman's minor scrapes, Paige bandaged them up.

"What's your name?" she asked.

The woman had yet to speak after she'd sat up and allowed herself to be cleaned off. In fact, it seemed that she had yet to blink. After hearing Paige's question, she twitched and replied, "Jennifer."

"What happened, Jennifer? Or should I call you Jen?"

Without meeting Paige's eyes, Jen nodded and said, "There was only four or five of us in here. We were eating lunch when they came."

"Who came?"

"The ones with the . . . the ones with the black . . ." Unable to finish her sentence, Jen reached up to brush her fingertips along her neck.

"With the markings on their skin?"

She nodded again. "I guess they were tattoos. They came in and they spread out and started looking us over. That's when I thought they were going to hurt us."

As Jen spoke, Paige removed one of the syringes containing the Nymar antidote from her kit and discreetly cleaned the needle with an alcohol wipe. "Then what did they do?"

"They had . . . they all had . . . they had long teeth. Fangs." Letting her head fall forward, Jen gave in to a sobbing fit that shook her shoulders and drained the color from her face. Fortunately, Paige had already stuck her with the needle and removed it.

"Some tried to fight them," Jen went on. "I think they even fought each other. One of them bit my arm," she added as she held out the arm that Paige had already cleaned and bandaged. "He was . . . I think he drank . . ."

"All right," Paige said. "What about the big one?"

Suddenly, Jen's eyes widened and she turned to look directly at Paige for the first time. "He came after most of us were dead! The ones with the tattoos were all talking after they were through with us. One of them said he was here, but I didn't know who they were talking about and I heard fighting in the kitchen." The more Jen talked, the more tears streamed down her face. Her voice streamed out of her in much the same way. "The ones with the tattoos started fighting each other. There were a few with guns and some more ran outside. There was screaming and . . . and ripping sounds. It was worse than what I heard in here. It was . . ." Her words devolved into an indecipherable series of gasps and sobs.

Rather than ask her to go on, Paige patted Jen on the shoulder and asked, "Can you stand up?"

"I don't know."

"Try for me, okay?"

With Paige's help, she was able to get up.

"Don't look around, Jen," Paige said. "We're going to get you outside. There's a fire in the kitchen, so you need to get moving. Just look at the front door and nothing else."

Although Jen was weak, she got moving once the F-word had been used. Fires had a good track record of motivating any animal, whether they were hurt or not, and Jen was no exception.

Cole watched through the window as Paige led her outside. Jen was about Paige's height, but outweighed her by at least thirty pounds. Even so, Paige carried her with ease and gently lowered her to one of the cement blocks marking the nearest parking space. When Paige walked back inside, Cole asked, "How is she?"

"She'll be all right. Are there any more breathing?"

Cole shook his head. "I can only see a few bodies that look human. The rest . . ." What he didn't need to say was that the rest were either leaking oily black liquid instead of blood or clawing at the ground with stiffening hands. Now that the diner was quiet, he could hear the sounds of dry snapping. The Nymar bodies had already become dry enough to crack and send flakes of skin into the air. Taking in the sight of it all, he wondered if it was good or bad that he could remain in that spot without puking his guts out.

"I've got some good news," Paige said after taking a quick survey of the bodies. "All these Nymar are real dead and Jen's still real human. She was bitten, but there would have been some of that black stuff in the wound already if a spore had been passed into her. I gave her a bit of the antidote anyway, but it's not like Nymar can just reproduce accidentally."

"That puts them one up on humans, then," Cole grunted.

Paige chuckled and took a closer look at the Nymar whose

spine had been ripped out. "Come over here. You should see this."

He stepped beside her and looked down.

Pointing at the black marks on the back of the dead Nymar's neck, she said, "Just so you know, you can always get an idea of what you're dealing with by looking at these marks. The older or stronger the Nymar is, the blacker the marks are."

"Wow. All this carnage and a lesson too. Lucky me."

"This is the job, Cole. I didn't plan on this, but here we are. You might as well learn something before we burn this place down."

Rather than air out the questions that reflexively popped into his mind, Cole set them aside and reminded himself he'd rather set fire to the place than allow anyone else to eat there. "All right. What next?" he asked.

"You got a camera on that phone of yours?"

"Not just a camera, but a four megapix—"

"That's a yes," Paige cut in. "Take pictures of everything you can and follow me." Without waiting for an okay from him, she walked over to another one of the human bodies. "This," she said as she pointed down to the corpse's decimated throat, "came from a Nymar feeding. And not one of those sexy, moaning ones you see in the movies. This was quick, violent, messy, and not at all voluntary. If the throat's torn up like this, that means the Nymar clamped down with those thick bottom fangs. When Nymar use those fangs, they're out for a lot of blood in a short amount of time. Whoever's on the receiving end of that won't be able to get away, and it's a miracle if they survive."

While snapping a few pictures, Cole asked, "So the Nymar came here and started feeding before these people could get away?"

"If that was the case, they wouldn't have missed Jen. This is more of a panic feeding. When Nymar are caught by surprise, feel threatened, or just in a hurry, they feed on whoever is nearby to make sure they've got all the strength they can to fight or do what they need to do. This is why we avoid fights in public. If you charge in without picking your spot and setting things up, innocents get slaughtered. Remember that, Cole."

He shook his head solemnly. "There's no way I'm forgetting this."

Paige reached into the gaping hole in the Nymar's back. After feeling around a bit, she withdrew her hand and wiped it clean on the Nymar's sleeve. "Henry went straight for the spore, just like everyone's been saying."

"I know it's on their heart, but . . . what is it?"

"Once it attaches, it spreads itself throughout their whole body. See this?" She rolled the corpse so Cole could get a good look into the hole.

He almost spilled his breakfast onto the floor, but he did notice something. "I'm no doctor, but it all just looks like mush in there. I don't even see any organs."

"That's right," Paige replied. "Once the Nymar attaches, it converts everything inside the person into one big organ. It's like a bug that's filled with one kind of juice. That's why, if someone might be infected, you treat them *quickly*. Once they turn, there's no way to turn them back. Not unless you can hollow them out and replace everything."

"Gotchya. Are we done? Jen's still out there."

After taking a look through the front window, Paige said, "She's still crying. She could use a little more time on her own." Squinting at the window, she reached out to swipe something that looked like yellow milk that had been spilled upon the glass. She rubbed it between her fingers, sniffed it, then said, "See this stuff here? This is the venom I was telling you about. It can paralyze anyone within a normal person's size. Even if it just gets on you, it can make you dizzy. If it gets in your eyes, that's really bad news. Smell it."

Cole sniffed at it and his stomach turned at the bitter smell. "What happens if I get that in my eye?" he asked.

"Did you?"

"Yes."

"When?" Paige snapped. "How much?"

"During the fight. It was—"

But Paige had already rushed to her medical kit and retrieved another syringe. She removed the cover, slammed it into Cole's neck and pressed the plunger. She then used the same syringe to roughly extract some of his blood.

"Is that sterile?" he snapped.

Paige held the syringe up to the light and examined it. She let out a breath and asked, "Did Misonyk spit this stuff on you?"

Even though he feared another needle in the neck, Cole replied, "Yeah."

"Hopefully I got to you quick enough, but you should steer clear of him for a while."

"You think?"

Paige nodded and stomped toward the kitchen. "Just go out front and check on Jen. Get her to the car and ready to go. I'll be out soon. With all the grease that's in this kitchen, torching it shouldn't be much of a problem."

"You said getting that stuff in my eye was bad," Cole said. "What's that mean?"

"Well, some Nymar can control someone for a few hours after they do that. It's only simple stuff like making them obey easy commands, but the Nymar's got to be close."

"You've researched this?"

"No," Paige replied, "but another Skinner has. There are nerves that run from the eye straight into the brain. I guess the venom works along those lines."

"Did this other Skinner figure out a way to counteract it?" he asked hopefully.

"He's still working on it, but it's been rough since he blinded himself."

"That's just . . . that's . . . that's really great."

"Go help Jen," Paige said. "She's about to wander away."

With his stomach still on spin cycle, Cole jogged out of the building and to the woman with the bandaged hand. Jen was leaning against the car and facing the highway. He approached her slowly and announced his presence by clearing his throat.

She jumped, but relaxed when she saw him. "Are you all right?" she asked.

Cole nodded and told her, "More or less. I was more concerned about how you'd answer that same question."

"I'm . . . well . . . I guess I'll be fine. Sooner or later."

Cole leaned against the car next to her and crossed his arms. "I know just how you feel."

"I saw how you fought those things. I was too frightened to move and you two came in to chase them off. I doubt you're afraid of much of anything."

"You wouldn't be so impressed if you saw the mess I left in there."

For a second Jen just stared blankly at him. Once she allowed herself to laugh, the tired woman quickly dissolved into a mix of trembling giggles and choking sobs. Cole eased his arm around her but didn't know what else to do. Judging by the way Jen turned and pressed against him, he was doing more than enough.

"Don't worry about any of it now," he said. "Just try to breathe."

Jen nodded and pulled in a few measured breaths. She held the air in her lungs and let it out as she forced herself to look back toward the diner. "Thank you so much. I wish I could find a way to thank both of you."

"And I wish we could have gotten here a little earlier."

Jen wrapped her arms around him and squeezed him so tightly that he began to see stars. The anaconda grip didn't let up until the crunch of boots against gravel approached the car.

"We need to get going," Paige said. Before she could say another word, she was nearly knocked off her feet by a hug from Jen that was equally as enthusiastic as the one she'd given to him. Paige smiled and rubbed Jen's back as the scent of burning grease drifted through the air.

"Good Lord," Cole said, catching sight of flames through the diner's front window. "We really do need to get going."

All three of them piled into the car and sped back to the highway.

"Why don't you call 911 before that fire gets too big?" Paige asked.

Cole took out his personal phone, flipped it open and then swore loudly. "No coverage. Freakin' Wisconsin!"

"Freakin' bad phone is more like it." Leaning to look at Jen in the backseat, Paige added, "So far, that phone of his makes a better camera than anything else."

"Ha ha," Cole grumbled. "It's also got some pretty decent

games on it." Before he could expound upon the virtues of playing Tetris during gridlock, he was connected to the authorities via Gerald's satellite phone. He called in the fire, pointed them in the right direction, then hung up.

"Now call MEG," Paige said. "She can make sure you don't get any calls from the Fraternity of Firefighters bugging you about tickets for their charity banquets."

"Huh?"

"MEG. Call MEG and tell her your number's now in the 911 system."

Finally, Cole nodded and said, "Oh, you mean MEG! Right."

Paige looked in the back and started to say something but was cut short by Jen's quickly upraised hands.

"Don't want to know," she said.

"Perfect," Paige replied, nodding, and shifted her eyes back to the road. "There's another gas station at the next exit. You can wait there for a while and then come for your car later."

Jen shook her head forcefully. "I don't want to go back there. If that means abandoning my car, then so be it. I left my purse back there as well, so I might as well complete the set."

Digging into the pocket of her jeans jacket, Paige took out a wad of money and handed it back to her. "Take this and get a bus ticket or a ride or a room or whatever you can. You need to call anyone?"

"No. Well . . . I can do that when I get cleaned up." Looking at the money, she asked, "Are you sure you can spare this much?"

"Yes. Take it. You want us to drop you off here or—"

"Here's fine," Jen said. Holding the money in both hands as if cupping a head of lettuce, she said, "That truck stop would be good. Aren't there usually showers there?"

Cole nodded. "Yep. And great food. Some of the best ham steaks I've ever tasted came from truck stops."

Jen smiled warily and stuffed the money into her pocket. She didn't say another word until they were braking in front of a store that appeared to be stocked with everything from country music CDs to pecan logs. Even then she seemed too tired to pull herself out of the car. Once she heard the sounds of hydraulic brakes, talking, and other signs of normal humanity, she perked up a little. "Thanks again," she said.

Paige waved. "'Bye. Take care of yourself."

"If you . . ." Cole kept the rest of his offer to himself, since Jen was all too anxious to get out of the car. He watched her go until she disappeared within the sprawling mecca of gasoline, beef jerky, and ridiculously strong coffee. Once the door had rattled shut behind the woman with the curly hair, he looked over to Paige and asked, "Do we need any gas?"

"Yeah," she replied as she backed away from the entrance and drove past the pumps, "but we'll wait until the next place."

"I don't think she'll say anything to anyone else. About us, I mean."

"Me neither."

"Should we even be worried about that?" he asked. "I mean, don't we swear anyone to secrecy?"

"It wouldn't matter if we did. Most people just want to forget whatever they saw so they can get back to what they were doing before." Paige sighed. "The ones who latch onto this sort of thing don't usually have a lot of credibility anyway."

Cole rolled down his window and let his arm dangle in the cold breeze. With Paige's window already open, a stiff wind blew through the car. Even though he could feel his fingers starting to tingle before the car even got up to speed on the highway, he let them dangle. The cold washed through him and made it difficult to focus on anything else.

It was nice.

"Should I call MEG now?" he asked.

Paige looked over at him and raised an eyebrow. She studied his face for just long enough to get Cole thinking there might have been something hanging from his nose. "Are you all right?" she asked.

"What?"

"You heard me. That was a lot to take in, even for me."

"Are you surprised I'm not back there eating a ham steak with Jen?" he asked.

Without hesitation Paige replied, "No, but still . . . it was a lot to take in. Are you all right?"

Slowly, Cole nodded. "It's just one more batch of strangeness heaped onto all the rest."

"It does seem to get heaped onto some of us more than others, huh?"

He shrugged. It was a lot easier than trying to figure out why things turned out the way they did.

"Call MEG later," Paige told him. "Our phones are all registered to fake names and addresses anyway. They can send you a new SIM card registered to another fake name and that usually does the trick. If it doesn't, there are plenty more phones out there. Just remember to think ahead whenever you—"

"When I use official Skinner phone lines to contact the authorities. Got it."

"I've got to admit, Cole. You impressed me today."

"Thanks. Now when do I get my own set of stakes?" He snapped his fingers and said, "You're not supposed to stake a Nymar through the heart! You're aiming for the spore attached to the heart, right?"

"Now, you learn, young one. But a stake won't kill it unless you hit that spore just right. The thing squirms around in there, so it's mostly luck if anyone gets a lethal hit. You stake a vampire and it may be able to live for a long time while the spore heals. A big hit will take a while to heal, but it can be done. Sometimes, if a Nymar gets hit too close to the spore too many times, the spore can pull some bone aside to hide behind. Don't forget that thing is alive inside of them. It's got a mind of its own."

"That reminds me," Cole said. "I shot Misonyk in the chest and it looked like there was solid bone protecting his heart."

"Yeah," she sighed as the day's events caught up to her in a single rush. "And that means we'll need to get real close and be real fast to take him out. It'll probably take an injection directly in the neck. How are your eyes, by the way? Getting any strange urges?"

"I wouldn't mind biting you in a few choice spots, but

that's nothing new." The moment that came out of Cole's mouth, he flinched. "Sorry, maybe I am possessed."

Paige did her best to keep from laughing.

"So," he said in a desperate attempt to change the subject, "there's no turning a Nymar back into a human. Doesn't the antidote cure them?"

"It reacts with the black stuff that contaminates their blood," Paige replied in words still strained by the laughter that flowed just beneath them. "Kind of like another virus that spreads inside and—"

"More technical jargon," Cole moaned. "I love it. So the antidote cures them."

"Once it gets into those black tendrils beneath their skin, it cures them just like cyanide cures depression."

"Oh."

"Don't worry about leaving a body either. When a Nymar dies, the thing inside them sucks up all the blood and water to try and stay alive. Whatever is left will crumble in a day or two on its own. Inject them anywhere other than the black tendrils and you'll either knock them out or give them a wound it'll take weeks to heal."

Suddenly, Cole felt as if the rest of the world was slipping away from him and he was standing on the edge of it all, just watching it go. Unfortunately, looking out the window or closing his eyes only made the dizziness worse.

Picking up on the change that had come over him, Paige asked, "Are you all right, Cole? You're pale and sweaty."

"I'm fine. I guess all of this is just catching up to me."

She kept her eye on him as much as she could without driving off the road. Even when she had to make a few jerky corrections to stay in her lane, she acted as if watching him was more important than plowing into oncoming traffic. "Are you sure about that? How are your eyes?"

"They feel fine. Maybe a little—"

They feel fine.

The voice was so subtle in the back of Cole's mind that he could have easily mistaken it for his own. He began to nod and say the words he'd thought of, but suddenly realized he hadn't thought of them. He shook his head and pressed his palms to his eyes until red splotches danced in the darkness behind the lids. "Maybe I'm not fine. I think Misonyk got to me."

No. It was nothing.

The voice drifted through Cole's mind like a gnat skittering into his ear, and was already gone before he had a chance to swat at the thing responsible for it.

"Yeah," he said. "He got to me. Maybe you should give me some more of that antidote."

Paige looked over at him once more and then pulled the wheel toward the right shoulder of the interstate. The tires screeched, skidded on the loose dirt on the shoulder, then the car came to a stop without a major incident. She got a few honks from some of the people who'd been directly behind her but ignored them.

"If you just tell me where the stuff is, I can inject myself," Cole said. "No need for all of this."

"What do you hear?"

"It wants me to tell you I'm fine."

"Do me a favor, Cole. Imagine telling me you're fine. Focus on it really hard."

He let out a deep breath and then thought about saying those words. He imagined saying them to Paige and then shook his head. "I can't focus."

Still studying him, Paige said, "Think about what you'd say as if you were singing a song in your head. You know what I mean?"

"Yeah. Actually I do." At first he started to sing those words. He stopped himself and then used that same inner voice to repeat them.

"When you imagine saying them to me, it doesn't matter if it's one hundred percent accurate," she said. "Just make sure the basics are in there and imagine it in a way that'll make it really vivid. It doesn't matter what you focus on, but it's got to be something you can truly hold onto. Think about it like you'd picture one of those games you design. Once you're locked in, let the words go through your mind."

Although he started off taking Paige's advice, the imagery wasn't sticking. It came and went like scrambled porn on a channel he hadn't paid for. The more he tried to zero in on it, the fuzzier it got. Then, perhaps drawing inspiration from the comparison he'd just made, he imagined Paige sitting there beside him in her sweats and halter top. He added a bit of water to her hair and beads of moisture running along those sexy freckles that were scattered over her chest and the image became clearer. Once he lost her clothes altogether and added more water running down her body, he was in business.

"I'm all right, baby," he said in his inner voice to the Paige that was naked and smiling back at him.

"Is it working?" the real Paige asked.

When he heard her voice, Cole realized it was working a bit too well. He shifted in his seat, thanked the god of denim that his jeans were loosely cut, then nodded. "I think so."

It's all right, he thought. *I'm just fine, baby.*

Very good.

Paige smiled in his mind, and when Cole focused on the real world, he found her smiling there as well. She nodded and placed her hands back on the wheel so she could pull onto the road and bring the car back up to speed.

"Misonyk is powerful," Paige said. "I've never heard of a Nymar getting this kind of range with any sort of mind control before."

"Aw, hell."

"Don't worry and don't think too hard about it," Paige said quickly. "It's tricky, but we can work with it. For the most part, a Nymar that's linked to someone can make out more of what that person is seeing than what they're thinking. He got to your eyes, remember?"

"Yeah," Cole said as he began squirming for a very different reason.

"He can read your thoughts, but only the ones you're broadcasting. You know, the ones you're really concentrating on? The kind of stuff a really good poker player might be able to read on your face if they looked at you hard enough."

"Okay."

"I can't give you any more antidote for a while, since you've already had some not too long ago. We don't want too much of that in your system. In the meantime, if Misonyk is tracking us through you, you can steer him away for a while."

"How do I do that?" Cole asked.

"First of all, don't look out the window anymore. Look down or at me or just close your eyes. I'm going to tell you directions that we want Misonyk to hear, and I want you to take in everything I say. Think about it really hard and try to put those thoughts out there."

"What if it doesn't work?"

Paige shrugged and smiled at him. "At best, it'll keep your brain busy enough that Misonyk won't get anything but static from you. At the very least, you should keep him away long enough for us to conduct our business with Prophet."

"Are you sure about this?"

"Yeah . . . well . . . sort of." She cut herself short and reached over to rub Cole's knee. "Just trust me, okay?"

Cole nodded and focused on the touch of her hand upon his knee. It helped feed his reserves when he imagined her hand drifting a bit higher up along his thigh. "Okay."

"We'll be heading north on 94 all the way up through Milwaukee," she said as if telling him a story that she thought was enthralling. "Around Milwaukee, things get sort of crazy, but we'll catch I–43 toward Fox Point. From there . . ."

While listening to her go on about interstates, turnoffs, and rest stops, Cole imagined that map in his head and the creeping red line that came along with it. Oddly enough, that red line calmed his nerves just as it had when he'd been flying over Canada. Paige's voice was soothing and she went into more than enough detail to add some texture to his mental map. His focus remained on that map thanks to the naked version of Paige he imagined pointing to it while bending at the waist or arching her back like a naughty meteorologist.

He wouldn't be able to watch the evening news the same way again, but at least he was finally able to relax.

Chapter 16

By late afternoon Cole and Paige were driving on a gray stretch of highway, beneath a gray sky surrounded by drab grasslands. Every now and then they would cross a grayish blue river and then it was back to more greenish gray. At least, that's what Cole caught from the reflected light that came through the window.

Once Paige ran out of steam in her storytelling, she trusted Cole to occupy himself and not give Misonyk anything worth looking at. He'd never been more thankful to have Tetris on his cell phone. Since he couldn't get a signal, his expensive device was reduced to making him swear out loud for a long block instead of a crooked one. He swore even louder when he accidentally looked up to give his eyes a rest and found himself staring at a sign announcing the river they were about to cross. It was some sixteen syllable Native American name that he couldn't pronounce, but he figured Misonyk might have seen it too.

"What's the matter?" Paige asked.

"I looked out the window. Sorry."

"It's all right. We're not supposed to meet Prophet for a while, so I've been tooling around in a big circle. You want to get something to eat?"

Rubbing his eyes, Cole grumbled, "I want a double burger with fries. If they don't have that, I'll have a chicken sandwich. But not grilled chicken. I want skin on there. If they have something spicy, I'll—"

He was cut off by the quick jab of a needle in his neck. "Damn!" he grunted. "Did it have to be in the *same spot* as last time?"

"Stop whining. Do you feel any better?"

After a few seconds Cole touched his eyes and then blinked. "Actually, yeah. There's no more itching or burning."

"You should be a spokesman for this stuff," Paige replied. "Side effects may include drowsiness, nausea, and diarrhea."

"Please tell me you're joking," he begged.

"More or less. It's been a while since your last dose, so you should be fine. Still hungry?"

They stopped at a fast food burger joint off of I–43. It was one of those places that had overpriced food to pay for the enclosed playground attached to it. At first Cole was just happy to be able to look around freely again. After he'd gotten something in his stomach, he and Paige sat outside to watch the sun set. Despite the romantic possibilities, they simply killed time before driving the rest of the way to wherever they were going to meet up with Prophet.

"So you don't think Misonyk can read my mind anymore?" Cole asked.

"Like there was much to read anyway," Paige shot back.

"I'm serious."

She took a few more fries from the cardboard container in her hand and stuffed them in her mouth. "I doubt he could read your whole mind," she said amid a spray of chewed potato. "But it's nothing permanent."

"How do you know?"

"Because if it was, the other Skinners who went through the same thing would all be dead. He might be able to sneak in there again, but he'll have to be real close to do it. If he's close, then it's too late to do much about it anyway. We're hoping to find Misonyk eventually, so even if he does pick up on us, it's not so bad as long as we get to hear what Prophet has to say."

Sitting perched on the edge of a curved plastic bench over-looking a string of gas stations and the ramp leading onto the interstate, Cole asked, "Does that ever bother you?"

"What?"

"Living like you're always one step away from a fight."

She shook her head and tipped the container back to empty the last, crunchy bits of fries into her mouth. "Nah." Tossing the container into a nearby trash can with a wide smile painted on it, she checked her watch and said, "Time to go."

"Should I keep thinking happy thoughts?" Cole asked.

She stood up and dusted the crumbs off the front of her shirt. "You shouldn't have much trouble with that, consider-ing where we're headed."

It was dark when they pulled to a stop again just under an hour later. They'd driven a few miles off the interstate and stopped at a spot without much more than a single building and a whole lot of garish neon to illuminate it.

Paige got out of the car. "Leave any weapons here," she advised. "There'll be metal detectors."

Cole could hear the thump of a nearby sound system rum-bling through the window, but couldn't see any occupied cars nearby. There were plenty of vehicles in the open lot, but not a driver to be found. He got out and spotted Paige walking toward the entrance of a purple A-frame building. The blinking pink neon sign over the entrance matched the bigger sign elevated on a post and facing the interstate. Both signs flashed, *Shimmy's Gentlemen's Club* in curved letter-ing. Cole craned his neck and looked up at the larger sign towering over the A-frame. Now that he was closer, he could see the outlines of women hanging from the tail of the Y. At the moment, those outlines merely sputtered with the crackle of failing neon.

He ran to catch up to Paige, but she'd stopped before pull-ing open the club's front door. When he got to her, he asked, "Shimmy's? Is it amateur night or do you just like—"

Paige brought her finger up to point at his face so quickly that she almost created a breeze. "Don't finish that sentence.

Prophet picked this place, not me. Do you have any of that money I gave you at the hotel?"

"No," Cole lied.

"Great. Just great."

Stepping through the front doors, they found themselves in a small, narrow room. Three of the four walls were covered in pictures of previous "Featured Entertainers" in various poses and glistening with baby oil. Although Cole wouldn't have admitted to it, he recognized a few of those ladies from features he'd downloaded on company time. A sliding window was built into the wall to the right of a blacked-out glass door, which led into the rest of the club. By the time Paige stepped up to the glass door and placed her hand on the panel with the words COME ON IN printed on it, a balding man with a light brown beard leaned over to look through the sliding window.

"That'll be twelve dollars for each of you," he said. When he got a look at Paige, he gave her a friendly smile.

She sighed and dug into her pocket for some money. Although the man in the window looked her over, it wasn't more than could be expected from any man who admired the sight of a petite brunette in tight jeans. When she handed some money through the sliding window, Cole beamed with enough pride to light up the darkest of the club's corners. The only thing cooler than hitting a strip bar with a woman like Paige was having that woman pay for his cover. But as much as he wanted to say something to commemorate the moment, he kept his mouth shut.

After receiving two tickets from the bearded man, Paige handed one to Cole and said, "This is good for your first drink. You try to buy a lap dance and I'll knock you out."

"Lap dance? Yuck," he said with an exaggerated scowl.

Not buying his act for a moment, Paige pushed the glass door open and walked into the club.

Shimmy's wasn't a big place. There was a pool table and dart board to the immediate left of the entrance, situated next to a counter that sold T-shirts and porno DVDs. An average-size bar stretched along the left wall and was tended by a big guy in a white shirt. At the moment, the only people sitting at the bar were women in slinky outfits and way too much glitter makeup to be patrons. The women smiled and waved to Paige and Cole as they walked by, but didn't move from their seats.

There was a small stage to the right of the bar, but it was currently dark. All the action was taking place on the main stage, which was straight ahead and surrounded by small tables. As far as strip bar stages went, it wasn't anything special. It had a pole in the middle, was lit by multicolored strobe lights, and was surrounded by a brass rail and chairs. Only a few of those chairs were occupied, but that was about to change. A busty, strawberry blonde, currently strutting toward the pole, was peeling off her bikini top and swinging it over her head to the beat of an old hip hop song.

"I take it you don't go to places like this very often?" Cole asked.

Paige kept walking toward the tables at the right side of the stage and had to shout to be heard over the thumping bass. "What?"

Now it was Cole's turn to shout. "Have you ever been here before?"

"Not this place, but the last time I met Prophet, it was in a shithole outside of Kansas City. This is actually a lot better."

"Really?"

She nodded. "I would have been hassled three times by now in that dive. This place is nice." As she said that, Paige returned the friendly nod she got from an approaching waitress.

"Hi guys," the waitress said. "Sit anywhere you like. Can I get you a drink?"

Paige handed over her ticket. "Jack and Coke."

"What about you, sweetie?" the waitress asked Cole.

"I'll just have a Coke."

She took his ticket and walked toward the bar. Even though she obviously had a nice little body, she wasn't dressed like she might be dancing that night. When Cole looked back to Paige, she leaned toward him and said something that was swallowed up by the bass of the music and the hoots of the men near the stage.

"What did you say?" he shouted.

"Your drink," she clarified. "I called you a pussy."

Despite the fact that he should have been at least slightly offended, he couldn't help but grin. There was just something about hearing Paige say that particular word in those particular surroundings that made him feel warm inside. Very juvenile, but very, very true.

"So where's this Prophet guy?" he asked.

"Just look for the buffet."

He wasn't sure where a strip club might set up its buffet, and he sure didn't mind having a look around. Dancers in all shades of hotness strutted from one table to another, bending down to stroke the customers' hands and ask for a private dance. The dancer on stage was down to a few bandannas wrapped around her waist and nothing else. Another woman stood at the edge of the stage waiting for the next song to start. And there, like a toad sitting in the middle of a flower bed, was the buffet.

As far as food services went, it wasn't much. There looked to be less than five items in all, and none of them seemed to have been touched. Cole amended that last observation when he spotted a man at a table next to the short bed of hot plates, hunched down over at least three dishes piled high with food. He couldn't quite make out the man's face, but pointed him out to Paige anyway and asked, "Is that him?"

She took her eyes from the stage and looked in the direction he was pointing. "Yep. That's him."

"Were you watching the dancers?"

"Come on," she said quickly. "Time for business."

"There's an ATM by the door, just in case you'd like—"

Shaking her head, Paige swung one arm back and effortlessly snapped her hand against a spot in Cole's midsection that robbed him of his next breath. By the time she made it to the table with the buffet's only fan, she was smiling warmly. "Hello, Prophet," she said. "Catch any food poisoning yet?"

The guy at the table was about a hundred pounds lighter than Cole would have expected for someone with so much food piled in front of him. A black man with short, clipped hair, he was dressed in old jeans and a dark, hooded sweatshirt. One leg was stretched out from under the table to stick a work boot a little too far into the common walkway. Cole narrowed the man's age to anywhere in the late thirties to early forties range, but the black light hanging nearby made that a difficult call to make. A narrow face and hooked nose all pointed down to a fairly well-trimmed beard.

"I've got business here this time around, Paige," the hungry man said. "I told you about the nymph I was tracking."

"Nympho?" Cole asked anxiously. "Point her out."

"No," Paige shouted over the music. "Nymph. Prophet always comes up with some stupid excuse to meet me at places like these. This time he's tracking woodland creatures."

"This one doesn't live in the woods, obviously," Prophet added. "Who's this you brought with you?" Sharp eyes sized Cole up in the amount of time it took for him to lift a callused hand. As far as Cole could tell, there were no scars on the man's palms.

As Cole shook the man's hand, Paige announced, "Cole Warnecki, this is Walter Nash."

Doing his best not to match the other man's iron grip, Cole said, "I've heard you also go by Prophet."

"The MEG guys came up with the name, but I don't know you well enough for you to call me that."

Cole raised his eyebrows and asked, "You're a psychic?"

"If you're expecting a prediction after this handshake, you're in for a real disappointment."

"Just tell me one thing."

"What?" Walter asked warily.

Cole glanced down at the plates, which he could now see were covered with mashed potatoes and some sort of goulash. "That food any good?"

Slowly, Walter's beard widened as the mouth beneath it formed a vaguely demonic grin. "Yeah, it's all right. All you can eat. Nobody ever tries the food in these places, but I figure it's gotta just be catered from somewhere so it should be fine."

"And here I thought men were drooling over the dancers," Paige grumbled as she sat down.

"Dancers are over there. Food's over here," Walter said. "No reason I can't have both."

Cole took a seat next to Walter and turned his chair so he could stay in the conversation while also watching the stage. Since one song was fading into another, the strawberry blonde was at the farthest end of the stage and reaching down to help the next dancer up. The new arrival was tall, dressed in an outfit made of purple silk scarves, and had long, coal-black hair.

"What've you got for us, Prophet?" Paige asked.

After setting down his fork, Walter reached into the large pocket sewn on the front of his sweatshirt to retrieve a small spiral notebook. He flipped the notebook open and studied the scribbles written there. "It's a place due west of a town called Milton, which is near Clear Lake. One of the MEG guys called me, since neither of you could pull yourself away from Chicago."

"Did I tell you how much I appreciate you taking up some of the slack now that Gerald and Brad are gone?" Paige asked in a sweet voice that Cole wasn't sure he'd heard before.

Walter ate it up with a smile and said, "Not until right now, but it's no problem. Anyway, the MEG guy's name is . . . Jarvis. He took me out to some creepy old house that had a pit in the back of it."

"Did you say a pit?" Cole asked.

"Yes I did, and I checked it myself. It could've been a basement or cellar at one time, but it's a pit now. He says he saw some messed-up-looking animals in there, but they weren't there when I was."

"You went to have a look inside?" Paige asked.

Nodding, Walter flipped the page of his notebook and angled his head as if he was squinting through a pair of bifocals. "It's a Half Breed den."

The smile that had been on Paige's face disappeared. "You're sure?"

"I may not hunt the damn things, but I've tracked down plenty for you guys over the years. There were Half Breeds living there. I could smell 'em. The pit looked big enough for three to five of them, but I wasn't about to crawl around to count the droppings for myself."

Paige nodded.

"Since Half Breeds like to run out in the open, I took a drive around that area," Walter continued. "There's a spot about five miles from the den that's got 'werewolf hunting ground' written all over it. It's some lake called Osh Kong . . . Koshconnong . . . what the hell is that?"

Paige leaned over and squinted at his notebook. "Lake Koshkonong. Is that right?"

He nodded and said, "It's a pretty good-sized lake and there's plenty of room for the things to run, which is what they like to do as the moon gets fuller. In any case, you should be able to bait one from there no problem. If they aren't at that lake, they'll be close enough to catch the scent."

"Okay," Paige said. "What else?"

"I've had a few dreams about werewolves, but some weren't werewolves. One looked like a black and gray cat, another looked like a panther, and one might've been a freakin' beaver or something, but they're all ugly and they're all pissed."

Paige laughed and glanced at Cole. "Sounds like Cole's girl. What else?"

"I'm serious," Walter said. "Something's going on with these things that's drivin' them crazy. I don't know when, but it's coming."

"What's coming?"

"Blood. Lots of it. Goddamned Armageddon, from what I saw. Now, it may not be as bad as all that or it may be worse, but there's a big fight on the way. I've dreamt it too many times for it to be bullshit."

Paige's eyes drifted toward Cole, but he was too busy studying the brunette on stage. She danced toward the pole as if she floating through water, and when she got there, she twirled around it fast enough to send the scarves wrapped around her fluttering through the air until they practically dissolved.

"Wow," he said.

Looking up at the stage, Walter smirked. "Yeah. That's Tristan. She's somethin' else."

"You were saying?" Paige reminded him. "Something about Armageddon?"

Walter pushed away his dinner and leaned back into his chair. "I've dreamt it plenty of times. There's a lot of fighting and plenty of dying. It's like the beasts just decide to come in from the hills and take over. They were even ripping through the pale kids like tissue paper."

"Pale kids?" Cole asked.

"You know . . ." Rather than finish his sentence, Walter pointed to the spot in his mouth where a Nymar's fangs would be.

"Do you have anything more specific?" Paige asked. "So far, you could be describing some sort of hunting raid. Those have happened plenty of times."

"This most recent vision was pretty specific. I saw it like I was watching a story on the news. Top of the hour stuff. Lots of gruesome pictures. Supposed to be some sort of massacre."

"Could it have been symbolic or something?"

Although Tristan peeled away a few scarves so the lights bathed every curve of her naked breasts in a soft, purple glow, Walter managed to take his eyes off her. It helped that she was shifting her focus to Cole. "Would I bother you with some symbolic crap?" Walter asked. "I didn't get an exact date, but there were scores for a Buccaneers game that isn't supposed to be played for over a week."

"You still watch the Bucs?" Paige asked as she shook her head. "Why the hell should I even listen to a man who does something like that? Anything else?"

Walter nodded. "The massacre was supposed to be in Janesville. It's a little town about ten miles away from that house with the Half Breed pit out back. That tying anything together for ya?"

Meeting Walter's eyes, Paige looked as if she'd finally let her guard down. "Were the bodies charred or—"

"Or vampires or werewolves or some other strange shit?"

"Yeah," she replied. "That sort of thing."

He shook his head. "All I saw was that they were all dead. Every last one of them. Like I said, it was some sort of news report. There were just bodies laying next to some dirty cement building, and cleaning crews were—" Walter stopped himself when he saw the waitress standing close enough to overhear. All the color had drained from her face.

"Can I . . . get you anything else?" she asked.

"No," Walter said with a grin. Once the waitress hurried away, he looked at Paige and grumbled, "Great. Now I'm gonna start getting treated like a freak around here. These girls all swap stories about the customers, you know. Especially the weird ones."

Paige shrugged and told him, "I think you earned that reputation just by being the only man stupid enough to eat from the buffet. And since you'll be on the weird list here, you might as well come along with us for a while."

Walter shook his head and chuckled to himself. He kept on chuckling as he picked up his drink and watched Tristan climb the pole all the way to the ceiling and then slowly turn herself upside down. "Every freakin' time. How many times do I gotta say no to this offer?"

"You've seen for yourself that things will only get worse. With Gerald and Brad gone—"

"That's enough of that," Walter snapped. "I burned out my conscience way too long ago for guilt to work on me. I don't mind our arrangement and I don't mind lending a hand after what happened to the old man, but you gotta be brain dead *and* stupid to pick a fight with these things on a regular basis. No offense, Cole."

"None taken," Cole replied as he tossed a quick wave toward the table and kept his eyes locked upon Tristan.

Paige looked in that direction as well and saw Tristan scaling the pole once more. This time the dancer made her climb with even less effort than it took most people to climb out of bed. Once she got to the top, she repeated her trick of turning upside down and then eased her way back toward the floor. Now that she was only wearing a fine layer of glitter, the trick was drawing a lot more applause. When she reached the bottom, Tristan let go and floated toward the stage so she could come to rest upon one hand. After that, she twirled effortlessly around the pole and above the floor as if she'd somehow switched off the laws of gravity.

"What the hell?" Paige muttered.

Cole shook his head as a wide smile crossed his face. When Tristan came to a stop, she was looking straight at him. Dollar bills were lined up on all sides of the stage, but she crawled past them and perched on the edge of the dance floor closest to him. She hopped up and snapped her head forward, whipping her hair with enough power to send a wave through the air and a torrent of applause through the crowd. Dropping backward, Tristan caught herself with one arm, arched her back and placed one finger on her inner thigh.

Just then, Cole swore he could feel her touching him in that exact spot. Tristan closed her eyes and let out a moan that somehow drifted through the pulsing techno music in a way that no human voice should have been able to do. Arching her back more and more, she let her hair brush against the stage. Her finger continued its upward journey between her legs and lingered in a spot that stopped the flow of singles onto the stage and started a flow of fives and tens. If she'd waited a bit longer before rubbing her fingertip along the little piercing in her navel, she could very well have gotten hundreds along with the pink slips to a few cars.

Cole's eyes widened as the ghostly touch worked its way through his body. Not only could he feel her fingers on him, but he swore his senses had been filled with a mix of perfume and the dancer's natural feminine scent.

"Jesus," Paige said as she propped her elbows on the table and rested her head in her hands. "I take it that's the nymph?"

"Oh yeah," Walter said with a wry grin. "Looks like you could use a smoke."

"So that means she's not only inhuman, but she's working some sort of spell on this whole place to steal money."

"Hey!" Walter snapped as he stuck a finger in Paige's face. "You keep yourselves busy with the werewolves and dangerous shit. If you so much as cause that lady to quit her shift early, I will personally end your life."

"Yeah," Cole gasped once he had enough breath to do so. "Me too."

Sitting upright, Paige picked up her glass and promptly emptied it. After pulling open the top button of her shirt so she could fan herself, she said, "If all she does is that trick, I might be able to look the other way." The flustered look that had been on her face before was replaced by a sly grin as she looked up and added, "But I couldn't guarantee the next Skinner that finds her will be so friendly. Some of our guys are downright nasty."

Walter shook his head and scooped up some goulash with a dented spoon. "You wouldn't hand some petty thief over to be executed, Paige. I know you better than that."

"Did you know I could arrange to give her a pass from anyone else who happened to spot her? But . . . that would only be a favor from one Skinner to another."

"And here we go again."

Suddenly, Paige looked genuinely appalled. "What ever do you mean?"

Shaking his head warily, Walter placed a cigarette between his lips and lit it. "You might want to worry more about your friend," he warned. "He's getting sucked in."

Sure enough, Tristan was leaning out from the stage and motioning for Cole to come closer with one slowly curling finger. He drifted toward her like a cartoon mouse being pulled through the air by a whiff of cheese, and by the time he got to the stage, he already had his wallet out.

"I've been coming to this place for a few weeks and I still have a hard time resisting that trick," Walter said.

"I could really use some help on this, Prophet," Paige said earnestly. "You've got some connections we could use to get supplies, you're a hell of a tracker, and you're good enough with a gun to keep us all alive."

"Gee," he grumbled. "I'm feeling all warm and wanted."

"Cole's doing good, but he's still new to all this. If there was just one Half Breed out there, we could've handled it. Any more than that and we're in a spot."

"Then let me keep track of that den until you get someone else to cover you."

Shaking her head, Paige replied, "I need to go there myself. Those Half Breeds have probably already killed someone, and they'll keep killing as they create more Half Breeds. Plus, there's something else out there."

"The pale kids?"

"An old Nymar. Ever hear of someone named Misonyk?"

Walter pulled in a breath and grimaced as if he'd put the wrong end of his cigarette into his mouth. "He's been stirring things up all around here. He's got that big freak with him too."

She nodded. "There's a price on his head. A big one. You'll get a cut if you help me bring him down."

"How much?"

"It's being put up by the Chicago Nymar. Those are some deep pockets."

Walter's lips curled into a smirk. Gripping his cigarette between his first two fingers, he leaned back and nodded toward the stage. A skinny dancer with smooth brown hair pulled into pigtails was prancing to the beats of an old Motley Crue song as Tristan gathered up her money. "Looks like your partner's goin' for the whole ride," he said.

Paige looked to the stage and spotted Cole standing at the opposite end, reaching up with one hand to help Tristan down the steps leading to the floor. "Dammit," she grumbled. "I'll be right back."

"Aw, let him have his fun."

After receiving a glance from Cole, followed by a shrug, Paige watched Tristan take Cole's hand and lead him toward another room, which was sectioned off by a black curtain. "Is she dangerous?" Paige asked.

"Only to a man's wallet," Walter replied. "Haven't you ever seen a nymph before?"

"Nope. Why are you tracking this one?"

"Some poor asshole handed over something he wasn't supposed to so he could pay for a trip to the VIP Room."

Paige chuckled and relaxed a bit. "If she's looking for anything valuable in Cole's pockets, she's in for a disappointment."

Chapter 17

Cole hadn't intended on agreeing to a private dance. In fact, from the instant he got up from Walter's table, he told himself he wouldn't be convinced to pay for anything more than another drink or two. But considering the fact that he could still feel Tristan's hands running along his chest beneath his clothes without her even touching him, he knew that saying no to her was going to be more than a little difficult.

When he'd walked up to the stage, he meant to give her a dollar and sit back down again. She had, after all, pointed him out and asked him to come over. Who was he to refuse a request from a naked woman with a body straight out of a daydream? When he got closer, he could see the smooth texture of her face accented by a set of very small diamond piercings: one in her nose and one on her cheek just north of the corner of her mouth.

"I'm ready for you," she'd purred when he approached the stage.

Even as those words reached into him to work their magic, he nodded and planned how he would refuse the inevitable proposition.

"Want to come with me for a private?" Tristan asked.

Without hesitation, Cole replied, "Yes."

She smiled knowingly, made her way along the side of the stage and got to the end just as the song was over. He met her there, and could feel Paige's eyes on his back. He turned around, shrugged, then allowed himself to be led away.

Tristan smelled sweet, but not as if she'd been dipped in body spray. In her heels, she was a bit taller than Cole, and led him toward a back room as if taking a puppy for a walk. There was some small talk, but Cole was more concerned with trying to remember how much money he actually had on him. Before he had too much time to ponder the many potential hazards involved with asking Paige for a loan, he was taken to a surprisingly nice back room. He was no expert in such things, but he wasn't expecting a plush, softly lit lounge filled with leather sofas and potted plants. Tristan was all smiles as she showed him to the biggest sofa, pushed him down, then climbed into his lap.

"Where are you from?" she asked.

"Uh . . . Seattle."

"You come here a lot?"

"Nope."

Still smiling as if he was spouting off supremely interesting bits of wisdom, Tristan sat with her legs draped across his lap. "Seattle's nice. They don't know how to deal with snow, though."

Amazed that she'd actually been listening, Cole replied, "They sure don't, do they? You ever been to Oregon?"

The next song was only slightly muted within the room, and Tristan shifted so she was straddling him as soon as it started. Her smile was just sweet enough to be infectious and just crooked enough to be genuine. "I love to travel. Mostly, I like northern California."

"Really? I never—" And then his breath was stolen from his lungs. Tristan grabbed hold of the sofa just behind his shoulders and started grinding her breasts up and down along the front of his body.

He could feel the touch of her hair against his face, which was followed by the brush of her lips against his earlobe. Her next breath was slowly let out to warm his neck as her fingernails slid perfectly through his hair. As much as he wanted to say something just to prove he was cool enough to keep talking, it didn't happen. He didn't even know what song was playing as Tristan writhed on him and then rubbed her nipples against his lips. As she moved higher, Cole leaned back to enjoy the view.

"No touching," she said with a playful smile and a little waggle of her finger.

He nodded and gripped the sofa as if in danger of falling off.

Thankfully, Tristan knew just how long to go before climbing down from his lap. She stood in front of him and slid her hands along her hips. With a little twitch, she twirled around and backed up against Cole's lap. From there she leaned back against him and reached over her shoulder to caress the side of his face. Looking down along the front of her body, he saw a stretch of heaven below her waist, accentuated by a dash of glitter. Tristan's eyes were closed, a faraway look on her face.

The song was fading, but she kept writhing in a smooth, up and down rhythm. Not only was it fun to watch, but Cole could once again feel the phantom touch of her beneath his clothes. Instead of spectral fingers teasing his chest or legs, he could feel something else entirely. At that moment, he had to look down to make sure he was still dressed from the waist down.

"I don't want to stop yet," she purred. "How about we go for a half hour?"

"Sure," he replied quickly. He didn't hear a price, but he would have agreed to pay no matter what it was. He did, however, hear another voice originating from the back of his mind.

Taste her.

Before he knew what he was doing, Cole followed the order he'd been given.

Everything happened very quickly after that.

Tristan was up, and with a little help from some bouncers, Cole was opening the side door of the club with his face. About a second later he hit a large trash container and was introduced to the ground. After the bouncers turned and walked back inside, the door slammed shut and Cole was alone to watch four men step from the shadows. They surrounded him and leered down with faces framed by serpentine black marks flowing up from their necks. One of them stepped forward and crouched down to Cole's level.

"Was she sweet?" Misonyk asked in the same voice that had hissed within Cole's thoughts.

That got a chorus of laughs from the other men surrounding Misonyk. Two of them were big enough to block Cole's view of the parking lot simply by standing shoulder-to-shoulder. Compared to Misonyk, however, the black markings under their skin were more like scribbles from a felt tip pen. The fourth man had an average build, which was mostly covered by a dark blue overcoat. There were enough bulges under that coat to make it obvious he was either heavily armed or trying to conceal some serious glandular issues.

Even though his climb was anything but dignified, Cole got to his feet and stood up. "If getting me bounced from a strip club is the best you've got," he snarled, "then that shit you spit on me must be wearing off."

"Ahh," Misonyk sighed. "Very observant. And since you're here now, I can fix that problem."

Cole tried to ignore the threat and buy himself some time. By the looks of it, he wouldn't be able to do that without getting a few bruises. Nodding toward the two bigger guys, he asked, "Are these the other ones who ran away from that diner like frightened bitches?"

"No. Only Edward and I made it out of there," Misonyk replied as he motioned toward his partner with the bulging overcoat. "The Nymar in this area needed to be shown what happens when I am displeased. Making you pay a similar price would be an even simpler matter."

Confident that Paige would be along soon, Cole forced himself to stand tall and regain some of the dignity he'd lost during his impromptu exit from Shimmy's. "Where's that freak job pet of yours? Don't you always need Henry along to back you up?"

Misonyk lunged forward so quickly that Cole could hear the Nymar's hand slice through the air on the way to his throat. The moment Misonyk's fingers clamped around his neck, Cole grabbed the Nymar's hand and tried to keep that grip from closing his windpipe. But though his intentions were pointed in the right direction, he didn't have the muscle to back them up. Before too much longer, his back scraped against the large metal garbage bin as he was hoisted onto his tiptoes.

"I can take my time now, Skinner," Misonyk growled. "I can make sure I do the job right so there's no way you can shake your mind free of me. I can command you to stay put and smile as I scoop the fat from your belly and burn it in your outstretched hands."

The venom was already dripping from Misonyk's fangs as he opened his mouth to show the curved set of teeth that slid out of his upper gum line. Even before Misonyk tried to bite, spit, or anything else, Cole could feel the Nymar's thoughts pushing against his brain like two oppositely charged magnets being forced together.

And then, strangely enough, he was reminded of a video game.

Actually, he was reminded of a specific game, one of the first he'd designed. It was called *Keeper of the Vault,* and it was a simple puzzler where one player was inside a box and the other was trying to get in. A secret he'd built into the game was a last line of defense that was also one of the greatest weapons. When one player finally broke into the vault, but before he could start sending in bombs to win the game, the defending player had one chance to send a bomb of his own through the hole the other had made. It involved a drawn-out combination of button presses, and ruined the game once it had become common knowledge among players, but it was a good idea at the time. And now it felt more like his only hope.

As Cole's strength started to fade, Misonyk's thoughts imposed themselves upon him. The Nymar drew closer while gathering a pool of venom onto his tongue. The corners of Misonyk's mouth curled into a victorious grin, and he forced an obscene taunt into Cole's thoughts.

As soon as Cole heard that foreign voice in his mind, he focused all of his concentration into one, desperate shout from his own inner voice to push Misonyk out.

The secret weapon worked a little better than he'd expected. As Misonyk released him, Cole was thrown onto his back to drown in a sea of alien memories.

One image that caught his attention was the eye of the Lord.

Chapter 18

The bastard had gotten lucky.

That was the only explanation for it. Like any other monkey that had more persistence than brains, the fool from Philadelphia had gotten lucky. Misonyk had heard about a fool who'd attacked Nymar and even a shapeshifter or two while surviving to tell the tale. Very lucky, indeed.

Misonyk had no trouble finding the man from Philadelphia for himself. As it turned out, the fool was also a coward who'd brought others along to help fight his battles. The others might have talked loudly, but they had shaky hands and frightened eyes. They came with weapons from the Old World, and most of them died like cattle. At the end of an exhilarating night, lightning was caught in a bottle.

Misonyk was blindsided by a stake that pierced his back. When he'd turned to get a look at the one who would make such a cowardly attack, he felt another stake pierce his side. That was followed by another, but none of them were deep enough to bring him to his knees. All those blows did was prove that the monkeys had listened to too many stories around their cooking fires before planning their little ambush. At one point Misonyk even thought he smelled garlic in the air.

That made him laugh.

When a spear was driven through his entire body to stop him in his tracks, he stopped laughing. The man from Philadelphia was at one end of that spear. The Nymar within Misonyk's chest was at the other.

Misonyk dropped. The spear was broken off so only an inch or so of wood protruded from his chest. After that he could only squirm and hiss as he was dragged to a filthy dungeon of a place that surrounded him with blasphemous markings, his ears stuffed with pompous words and his nose filled with the stench of feces.

For years he lay on that floor as men with smug faces came and went. At first they'd preached to him and asked why he did what he did, how he'd become what he was. All Misonyk gave them was profanities in every language he could remember. When he'd gathered up enough strength to spit at one of them, the putrid jailer actually collected the mess from his own face and saved it. It seemed the monkeys enjoyed wallowing in the filth of others just as much as they enjoyed wallowing in their own.

All the while, Misonyk could only think one thing: the bastard from Philadelphia had gotten lucky. It was the only thing that could explain how that fool had struck such a blow. While luck might have played a part in putting that spear through his chest, there was no word to describe what possessed those monkeys to lock him in a room and prod him for their own amusement rather than finish him then and there.

Every so often the pompous men would visit his cell wearing butchers' coats and gloves so they could carve off pieces of him and then leave. Misonyk was impaled with steel spikes. He was drained of his essence one drop at a time. He was cut open. His hair was plucked from his scalp. Holes were bored into his head. But he took none of those things to heart. The monkeys, it seemed, even committed such atrocities to their own kind. Misonyk could hear the human prisoners scream, even though he wasn't willing or able to make a sound of his own.

One day blended into another, and the only way he knew time was passing was because of the hole that had been cut into his ceiling. He'd heard the monkeys chattering about him burning away in the sunlight, but that never happened. While his skin might have crisped in the summers, his eyes eventually got used to the glare and his body became accustomed to the warmth it usually shunned.

As he lay there, growing numb to the endless violations inflicted upon him, Misonyk became skilled at playing the part of a dead man. He allowed his eyes to glaze over and his body to remain as still as he'd been when he was first dropped onto the floor. That way, the monkeys became more relaxed around him. Even as they stuck their hands and faces within biting range, they chattered about the other patients in nearby rooms. Apparently, the room directly across from his contained a very special case.

The voice coming from that room screamed much louder than the rest. It grew wilder as the days wore on. In time it became feral.

According to the idle chatter of the lazy monkeys who tormented Misonyk, the wild patient had also been dragged to his room by the fool from Philadelphia. He was a young man who screamed and bit and scratched at the orderlies that came to clean out his room. He choked on his food and gnawed on his own fingers. There was even talk that he wasn't a man at all. And after a few patient years, Misonyk arranged for a very personal introduction to that troubled young soul.

It happened on a day that started like any other. Before his door was opened, Misonyk tested his muscles to see if they would move. The spore inside of him was still punctured, but it was slowly healing around the chunk of wood that remained in his chest. Perhaps in a few more months he would be able to stand.

This time, however, it was no orderly that came to torture and humiliate him. It was the man from Philadelphia himself. The fool was as tall and brutish as Misonyk had remembered. His graying hair was gathered behind his head in a thick ponytail by a short length of twine. Even the whiskers sprouting from his gaunt face reflected how time was having its way with him. Until he'd actually seen how the years had scratched that face, Misonyk wasn't aware that he'd been laying on that floor for so very long.

Stomping over to Misonyk as two of the regular orderlies filed into the room, the fool dropped to one knee and grabbed his face in one hand. Misonyk tried to struggle, but the lucky bastard responded by grabbing and twisting the stake in his chest as if working a lever. When Misonyk was almost unconscious from pain, the fool from Philadelphia stuck his fingers into the swollen sack under the left side of Misonyk's tongue and pulled the delicate Nymar seedlings out from where they naturally collected. The seeds of his species might have gathered in a different spot than they did for humans, but that spot was just as sensitive for a Nymar as it was for any man. Misonyk tried to clamp down on the fool's hand, but his jaw was already held in place by a rusted metal wedge.

No one, human or Nymar, had ever wounded Misonyk that way. The pain spiked from that protected sac under his tongue, all the way down to the spore attached to his heart. Even through all of that, he was able to hear the fool's voice.

"I imagine this hurts you," the fool from Philadelphia said. "But I have also gathered that you quite enjoyed raping the women of the nearby towns until they'd lost too much blood to provide you with a meal."

That one made Misonyk smile. Such fond memories would sustain him for several more weeks in that room.

"I would imagine their spirits are enjoying this show very much indeed," the fool said as he pinched the nerves that attached the seedling gland to Misonyk's jaw. The man then tore the sac loose and held it out far enough for Misonyk to see it before he finally cut the last remaining nerve with a quick swipe of a short dagger. "You'll roast in hell for the sins you committed against all those good people, but not until I'm through with you. At least you'll do some bit of good before you rot away." Looking over to the other men who had filed into the room, he held the sac out until one of them stepped forward holding a glass jar that was half full of a cloudy liquid.

Once the sac was dropped into the liquid, the other man asked, "What should I do with this, Mr. Lancroft?"

The fool from Philadelphia made sure to lock eyes with
Misonyk as he replied, "Take it to the lab inside the mansion. And be careful. It'll take a long time to collect another batch like that. Personally, I'd rather kill this piece of
manure rather than keep him alive that long."

The rest of the men nodded and backed out of the room.

The fool from Philadelphia knelt down so he could look
into Misonyk's eyes. He pushed the lids open and even
pulled the Nymar's lips up so he could get a look at the fangs
extending from the gum line as he removed the wedge. Misonyk snapped, but the fool's hand was pulled back with re-
flexes that were marginally impressive for a human.

"Lancroft," Misonyk hissed.

The fool nodded and stood up. As he stepped out of the
room, he turned to face the men in the hall. "Keep an eye on
the vampire and see what's bothering Henry. Work up a new
schedule so both of them can be observed for any changes."

"Yes, sir."

Misonyk reached his decision as one of his keepers was
about to lock the door to his cell. Before the men could get
too far away, he pushed out a loud breath and used most of
his strength to scrape his leg against the floor. Thankfully,
that was enough.

"See if he needs to be tied down," he heard Lancroft say.
"I've got to look in on a few of the others."

"Yes, sir."

One of the remaining orderlies came back to Misonyk
and stared down at him from a safe distance. Misonyk could
practically taste the fear dripping out of him. Forcing himself
to groan and turn his face to one side was enough to draw the
curious monkey closer. When the orderly was close enough,
Misonyk faced him again and spat venom into his face. After
all the time he'd been laying there, he had collected more than
enough in his throat to get the job done. Like a good, frightened
little animal, the orderly rubbed at his face and eyes to make
sure plenty of the cloudy fluid got where it needed to be. Mere
seconds after wiping himself off, the monkey responded to
the intense glare in Misonyk's eyes.

Come . . . closer, Misonyk thought. Each syllable grated

against his agonized mind, but proved to be worth the effort as the orderly leaned forward.

Misonyk could have sunk his fangs in then and there, but he resisted. He could have ordered the man to remove the remnants of the spear in his chest and help him up, but Misonyk was too weak to put up the fight that would be necessary to get him outside of Lancroft's walls. Since it would take a long while to produce more venom, he used the chance he'd been given.

Get those spores. When Misonyk saw the confusion on the monkey's face, he added, *The things in that jar. Take them and give them to the wild man across the hall. You will tell Lancroft the jar was dropped. Do you understand?*

The orderly glanced toward the door and nodded.

Come back . . . every day, Misonyk ordered, putting as much power into his thoughts that his weakened body could manage. *Blood you take from me . . . will be shared with him.*

It took all of Misonyk's strength to project so many words, but he got them out. The monkey left and pulled the door shut behind him. Even after he'd been locked into his room, Misonyk could watch from his new puppet's eyes as the jar was retrieved and then brought to the room across from his. Henry fought and screamed, but the puppet carried out his task. A few of the monkeys came to help and might have been killed by the wild man, but Misonyk knew that would only leave Henry with some much-needed sustenance. Eventually, the fighting stopped and Henry's shouts were silenced.

Before long Misonyk's eyes snapped open and he fought the urge to scream. It wasn't normally possible for a Provider to pass along more than one seedling at a time, so that added a few more voices to the hellish symphony already filling poor Henry's thoughts. The connection was made. The spores had been fed to Henry, but now Misonyk found himself in the mind of a madman. It didn't take long for him to learn that Henry was no man. He was a creature struggling to find his new shape. A creature with a head full of demons preventing him from taking his true form.

Misonyk closed his eyes and tried to block Henry's screams from his mind. The spore required time to nest.

* * *

Time crawled along.

The wild man grew wilder. Although he wasn't progressing as Misonyk had expected, Henry was indeed able to hear the thoughts that he sent him.

Lancroft and his helpers continued to check in on him to see about harvesting spores to replace the ones that had gone missing, only to find that some parts of Nymar physiology were slower to heal than others.

The link between Henry and Misonyk was strong, thanks to the multitude of spores forced into Henry's body, but it wasn't a normal transition from man into Nymar. Instead, the process was slowed by something else. The wildness inside of Henry kept any of the Nymar spores from embracing his heart as they so desperately wanted to do. The spores continued to grow, however, and were consistently fed as Henry got his hands on more and more of Lancroft's men. Soon, Henry was strong enough to start digging.

Poor Henry. He loved his room, but Misonyk pressed him to find a way out. When the monkeys couldn't get close enough to touch Henry without losing a piece of themselves, they started firing their weapons into Henry's beloved room. They even tried to starve him and beat him into submission. It was even rumored that somewhere along the way one of the workers had snapped poor Henry's neck.

Throughout this time, Misonyk comforted Henry as any good Lord should. When the explosions came and the floors above Misonyk's cell collapsed, the only thing he or Henry could do was listen.

Years later, as Henry kept screaming and scraping at his walls with torn and bloody fingers, Misonyk urged him on. The wolf inside of Henry kept him alive. It also forced the spores inside of him to squirm in his belly, wriggle between his organs, and occasionally fight one another like eels trapped within a suffocating prison. That struggle turned out to be a blessing, since it kept Henry awake day and night for years on end so he could continue digging.

By the time Misonyk heard the crumbling of shattered stone and the splintering of reinforced wood, the spear in his chest had almost rotted away. Since there was nothing on which to feed, it was all Misonyk could do to keep himself alert and ready to move in the event that Henry finally fulfilled his Lord's command.

That day came after over one hundred years of imprisonment.

Misonyk could smell Henry's fetid hide and hear his nonsensical ravings as he'd scraped at the door that had been shut so long ago. As soon as that door gave way, Misonyk wanted to pounce upon the man who'd opened it and drink until he could feel the spore swell once more within him. Instead, all he could do was lay beneath the dust that had formed a filthy cocoon around him and wait to see Henry with his own eyes. When he did, Misonyk almost felt sorry for the poor wretch.

Almost, but not quite.

Henry's body swelled and shrank, unable to stop as long as the Nymar spore fought the beast inside of him for sole ownership of the man's soul. Somehow, Henry managed to stand before Misonyk as his head dangled at the end of a broken neck.

"God?" the wretch whispered.

Misonyk turned his head, but just enough to crack the thick layers of filth encrusted upon his neck. *You must heal me,* Misonyk thought. *And then we can walk together.*

For a moment Henry simply gawked down at Misonyk. After he moved closer, Henry's eyes finally settled upon the remains of the spear lodged in Misonyk's chest. The pain Misonyk felt as the remains of Lancroft's weapon was pulled free was the best thing the Nymar had felt in all of his years. Pressing his hand against the phantom splinters marking the spot where the spear had resided for all that time, he stood up and smiled at Henry.

The sounds of a changed world drifted from above the ruins of Lancroft. Machines rumbled and humanity bleated their nonsense without so much as a thought as to who might be listening. Misonyk was hungrier than he'd ever thought possible. *Stay here until I come back for you.*

"Then can I walk?" Henry grunted.

You'll be able to run.

Chapter 19

Cole staggered back and bounced off a wall. The back of his head cracked against brick, which made everything around him blur. When he blinked and struggled to regain his balance, he was no longer seeing through Misonyk's eyes or on Lancroft's floor. He was outside in the cold night air as the familiar thump of bass echoed behind him.

"What did you do to him?" Paige shouted as she moved to catch Cole before he bounced off anything else.

Misonyk stepped back and was immediately flanked by the two larger Nymar with him. "Nothing yet," he said.

As Cole steadied himself, Paige stepped in front of him. "And if you try to get your hooks into him again, I'll kill all of you right here and now."

Although the men flanking Misonyk were waiting for their orders, Misonyk looked as if he was merely deciding which part of Paige he should rip off first. "You should know better than this, Skinner," he said. "Defy me any longer and if Henry doesn't kill you, my sect will complete the task."

"I'm betting these four assholes and that freak are all the sect you've managed to scrape up. If you think that's enough to keep the cops busy, then just keep making noise until they get here."

Eyeing Cole furiously, Misonyk wheeled around and headed for the parking lot. While the two bigger Nymar followed him, the one in the bulky overcoat stayed behind. As the pounding rhythm inside Shimmy's faded from one rap song into another, the remaining Nymar reached beneath his coat and brought out a weapon that looked like a cross between a shotgun and an automatic rifle. The wide black barrel was easy to recognize, but the drum beneath the barrel gave the shotgun more of an edge. Cole might not have known exactly what the shotgun was called, but he made a note to find out and use it in the next game that called for big holes to be punched through things in a loud fashion.

Paige crouched a bit and reached toward the side of her boot where her club was hidden within its pouch and beneath her jeans. "Just leave," she said. "That is, unless you want this to get real messy real quick."

Although the gun-toting Nymar didn't seem impressed by her threat, he backed up a step anyway. Once a car rolled up behind him, he got inside and didn't shut his door until the car was moving too fast for him to keep his gun aimed at Paige.

"Stay right here, Cole," she said. "I'll make sure they're gone and then I've got to have another look around. As soon as I know it's safe, I'll bring the car to you."

Cole allowed himself to slide down against the wall until his butt hit the cold ground. Pressing his hands against his forehead alleviated some of the throbbing in his skull. After rubbing his face and eyelids, the only moisture he felt was from the perspiration that had begun to work through his skin. Apparently, Misonyk had been too surprised by his mental maneuver to spit any more venom at him. A few minutes later Paige stomped from the front of the building to close in on the garbage bins.

"I swear to everything that's holy," she growled, "if one more man stares at my chest tonight, I am going to plant my boot in his ass! Would you believe some assholes in the parking lot were too busy watching me to notice which way Misonyk went?" Putting her hands on her hips and looking around as if searching for someone to hit, Paige took a few more breaths and asked, "You all right, Cole?"

"Yeah. I was just—"

"Good," she said. "Now let's get out of here."

"What about Misonyk? Is he . . . gone?"

Paige hooked a thumb toward the main parking lot and said, "They left, but something else was sniffing around here. It may have been another Mongrel or it may have been something worse. Whatever it is, it's gone too."

"And I thought you'd be anxious to follow them."

"Don't need to. Prophet's agreed to help us and should be tailing Misonyk right now. He also gave us some real good leads that point us to a spot west of here, so that's where we're going. Now why don't you tell me what was happening with you. When I heard you got bounced, I came outside and saw you and Misonyk having some sort of special moment."

Cole followed her back to the parking lot, but couldn't shake the feeling that someone else was going to jump him at any second. He started telling her about what he'd seen when Misonyk attempted to enter his mind again, but gave up once they reached the car. "Wait a second. What was sniffing around here?"

"It was a shapeshifter. It was too far away for me to tell what kind, but it was a real big one with black fur. It could have been just trying to draw me out far enough to take a run at me, but there's no time to worry about that. We need to get moving."

"Could it have been Henry?"

Page shook her head. "I doubt it. No shapeshifters can change their markings that much."

"He's a lot more than just some shapeshifter."

Now that she'd settled in behind the wheel, Paige looked over at him with an intense glare. "What did you find out?" she asked. "Did Misonyk do anything else to you?"

Shaking his head enough to rattle his aching brain, Cole dropped into the passenger seat. "He didn't get any more of that shit on me, but I still got that asshole rattling around in my head. Or . . . maybe I was rattling inside of his."

"All right," Paige grunted as she threw the car into gear and sped toward the interstate. "Start talking."

Cole told her what he'd seen from start to finish. When he was done, he added, "I shouldn't have even left the table back there. This is my fault, Paige. I'm sorry."

She sighed again, but looked over at him reassuringly. "Don't be sorry, Cole. There was nothing you could have done. Nymphs have been tempting stronger men than you for a real long time."

"And what about Misonyk being able to track us?"

"If Misonyk went through the trouble of bringing you to him, his hold on you must have been weakening. But that's only the start of it," she added. "There's rumblings at the top of the food chain that is way over our heads."

"How far over?" Cole asked.

"You don't want to know."

The rest of the ride passed in relative silence.

Misonyk's presence in his mind was gone.

The shapeshifter with the black fur was nowhere to be found.

Apparently, those at the top of the chain didn't need to explain themselves to the lower links.

The hotel they stopped at was just off the highway in a place called Big Bend. For some reason, Cole had expected to spend the night in a rat trap with bugs on the walls and rusty water in the pipes. Instead, Paige had pulled up to a place that might even have earned a star or two more than the Afton Inn. And yes, it served free breakfast.

As soon as she unlocked the door to their room, she stepped inside, dropped her bags, and headed for the bathroom. "Walter should be here before long," she said through the door. "I need to get the stink of all that cigarette smoke off of me."

Cole pulled his collar up so he could take a whiff of himself. Although the odor of stale smoke permeated his clothes, there was still more than enough of Tristan's scent to overpower it. He savored the sweet smell and the memories that came with it until the other odors crept back into his nose. "I thought you said Walter wasn't a Skinner."

"He's not," Paige replied through the bathroom door. "He's

only along this time as a favor." After that, the bathroom filled with sounds of water running through the shower, mixed with a few contented sighs.

Cole sat on the edge of the bed, turned on the television and flipped through some reruns. He dug the phone from his pocket and thought about giving Jason a call just to let him know he was still alive. There was still the matter of fixing those bugs for *Hammer Strike,* but the phone's battery died before he could scroll through his stored numbers.

"Cole?" Paige said, while sticking her head out from the bathroom. "Could you bring me my bag?"

"It's right there," he groused as he shook his phone in the misguided belief that he could somehow frighten the battery into charging up again.

"I know, but . . . oh never mind." Stomping out of the bathroom, she clutched a towel to her chest and walked over to the bags that had been piled beneath a colorful sketch of oversized leaves. Her hair was wet and pulled behind her head, showing off her high cheekbones and the crooked line of her nose. Even though her expression was on the per-turbed side, it somehow worked when combined with the quickness of her movements and the water that had beaded upon her skin.

Cole watched her discreetly while playing with his phone, but realized his subtlety wasn't quite up to par when he saw the annoyed roll of her eyes. Shaking her head, she clutched her bag so it held her towel against her stomach as she turned on the balls of her feet and stomped back toward the bath-room. The damp towel spun with her and kept her front covered pretty well. Fortunately for him, the towel wasn't wrapped all the way around and he was given a quick, glori-ous peek at her back. Paige's wet hair hung down to a spot just below her shoulder blades. The smooth curve of her spine was surrounded on both sides by taut muscle that led his eyes to the perfectly rounded curves of her buttocks.

After she'd disappeared into the bathroom, Cole tossed his phone onto a nearby table and walked over to the plas-tic bag from the outlet clothing store they'd hit earlier that day. Before he could pull the tags off his new shirts, the bathroom door swung open and Paige stepped out wearing a baggy T-shirt and a clean pair of cutoff sweatpants. "No Walter yet?" she asked.

"Not unless he's got some of that invisible crap on him. By the way, I've got an idea for that."

"Save it," Paige snapped as she plopped down on the bed and searched for the TV remote. "I'm too tired." While she flipped through the channels, someone knocked on the door. "Could you get that?" she asked.

"Is this some sort of initiation thing? The rookie gets to do all the grunt work?"

With a cute grin, Paige replied, "Yep."

He stepped up to the door and put one eye to the peephole. All he could see through the cracked fish-eye lens was a tall figure in a long dark coat. The man had a large suitcase in each hand and what looked like an overstuffed gym bag under one arm. Without setting any of the bags down, the figure tapped his foot against the door and waited.

"That you, Walter?" Cole asked.

Behind Cole, Paige reached for another one of her own bags and found a .45 pistol.

"Yeah it's me," the man outside grunted as he lifted his chin to show his face to the door. "And you're about to get a real good look at my ass through that peephole if you don't open the damn door."

Cole opened the door, but Paige didn't lower her gun until she could see Walter's face. At the moment, that face wasn't happy.

"Sorry about that," Cole said. "Just being safe. Need any help with those bags?"

"No, I've got 'em. Thanks for ruining Shimmy's for me, by the way. I'm probably banned from there now. Got a place for me to set these down?"

"Anywhere you like, Walter. You want some coffee?"

"Already had plenty. How do you think I scrounged up all that gear Gerald left behind and made it here so quickly?" He kept talking as he set up his cases so they were all evenly spaced on the bed that Paige wasn't on.

"You did follow Misonyk, right?" she asked.

Walter nodded. "Long as I could. That car was headed west when I lost it, but that means they were headed toward Janesville."

"So they lost you?" Paige groaned.

"They sure did. Oh, and they also had a running head start and could see damn near anyone pulling away from that parking lot in their rearview mirror. You want to hold that against me too?"

Reluctantly, Paige shook her head. "Sorry. Thanks for trying, Prophet."

"Wish I could've done more, but I should be able to pick up on them later." Tapping his temple, he added, "I know where they're going, remember?"

"Oh," Paige grumbled skeptically. "That's right."

Motioning toward the second large case, Walter added, "The Brown rifle is in there. It's not the .50 cal, but it should do all right."

"Oooh," Cole purred as he reached out to touch the rifle. "I've been using these since *Sniper Ranger 2*! Can I have a look?"

"You were a Ranger?" Walter asked.

"Oh, no. *Sniper Ranger*. It's a video game. I . . . uh . . ." The more he spoke, the more he wanted to go stand in a corner. "I design games. Never mind."

"If you designed *Sniper Ranger 1*, you've got some answering to do. The specs for most of those weapons were ridiculous."

"I know!" Cole replied. "I researched them all for *Two* and tried to make it more realistic."

"I'll have to give that one a try," Walter said. "Go on and see how she feels, since you may just have to use it."

"I don't want to brag, but I have fired one of these before and I was pretty good," Cole bragged.

Looking over to Paige, Walter said, "The rounds are all coated in the antidote, so it really doesn't matter where they hit. If it's a Nymar, it'll feel it."

"I said I was a good shot," Cole repeated.

"Then hit them in the heart and you may kill one," Walter explained. "I won't guarantee it, though. If you do have to go up against a human, that thing'll drop 'em just fine. A shapeshifter, though . . ."

"Speaking of shapeshifters," Paige said as she handed over one of the bundled towels she'd collected from the last hotel room Cole had rented. "Think you can get this to Daniels?"

Walter carefully unfolded the towels, dipped his fingers into the greasy residue and whistled. By this time, the towel looked as if it had a shimmering void in its center. "Oh, he'll have some real fun with this. It'll take me a little while to find out where he went, though."

"Take your time, but I've got first dibs when he does come up with something," Paige insisted.

"Of course." While folding up the towels as if swaddling a baby, Walter nodded toward the gym bag and said, "There's more antidote in there, but use it sparingly. It's just what was left behind by those guys heading out to Philadelphia. They mentioned something about Nymar being able to ingest more and more of the stuff. Could be an immunity or possibly some sort of vaccine."

Rolling onto her side, Paige furrowed her brow and asked, "Any reason you didn't mention a Nymar vaccine before?"

"I pass on what I hear to MEG. Don't you check in with those guys?"

"Yeah," she said with a dismissive wave, "but they're kind of . . . creepy."

"They know their tech, Paige," Walter scolded. "They also do a damn good job of putting up with the likes of you. You shouldn't give 'em such a hard time."

"Wait until you get hit on by every geek that answers the phone over there and see how you like it."

Walter smirked and said, "Well, maybe if you use your sexy voice, those creepy guys will help you circulate these," he said as he handed her a piece of paper that had obviously been torn from a small, spiral notepad.

"Are these the new lottery numbers?" she asked.

"Oh, yeah. Real winners too. I can feel it."

Cole set the rifle down and lovingly patted the stock. "Lottery numbers? Did you get those from another dream?" When he didn't get a joking response, he snapped his eyes back and forth between Walter and Paige. "Did he? Seriously?"

Walter nodded.

"Don't get so excited," Paige said. "He's only right less than half the time. As long as we spread the numbers to different people around the country, the big hits barely even make the news and we're all set up for a while."

Cole's skeptical grin slowly faded as he thought about all the times over the years when he'd seen reports of a bunch of people hitting the lottery and dividing the jackpot to something much less impressive than the whole amount. "I always wondered how that happened," he muttered.

"What's gonna happen," Paige chided, "is that you got to make a whole lot of calls to a whole lot of people to spread a whole lot of numbers. Consider it another one of those initiation things."

"I thought MEG was going to do that!" he said.

Paige shook her head and waggled the paper at him. "MEG does a lot for us, but those guys love their websites. If these numbers found their way onto one of those, they'd be worthless even if every single one of them hit. By the way, you won't be e-mailing them either. Phone calls only. I'll give you the numbers."

Once Cole had taken the paper from her, Paige began sifting through one of Walter's cases. When she reached the bottom, she looked up and asked, "Didn't Gerald leave an armor kit with you?"

"I only have one pair of hands," Walter replied patiently. "See why I meet her at the strip bars, Cole? She's always willing to get in and get out real quick. Meeting in the real world only leads to me mixing up another batch of something or bugging one of my suppliers for something else. Makes me wish for the old days before you folks knew I could get my hands on this stuff."

"You could always just join up with us," Paige said as she picked up the TV remote and flipped through a few channels. "I could sure use the help, with the massacre we're trying to avert. I still need to check up on that Half Breed den and then try to make it to Janesville with time to spare."

"Fine," Walter said as he motioned for Cole to follow him out of the room.

Paige nearly shot up from where she'd been resting. "You're going to help us full-time?" she asked hopefully.

"I'll cruise into Janesville, find that Nymar who left you in the dust tonight, see what I can see about a massacre, and then point you in the right direction when you're through cleaning out that den. You'll owe me, and I still want a cut of that money being offered by those pale kids in Chicago. Now, I've got some more cases to haul up from my van and I don't intend on doing all the lifting myself." With that, Walter turned and left the room.

"I'll give him a hand," Cole said. When he reached the door, he stopped and turned to look at Paige. She was laying on her side, propping up her head with one arm while using her free hand to work the remote. "Walter seems like a big help."

"He is."

"So what's the difference between what he's doing and what he'd do if he was an actual Skinner?"

Slipping back into her kung fu master voice, Paige replied, "Bringing sword to battleground and wielding it are two very different things, young one."

Chapter 20

Paige woke Cole early the next morning. Walter was already gone, but was supposed to meet them at the pit just west of Clear Lake. Cole grabbed some complimentary bagels and coffee from the lobby on his way out and then loaded up the car. Since it was early enough for the haze of dawn to still be thick in the air, he didn't mind letting Paige drive. In fact, he felt pretty good just to be in some clean clothes. It wasn't a long trip, but he still managed to fall asleep somewhere along the way. When they arrived, they spotted one van parked in front of a deteriorating old house. It was a large, boxy model from ten years ago that had plenty of room inside and plenty of rust on the outside.

The engine of Paige's car was still ticking when the driver's side door to the van's swung open and Walter stepped out.

"You found the place," he said. "There's a pile of rocks and crap out back. The pit's in the middle of it all. You can't miss it."

Paige stretched her arms as if about to embark on a leisurely morning stroll. "Can't you show us where it is?"

"I'm just acting as the scout on this one, remember? You guys are the ones who're crazy enough to poke these man-eaters with a sharp stick."

"I thought you said you'd be able to give us more help than that," she reminded him.

Walter cocked his head to one side in preparation to defend himself. "I know what I said, Paige, and I'll be able to help you even more than I thought. I had the same dream again last night and I managed to write down a few things."

"What kind of things?" Cole asked with genuine curiosity.

Grateful to have a more receptive ear, Walter turned to him and replied, "I saw the news report about that massacre again, but there was someone reporting on the scene this time. She was at a park in Janesville and there was some big ugly building in the background. I got a much clearer look at it this time around."

Paige let out a short grunt of a laugh. "Real helpful."

"Yeah," Walter snarled. "It is. Janesville isn't a big place. I looked it up and there are only about six parks and a few golf courses, so it shouldn't take me long to drive around and see which one matches what I saw."

"How long would something like that take?" Paige asked.

He shrugged. "I should have it narrowed down to a few possibles by the end of the day. By the end of tomorrow, I could have the spot all picked out."

Even though Paige was raking her fingers through her hair with almost enough force to pull it out at the roots, Cole was nodding enthusiastically. "Fine, Walter," she said. "Check out your hunch. Did you get the rest of those things we needed?"

"Everything that was in Gerald's personal stash," he replied. "He might've given some stuff to some other partners, but this was all he wanted me to keep in my van. I'll leave it here for you."

Paige nodded. "He always trusted you, Walter. Wait a second. Last night you said you had to go scrounge for that stuff."

"I stopped back at Shimmy's," Walter admitted with a shrug. "I've still got other jobs to do, you know."

"Go check out Janesville," she said without the annoyed tone that had been in her voice before. "Give us a call as soon as you find anything. Even if you don't find anything, check in tonight."

"Yes, ma'am," he replied with a quick salute. He tossed a friendlier wave to Cole as he headed for his van and unloaded a few things from the back.

Paige walked toward the house with quick, purposeful steps and stopped at the front door. "Do we have this place to ourselves?" she shouted toward the van.

"Apart from the Half Breeds sleeping out back, yeah," Walter shouted back. "The owners think the MEG guys are conducting one of their investigations over the next few days."

Suddenly, Cole became very uncomfortable with the fact that their voices rolled through the air with the subtlety of an incoming thunderstorm. Even as he jogged to catch up to Paige, he winced with every crunch of his hiking boots against the gravel. "Didn't you say Half Breeds are werewolves?" he asked.

"Yep," she replied as she stepped into the cavernous foyer of the mansion. "Real nasty ones too."

"Then shouldn't we be quieter?"

She considered that for a moment. Leaning forward, she lowered her voice to a stage whisper and said, "I think Prophet's losing his mind."

"You don't think there are any Half Breeds here?" Cole asked hopefully.

"I believe what he sees with his own eyes. What he dreams, though . . . that's another story. If there is a den here, any city within miles of it is in trouble. All that massacre talk could've just been run of the mill extrapolating. Psychics pull that shit all the time."

To drive the sense of foreboding even further into him, the next thing Cole heard was the spinning of tires against gravel and the howl of the old van's motor. The van sped away quickly and noisily. Once it was gone, the only sounds within the mansion were the tapping of his and Paige's boots against the dirty floor, and the rustling of wind through broken walls.

While it was much too late in the year for it to be warm in Wisconsin, the air seemed even cooler inside the mansion. Cole walked along a path that was fairly well marked by new boards upon the cracked floor. Sawhorses connected by plastic tape kept them from wandering too close to crumbling banisters or a dangerously weak section of ceiling. Even with all the precautions set up, however, he couldn't help but feel he was tempting fate just by being in that place.

"How are you doing over there?" Paige asked.

"Funny you should ask."

"Are you hearing Misonyk's voice again?"

Cole blinked and had to struggle to pull himself off one line of thought and onto another. "No. Didn't you already take care of that?"

She reached out to push aside the sheet of plastic that separated the kitchen from the backyard. "If you feel even the slightest twinge that Misonyk may be around, you let me know. This is important."

After taking a few steps into the sprawling land behind the mansion, Cole saw the pile of rocks that Walter had mentioned. He also saw a spot where the rubble dipped down into what could very possibly be a hole or a pit. There wasn't more than twenty to thirty yards between the back door and the start of that rubble, but he suddenly felt as if it was several miles away. "This is it," he muttered.

"We don't know that yet," Paige replied as she curled her fingers in to scratch her palms. "But I think we're pretty close to something."

"No. I mean this is it for me. I've come so far that I won't be able to go back. I either get hunted down by these things or I hunt them."

Paige shrugged. "That's how it is for all of us. Things may not have gone very smoothly here, but I couldn't have gotten this far on my own. Just having someone watching my back has been a big help. Something's happening and we're going to need all the help we can get when the time comes."

Cole didn't have to ask if that time was drawing near. He could feel it approaching through the chill in the air, all the way down to a subtle rumbling that seemed to be coming from miles beneath his feet. It might not have been measurable by any scale, but it was there. He could feel it stirring in the back of his mind like the wind rattling the loose boards behind him.

"Okay," he said as he walked forward to stand beside Paige. "But if I'm going up against another werewolf, I want a weapon."

"Let's get a look first. Then we'll get you armed."

Although the sky was darkened by hues of gray and blue, the sun was poking through the clouds to cast its light onto the cluttered mansion grounds. That combination gave them a dreary, washed-out hue that smeared the natural colors into a mixture that looked every bit as slippery as it felt. Morning frost had settled in beneath the loose rocks at the top of the rubble. As Paige and Cole climbed over the heap, they leaned down to support their weight with their hands as well as their feet. That way, when they were able to look into the hole on the other side of the ridge, only a few bits of dust trickled down to announce their presence.

Cole couldn't see very much in the shadows below, but he could hear something that reminded him of a train chugging through the far end of a tunnel. As his eyes adjusted to the darkness in that hole, he could just make out a few shapes down there. The little bit of light that did make it all the way to the bottom was just enough to show a few skinny limbs with strands of wiry hair sprouting from them in irregular patches. Judging by the way the shadows moved, the chugging he'd heard was several sets of haggard breathing.

"Is that . . . alive?" he asked.

"Yep," Paige told him. "Both of them are."

"I only see one."

She scooted in closer to him and placed her cheek against his so she could follow his line of sight. "There," she said as she reached out with one arm. "See the other one?"

For the moment, he couldn't help but look over at Paige's face. Now that he was this close to her, he could make out a faint array of freckles running along the upper curve of her cheeks that had faded until they were almost invisible. She looked back at him then, surprising him. Oddly enough, considering their circumstances, she was smiling.

"Down there," she said softly. "Look."

If he had been pulled from his thoughts any quicker, he would have gotten the bends. By the time he shifted his gaze back into the pit, something at the bottom stirred within a messy bed of leaves. Hairless, twisted legs kicked at the dirt and jagged nails scraped against rock.

"What are they?" he asked.

"Half Breeds."

"But they don't look like werewolves. They don't even look like they can stand up."

"They sleep during the day," Paige replied. "When the sun's out, they shift back into this form. If they get worked up, they can shift into their wolf form. They almost always change at night, and full moons are the worst."

"When do they turn back into people?"

Paige slowly shook her head. "After they change the first time, they never change back into people. I don't like the looks of this."

"Tell me about it," he grunted. "They look like big rats that were shaved by a cheese grater."

"There should be more of them. Walter was right. That den's big enough for three or four more of those things."

"Three or four *more*?"

After nodding a few times, Paige crawled away from the edge of the pit. "Half Breeds like cramped spaces and don't pick large dens unless they've got the numbers to fill them. The rest must be out somewhere. If they were too far away to get back here when the sun came up, they probably dug in wherever they wound up to sleep through the day."

"Can you find them?"

She shook her head. "Only if I got real lucky. Half Breeds can run a long ways in a short amount of time."

"What about Lake Koshkong or whatever that place was that Walter mentioned?" Cole asked. "You think they're there?"

"Could be. This looks like it's probably their main den, so they'll all wind up back here. The bad news is that they may have picked this place for another reason."

"Like what?"

Paige shrugged as she backed away from the opening and got to her feet. "They could be sticking close to whatever is acting as the alpha for that group."

"Is there any good news?"

"The good news is that we've got some time to get you your weapon."

Cole practically jumped to his feet as he followed her down the side of the heap. "I really can use that rifle. I could also carry that Blood Blade. After all, I did carry the thing all the way from Canada."

"I've got a better idea," she said. "Pick out a stick."

After all the walking, climbing, and crawling he'd been doing, Cole was sweating beneath the layers of discount clothing he'd bundled around himself. He scratched at a spot where wool scraped against damp skin and grunted, "Huh?"

Leading the way toward the edge of the grounds, Paige said, "You heard me. Pick out a stick. It's going to be something you use for a weapon, so make sure it's a good one."

"Didn't you bring the Tactical Rifle?"

"You need a stick."

Cole looked around as if he expected a camera crew to jump out and start laughing at the dumbfounded expression on his face. All he saw was a lot of brown, swaying grass and a few clusters of rocks scattered throughout the fields that went on for miles before reaching the interstate to the west. The pile of rubble was still where he'd left it, and the mansion was beyond that. "I don't get it."

Paige pulled in a deep breath, bent at the waist and pulled out the twin clubs that she kept sheathed on the sides of her boots. "Here's what I picked when I was in your spot. You've seen us fight with these. You're going to need your own."

The expression on his face shifted from dumbfounded to terrified. "Please don't tell me I'm going to fight this werewolf with a stick."

"You've come this far, Cole. Think about when you saw Gerald fight that Full Blood. Think about when you saw me fight that thing in the diner. You want to know how to bring these creatures down? I'm going to show you. You've been lucky so far, but if you don't get trained real quick, you're going to be real dead. I honestly don't want that to happen. Shapeshifters and even Nymar can take a hell of a lot of damage from gunfire. Sometimes, the biggest guns out there don't do jack. Skinners may have only developed one weapon for themselves, but it works really well. Just trust me and pick out something so we can get started."

Cole's eyes wandered toward the trees to the south and the pile that had already gathered at the base of those trunks. Before he could take one step in that direction, he was interrupted.

"Actually, dead wood won't work for this," Paige said. "The process only works on something with a bit of life left in it. It's got to be freshly cut or uprooted for it to be any good."

Suddenly, he felt something swell up inside of him that made him turn away from her and shout, "This is fucking crazy!" Shooting a glance toward the pit, he bit his tongue and listened for any trace of the ugly things at the bottom of that hole. All he heard was the wind. "I can't do this," he said in a measured, quieter tone. "I thought I could, but I guess . . . I'm just not . . . I'm just . . . I'm just some asshole who designs video games for a living and scratches my ass on the weekends. I don't *do* anything. I don't even know why you or anyone else thought I could be some kind of fighter."

Paige listened and her brown eyes watched him with gentle interest. Her face seemed softer than ever before. When she reached out for him, her movements settled his uneasiness before her fingers had fully wrapped around his wrists. Once she had him, she held onto both of his arms and pulled him closer so she was certain to keep his attention.

"Listen to me, Cole," she said. "You're the ninth person I've tried to train since I've been accepted as a Skinner. Two of those others are out there doing their part right now. The other six ran away crying when they got a look at what they were supposed to be hunting."

"Yeah, right," he grumbled.

Her grip on his wrists tightened and her eyebrows shifted just enough to show the first traces of a glare. "Crying, Cole. Some screamed. Some sobbed. Some just ran. You've had plenty of chances to run, but you haven't. You've done the best you could with what you had, and to be honest, you haven't had much."

"Gee. Thanks."

Although she smiled a bit, she didn't loose any of her intensity. "This is going to sound a little corny," she continued, "but there is such a thing as a warrior's spirit. It's in legends from all over the world and it separates the people who stand and fight from the ones who run and hide or sit and watch. It's nothing supernatural. It's just something that some people have and some don't."

Cole finally did look away from her and toward the nearby patch of trees as he said, "A lot of my friends joined the military after high school. A few joined the Navy and one wound up in the Air Force, but one became a Marine. No . . . he *was* a Marine. It's like he was always a fighter. Didn't care about the pay or benefits. He just knew where he needed to be."

"Warrior's spirit," Paige said.

"You're right," Cole said with a nod. "That does sound corny."

More clouds had rolled in, making the sky look more like something that would get under his fingernails if he reached up and scratched it. Either he'd stopped thinking of his apartment and job back home, or he'd just lost the last strands of common sense that had clung to his brain for so long. Whatever it was, he felt confident enough to take Paige's face in his hands and kiss her the way he'd been planning for far too long.

Her lips were soft and just moist enough to glide over his mouth as he settled in to a comfortable spot. Once his head was tilted just the right way and he'd pulled in another breath, he leaned in closer and slipped his hands through Paige's hair. As the kiss wore on, she melted against him. His hands wandered down to settle on her hips, allowing him to feel the muscles tensing beneath her clothes. Standing on tiptoe, she finally allowed herself to lean back into the arms that were now wrapped around her.

"There's a Half Breed out here, you know," she whispered while Cole's lips wandered from her mouth to her chin and then to her neck.

"Yeah," he said as he nibbled a spot just beneath her ear. "Two of them."

"They're werewolves. Really fast and really . . ." She had to pause as Cole hit a spot that took away her next breath. Finally, she was able to say, " . . . and really mean."

"I bet they are."

Tightening her grip on him, she started to unbutton the front of his shirt. Once she had it open, she slipped her hands beneath the material and ran them all the way along his ribs. "They can smell us if they're awake," she whispered. "Maybe even hear us."

Suddenly, the trees didn't seem as far away as they had a few seconds ago. Before he knew what was happening, Cole had Paige backed against one of those trees and was pressing himself against her. He could feel her soft, warm lips on his chest as her hands continued roaming beneath his shirt. The cold air snuck in as well, adding another layer of sensation to those already rolling through him. As he moved closer to her, she arched her back and lowered her arms so she could grab hold of the tree beside her.

"I think you found my stick," Cole whispered.

A relaxed smile curled Paige's lips up at both edges. "Not yet, but give me a second."

"No, this tree," Cole said as he ran his hand along her arm to the tree she was gripping. "This actually reminds me of something."

Paige's eyes had been partly closed, as if she was dreaming. When she snapped them open, she was clearly awake. "What? Oh, you mean this?" She turned to the side and looked at what she'd been holding. The tree was actually more of a sapling compared to the others in the area. It was a bit taller than her, with a trunk as thick as a baseball bat and branches that had been picked clean by the crisp autumn winds.

Although Cole was leaning more toward the sapling, his hand was still upon Paige's hip. He glanced at her and caught a flush in her cheeks that didn't have anything to do with the weather. "You know something?" he asked.

"What?"

"This is the first time you're not the one leading me around."

Paige lowered her head and pulled in a deep breath before nodding slowly and then turning away from him completely. Before he could get too worried, she turned back around to show him an embarrassed smile. "All right. If you want to keep strictly to business, that's fine."

"Oh sure," Cole chuckled. "As if you would have done anything else with those things sleeping right over there. I appreciate you not kicking my ass or anything for getting carried away like that, but I shouldn't have started anything we wouldn't be able to finish."

Drawing the club from her right boot, Paige tightened her grip on its handle and held on as the wood stretched out and curled at the end to form the curved sickle blade that Cole had sworn was another weapon altogether. With one powerful swipe, she cut the sapling at its base and then lowered her arm. As she loosened her grip on the sickle, it flowed back in on itself to become the simple club it had been before.

"I may be a screamer," Paige whispered, "but we could've done a whole lot out here before we'd ever wake up one of those Half Breeds."

Cole's eyes darted back and forth between her, the tree where she'd been pinned, and the sapling that now lay at her feet. "Don't kid around like that, Paige. It's cruel."

Dragging the tree behind her, she brushed against his body just long enough for Cole to feel the curve of her hip as she passed him by. "Who's kidding?"

Chapter 21

When Cole saw the way Paige handled a hunting knife, he couldn't decide whether he was aroused or uncomfortable. It was a distinction he hadn't had to make since the tight gym shorts he'd been forced to endure in junior high. She wielded the blade with speed and efficiency as she whittled the sapling down to his specifications. While she did that, he was given the task of patrolling the property. After glancing a few more times into the dark pit where the bizarre creatures were still sleeping, he became accustomed to the sight of them. Over the next hour and a half or so, the cold air seeped under his clothes and brought a silence to the area that normally only came in the dead of winter.

Rubbing his hands together while hunkering down to watch Paige some more, he asked, "Can weapons like this hurt a Full Blood?"

"Yes, and that's saying a lot," she replied without allowing her hands to lose the rhythm she'd built up. "There's only three things that we know of that can kill a Full Blood and this is one of them."

Cole's face darkened as he thought about what he wanted to say. As much as he wanted to bite his tongue, he couldn't keep from telling her, "It didn't help Gerald very much."

If Paige was fazed by that in any way, she didn't show it. "That's because he wasn't prepared. You take any boxer and tell him he's training for a featherweight match and then toss his narrow butt into a ring against a heavyweight who's carrying a sledgehammer in each hand and that boxer won't have much of a chance. He's got weapons, but they're just the wrong ones. I won't lie to you, Cole. Even with the proper weapons, we're a hell of a long way from having the upper hand."

"But there's got to be a better way than swinging a spear at them," he insisted.

Paige sat with her back against a tree so she was facing the pile of rubble behind the Lancroft mansion. She and Cole had moved farther into the trees so nothing could get behind them without rustling several yards of dead leaves or shaking a whole lot of dry branches. As she got back to her work with the knife, she said, "We can treat bullets to hurt some of these things, but not Full Bloods. Charmed weapons like that Blood Blade do a lot of damage, but the Gypsies who craft them don't part with their secrets."

"I'd think anyone who could make those weapons would want to get them to the ones who can use them."

"Yeah," she grumbled. "That's how you'd think it would work. Those families do things their own way and don't get along with Skinners too well. It's some sort of feud from a long time ago, but all I care about is here and now."

"We've got a Blood Blade here and now," he pointed out.

She shook her head definitively. "I can't risk anything happening to that. That Mongrel in Canada was supposed to have two Blood Blades. Full Bloods are known to collect the things just to keep them away from us, which was probably what brought that one running to Gerald and Brad. I've got plans for this blade and I can't risk anything happening to it. Gerald didn't believe in my idea. He thought the blades should just be used for fighting, and too many other Skinners agree. We don't need the Blood Blade yet."

"So those blades are the best way to kill one of those things?" Cole asked.

Shaking her head without taking her eyes from her work, Paige said, "The only surefire weapon to use against any supernatural creature is another supernatural creature. Nobody knows the specifics, but they can tear each other apart just fine. It may be some sort of natural balance, but it didn't help us until a Skinner from a couple hundred years ago came up with what I'm about to show you."

"Will you show me how to get that stick to change shapes like yours did?" he asked.

"I can turn this stick into something that will hurt a Half Breed. That's all we've got time for. Normally, I wouldn't even bring you on a hunt like this, but we don't have a lot of choice right now. We're the only two Skinners within a couple hundred miles."

"What about Walter?" Cole offered weakly.

"I counted him as half and you as half."

Although that bent Cole's nose out of joint, he quickly snapped it back into place. "You were probably being generous where my half was concerned. Will you at least show me how to swing that stick?"

"Sure," she said as she tossed the trimmed sapling at him.

The stick was somewhere between four and five feet long, and still fresh from getting its bark peeled off by Paige's hunting knife. It felt a little damp in his hands and had plenty of give when he swung it back and forth. Even though the ends had been whittled down to points, he still would have been more confident wielding a broomstick.

"You sure this isn't another initiation joke?" he asked.

Circling him in slow, measured steps, Paige spoke in a soft voice that made it sound as if she had her eyes closed and was describing something from a dream. "Try to imagine fighting a Full Blood," she said from behind him. "Or imagine fighting that Mongrel. You know how well you can move. You know how fast or slow or strong or flexible you are. What kind of weapon do you think you'd use?"

"When fighting a Full Blood?" he mused. "I'd call in an air strike. Or how about a nice red button with a few nukes on the other end of it? That sounds good."

Paige laughed under her breath and then calmly said, "Turn around."

When he turned, he could hear the subtle brush of feet

against the ground, which didn't at all match the sight of Paige stepping forward while swinging both of her clubs at his head. He let out a surprised grunt and turned at the waist while swinging the sapling up in both hands to protect his face.

Stopping less than an inch before hitting him, she completed her attack by lightly tapping his forearm with the short blunt clubs. "There you go," she said. "You should fight the way your instincts want to fight. You'll need a two-handed weapon." As she ran a club along the edge of his arm that was facing toward her, she added, "And see the way this arm is turned more than the other? You should be able to shift the weapon to block with that arm, but you'll be able to use it either way."

"Actually," Cole said, "there was this one weapon I designed for *Hammer Strike* that had these—"

Paige cut him short with a politely raised hand. "Is it about this size?" she asked as she tapped the sapling he was awkwardly gripping.

"More or less. Don't you remember when I told you about *Hammer Strike* while we were driving out from Chicago?"

"No."

"Before we got to the outlet mall," he added. "You know. It was the game with the Cerberus."

Slowly, Paige began to nod. "Oh yeah. You got going about that a couple of times, but I sort of blocked you out. Here," she said as she tossed the hunting knife to him. "You should do the carving."

"I really don't know how to carve."

"You know how to whittle?"

"Barely."

"Same idea," she said. "Just sharpen the ends the way they should be and get it down to the basic shape you're after. I'll check on you later."

"What about the Half Breeds?" Cole asked.

After glancing at her watch and then looking up at the bright gray sky, she replied, "I'll check on them too, but they won't be going anywhere until the sun starts to go down."

"So they stay out of the sunlight completely? Does it hurt them or something?"

"If you looked like a peeled grape, you'd probably stay out of the sun too. Besides, they'll be resting up for a good run tonight."

Cole caught her looking up toward the sky again. "Full moon?" he asked.

She nodded. "Yeah. Unfortunately, that legend's true. Now get to whittling."

By late afternoon Cole's feet were covered in wood chips. His hands were bleeding from several cuts and splinters and his arms ached so badly that he prayed for them to fall off. In his lap, the fruit of his labor rested like a pathetic mockery of the feeble efforts that had produced it. The crooked stick was pointed at both ends and shaped roughly like a thick bow. One end was thicker than the other and had the beginnings of a notch carved into it.

"Behold," he said as he held up the length of wood for Paige to see. "I shall name it . . . aw, this thing sucks."

She sat nearby, with cases she'd unloaded from the car on either side of her. As the day had worn on, smells had drifted through the air from one of several holes she'd dug into the cold soil. Each of those holes had a small clay pot set into it. Now, she stood up, dusted herself off, and walked over to sit beside him. "What's wrong with it?" she asked.

"First of all," he replied as he tapped the rough notch, "this is supposed to be like two points split apart. Maybe it's stupid, but it looked really cool in the—" Before he could finish his criticism, metal sliced through the air as Paige swung the hunting knife straight down toward the stick. The blade landed in the notch with a solid *thunk* and caused the wood to split another couple of inches down.

After twisting the knife to separate the two halves a bit more, she asked, "Is that more like it?"

Cole looked at that end of the stick and nodded as he compared it to the forked tongue model of his favorite melee weapon from *Hammer Strike*. "Yeah! I don't know if it'll do a lot of damage, but that's the look of it."

Taking the whittled piece of wood from him, she hefted it in both hands and nodded. "This isn't bad. See if you can get these points a bit sharper, though," she said, handing the wood back. "Then it'll do plenty of damage."

Cole rested the bow-shaped stick across his lap and got back to whittling. Once Paige returned to the clay pots she'd partially buried, he asked, "So, I had this really great dream where I kissed you and you seemed to like it. It seemed real, but I guess you weren't there."

"I was there," she said quietly.

"Maybe it wasn't a dream, then. Maybe it was a mistake?"

"I hope not," she replied as she lowered her head and kept stirring the mixture at her feet. "You surprised me and I ran with it, but maybe it wasn't the best time. Then again, who knows when there'll be a better time?"

"For tomorrow we die," he declared. "Is that it?"

"Could be tomorrow. Could be tonight. Maybe I've just been living day to day for too damn long." She shook her head just enough for her hair to slip down into her face. "You probably think I'm such a—"

"Hey," he cut in. "If you can help me turn this piece of crap I whittled into anything more than a glorified toothpick, I'll think you're a miracle worker."

Paige looked at him without saying a word. Slowly, the frustration in her eyes faded away. After holding onto the silence that stretched between them for a few more seconds, she lifted a small bowl from the dirt and moved over to sit beside him. She reached out to take a small rag from one of the nearby cases and dipped it into the concoction. Cole watched her, savoring the grace in her movements, which brought out the sublime in even the most mundane of tasks.

"This is a resin made from a recipe that dates back to the 1600s," she said. "I don't know the name of the Skinner who cooked up the first batch, but I will tell you it works real well."

"Do I need to learn how to make it?" he asked.

"Yes, but not tonight. This just needs to be worked into the grain of the wood in a thick, even coat. Here," she said as she carefully handed it over. "This is your job."

"Should I get any on me?"

"Only if you don't mind losing the use of your fingers." Paige smirked as she saw the panic that drifted across his face.

As soon as he got a look at that grin, Cole relaxed and simply held onto one end of the stick as he applied the resin like a coat of foul-smelling varnish. Before he was three-quarters done, he could hear something creaking and snapping like bones being bent until they broke.

"Is that supposed to happen?" he asked.

"Yeah," Paige told him. "That's the resin soaking in."

Cole looked down at the stick and noticed how the sunlight was reflecting differently along the surface where the resin had been applied as opposed to where it hadn't. While the end he was using as a handle still felt like freshly cut wood, the treated areas looked almost petrified.

"Coat the rest of it," Paige instructed. "End to end. Top and bottom."

Only about a minute after the rest of the coat had been applied, she took the stick from him and tested to make sure the varnish was dry. "Show me how you'll wield it," she said, and tossed it back to him.

Cole caught it and hefted it in his hands. Not only was the resin dry, but it made the stick somehow feet lighter and stronger at the same time. Holding onto it stick so the bowed angle arced away from him, he said, "I guess like this, but I could always switch it around."

"You'll hold it the first way," Paige told him. "That's going to be more effective. Now hand it back. Quickly."

He gave the stick back to her and watched as she used the hunting knife to hack at a few spots halfway along the length of wood. She split off a few thin sections, peeled them back, then dabbed more resin onto the spots of fresh wood that had been revealed. After repeating the process several more times in a few different spots along the length of the stick, she dropped the rag and tossed the hunting knife so its blade stuck into the dirt. Gripping the stick between the barbs she'd created, she dipped the barbs into another one of the pots she'd been using to create one of her potent mixtures.

"When the time comes," she said, "this weapon will save

your life. It will be an extension of your own body. It will be the only weapon you'll need." As she lifted the stick, a clear, glistening string extended from the barbs to the pot. It was broken by her finger, which she then used to smear the resin a few more places. "When the time comes, you'll hold the weapon just like you showed me."

"Those spikes are gonna get in my way," Cole pointed out.

She looked up at him and nodded once.

He furrowed his brow and studied her face. He didn't exactly like what he saw. "You want me to fit my fingers between the spikes?"

"The thorns will cut into your hands, but try not to think about that," she explained as she handed the weapon to him. "It's a necessary part of the process."

Glancing between those thorns and Paige's hands, Cole could see the thick layers of scars that marked her palms. He suddenly recalled seeing similar scars on the palms of almost every other Skinner he'd met. "I need to tear my own hands open every time I use this thing?" he asked.

Paige shook her head reassuringly. "Not every time. Trust me, it looks worse than it is. Just to get the feel of it, hold the weapon up like you're blocking something."

Tentatively placing his hands around the spot that had been carved into a rough grip, he felt the wooden barbs press against his palms. "When's the first time I'm gonna have to do this?" he asked through gritted teeth.

Without a moment's hesitation, Paige drew one of her clubs and cracked it against the middle of the stick, causing some of the thorns in Cole's handle to snap against his hands. The rest pierced his flesh and dug into the meat of his hands.

"Holy . . . God . . . that hurts!" he moaned.

She dropped her club back into her boot and leaned forward to examine his hands. Just when it seemed that she was going to tend to his wounds, she pulled the weapon up from his palms and then forced it back down a bit farther. This time Cole was too shocked to make a sound.

"That's not so bad," she told him. "We got what we needed

on the first try. I know someone who had to go four or five times before he got so much blood drawn." As she spoke, Paige lifted the weapon until all the thorns came free of Cole's hands. The ones that hadn't snapped were coated with a slick layer of blood. A few of the broken ones remained lodged in his flesh.

Cole's mouth hung open and he held his hands out. Most of the color had drained from his face as his fingers slowly trembled and curled in and out like squirming caterpillars. "What in the *hell* was that for?"

Having already gotten herself situated on the ground with her legs bunched up beneath her, Paige dipped one rag into the second of her concoctions. "It connects you to your weapon. It'll also toughen you up. Bring me the small vial on top of the case over there," she said.

Cole pulled the largest of the broken splinters from his palm and flexed his fist to work the pain out. It stung like hell, but the pain was seeping into him and becoming easier to bear. After finding the vial she'd requested, he asked, "Do I want to know what's in this?"

"Diluted Nymar venom. I'm going to mix it with your blood on these thorns so your weapon will bond to you and eventually respond to your commands."

"What sort of commands?"

"One thing at a time, young one. Come over here and watch what I'm doing. You're going to need to learn this."

"What about the Half Breeds?" Cole asked.

"We've got another few hours before they wake up. I just hope to teach you a few basic moves before then."

"How long before I need to fight?"

Paige looked up at the sky to check the moon and then looked at her watch. "Like I said . . . probably a few more hours."

After modifying Cole's weapon with her hunting knife, she tossed it back to him. Although the thorns on the grip were either cut off or trimmed down, the remaining ones were sturdier and a bit sharper than their bigger brothers. Cole listened as she gave a quick rundown of what she was doing.

"Something in Nymar venom allows them to control some-one the way Misonyk controlled you," she explained. "Basi-cally, this resin mixed with a little diluted venom allows us to control our own weapons. It'll only work for you, though. For everyone else, this'll just be a stick."

"And for me, it's something that shreds my damn hands anytime I want to use it."

Paige shook her head slowly. "The venom is diluted with Nymar saliva—"

"And it gets better!"

"That saliva," she cut in, "has a weak healing property."

"Healing?" Cole asked.

"Nymar can heal up their victims a little bit, just to make sure the throats get ripped open enough to feed but not enough to kill."

"That's nice of them."

Meeting his eyes, Paige said, "A beating heart makes it easier for them to get more blood from the veins. That's all there is to it. For our purposes, it keeps our hands from being ripped apart too badly. But," she added as she held up her own hand to show him the scars on her palm, "it's not perfect."

Once the weapon was treated with the venom and another coat of the varnish, Cole was put through a few paces to practice using it. Thankfully, Paige allowed him to grasp the weapon with his fingers between the barbs instead of on top of them. He wasn't allowed to bandage his hands, however. More blood needed to soak into the resin. Tightening his grip on the weapon, he got used to the feel of it as she slowly swung one of her clubs at him. The two weapons knocked together, allowing him to feel the sturdiness of what had so recently been a sapling.

"So how come my weapon isn't half as cool as yours?" he asked.

Paige sped up her attacks and watched every one of Cole's movements. "Because it's not finished. Even so," she added as she snuck in a lower swing, "it'll never be as cool as mine."

"Just because you've got some magic kind of wood that changes shape."

"We'll get to that part later. Right now, just try not to hurt yourself."

They spent the next half hour with Paige attacking and Cole defending in one of two basic ways. After that, they switched roles and practiced for another hour with her showing him two simple ways to attack after each defense. When she finally called for him to take a break, he was ready to collapse.

"You ready to meet your first Half Breed?" she asked.

Cole tried to laugh but could only manage a few short-winded gasps. "Just as long as . . . you don't expect me to . . ."

"Oh, you'll be fighting," she said before he could finish his sentence.

His mouth hung open but no words came out. After a bit of coaxing, he finally managed to spit out, "Unless a Half Breed is some sort of rabid dachshund, there's no way I'm ready to fight!"

Even though she'd been working twice as hard as Cole throughout their sparring session, Paige was practically jumping out of her skin for more. "It's not about the moves," she told him. "It's about the warrior's spirit, remember?"

"I thought that was just inspirational bullshit."

She shook her head as a hungry smile drifted onto her face. "The Half Breeds will be coming for us as soon as they wake up."

"You can't seriously expect me to do this. We've only been practicing for a couple hours. How good can anyone be after a couple hours?"

Paige eyed him for a few more seconds before easing up on her stance. "Fine. Would you feel better if I told you there's a shotgun in the case behind me?"

"Is there?"

"Yep."

"Then yes," Cole sighed. "I feel much better."

"You'll still need to be ready to use some of those moves I taught you. All you're doing is stabbing like it's a spear. If a caveman could figure it out, I think you'll do just fine. It's getting close to nightfall," she added. "That means we still have time to get into that pit and introduce ourselves."

Some of the supplies that Paige took from the case included a flashlight and hunting knife for each of them, some rope, and a plastic container about the size and shape of the one he had used for his retainer when he was in eighth grade. When he opened the plastic case, he saw two sculpted glass vials and a syringe. One of those vials was very familiar.

"That's your Resurrection Vial and dose of antidote to reverse it," Paige explained.

"What about the other one?" Cole asked as he eyed the vial that had a single delivery needle as opposed to two.

"That's what you take if you get mauled by a shapeshifter and survive," she told him. "It'll kill you quick and painlessly."

"Jesus, you Skinners are morbid."

"Just safe," Paige said as she pulled out a false bottom from the larger case, then removed two sawed-off shotguns. "If you ever see how a Half Breed changes, you'll know the alternative is a hell of a lot better." She handed one of the shotguns to Cole and took the other for herself. Both had a mesh strap that allowed the weapons to be slung over their backs so their hands were free. Leaving the rest of the supplies in the clearing, she led the way to the pile of rubble. "When you use that weapon," she explained, "grab hold of the thorns tightly. It'll be quick and may even fire you up."

"Stick versus shotgun? That sounds like an easy loss for the stick to me."

Paige dropped to one knee once she got to the edge of the pit. Looking down to make sure the gnarled creatures were still laying in their spots, she whispered, "You empty both barrels into a Half Breed's head or chest and you should put it down. Of course, they do have a tendency to rip apart everything in the vicinity when they're wounded, so no wild shots."

"If this is payback for me getting frisky a while ago, it's a bit extreme."

"No, no," she said with a sexy grin as she tied a length of rope to a stake she'd pounded into the ground. "I get pretty frisky on full moons too. It's a shame you didn't feel your wild side a bit more when we had the time."

Before Cole could reflect upon what could have been, she was gone. She'd simply grabbed hold of the edge of the pit, swung her legs over, and dropped into the shadows with the rope trailing behind her. He glanced up at the darkening skies. There were still clouds overhead, but they'd thinned out into tattered, smoky shreds. The sun had dipped below the horizon, which allowed a good portion of its light to sneak in beneath the clouds and wash over the rubble and neighboring mansion. When he craned his neck a bit more, he could already make out the pale shape of the moon hanging back like an actor waiting for his cue. He looked into the pit and was stricken by the vast contrast between that dirty hole and the sky above it.

He expelled the breath he'd been holding, dangled his legs over the edge . . . and dropped.

Chapter 22

Cole's feet smacked against the dirt with a jarring impact. Pain shot up through his ankles, burned all the way past his knees and settled into his hips. Switching on his flashlight, he scraped his foot against the ground and took a look at the ground beneath him. The first few layers of dirt on the floor came away easily to reveal smooth, evenly placed bricks. He then saw that the hole wasn't actually a pit, but the remains of an old room.

One side of the room was piled high with a mixture of broken bricks, dirt, and rotted beams similar to the rest of the rubble aboveground. There was a distinct odor underground, however, which was only made worse by the mangy, deformed creatures sleeping noisily against one of the only walls that had remained in tact. Paige was in that area, covering most of her flashlight's beam with the palm of her hand. The light she cast was muted and reddened from being filtered through body.

"I see two of them," she whispered. "What about you?"

Cole's first reaction was to look away from the closest Half Breed, as if the creature was some pathetic collection of remains laying on the side of the road after being decimated by a passing truck. It had looked strange from a distance, and was only stranger now that he was close enough to hear every last one of the thing's rasping, grunting breaths.

Pale skin varied in texture from smooth spots along its back to callused and wrinkled patches along its limbs and side. Its face looked like something sculpted from wet clay by someone who couldn't decide if they were making a pig, a dog, a person, or a monkey. Half of a snout emerged from between misaligned cheekbones and slanted to one side as if it had started to melt and then cooled. A thick, meaty tongue lolled over its crooked jaw. Some of its teeth were dangerously sharp and others blunted and broken. Greasy hair sprouted in tufts that didn't even come close to covering its wrinkled privates or sagging teats.

One of the creature's hands sprouted wrinkled, clawed fingers. The other was definitely some sort of paw. Both of its feet were drawn up close to its torso, where they twitched and wriggled in fits of sleep. As Cole's eyes wandered along the length of the creature's body, he couldn't help but wonder if the jagged bumps in the thing's flesh were some sort of growth or broken bits of bone poking up from beneath its flesh.

"I've got one over here," he reported. As he spoke, he noticed the chewed-up flaps of skin over the creature's ear holes twitching a few times before coming to a rest. "Wait a second," he added as his flashlight wandered toward a dark corner to reveal another figure huddled on the ground. "Make that two."

"Damn," Paige hissed.

Cole moved in a slow crouch to keep his head from knocking against the fallen supports that kept the ceiling from collapsing into the pit. He didn't have to go far before noticing something about the sleeping figure he'd just found. "This one's human," he said. Upon spotting the dirty jeans, flannel shirt, and neon yellow vest wrapped around it, he asked, "Didn't Walter mention something about a survey crew that was supposed to be coming out here?"

Paige's voice was faint as she whispered from another section of the pit, "Yeah, but they were supposed to stay away for a few more days."

"Looks like they didn't follow orders."

When Paige shined her light on the figure laying in front

of Cole, she illuminated the face of a man somewhere in his forties. His hands were clasped to a gaping wound in his chest. Blood had dried into a crusty paste that held his arms in place. His eyes were partly open, but clouded over and unresponsive to the light.

"Oh God," Cole moaned. "He's hurt. He's gotta be dead."

"Come over here," she said. "That body's probably just there for a snack."

He was all too happy to turn away from the gruesome remains and walk toward her light. Along the way, he nearly tripped over a section of broken wall that protruded almost a foot from the floor. It wasn't hard to find other sections hanging from the ceiling directly overhead like rocky growths inside a cave. Swinging his flashlight along the ceiling, he said, "Looks like this used to be divided into smaller rooms. Maybe it's some sort of basement?"

"There's more this way," Paige replied from a crooked doorway supported by crossed pieces of lumber that seemed to have fallen there when the rest of the place collapsed. Shining her light through the doorway, she added, "Looks like a whole hallway. A lot of it's in bad shape, but we should be able to get through."

"Great. Let's just get the hell out of this pit."

"Not until we put those Half Breeds down," she said.

Cole wanted to keep moving, but Paige was blocking the way. Judging by the intensity of her stare, she wasn't about to step aside any time soon. Doubting that he could force her to move, he nodded and said, "You're right. These things have already killed one guy and they'll only kill more."

"Just one? You might not want to look in that corner."

Following her eyes to the corner to his left, Cole found a collection of bones scattered among bits of clothing matching the outfit worn by the dead guy in the opposite corner of the room. "All right," he sighed. "There's the rest of the survey team."

"If Henry is any kind of Full Blood, he could have made any one of these things. As long as all of them are out hunting, there'll be even more. Let's clean these things out now before they wake up."

"Should I use the shotgun or the stick?"

"The stick," Paige told him. "The wood needs to absorb shapeshifter blood, and the shotgun will only wake the others up."

"Got it," Cole snapped before he lost his nerve. "The stick it is." He reached over his shoulder to take hold of the weapon, which now had the feel of lightweight metal. After getting his shirt snagged by the forked points at the bottom a few times, he finally managed to wield it using both hands. He felt more than a little comforted just having the strange weapon in his grasp. He got an additional boost of confidence when Paige stepped up beside him with her own weapons drawn.

The two closest Half Breeds were laying against the wall facing the doorway. Both creatures sprawled with their limbs at awkward angles and their heads tucked in against their chests. Of course, it would have been difficult to think of a position where the creatures would have looked comfortable.

Paige approached a Half Breed and tightened her grip on one of her clubs. Now that Cole knew what to look for, he had no trouble spotting the trickle of blood as the barbs in her handle dug into her palm. A few seconds later, the blunt end of the club stretched out to form a pointed stake. Holding the stake over the top of the Half Breed's spine, she whispered, "We'll take these two out together so one won't get a chance to wake the other. One quick, strong stab here will put them down quickly and quietly."

"What about that one?" Cole asked as he nodded toward the other end of the room, where the third Half Breed was laying.

"These two first. After we take out that other one, we can see what else is down here. You ready?"

Cole stood beside her and turned his weapon around so the single spearhead was pointed at the base of the creature's skull. Just then, the creature twitched and kicked. Looking down at the pathetic thing, Cole realized he'd never killed anything bigger than a spider. The longer he waited, the more inadequate he felt for only having been exposed to his little bit of rushed training.

Picking up on his hesitation, Paige kept her own weapon steady and asked, "What's the matter, Cole?"

"Why don't we just shoot them? Wouldn't that be quicker?"

"You miss the perfect spot and they won't go down," she warned him. "You wound them and they'll be even more of a goddamn nightmare than when they're hungry. They'll kill just because they're pissed, and it won't be pretty."

"What about pulling out these supports?" he asked. "We could cause a cave-in that would—"

"That might just bury them until they get really hungry and manage to dig themselves out again. These things are killers, and this is the quickest way to get rid of them."

Cole tightened his grip on his weapon and raised it again. He looked down at the Half Breed and saw a mangled rat that was bigger than a German shepherd. He saw twisted limbs and broken bones. He even saw what could have been a tattoo on the thing's left shoulder blade.

"What if I miss? What if I—"

"Dammit, Cole! Kill it!"

Paige's voice echoed through the pit. It was all she could do to break through the haze settling into Cole's brain, but it was also enough to wake the animals laying on the floor.

Paige's Half Breed shook its head and rolled onto its belly so it could get its legs beneath it. The thing managed to stand up halfway before her stake was driven through the back of its head, instantly snuffing out the light that was flickering in its eyes. The Half Breed twitched and then dropped into a heap of bones and muscle.

Beneath Cole's weapon, the other Half Breed pulled in a quick breath and let out a wet hacking sound that was part bark and part cough. Its eyelids snapped open to reveal milky yellow eyes that found him in less than a second. It opened its mouth, showing him pointed fangs that pushed their way out through shredded gums. Suddenly, Cole realized the creature was scrambling to its feet with its body pointed away from him and its head twisted 180 degrees around to let out a strained snarl.

Acting out of pure reflex, he jabbed his weapon downward, but buried the single spearhead into the meaty portion of the thing's neck instead of the spot Paige had singled out. Ignoring the sharpened spike gouging into its flesh, the Half Breed snapped at Cole with enough ferocity to clip its own tongue in half. The only thing keeping it from eviscerating him was the spearhead that all but pinned it to the floor.

"Keep it there, Cole," Paige said. "Nice and steady."

In the space of a few seconds he could feel the resistance from the creature growing stronger and stronger. Fur was sprouting from its back, and the ridges beneath its skin were smoothing out to disappear under thick layers of muscle. "I won't be able to hold it much longer," he warned.

Paige's weapon shifted into the sharpened sickle, which she swiped across the Half Breed's throat and opened its jugular. Now, Cole struggled to hold the creature as it thrashed and then finally slumped to the floor. Lowering his arms, he placed one foot on the Half Breed so he could pull his weapon free. Behind him, frantic steps scraped against the dirty floor, followed by the impact of something heavy knocking against his back.

Cole fell over and skidded until he hit the wall. His weapon was knocked from his hand and disappeared from sight. Even before he could figure out how he'd landed, he reached for the shotgun slung across his back. The moment his finger found the trigger, he saw the third Half Breed crawling toward him. The creature was trembling like a drowned cat, fur spewing out to form a thick coat over its skin. Claws snaked from the ends of its paws and its gnarled face took on a distinctly canine shape. When the Half Breed opened its mouth to let out a vicious snarl, Cole pointed his shotgun at it and pulled the trigger. The gun bucked in his hands and let out a deafening roar, sending a load of buckshot into the Half Breed's face.

Blood sprayed onto the wall behind the creature as it staggered back to bump against the filthy bricks. It caught most of the buckshot in the mouth, losing a portion of its lower jaw and several teeth in the process. Its feet were still forming, which made it even harder for the creature to keep its balance when it stepped into a nearby pile of chewed body parts. Cole wanted to take another shot, but the gun in his hands was empty. Instead of being able to pump in another round, he had to open the breech and manually fit in two more shells. Swearing under his breath, he discarded the spent firearm.

"Your weapon's over there," Paige said as she shoved past him and faced the disoriented Half Breed. "See if you can get it!"

Cole looked around and spotted his spear under the hole that led back up to the mansion grounds. Scrambling toward it, he saw more movement coming from the end of the room that was filled with debris. A faint voice also came from that direction.

"Someone . . . please help . . ." the voice groaned.

Cole hurried to that end of the room, figuring Paige had things well in hand. After crossing beneath the hole that led outside, he saw what he'd previously thought was a corpse in a yellow safety vest. Not only was the man alive, but he was crawling toward him, fingers scraping against the floor and eyes locking onto his with desperation that bordered on the fanatical.

"Please . . . you gotta . . ."

"Don't move," Cole said. "We'll help you!"

Suddenly, the snarls behind Cole turned into a muted gurgle. After that, something heavy hit the floor.

"Stay away from him, Cole," Paige commanded.

But Cole was already reaching out for the wounded man. He would have been able to get to him if Paige hadn't rushed over and pulled him back. She was saying something in a hurried series of words, but he wasn't hearing any of it. She struggled to pull him even farther back, but he reflexively wanted to help the man on the floor. And then, when he heard the first wet pops coming from the man's body, he couldn't get himself to look away.

The man was on all fours, convulsing uncontrollably. His fingers clawed at the ground and his feet thrashed against the unforgiving surface. When that first crack sounded out, the front part of the man's body fell forward. After the next pop, his forearm folded in the middle and caused that shoulder to slap against the ground. Still propping himself up with his other arm, the man pushed against the ground and kicked his legs out as more of his bones cracked and sent jagged splinters up through his skin.

Craning his neck until he reached its limit, the flailing man looked at Cole. By the time his eyes locked upon the sliver of darkening sky that could be seen through the hole in the ceiling, his face exploded outward to form a ridged brow and blunt snout. For the first few seconds, the man's head appeared to have been crushed and reshaped by a set of cruel, invisible hands. The rest of his body continued to spasm as more and more of his bones were snapped into pieces inside of him.

It was a sound Cole would never forget.

The man on the floor struggled to pull himself up. Tears rolled down his face and the pain in his eyes was almost unbearable to witness. Even as he tried to reach out for Cole, his hand was reduced to a rubbery mass of broken bones encased in skin that somehow refused to tear. The convulsing figure struggled to look up, until the life in his eyes faded away and he allowed his head to droop. From then on the twitching and flailing of his limbs made him look more like a puppet being swung at the end of its strings. The human inside the thing gave no more resistance, since his body was too shattered to obey its commands anyhow.

And then, somehow, the man looked up.

Muscles writhed and twitched as the nubs of broken bones were pulled back down into him. His entire shape stretched out and reformed into something more like the other wretches that had been curled up at the bottom of the pit. Cole took one step back before his legs gave out beneath him. Paige shouldered him to one side so she could rush forward with her weapons already swinging for the creature's neck. The eyes that met Cole's were no longer those that had been begging for help a few moments ago. They were cloudy, yellow and vacant. The voice that came from the thing's reformed mouth was an inhuman scream that mercifully ended as both of Paige's weapons slashed out and across to sever the newly formed Half Breed's skull from its body.

Cole couldn't move.

He could barely even breathe.

Offering her hand to him, Paige said, "There was nothing we could do for him, Cole. He was dead as soon as he started to change."

"But . . . he asked for help. He . . . he was looking at me," Cole stammered. "He was alive."

She shook her head. "If a werewolf hurts you without killing you, it's probably infected you. Someone like that can only be helped within the first few hours after they were hurt, and even then it's hit or miss. The first time they change, it breaks every bone in their body. We know," she told him with confidence. "We've looked for ourselves."

After what he'd already seen, Cole didn't want to press her for details.

"Are you all right?" she asked.

He looked down at the gruesome remains of the man in the yellow vest. The body wasn't even close to human. Those dead, yellow eyes still gazed out into nothingness. Cole knew he'd probably be seeing those eyes for a long time to come.

"Do you still want to check out this place or would you rather wait up top?" Paige asked.

Cole nodded once and looked around for his weapon. "Are there more like these things around?"

"Yeah. And every one of them can make more."

"Then I'm coming with you." Shaking his head solemnly, he added, "Nobody deserves to suffer like that. It was . . ."

"I know," Paige said.

Standing in that spot, Cole moved his eyes back and forth. The last hints of sunlight trickled down through the hole over his head in a dark red haze that faded by the second. Focusing on one of the walls, he asked, "Where's a flashlight?"

"I've got one."

"Shine it on that wall right there."

Paige holstered one of her clubs and quickly flicked the switch on her flashlight. Even before the wall was illuminated, Cole moved forward and reached out to brush away some of the dirt and cobwebs encrusted on the cracked vertical surface.

"These markings," he whispered. "Do you know what they mean?"

Paige stepped forward and lowered her flashlight so the beam wasn't reflecting directly off the wall. After studying the markings for a few seconds, she said, "I don't know exactly what they mean, but they're close to the ones on the Blood Blade."

"Is it some sort of language?"

"It could be some kind of ceremonial script or possibly an old Gypsy dialect."

"But you can't read it?"

Chuckling once, Paige replied, "I can teach you plenty of things, but ancient languages and ritual symbols are out of my league."

Cole tapped the wall and glanced around. "I've seen this room. Not the way it is now, but when all the walls were up and the building wasn't collapsed. This was the room where Misonyk was kept. This is where he was laying when he had the spear through his chest."

"Are you sure about that?"

"I remember those symbols. He used to look at them when he was laying here. I saw it." Cole shifted his eyes down and began scraping at the floor with his foot. The dirt had formed a thick shell over the floor. Although he'd hoped to see some sort of trace left behind from the vision he'd taken from Misonyk, all he uncovered was more cracked bricks.

"You're starting to sound like Prophet," Paige grumbled. "Why don't we see what else is in this place and get out? There's got to be more Half Breeds on their way. They wouldn't just abandon a den as good as this one."

"Oh yeah," Cole said as he looked around at the bloody remains scattered upon the dirty mat of soil, broken rock, and dead leaves. "Prime real estate here."

Paige held her flashlight in one hand and one of her clubs in the other. Now that he knew what was along the handle of those clubs, Cole had to admire her for wielding it so fearlessly. He found his own weapon and picked it up, careful to slip his fingers between the thorns rather than place his hands on top of them. Since the danger seemed to have passed, there wasn't a reason to maim himself just yet.

"I think there's an infection from that stuff you used to coat those thorns," he grumbled as he followed Paige out of the room. When he checked his palm, he found the wounds irritated but mostly closed. "It's healing up pretty good, but my skin is burning. I don't think this is good, Paige."

Heading for the doorway that led from the room, she said, "Your blood bonds you to the weapon and also to the venom. Everything Nymar reacts to human blood anyway, but you can't feel it until you get close to an actual spore."

"So there's a Nymar nearby?"

She nodded. "Just think of it as an early warning system. It'll work with shapeshifters too, now that you've added some of their blood into the resin."

"Wow," he said with genuine admiration. "Did you guys happen to get a Skinner who was also a chemist?"

"No, a couple dozen Skinners worked on the formula for God knows how long before it was perfected. There just happened to be some useful side effects."

"Were there any bad side effects?"

"Oh yeah," Paige whispered. "But you probably don't want to hear about those."

She walked into a crumbling, dirty hallway beyond the door that led out of the Half Breed den. Taking a few more steps, she swung her flashlight, illuminating the walls and ceiling, which were in somewhat better condition than the room they'd just left. The hall ended a few paces to the right, blocked off about ten paces to the left by tightly packed debris that had settled into a solid barrier.

Having found his flashlight, Cole shined it on the obstruction at the left end. It didn't take much searching to find the blackened scorch marks that formed a ring all the way around the rubble blocking the rest of the hall. "Looks like there was a fire," he said while brushing his fingers along the wall. "Maybe this hallway was blasted shut. Whoever did that must have really wanted to be sure nobody else got in here."

"Or maybe they didn't want someone getting out," Paige added. "Take a look over here."

The wall separating the pit from the hallway was buckled and cracked. Most of the doors had been wedged into their frames by the shifting of the building around them. The room she was pointing at didn't even have a door. It was directly across from Misonyk's old cell, and judging by the sounds coming from inside, it was currently occupied.

"Do you hear that?" Paige asked.

Cole nodded. "Should I get the shotgun?"

"No. I've still got mine. But," she added as she took a look into the next room, "I don't think a gun will do either of us any good."

Cole's hand reflexively tightened around his weapon. Some of the thorns scraped against his fingers, but he was more concerned by the way the irritation in his hand suddenly felt as if someone was holding a match against his skin. The wheezing voice coming from the next room, however, was more than enough to distract him from a bit of pain.

While keeping her flashlight pointed into the room, Paige held her weapon so the curved blade was ready to be swung.

As he followed her into the room, Cole noticed the etchings on the outside of the door frame. They were similar to the strange letters he'd seen in the other room, but the symbols inside this one had been scratched and clawed until they'd almost been gouged from the brick. Somehow, the marks still showed up like stubborn water stains in a leaky basement. The room stank of urine and worse. There were no furnishings or anything else in that cramped space apart from a few short bones on the floor next to the door and a large figure rocking anxiously in the opposite corner.

The beam from Paige's flashlight played along the walls and reflected off the smooth, rounded surface of Henry's corner. Even though it appeared to have been made from the same brick as the rest of the walls and floor, that corner had been worn down to glassy perfection, which hugged Henry's body like an old rocking chair. Although that body was more compact than the last time Cole had seen it, Henry's flesh was still gnarled and twisted into something alien and unnatural. A hole in the ceiling opened up to show the bottom of a pile of rubble that could very well have been the same pile he'd scaled while searching the mansion grounds. Dirt trickled in to patter upon the floor in a dusty drizzle that blended nicely with Henry's voice.

"I'mGod'sfavoriteHespeakstomeandtogetherwemake-harmony," Henry mumbled in a single, continuous stream. As he spoke and rocked, his head lolled back and forth with a hypnotic rhythm. His lips twitched and his mouth hung open to reveal a few sharpened teeth that had pushed through his jaw and split apart several of his old teeth in the process. "SitandwaitsitandwaitsitandwaitwaitwaitforGodto-callmyname."

Paige stepped into the room, keeping her hands where Henry could see them. When she spoke, it was in a soothing voice that almost blended in with Henry's seamless mumbling. "Where's Misonyk?" she asked. "Where is he?"

When Henry shook his head, the disconnection from his spine made it difficult for him to stop. "I made a friend," he said in a slower, clearer voice. "He's . . . like me."

From behind Cole, a coarse howl rolled through the subterranean confines. It was definitely coming from outside, but that didn't make Cole feel any better. The howl didn't sound like it came from an animal nor did it sound like it came from a man. It was more like the sound a demon would make while getting its bony wings torn off. After the first hellish roar, it tapered off into something more familiar.

Familiar, but still unnerving.

"Uhhh, Paige?" Cole whispered.

She waved quickly at him and nodded. "Can you hear that howling? Are those more like you, Henry?"

Curled up in his corner, Henry looked as if half of his body mass had simply folded in on itself. His arms were wrapped around his knees and his chest heaved with strained breaths. When he rocked forward to get a closer look at Paige, it was easier to see the deep groove that had been worn into the corner behind Henry as well as beneath him. "They weren't like me. Not at first. God told me to hurt them, so I did. He said they'd help us, and they will. They did. They like to run with me. They . . . like me."

"How many did you hurt?"

"Don't know. God didn't teach me to count. God told me about you," Henry said as he bared his teeth. "He said you wanted to kill me." Furrowing his brow, he clenched his eyes shut and let out a groan that boiled up from the back of his throat. "You tried to kill me! I remember!"

Paige held her weapon behind her back. "I want to hear about God," she urged as she took a few steps toward Henry's corner. "What did God say? Where is he?" When she saw the happy gleam in Henry's eyes, she added, "Can you take me to him?"

Henry kept trying to see what was happening in the shadows behind her, but Paige pulled his attention back to where she wanted it to be.

"I . . . didn't mean to make her," Henry said.

Paige narrowed her eyes and asked, "What?"

"I was looking for someone. She reminded me of the pretty lady from the saloon."

"Saloon?"

Henry nodded, but could only manage a slight bob before letting his head swing along its normal course. "The golden-haired one. She . . . so pretty. Her friend was so pretty. I thought she missed me. They all screamed at me. Just like they did the first time I . . ." Henry's eyes shifted and his brow twitched. On anyone else the expression would have seemed vaguely contemplative. On Henry it looked as though a caterpillar was slowly crawling beneath the skin of his forehead. "I don't . . . I don't . . . I hear His voice now. I hear him!" Suddenly, Henry twitched and he flopped into his corner as if he meant to curl into a ball of filthy, knotted muscle. "God don't like it when I think too hard. Agoodmanobeyshis-LordandhonorsHimwithswiftstepswhenHecalls." In a voice that had suddenly cleared, Henry said, "I'm hungry. God will provide! Godwillprovide! I'm so hungry."

When he pulled himself to his feet, Paige shouted, "Henry, no! Stay here! Tell me about God!"

But her words were lost amid whatever else was swirling

through Henry's mind. He shoved past Cole and ran across the hall. Cole looked into the den and was just in time to see Henry squat beneath the hole leading outside and then jump straight up through it.

"Cole?" Paige called out from behind him. "Did he get away?"

"I sure as hell couldn't do much to stop him!"

"Grab one of those Half Breeds," she said as she anxiously patted Cole's chest, "and I'll help carry it to the car."

"You want to bring one of those dead things with us?"

"That's right. You made it this far, so don't punk out on me now. We need to get moving. Half Breeds only howl for a few minutes before they start hunting, and we need to make sure we don't lose sight of them." She made a straight line for the Half Breed directly beneath the entrance in the ceiling. "This one's perfect," she said while pointing to the werewolf carcass as if it was the prettiest Christmas tree in the lot. "Hand him up to me and we can get the car started before the rest of those things start running."

"What in the hell are you talking about?"

"Just do it!" she growled with more ferocity than the monsters outside.

Chapter 23

The phone in Cole's pocket chirped in its familiar way. Despite the squealing of the tires against the pavement and the dangerous pull of the steering wheel in his hands, he reflexively dug the phone from his pocket and flipped it open. Angrier at himself for answering the damn thing than he was at the actual ringing, he snarled, "Yeah. What is it?"

"You guys doubted me, but I found the place," Walter said from the other end of the line.

"What?"

"I'm in Janesville. I've been scouting all the parks all day long and I finally found one that fits my vision!"

Turning his head away from the phone, Cole announced, "Walter found his park."

Paige was in the backseat with the dead Half Breed across her lap. Although the werewolf had shrunken a bit since it was killed, it didn't shift all the way back to the putrid, gnarled thing it had been while it was asleep, and it was still a long ways from anything human.

"Great," Paige said as she pulled up a handful of the werewolf's fur and started cutting it away with her hunting knife. "That just gives us a fat load of nothing, since we've already found our own way to get to Misonyk."

Cole looked out the window at the stretch of I–39 he was currently using as his own personal autobahn. With the sun long gone and the full moon hanging overhead, the road was only illuminated by an occasional streetlight and the rare billboard. The pale light coming from the moon was enough to put a nice glow on Henry's back as he launched himself into the air to cover the ground at anywhere from ten to twenty yards per jump.

"Yeah," Cole said. "Paige says great job."

Walter dropped his voice until he was almost drowned out by the roar of the Cavalier's motor. "A bunch of Nymar are gathering, and it looks like one's in charge. He could be Misonyk. From what I can see, it looks like a lot of these guys are freshly turned."

Suddenly, another shape bolted from the side of the road and flashed into Cole's side mirror. The Half Breed was one of two others that had showed up to howl at the moon near the ruins of Lancroft's East Wing and had yet to stray too far from Henry. When the werewolves originally bolted from the mansion, they headed south. Although Henry stuck fairly close to I–39, the Half Breeds came and went like flickers of shadow across the surface of a choppy lake.

"We should be there pretty soon," Cole said. "Which park is it?"

"Palmer Park near I–39. You can't miss it. Just turn off at—"

Suddenly, one of the Half Breeds dashed across the interstate in front of the car. Cole had to pull the wheel hard to the right to avoid hitting the werewolf, which caused him to swerve almost directly into a roadblock of twisted muscle. Henry sat in the middle of Cole's lane. At the last second, Henry hopped back and swatted at the Cavalier as if the car was a pesky insect.

"What the hell are you doing?" Paige shouted. "I'm working with sharp objects back here!"

Cole gritted his teeth and swerved back onto the road. Henry leapt over the Cavalier to land a few yards ahead of it. The moment his feet hit the ground, he was running again. "Gotta call you back," Cole said into the phone before he flipped it shut and tossed it onto the passenger seat. Squinting into the rearview mirror, he made sure Paige hadn't cut anything that wasn't supposed to remain attached.

The backseat was all but filled with dead werewolf. The Half Breed's front two legs were wedged between Cole's seat and his door, the curved claws scraping against his left leg. Its hind legs were wedged in a similar fashion between the passenger seat and that door. Paige sat with her legs tucked beneath the carcass so her hands were free to work. The details of that work became a little clearer when Cole heard something that sounded like thick, wet canvas being ripped apart.

"You might want to crack the window," she said.

Before Cole could take a closer look, a smell hit him that made him regret that he had to breathe at all. "Good Lord!" he groaned as he lowered the window. "Are you cutting that thing open?"

"Just taking some of the fur," Paige said. "Skinner isn't just a clever name, you know."

"Jesus. I think I'm gonna puke."

"It's not as bad as all that. If you'd like a lesson in what makes a Half Breed tick, I could point a few things out for you."

"No thanks," Cole said as he twisted the wheel once again to avoid another of the Half Breeds. "I'm getting a good enough look for myself."

Paige glanced through the side window and then twisted around to look out the back. She cursed loudly and shook her head. "The rest of them are splitting off on their own," she said.

"Good! Maybe they'll stop trying to run me off the road!"

"Not good. Not good, at all. If they split off, they'll just go hunt somewhere else. We'll have to come back later to track them down."

Before Cole could think too much about that, he caught sight of Henry landing a ways ahead of him on the side of the road. Henry turned and hunkered down a bit, his eyes glittering in the glare of headlights before he sprung toward the car with his arms held wide open.

"Oh shit," Cole grunted. "Hang on!"

Fortunately, Paige didn't have much room to move. She

stretched her arms out and braced herself as Cole slammed his foot against the brake pedal to throw the Cavalier into a fishtail. He struggled to straighten the vehicle's course, but that didn't seem like such a great idea either.

Henry waited for him in the middle of the interstate. Swelling up to somewhere over seven feet tall, he lowered his shoulder and ran toward the car like a linebacker that had been deprived of red meat a month before Sunday's game. Focusing so much upon Henry and his fight with the steering wheel, Cole almost didn't notice that he was about to cross lanes and swerve into the path of an oncoming semi.

Spouting a blasphemous mixture of profanity and biblical references, he hit the gas, turned into his skid and steered across the other lane. He headed straight for the opposite shoulder and somehow managed to correct himself before going any farther. The semi rumbled past him while blaring its horn. Cole built up speed along the shoulder and looked for a chance to swerve back onto his own side of the road. There was another car behind the semi, which flipped on its blue and red lights as the entire car spun around to come after him.

"Of *course* it's a cop!" Cole shouted. "What the hell else would it be?"

Twisting to look out the back window again, Paige said, "I don't see a cop."

"He's making a U-turn and coming after me."

"Then just gun it and get back over. You've got plenty of time to lose him." With that, she sliced off another layer of fur and held it up so she could set it on top of the rest she'd collected.

For the first time, Cole got a clear look at what she was cutting. Although most of it was thick, wiry fur, it was attached to a thin layer of skin. Most likely, that explained the smell now filling the car. The actual werewolf carcass wasn't as butchered as he had expected. The spots where Paige had been cutting were marked by skin that looked more like bare, leathery parchment. "I thought you were skinning that thing," he said.

"The fur is what stops most of the bullets," Paige said.

"Deeper layers of skin are too tough to cut. How about you watch what you're doing and let me handle this?"

Cole swerved into the right lane and looked around for Henry. Between the werewolf being skinned in the backseat and the creature that was out to tackle his car, he found it somewhat difficult to focus on something as normal as steering. Seeing police lights flashing in his rearview mirror, he said, "That cop's catching up to us."

"It might be better if he did," Paige replied. "Half Breeds do enjoy their bright, shiny things."

Still watching the road behind him, Cole winced as he saw Henry veer off to rush the police car. Henry's shoulder slammed against the cruiser and knocked it several feet to one side. "Dammit!" Cole snarled as he slammed on his brakes.

"What the hell?" Paige shouted from the backseat.

Ignoring her, Cole put the Cavalier into reverse and got it rolling backward down the interstate. Paige kept cutting while leaning over to clear his line of sight. Pushing the reverse gear to its limit, Cole backed toward the damaged police car as fast as he could.

Henry had brought the cop to a halt and was slamming his fists against the officer's hood while bellowing wildly. When the cop fired a few shots at him, however, things took a turn for the worse. Henry screamed loud enough to be heard over the whine of the Cavalier's reverse gear and stampeded the police car to push it off the road completely.

Paige straightened up to look out the rear window, giving Cole another good view of the dead werewolf. Now that it was missing a good portion of its fur on one side, he could see the line of the creature's rib cage. Instead of the smooth ridges of bone, the Half Breed's ribs were dotted with bundles of ropy material at several places. Even with such a quick look, he didn't have trouble envisioning muscle or sinew bunched at those spots to hold the Half Breed's skeleton together.

Henry and the Cavalier's rear bumper collided with a jarring crunch, stopping the Cavalier in its tracks and nudging Henry a step or two away from the police car. Just as he thought Henry was about to fall over, Cole saw the hulking figure stagger off the shoulder of the road and then jump straight up. A dent almost as big as the Cavalier's hood buckled over Cole's head as Henry landed on top of the car. After that, Henry's gnarled, twisted hands began pounding against the windshield.

"All right!" Cole said as he put the car back into Drive. "Hang on!"

Paige lowered her head and braced herself as Cole hit the gas and got the car rolling forward.

"I've always wanted to shoot up through a car roof," Cole said. "Now's my big chance! Hand me a gun."

Shaking her head, Paige said, "If we could just shoot him, this wouldn't be such a— *Look out!*"

A muscular arm reached down to try and grab Cole through the driver's side window. Leaning in the opposite direction, Cole twisted the steering wheel back and forth to shake Henry loose. After a few attempts, Henry dropped down from the roof, hitting the pavement in an awkward heap.

The moment he found Henry in his rearview mirror, Cole watched him pull himself up and leap into the air. The twisted figure landed in front of the Cavalier with a heavy thump and then jumped farther down the road.

"He's headed south again," Cole said.

"Good. What about the Half Breeds?"

Cole looked around, but could only see a few scattered streetlights and a whole lot of inky blackness on either side of the road. "They're gone. Should I go check on that cop?"

"If they were close enough to hurt him, we would've seen them by now. Just keep following Henry."

"He's getting too far ahead!"

"Then just go to Janesville," Paige replied. "Looks like whatever is about to happen will be happening there. After all the grief I gave Walter about the massacre, I'll never hear the end of it if he's right."

Checking his rearview mirror as he stomped on the gas pedal, Cole asked, "You think there's gonna be a massacre?"

"Hopefully we'll be able to prevent it," she said. "Now that I got my hands on this little beauty here, we should stand a pretty good chance against Henry, Misonyk, and however many local Nymar he managed to scrounge up. After what he pulled at that diner, there's just as good a chance that those locals will be out to kill Misonyk too. If it's true that the lie's been shot down like your Mongrel girlfriend said, Misonyk and all the other Nymar must be getting ready for a fight."

"So what's the big lie?" Cole asked as he fixed his attention to the road and enjoyed the rush of fresh, cold air against his face. "Professional wrestling is really fake?"

"You know how the Nymar talk about their covens or clans or sects?" Paige asked. "They claim to rule Chicago and just about every other city worth ruling. They're supposed to patrol the streets and know about everything that happens while they live forever and rule from their skyscrapers."

"Yeah," Cole replied. "None of those guys can say two words without throwing that crap at you."

"That's the thing. It's crap. Every last word of it. The Nymar can barely hold together loose associations with each other. They might be able to manage a gang here and there, but that's about it. As far as holding a city . . . that's just a joke."

Cole waited a few seconds, glanced out the windows to see if they were being followed, then looked into the rearview mirror again. "That's it? That's the big lie?"

Paige chuckled as she took a folded bundle of black plastic from her bag. "That's all they need to keep anyone who finds out about them quiet. Some poor fool who got bitten starts to panic but shuts up if he thinks he's got to worry about some bunch of undead crime lords. Most humans are too frightened to go against one Nymar, but the thought of a whole society of them carries a lot of weight even with some very influential people."

"But from what I've seen, there *are* a whole lot of them," Cole pointed out.

"Sure, but they're not organized," Paige replied. "There are a whole lot of drug addicts too, but they're not about to get together and rule a city from the shadows. What it all comes down to is that Nymar are junkies. They're dangerous and more powerful than some poor schmuck who's hooked on crack, but they're still junkies. A few of them are craftier than the rest and some of them kill rather than just feed. Those are the ones we're after. I would've told you sooner, but I had to wait until I knew you were coming along for the whole ride."

Laughing as he passed a green mileage sign, he said, "That ride's almost over. Only about five more miles until we hit Janesville."

"You've got to realize how important it is that you don't talk about this where anyone else can hear," Paige said as if she was alone in a quiet room with Cole instead of talking from the back of a speeding car with a dead werewolf across her lap. "The Nymar's supposed infestation of the cities is what keeps the Full Bloods from making a move of their own."

"I've seen one of those things," Cole shot back. "You can't tell me they're afraid of Nymar."

"Maybe not afraid, but a whole swarm of Nymar can bring a Full Blood down if they do it just right. It's not pretty, but Nymar and werewolves are both supernatural and they can most definitely spill each other's blood," Paige said as she pulled a few of the Half Breed's teeth. "The Full Bloods stay in the woods because it's easier than trying to invade a city held by both humans and Nymar. Full Bloods may be damn near bullet-, fire-, and everything-else-proof, but Skinners and the Nymar are their only real threats. We figured out the Nymar's bluff some time ago, but if the Full Bloods bothered to do the same thing, they might just decide to take a run at the more populated parts of the world."

"I don't know," Cole said. "Sounds like a stretch to me."

"All right. What do you think would happen if all of America's enemies found out we'd made up three of the four branches of our military?"

Wincing, he muttered, "Point taken."

"The Nymar also think their bullshit has been keeping Skinners in line. For years they've thought that the only reason we haven't stormed in to clean them out is because we're afraid of going against the big, dark overlords." Paige spoke those last words with no small amount of sarcasm. "As long as they think they've got us snowed, they won't look hard enough at us to know they outnumber us by at least twenty to one."

"Same lie, different liars, huh?" Cole asked.

"It's not a great system, but it's been holding things together for a long time. If the Full Bloods and other shape-shifters aren't buying it anymore, it may just explain why they're getting so restless. Mongrels usually stick to their own packs, but now are prowling into your hotel room. Half Breeds don't obey any rules, but Full Bloods sure never bothered sneaking as far into civilization as the one I saw outside of Shimmy's."

"You're sure that was a Full Blood?"

"Yeah."

"And what are we going to do about Henry? You plan on gagging him with all that fur you collected?"

Paige let out a breath and began stuffing the werewolf fur into a casing that resembled two plastic trays held together by nylon straps. Considering the weight on her lap at the moment, the simple movements weren't easy. "I've got some ideas about him. Did you see any black markings on him anywhere?"

Even though it was difficult to focus, Cole had seen Henry enough times to have his face imprinted on his nightmares for a good long while. "Actually, no. Henry's pretty messed up, but not like the Nymar."

"And if there are a bunch of spores in him like you saw in that vision you snagged from Misonyk, then that would explain why Henry feeds off of other Nymar the way he does. If his own spores aren't attached to his heart, they can't feed on his blood. They must be leeching off of him for whatever food they can get."

"And so," Cole added as he swerved around a slow moving SUV with Iowa plates, "he's got to eat healthy Nymar spores that are filled with all the stuff they'd get if he fed the way Nymar are supposed to?"

"Exactly! Kind of like when you crave peas even though you hate peas and it turns out your body just needs whatever is in peas. Does that make sense?"

"It actually does," he replied. "And that scares me. Also, I'd really like some peas. But I don't know if you should take what I saw in that vision too seriously. For all I know, I could've been seeing whatever crap Misonyk was thinking at the time."

"Henry's a mix of Nymar and shapeshifter, all right. I was close enough that I could feel it." Paige had pulled apart the plastic plates and placed the Half Breed fur between them. Now that she was fastening the plates together, the whole thing looked like some sort of vest.

"Is that what I think it is?" Cole asked.

She grinned and nodded. Holding up the harness to show him, she said, "Standard level two body armor on either side, with a bit of goodness on the inside. Together, it'll stop a few bullets, uncharmed blades, and even withstand a hell of a lot of punishment from claws and teeth of the supernatural variety. There's a better way to put one of these together, but we don't have time. This should hold up well enough to get me through the night. Since Henry is probably on his way to Misonyk, and Misonyk is probably trying to take over this area, it's a safe bet that I'll be wading into a whole lot of trouble."

"I thought you said Nymar couldn't take anyplace over," Cole pointed out.

Paige shrugged and pulled the black plastic vest over her head. The two sets of black plates on front and back were sealed by a zipper, making it look like something worn by members of a SWAT team. She looked up and smiled at Cole in the rearview mirror. Even with all the layers of blood, sweat, and dirt coating her face, she still managed to look cute. "There's always some crazy bastard who wants to make a play for the big time. It doesn't mean they can actually pull it off. Chicago's got a knack for attracting men like that."

"Massacres and all," Cole replied as he steered for the on-coming exit. "Why don't the Nymar just take over the cities for real?" he asked. "I mean, they're fast and strong."

"Not fast and strong enough to go against the butt-load of guns that would be pointed at them by cops or the military if they made a move like that. Besides, there's just not enough of them. If there's one thing the Nymar know, it's math. They need human blood to replace the blood their own spores burn up, so they need to keep humans around. They're no better at internal power struggles than humans are, so the best solution is to keep their numbers limited."

"Did you say 'butt load'?" Cole asked

Paige shrugged and shared a laugh with him. "Technical term. You'd better get Walter on the phone."

He slowed down while reaching over for the phone. After Walter picked up, Cole hit the button for the phone's speaker and held it near the rearview mirror so everyone could have a nice little chat.

"Where the hell are you guys?" Walter asked.

"Almost there," Cole replied.

"Has Henry showed up yet?" Paige asked.

Even though they were at opposite ends of the digital connection, Cole swore he could picture the expression on Walter's face. "He's supposed to be here and you're not?" Walter snarled. "I'm not a fucking Skinner, remember? I'm doing this as a favor. I'm not about to hold off an army of vampires along with some freak job that rips through bodies like toilet paper! Have you checked your laptop lately? That diner's on the news! There's pictures on the Internet! They're saying there was a grease fire, but I know dead Nymar when I see them. I should've known better than to put my ass on the line like this. Skinners attract this kind of gruesome crap like—"

"Take a breath," Paige said. "We're not going to leave you there on your own. In fact, we're almost there! Will you at least be able to cover us from a distance? You still have that rifle, don't you?"

After a pause, Walter said, "Yeah, but who's gonna cover me?"

"I will," Cole said. Noticing how Paige looked right back at him with genuine surprise on her face, he said to her, "Thought I'd save you the hassle of volunteering me."

She smiled and rubbed his shoulder. "We won't forget this, Prophet," she said to the phone.

"Just don't forget about my cut of that bounty money. In fact, I should get a bigger cut! And you'll still owe me for this no matter how much cash you throw my way."

"You got it," Paige replied without hesitation. "What's the situation there right now?"

For a moment, Cole thought Walter might have hung up. Then a heavy sigh crackled over the speaker and Walter said, "The pale kids are still drifting in to some sort of meeting. You should have a little time before anything happens, but that might all change once Henry gets here. I'll show you where to make your entrance and then hang back to cover you. If things get too hot, I'm out of there. You two can have your blaze of glory."

After Walter rattled off a quick set of directions, the connection was cut and Cole snapped the phone shut. Now he just needed to refrain from thinking about what was left to be done, and he might just make it to Janesville without getting sick.

Chapter 24

Upon driving into Janesville, Cole followed Walter's directions and stopped along the side of the road within sight of the interstate. Palmer Park was directly ahead of them, lit by moonlight that fell onto the treetops like dusty snow. Leaning against the Cavalier's trunk, Cole surveyed the area. Even though Janesville seemed like a nice enough place, something about it struck him as odd. It took a few moments for him to put his finger on the cause of that feeling, but he eventually did. "It's so quiet," he said.

Paige sat on the ground with her back against the bumper, Cole's weapon across her lap. The werewolf carcass was still in the backseat, but had been covered with an old wool Army surplus blanket. Having retrieved something she'd cooked up back at the Lancroft estate, she was now adding another ingredient and swirling the mixture in a Tupperware bowl. She looked around and replied, "We're in dairy country. Did you expect Mardi Gras?"

"No, but it's not that late. So far, I've only seen a few cars and nobody out walking around. I don't care where you are, there's always *someone* out doing *something*."

"It always gets like this when too many of them get together."

"Them? You mean Nymar?"

"Nymar, shapeshifters, especially werewolves. People

may not know about all of those things. They may not even
believe in them. But when too many predators get too close,
there's something in the back of every animal's head that
tells them to stay where it's safe."

Looking into the bowl in Paige's hand, he asked, "Is that
blood?"

"Yep."

"Blood from that Half Breed?"

She nodded. "Hand me a towel."

The trunk was ajar, and Cole turned so he could reach into
the gym bag at the top of the pile. The first towel he could
find was a familiar white bundle of starched cotton.

"Not that one," she said. "That's got the invisible Mongrel
stuff in it. Try one of the blue ones."

There would have been a time, not too long ago, when
hearing someone refer to an invisible anything would have
raised his eyebrows. Now he simply dug around until he
found the blue towel. Once he handed it over, he watched
Paige dip it into the mixture and apply it to the thorns on
his weapon as if the stuff was just another kind of dark red
varnish.

"Is that what makes your weapons change shape?" he
asked.

Without looking up from what she was doing, Paige said,
"That's right, but don't get excited. It takes a lot more than
one coat before you'll see so much as a twitch."

"Shouldn't I be watching how you do that?"

"I'll show you when we have more time. You'll be doing
this a lot. What you need to do, though, is hold this weapon
so these thorns actually break those soft little computer boy
hands of yours. You'll need to get used to it. Don't worry,"
she added, gently rubbing his arm before handing over his
weapon. "This is one of the oldest Skinner rituals there is.
The kinks have been worked out over the last couple hundred years or so."

Cole flipped the weapon around a few times. It seemed
lighter and more balanced. He placed his hands over the
thorns and thought about trying to drive them into his palms
right then and there, just to get it over with. The first time

had been an accident, but the thought of doing the deed on purpose hit a block in his head that prevented him from following through.

It was simple. All he needed to do was grab hold of that weapon and tighten his grip enough to drive sharp pieces of wood through his flesh.

Nothing to it.

The longer he kept his hands on top of those thorns, the sharper they felt. Before he could force himself to kick down that mental roadblock, another vehicle rolled up alongside Paige's Cavalier. It was Walter's van.

Walter pushed open his door, hopped out and walked over to them. Pointing toward the park, he announced, "There's a bunch of Nymar gathering at an old parking garage off Palmer Drive. A few of them headed up north toward Ruger Avenue, but most of them are staying in the park. Misonyk and his bodyguards went inside the garage a while ago and haven't come out yet. Some big freak that looked like a messed-up Full Blood jumped in all the way from the interstate. I'm guessing that's your Henry."

"Sounds like it. How do you know he's part Full Blood?" Paige asked.

"I've tracked a few in my day," Walter said. "This thing's got the same build and the same power in his stride. Whatever he is, he sure as hell doesn't have the smarts of a Full Blood."

Nodding quickly to what Walter told her, Paige asked, "And you're sure about the rest?"

"As sure as I could be, considering how much time I had to do the job. Janesville is a nice town, but not a very big one. Even if those pale kids move, it shouldn't take long for you to pick up on them. So what's the plan?"

"Real simple," she replied. "We're going in to pay Misonyk a visit before he can set Henry loose on the Nymar in this town as well as any humans who don't clear Henry's path. Misonyk seems to be controlling Henry through some sort of mental link, so killing Misonyk should cut that link."

"What then?" Cole asked.

"If I can find a way to stuff enough antidote down Henry's

throat to kill anything Nymar inside of him, I should be able to take him down like any other shapeshifter."

"Should?" Cole asked. "Have you ever fought a Full Blood without another experienced Skinner helping you out?"

Paige tightened the straps holding her body armor in place and then proceeded to check the rest of her equipment. "No, but unless you've got a better idea, that's all I've got." When the armor was situated, she removed a revolver from the trunk and handed it to Cole along with plenty of spare ammo. "These bullets were treated with Nymar antidote," she said. "It'll hurt them, but it won't kill them unless you get a direct hit in the spot where the spore's attached to their heart. You have the right ammunition for that rifle of yours, Prophet?"

Walter nodded.

"Good. These things look tough, Cole, but it all boils down to bringing the right tool for the job. We've got the right tools, now we just need to do the job."

"Are you sure that vest will hold up?" he asked.

"Oh, yeah," she said as she knocked her fist against the re-inforced section of the harness. "This is where we honor the spirit of the person who was killed when they were turned into a Half Breed. This is where we take the power from one monster and shove it right down the throat of another."

Just when Cole thought he'd seen the extent of how twisted his world had become, another layer had been stripped away.

"Crazy but effective," Walter said with a shake of his head. "That's a Skinner for ya."

Chapter 25

The parking garage looked like something that had been built on a whim and then left to be used for graffiti practice. It was three levels of weathered concrete, covered with more than enough spray paint to keep anyone from thinking they'd ever get their car back after being stupid enough to park it there.

Poorly lit and closed in by metal grates over the main entrance, it was situated in the middle of Palmer Park, which was about 150 yards from the tree Walter had picked for his perch. During the warmer months, it would have been next to impossible to watch the garage from that spot. But since the branches were bare and the moon was full, Walter had a pretty good view once he climbed into a tree. There was nobody else in that section of the park at the moment, lending credence to the theory that the locals were following their natural instinct to give the predators some room. Cole knew that instinct was very real, because it currently screamed inside his head like a maladjusted car alarm.

"I don't like Paige going in alone like this," he said as he paced back and forth beneath Walter's tree. "I should be with her. I'm her partner."

Walter sat no more than six feet off the ground, which was more than high enough since there were only dead branches to obstruct his view of the garage. Most of his weight was supported by a thick branch, and he sat with one leg dangling against the trunk. "She knows what she's doing," he said as he peered through the scope of the Brown Precision Tactical Rifle.

"I know she does, but I should still be there to help."

"You are helping." Walter kept glancing over his scope and through it again so he could make minor adjustments to the lenses and the angle of the sights. "By covering me, I don't need to look away from this scope, which means I'll be able to cover her. I'm sure she'd rather have it this way than needing to worry about you."

The whole town seemed to be asleep. When he looked around the park, Cole saw nothing but frosted grass, bare branches, a few benches, and a locked public restroom.

Staring through the scope, Walter asked, "Do you see Paige yet?"

Cole focused his attention on the road leading up to the parking structure. Although he'd seen her heading that way a while ago, there was no trace of her now. He told Walter as much and continued pacing around the tree.

"Just let me know the minute she shows. I'll keep an eye on the garage. It doesn't look like there's much of anything going on there either. I count at least four Nymar inside. Possibly five. There's more than that sneaking around, though."

"What are they doing?" Cole asked. "Is it some kind of meeting?"

Walter shook his head without moving it more than a centimeter in either direction. "I just track 'em and point you guys in the right direction."

"Why even do that much?" Cole asked.

This time Walter did look away from his scope, to fix his eyes on Cole. "Excuse me?"

"I kind of got pulled into this, but nobody forced me to stay. If you don't want any part of it, why don't you just leave?"

Slowly, Walter shifted his eyes back to the scope. "I spent a good amount of time in law enforcement, so maybe I'm no stranger to seeing hopeless situations. A man's gotta do what he can."

"So why not be a Skinner?" Cole asked.

Walter shifted against his branch. "I've also seen plenty of men think they could save the world and only wind up getting chewed up and spit out by it. If a man gets lucky a few times and survives a few bad calls, he gets cocky. Once he gets cocky, he gets killed. Think whatever you want about me, but you Skinners must be awfully cocky to keep going against these creatures. Learning about them is one thing. Pissing them off on purpose is another."

"Yeah? Well . . ." Cole tried to put together a good comeback but could only grumble, "That actually makes sense."

After a few quiet seconds, Walter asked, "What about you? From what I've heard, you were there to see what happened to Gerald and Brad. If it was a Full Blood, it couldn't have been a pretty sight."

"It wasn't, but I survived because of them. Gerald asked me to do him a favor and I wasn't about to refuse. After that . . . I don't know. Things just sort of fell into place."

Walter smirked and nestled his cheek against the side of his rifle. "See what I mean? I've seen it with Skinners just as much as I've seen it with cops. They luck out of a few bad situations and they think they're untouchable."

"Lucky?" Cole asked. "If I was lucky, I'd be back home, playing my games, secure in the knowledge that werewolves and vampires were just cool characters in them. I've already seen enough to blow that to hell, so now I've got to do something about it."

"You do, huh?"

"Yeah," Cole said reflexively. He took a moment to think it over and then nodded again. "I do. If I left now, I'd only feel guilty every time I heard about some wild animal attack or bizarre murder on the news. I'd wonder if it was one of those creatures that did it, and then I'd wonder if I could've kept it from happening."

"You won't be able to prevent all the killing, you know."

"Sure, but I can try."

Shifting to get more comfortable in his spot, Walter said, "I suppose we all just gotta do what we can. Right now you gotta keep your eyes open because one of the Nymar is talking to a few others inside that garage."

"Is it Misonyk?" Cole asked anxiously.

"Big bald guy with black marks running up to the top of his head?"

"Yeah," Walter said. "And it looks like he's about to step outside."

"Shit," Cole snapped. "I can see a bunch of them walking toward the front of the garage. Paige is approaching from the other side of the building."

Already shifting his aim to the wide entrance of the parking structure, Walter nestled the rifle's stock against his shoulder and adjusted his cheek in its spot beside the scope. "I see them."

"What should I do?"

"You know what to do! Paige can take care of herself. Just keep your eyes open for anyone coming at us and I'll let you know when I hear from her."

Although he wasn't the one who got to use the sniper rifle, Cole wasn't completely overlooked in the firearms department. The revolver he'd been given was a .44 loaded with rounds that had dark streaks running through them, making them strangely similar to their intended targets. He checked again to make sure the revolver was loaded, then dropped the .44 back into the holster under his arm. He then picked up his wooden weapon, which had been leaning against a tree, and held it like a spear. There was nobody close enough to be of much concern to him or Walter, so he held the spear with his fingers around the barbs. There would be plenty of time to bleed later.

Paige walked up to the parking structure and immediately spotted the reception committee that was headed toward the front entrance. From within the garage, several men and a few women pushed on the metal grate so they could slip through a gap where it had fallen off the track built into the cement doorway.

The men and women who swarmed toward the garage were extremely pale, which meant they were hungry. Their markings were gray, skinny threads stretching beneath their flesh and extending all the way to their hands and up to their chins. The Nymar were definitely fresh kills. Their spores had settled in, but were still stretching out to probe theirs new hosts.

"Here they come," Paige said just loud enough for her voice to be picked up by her earpiece. "They're freshly infected. Looks like Misonyk has been expecting trouble."

"I got 'em," he replied. "Just try to draw them out into the open so I can get a clear shot."

The shotgun in her hands was a pump action that could hold half a dozen specially packed shells. She pumped the first round into the chamber, put the shotgun to her shoulder and aimed at the closest target.

"Where's Misonyk?" she shouted. "He and Henry are all we want."

The Nymar approaching the garage stopped and looked at Paige while flashing fangs that were still bloody from cutting through their gums for the first time. Despite their tough act, they were obviously taken aback by the fact that she wasn't scared by their display. The first woman to crawl through the grate was a bit taller than Paige and had skin the color of ash. She looked at Paige with wild, hungry eyes and opened her mouth to hiss and show the set of thinner upper fangs next to her primary ones. Her markings were darker and thicker, which meant she'd been infected a lot longer than most of the others in the vicinity.

"Misonyk is beyond your reach!" the ashen woman screeched. "He controls the Full Bloods and soon he'll control the Nymar."

"Where is he?"

"Protecting us. Teaching us."

"You think so?" Paige asked. "Maybe you should ask the Chicago Nymar about how much bullshit Misonyk's feeding you."

The ashen woman scowled defiantly. "We have all seen the power from drinking souls. We will spread from this city and bring true unity to all of our kind!"

Although Paige listened to what the Nymar woman was saying, she was distracted by what was just inside the garage. Stacked up against a booth where parking fees had once been collected, there was a pile of bodies in clothing ranging from uniforms to mismatched coats and boots. Since the bodies weren't much more than dried husks, she knew these Nymar had been making good on Misonyk's threats.

"Misonyk has shared his memories of you with us," the ashen woman said. As she spoke, the other Nymar grinned as if they were all in on a private joke. "If you start running now, you might just get away before we catch you. I still don't know if you'll ever be able to outrun the Full Bloods when he calls them down like a—"

Without so much as a wince, Paige pulled her trigger and fired a thundering blast into the woman's head. Since the Nymar had closed the distance between herself and Paige to less than ten feet, the shotgun blast nearly decapitated her. She fell to the ground and writhed as the Nymar within her slithered out the gaping hole at the top of her neck. The eel-like creature made it less than a foot before it had absorbed all the fluids in the woman's body in a useless effort to heal the grievous wound. Once the fluids were gone, the body cracked like a section of desert floor.

Paige ejected the spent round and pumped in another. More Nymar sped through the break in the entrance grate and then scattered to flank her. The new arrivals who'd been approaching the garage from the outside moved erratically rather than coming at her head-on. Instead of wasting a round in trying to catch another head shot, Paige lowered her aim and fired into the middle of the crowd streaming from the garage. The shotgun pellets tore through two of the closest Nymar and then spread out to rip into a few more behind them. The pale faces constricted with shock and pain as antidote-infused lead shredded them, but their bodies were already knitting back together.

Nymar rushed at Paige from both sides as she managed to fire two more shells at them. The first one missed completely, but the second knocked one man down. The color of his skin was a bit darker, but that was merely a remnant of his living visage. As the Nymar healed, his skin paled and he became hungrier. When he caught sight of Paige, he ran at her twice as fast, and was dropped by a high-powered round that had been fired from an entirely different section of the park.

"Thanks, Walter," Paige said as she swung the shotgun so

its stock caught a Nymar in the side of the head. The undead man recovered quickly and lunged forward to bite her neck. She dropped to one knee, pulled her clubs from the sides of her boots and rolled backward before anyone got close.

"I'm going after her!" Cole shouted.

Walter levered a fresh round into his rifle and sighted through the scope. "You do that and you'll leave me open. Stick to the plan."

"But Paige is outnumbered!"

"You guys are always outnumbered," Walter replied as he calmly fired another shot.

Cole was debating on whether he should argue or just run for the parking structure. Both options were pushed aside when he spotted movement in the corner of his eye. He looked over to find two shapes racing toward him from the surrounding shadows. All this time, he thought he'd had a good feel for the park. Now he felt as if he'd just been dropped into alien territory. "Someone's coming," he said.

Walter's reply was as calm as it was stern. "Just don't let them get to me." He didn't so much as glance down at Cole, even as the impact of feet upon cold grass rumbled through the ground.

Misonyk and one of the muscular bodyguards from Shimmy's scrambled forward in a low crouch. The bodyguard snarled while extending his arms and balling up thick, meaty fists. As he approached, Misonyk showed Cole a wide smile, complete with both sets of fangs protruding from his upper jaw.

"So you have chosen to stand your ground," he said as he glanced at the weapon in Cole's hands. "I'm always happy to send another Skinner from this world." He then shifted his eyes toward Walter and snarled, "Kill him before he fires another shot!"

The bodyguard ran toward Cole, but leapt into the air at the last moment.

Shifting his grip to hold onto his weapon more like a golf club, Cole swung the spear upward and snagged the bodyguard's foot with the two points at the bottom of the grip.

That was enough to divert the airborne Nymar's course and bounce him off the trunk of the tree next to Walter's.

Walter kept the rifle to his shoulder and fired whenever a target presented itself. If he had any doubts regarding Cole's ability to protect him, he didn't voice them.

Tightening both fists around his weapon the way Paige had shown him, Cole swung in a low arc that cut across Misonyk's ankles. The blow caught the Nymar by surprise, but only caused him to stumble back half a step. Then he straightened and lashed out with one hand. The Nymar's nails were short, jagged, and sharp enough to slice through the air like tempered steel. Cole leaned back to avoid getting eviscerated and saw Misonyk's other arm coming straight down toward his face.

It was nothing but reflex that brought both of Cole's arms up to block the incoming swing with his weapon. Misonyk's fist landed like a sledgehammer, sending a shockwave all the way up to Cole's shoulders while also burying the weapon's thorns into his palms. At first Cole felt numb, then the pain hit him in a white hot explosion that caused his vision to blur around the edges. Gritting his teeth, he pulled one end of the weapon back while pushing the other end forward to drive the twin spearheads into Misonyk's midsection.

Misonyk hopped backward while pressing a hand against the bloody gashes that had been torn across his stomach. As he bared all three sets of his fangs, the muscles in his jaw strained as if every one of his teeth were separate entities that hungered for Cole's blood.

Cole's rage grew as those thorns pulled and twisted within his hands. When he caught the bodyguard approaching Walter's tree, he was glad to have another target on which to vent some of the fire that had been sparked within him.

The bodyguard bent at the knees and launched himself toward Walter's legs with both hands open. In doing so, he left himself open for the impact of the single spearhead that Cole drove all the way up between his ribs. The Nymar opened his mouth to scream, but only half a grunt came out. The bodyguard's arms and legs flailed, losing their grip on the tree.

Cole drove him to the ground and pulled the sharpened end of his spear free, just as Misonyk's arms wrapped around him from behind. With the fire still raging through him, Cole twisted his upper body back and forth until he gained some leverage. At the first cold touch of Misonyk's deadly lower fangs against his throat, he leaned forward and drove the lower end of his weapon down and back to take a chunk out of Misonyk's right shin. As Misonyk cursed and fell back, the bodyguard rose up to renew his attack. Cole pulled one hand free so he could draw the .44 and fired several shots into the bulkier Nymar.

The gun slipped within Cole's bloody hand, but his target was nearly at point-blank range. Each bullet knocked the bodyguard farther back and kept him off balance. Even as the .44 was still bucking against his palm, Cole could see the bodyguard's wounds closing up like little, toothless mouths puckering beneath the holes that had been blasted through the Nymar's clothes. Finally, he fired a round that glanced off the big man's head and sent him spinning on one heel and flopping to the ground. Cole knew better than to assume the bodyguard was dead, but the Nymar was obviously stunned. Turning back around, he reflexively fired his last round when he saw Misonyk fly at him like something launched straight out of hell.

His shot caught Misonyk in the chest and tore open a gaping wound, but didn't do much to slow the Nymar. Misonyk knocked him down and dug his claws into the fabric of his jacket. As he wrapped his hand around the barrel of the .44, steam erupted with a noisy hiss as heated metal met bare skin. Without showing the slightest reaction from the burn, he yanked the .44 from Cole's grasp and tossed it away.

Jagged fingernails scraped against Cole's chest as Misonyk pushed him down. What worried Cole more was the strength behind those fingers, which was enough to hold him against the grass without any hope of wriggling free.

Gritting his teeth, he brought his weapon around to hit Misonyk in the ribs. For the first time, he was thankful for the thorns connecting the weapon to his hand. Without them, he would have surely lost his grip on the specially treated spear. One of the two sharpened points dug into Misonyk's side, landing within inches of the first wound Cole had given him. The Nymar bared his teeth like a wounded animal and swiped at Cole's face, but quickly pulled his hands back to protect him-

self from the next swing. Cole turned his head when he saw
the Misonyk's jagged nails slashing toward him, and he felt the
breeze as those claws passed less than an inch from his cheek.

Since the bodyguard was still pulling himself up and Misonyk was backing away, Cole scrambled to his feet and gripped
the spear in both hands. "Walter! How's Paige?" he asked
quickly.

Walter fired another shot and reached into his jacket
pocket for more ammunition. "You don't want to know."

The newly infected Nymar knew how to bite and snarl,
but they were still uncomfortable in their own skins. Their
spores had yet to spread fully throughout their bodies, which
meant they were slow to recover after taking the damage
Paige was dishing out.

She held a club in each hand and kept her stance low. The
weapon in her right hand had shifted into a sickle, while the
other had extended into a stake with a sharpened point on
either end. That way, she could hit one Nymar after another
in a series of quick, flowing movements. After putting one
of them down with a stab to the chest, she managed to crack
a few skulls with the side of her other weapon. Walter had
dropped a few of the Nymar, killing at least two, but that left
plenty more for Paige to contend with.

They came at her in waves, flailing madly with claws that
were too new to be sharp but still strong enough to shred
through the layers of clothing protecting her arms, neck, and
back. Only a few of those claws were quick enough to cut
her skin. The rest were deflected by her weapons or scraped
along the protective black body armor. She didn't even feel
the attacks that bounced against her torso, thanks to the
layer of werewolf hide, which was strong enough to make
Half Breeds among the most feared animals in creation.

Most of the Nymar relied upon their bare hands or a few
small weapons to attack Paige. A few bullets whipped past
her or slammed into her vest, but Walter focused his aim on
the Nymar who'd brought guns. Paige remained in motion
so she could always attack, while also making herself a difficult target to hit. As soon as she spotted a Nymar who had

thick, muscular arms marked by the gray tendrils beneath his skin, she bent down low and raked her sickle against the back of his knees, cutting his hamstring and sending him to the ground. She then buried the sharp end of her double-ended stake into the heart of another attacker, a blow that landed perfectly and put a look of stark terror onto the Nymar's face. Its eyes shifted from those of a hungry demon to a tired victim grateful to be released from the twisted shell that had once been his own body.

Suddenly, the Nymar all jerked their heads around as if they were hearing something well out of Paige's range. She scrambled away from the group and was barely able to brace herself before Henry leapt from the top of the garage to land with the crunch of bare feet against broken pavement. He pulled himself mostly upright and then took in as much of his surroundings as his wobbling head would allow.

Henry opened his mouth and let out a loud groan. Just then, a bullet from Walter's rifle whipped through the air and snapped Henry's head around. Since the fresh Nymar seemed to be more scared of Henry than of Paige, they scattered like a flock of birds flushed from the same bush. That bit of motion was enough to catch Henry's eye, and he pounced on the first one that got within his reach. Consumed by a pained frenzy, he ripped open the hapless Nymar's chest in one swipe.

Paige knocked aside the fleeing Nymar and summoned the will needed to change the shape of the stake until it curled around into another sickle. While Henry crouched over his dinner, Paige rushed at him with both weapons held at the ready.

Henry reared up. The Nymar spore he'd pulled from the man on the ground still hung from his mouth as he swung a fist at Paige. She ducked under the powerful swing and sank one of her blades into Henry's thigh. After that, it was all she could do to hang on for the ride.

Henry spun around like a dog chasing its tail and kept swinging at Paige, who was attached to him by the weapon embedded in his muscle. She twisted and ducked while his own movements kept her out of his reach. All the while, he kept gnawing on the oily black thing between his teeth. Hanging on as best she could, Paige tried to get the impaled weapon to shift again. Before she could do so, Henry's ape-like hand slapped against her arm and knocked her away with enough force to rip the weapon from his own flesh.

Henry staggered and rubbed at his eyes. The color drained from his face as he stared directly at Paige and groaned, "Hungry." Then he clamped a hand around her throat. He'd moved so fast that she didn't even realize he had her until her feet were off the ground and her back was being slammed against the wall of the parking structure.

"He's got her!" Walter shouted as he fired, worked the rifle's lever, and fired again. When Misonyk's bodyguard pulled himself up, Walter quickly worked the rifle's lever, lowered his aim and pulled the trigger. The round exploded from the rifle at such a high rate of speed that it cut through the body-guard like a laser beam.

The bodyguard stared up at Walter with one good eye and another that had just been turned into a messy hole. He opened his mouth to bite down on Walter's leg, but instead felt the stock of Walter's rifle crack against the bloody hole in his eye socket. Dropping to his knees and pressing both hands to his face, the bodyguard howled in pain and fought to regain his senses.

Cole kept his eyes on Misonyk, but also caught sight of an-other shape rushing in from the darkness. He didn't have to look over there to know that the burly figure was the second muscle-bound bodyguard coming to join his master. With Misonyk closing in on him, Cole reached into his jacket for one of the antidote syringes Paige had given him. Although he was fairly quick on the draw, Misonyk knocked the sy-ringe from his hand in a blur of motion. Before Cole could reach for another syringe, Misonyk extended his arm and slashed at his jacket, tearing away that entire pocket.

"You disgust me," Misonyk said as he threw the syringes to the ground and stomped them under his heel. "Chicago is practically mine and I took this place over in a matter of days. Now that Henry has provided some wolves to fight for my cause, I'll be able to make every last one of you sadistic, godless Skinners pay for the pain you've caused."

Listening to the howls and screams coming from the parking structure, Cole expected to hear sirens or some other sign of a police presence. Instead it seemed as if the entire town was curled up and ignoring the battle being waged within its boundaries.

"Henry will feed and allow me to claim this city for my own," Misonyk growled. "He should be done with that bitch of yours before my partners have finished dealing with this town's police."

"And maybe you and that big, crazy hunchback of yours should lie down in another hospital room so you can whisper in each other's ears," Cole replied. It wasn't his best insult, but it was good enough to get an angry twitch from Misonyk. "Then you can play God all you want with the one person on this planet that's crazy enough to believe you."

He could see that his words prickled against Misonyk's skin. The corners of the Nymar's eyes kept twitching and his lip jerked upward as if it had been hooked by a fishing line. He walked toward Cole slowly, but snapped his hand out to grab the weapon in Cole's hands and take it away as if he were disarming a small child. When Cole turned and started running toward the car, Misonyk laughed.

"I admit, I didn't think you'd take me up on my offer to run," he said. "The Skinners must surely have fallen since the days when Jonah Lancroft was among them. Or perhaps that was a fluke. Perhaps you have always been an order of morbid braggarts who pick at carcasses and then strut about as if they are to be feared."

Cole made it to the car and got the trunk open. Knowing he wouldn't have much time to work, he rummaged through the towels stuffed on top of Paige's cases. He took out the plastic retainer case she'd given him, opened it and managed to find the thing he was after. His hands worked feverishly as blood from his palms soaked into the white towel. Within seconds he could hear footsteps behind him that were quick enough to have come from a rat scrambling across a hardwood floor.

"My offer was for you to run, Skinner," Misonyk practically whispered into his ear. "Not for you to dig out another toy to be used against me." Grabbing Cole by the shoulder and spinning him around, he looked to the second bodyguard and growled, "Search him."

Cole raised his arms high over his head and dropped Paige's towel. Looking past the two Nymar, he saw Walter still in his perch, glancing nervously back at him. He looked away from Walter as the bodyguard roughly patted him down.

"I cannot abide a coward," Misonyk sneered.

The bodyguard's fangs extended from his gums, and the muscles in his jaw twitched with the anticipation of sinking all three sets into fresh meat. No venom dripped from the slender set of fangs, making it clear he wanted Cole to spend his last moments kicking and flailing.

"Did you ever tell any of your followers how much you cried when you were laying on your back on Lancroft's floor?" Cole asked before the bodyguard could get any closer.

With a subtle motion from Misonyk, the bodyguard froze.

The air was cold against Cole's face, and the chaotic sounds from the garage rumbled through the park. Sirens and gunshots finally echoed from farther down the street. Cole even thought he could hear tires squealing and people shouting, but that was just background static. As Misonyk leaned in closer, Cole's ears filled with the pounding of his own heart mixed with the mad Nymar's voice.

"What . . . did you say?" Misonyk asked ominously.

"I saw your memories," Cole said in the steadiest voice he could manage. "I saw how you laid on that floor with Lancroft's spear in your chest, crying like a little . . . like a little bitch every time Lancroft or one of his men would do whatever the hell they wanted to you." Even though he somehow got his words out, Cole thought his own nervousness might overtake him. Sweat pushed out of his face when he added, "I'll bet you liked it. Maybe that's why you want to find more Skinners. Maybe you just miss the days when Lancroft would—"

Misonyk's hand clamped around his throat in the space between heartbeats. Jagged claws pressed against his windpipe, turning Cole's head so he was forced look directly into the Nymar's twitching eyes. Cole let out a breath that caused his body to droop within Misonyk's grasp. That way, he was able to line up his left hand with the thick black tendril that ran beneath Misonyk's skin and reached all the way to the top of his scalp. Then, using every bit of strength he had, Cole delivered a single blow to Misonyk's neck.

The Nymar hadn't seen it coming.

Wincing at the quick pinch in his neck, Misonyk looked down at Cole's fist. Something shimmered within Cole's grasp, as if the pale moonlight had wrapped around it instead of shining directly upon it. Only when he shoved away from Cole did Misonyk see his own black, oily blood dripping from the end of a needle that appeared to hover in the air beneath Cole's fist.

"What? What's . . . ?" Misonyk stammered as he reached for the aching spot in his neck.

Cole knew he should run, but he couldn't resist holding his arm out and wiping away the greasy residue that he'd smeared onto the antidote-filled syringe from his emergency kit in the scant moments before Misonyk had gotten to the car. If those towels with the Mongrel substance hadn't been at the top of the pile in the trunk, he might not have had enough time to fully cover the thin plastic tube. Fortunately, Paige had collected more than enough from the trashed hotel room.

Misonyk's hand twitched, and Cole was just fast enough to slap it away before it could close around his throat. The Nymar leaned his head back and started to let out a pained grunt, but quickly began to gag on the venom he'd collected in his mouth. Coughing and staggering a few more steps, Misonyk dropped to his knees and grabbed the earth beneath him as the distant sirens grew louder.

Hacking up a strained laugh, Misonyk said, "The wheels are . . . already turning. I am the only one who could . . . control the fire that has been lit. And when your authorities arrive, the monkeys you try to protect will . . . throw you into a cage . . . just as they did to me."

Walter had climbed down from his perch and walked up to Cole while keeping his rifle trained on the remaining bodyguard. "He's right. There's a bunch of cops headed this way. Whatever was distracting them before isn't holding them back anymore."

"And they will . . . find bodies," Misonyk promised. "Here and . . . more in the years to come."

Although still holding his head up, Misonyk was losing the strength to keep it there. Death wrapped its arms around him, starting at the spot where the antidote had entered the vein in his neck. A pale gray shadow spread throughout his body while draining the moisture from Misonyk's skin. The thick black markings beneath the Nymar's flesh dulled like paint left too long in the unforgiving elements. A faltering breath escaped Misonyk's throat and the tendrils dwindled into thin, quivering lines.

Since he'd dropped the syringe and didn't have another to replace it, Cole picked up his double-ended spear and faced the remaining Nymar.

The bodyguard stalked forward, but as his employer crumpled to the ground like a broken cement statue, he backed away from Cole so he could run into another section of the park.

Turning to Walter, Cole asked, "What's going on with Paige?"

Walter had his rifle reloaded and against his shoulder. "There's enough cop cars headed toward this park to form a parade," he said while pointing his scope toward a part of town that had suddenly become very active. "Looks like they're chasing someone. Aw, hell! Someone's already firing back at them!" Placing a finger to his earpiece, he spoke in a quick rush. "Paige? Can you hear me?"

Henry held Paige against the garage in a way that prevented the other Nymar from getting to her. Then again, the other Nymar weren't her main concern.

"Hungry," Henry groaned as he sniffed the oily blood on her neck and the front of her jacket. "So . . . hungry." With that, he slammed her even harder against the wall. His claws scraped against her torso and his teeth gnashed against her stomach in a flurry that peeled away the outer layers of body armor before getting to the thin layer of werewolf hide beneath it. The Half Breed fur absorbed some punishment from Henry's attacks, but more of the impacts were getting through the heavy plates that lay against her body.

A voice drifted through Paige's head that made her wonder if Henry was doing more damage than she'd originally thought. She slammed the side of one weapon against Henry's temple in a blow that would have dropped most men. He reeled a bit from the impact but quickly recovered. When a freshly turned Nymar got bold enough to try and tear off a piece of Paige for himself, Henry slapped him away like he was swatting a fly. Paige took advantage of the small opening to deliver a blow to Henry's other temple with her left weapon. It didn't do any damage, but moved him back just enough for her to pull away and use her clubs.

The scent of Nymar blood was thick in the air as she used the sharpened ends to deliver one uppercut after another. Henry's misshapen face swung back and forth like a speed bag but was tough enough to withstand her assault.

And then, like a gift from above, a bullet whipped through the air to tear off a chunk of Henry's scalp. Backing up a few steps, Paige heard the sirens in the distance. She couldn't see the flashing lights yet, which meant she still had a bit of time before adding the police to her laundry list of problems.

Henry's torso swelled, and his ribs creaked outward to accommodate the swelling. He reared up and swung his loosely attached head to holler at Walter's section of the park. When he started to turn toward Paige, she hopped sideways and then jumped forward with her left arm extended. The straight point of her left weapon dug into Henry's skin, glanced off one rib, and tore a deep scratch into his side, which she used as a target for the sickle in her right hand. Her aim was true and the curved blade sank in almost a quarter of an inch.

Activity from the streets behind the parking structure was intensifying. Sirens blared, voices shouted over loudspeakers, and shots were fired.

Henry let out a pathetic whimper, took one limping

step forward and then was hit in the side by another high-powered rifle round. That shot was followed by another, which dropped him to one knee. Paige circled around so she could get a look at Henry's side without being in the line of fire. One more bullet whipped through the air and landed with a distinctive hiss as the round's coating reacted with Henry's Nymar-infested blood.

Paige took one of the syringes from her jacket pocket, popped off the cap and rushed toward Henry to give him the injection. When she slammed the syringe down on the wound, she felt the needle snap like brittle straw against him.

"All right," she said as Henry snarled at the incoming sniper rounds. "Looks like I need to hit a softer spot."

She dropped her left weapon back into its holster on her boot and focused her attention on the weapon in her right hand. Once the point of that stake was down to something close to a needle, she cocked it back, reached under her jacket at the small of her back, and twisted her body around in a tight circle. The lightning-fast movement snapped her arms around like whips. When her left hand emerged from beneath her jacket, it was wrapped around the handle of the Blood Blade. Her momentum allowed her to slice through the skin along Henry's ribs and cut through several layers of hardened muscle. She drove her right arm forward to send the finely honed point of her stake directly into the deep wound she'd just made. Henry was already starting to heal, but Paige was just fast enough to drive the stake into the wound and bury it several inches between his ribs. From there, she closed her eyes and willed the impaled end of the weapon to split apart into three separate sections.

When Henry arched his back and let out a bellowing cry, Paige knew the weapon was doing its job. She could feel the petrified wood changing shape as if it was an extension of her own arm. While that should have been enough to bring Henry down, it was only adding fuel to his fire. She cocked her left arm back so she could do even more damage with the charmed blade. Before she could land the blow, however, the back of Henry's fist caught her in the shoulder with enough power to knock her loose and pull the stake free. Because the stake had blossomed inside of him, however, it snagged muscle, tore flesh, and even chipped a few ribs on its way out.

For a moment Henry was dazed. He looked down at a hole in his side that was big enough to expose half his rib cage. A living flood of Nymar spore was spilling out of him. At least four of the slimy black things slipped out of his body, each one sending out gelatinous tendrils to grab hold of whatever they could to pull themselves back inside.

Paige grinned and retrieved the final syringe from her pocket. Closing her fist around the plastic tube, she buried the needle directly into one of the spores and jammed her thumb down on the plunger. The antidote was quickly absorbed by the Nymar spore, eating it from within and exploding outward to disperse the rest of the antidote among the remaining spores within Henry's torso. One by one the spores sizzled and popped, until Henry's entire system was exposed to the antidote.

For the next few seconds, Henry clawed at the ground and scraped at it with his feet. His mouth opened but he clamped it shut again and winced as the deadly process continued inside of him. When he lost the strength to hold himself up, he dropped to his belly and curled up so the hole in his side was facing the sky. The bulbous growths under his flesh had flattened to give his body a more familiar shape. And when the last Nymar within him was dead, the hole in Henry's side began closing up. Already the blood flowing from him was losing its black, oily tint.

"Can you hear me, Paige?" It was the voice again. Now that she didn't have an insane monster trying to rip her heart out, she could understand it a little better.

Touching her earpiece, she replied, "Yeah, Walter. We've got some cops headed our way."

"I know. Misonyk's dead, so get over here and we should be able to get out before things get too hot."

"Great. Have you noticed what's happening to Henry?"

After a slight pause, Walter said, "Looks like you got him. Great!"

Paige shook her head and took a tentative step toward Henry. Although some of the Nymar were still near the garage, they backed away as well. In a few more seconds they turned and bolted from the area like dogs that reflexively knew when it was time to cut and run. "It looks like Cole was right," she whispered. "Henry is a Full Blood. Now that the Nymar's out of him, that's all that's left."

"Then kill him!" Walter shouted. "Do your Skinner thing and finish him off. Whoever or whatever the cops are shooting at, they'll be at the garage in—"

"I realize what's happening, Walter! But there's something else—" Suddenly, a burning pain scorched Paige's palm. She pulled her hand away from the earpiece as if she'd accidentally touched an open flame. The Nymar in the vicinity had made the scars from her weapons itch as if there were ants crawling beneath her skin. Henry's presence had caused a reaction that was distinctive but muddled. This, however, was something much more powerful. It was also something that she'd only rarely felt before.

"Paige?" Walter said in a cautious whisper through her earpiece. "Look at the roof of the garage."

When she looked up, Paige spotted a hulking form crouched on the edge of the roof. It glared down at her with brilliant, glittering eyes and let out a low growl that rolled like thunder through the cold night air.

Chapter 26

"A Full Blood?" Cole said. "I thought those things stuck to the woods!"

Walter had his scope trained on the massive shape that had appeared at the edge of the garage roof. Its fur was so black that it was difficult for him to make out an exact shape, but the brilliant eyes and long, massive fangs were more than enough to stand out from the shadows. As it leaned forward to part its lips in a warning snarl, the creature's shape became even more distinctive against the somewhat lighter background of the cement roof. Its head and movements were those of a giant wolf, but its upper body had the mass of a grizzly bear.

"It's a Full Blood, all right," Walter said. "A big one too. That's probably what scared away the rest of those Nymar."

"Shouldn't you shoot it or something?"

"My ammunition is treated for use against Nymar. I'd only piss it off."

"Do you have any Full Blood rounds?" Cole asked hopefully.

"There are no Full Blood rounds."

"Aw, shit."

"Yes," Walter replied calmly. "I'd have to agree." He tapped his earpiece and said, "You see it, Paige?"

"I see it," she replied in a harsh whisper. "The Nymar saw it, and soon a whole lot of cops will see it too."

"How's your armor?" Walter asked.

Paige felt the shredded remains of her vest. Beneath the tattered outer layers, there were a few strands of fur attached to uneven ribbons of werewolf hide. "Just enough left to get me in trouble," she said while removing the vest and tossing it, with the hope that the Full Blood didn't already know she'd worn the skin of its distant brethren.

The Full Blood gripped the edge of the roof with thick, yellowed claws. Though it was hardly moving, it held on with more than enough strength to send pieces of broken cement clattering to the ground below. It slowly shifted its head to take in the sights with eyes that sparkled like two out of the millions of stars hanging motionless above it. Large pointed ears pricked up at the sound of approaching sirens.

From the corner of her eyes, Paige could see the flashing blue and red lights of police cars that rounded a corner and sped toward the parking structure. She didn't see the solitary man that had been running ahead of the cars until his feet clapped against the cement path leading to the garage's entrance. It was Edward, the third of Misonyk's bodyguards. Unlike the previous times Paige or Cole had seen him, he now had his coat open to reveal several pistols and a few MAC-10s hanging from large rigs beneath both arms. Edward also had a small machine pistol in each hand and a wild look in his eyes as he quickly soaked up the carnage in front of the garage.

She didn't need to read minds to know the gun-toting bodyguard wasn't happy with what he saw. As soon as he spotted the dead Nymar strewn on the ground, Edward raised both guns to extract some payback. The fact that Paige was standing in the middle of all those bodies sparked a bit of fire in his eyes, but the sight of the Full Blood snarling at him from on high was enough to push him right over the edge.

Edward bared his teeth as all three sets of fangs extended from his jaws. He fired both guns in his hands and leapt for the parking structure's second floor.

Letting out a quick, panting breath, the werewolf streaked along the top of the garage and practically flew off the side so he could collide with the Nymar in midair. The Full Blood hit the bodyguard in the chest with both front paws and sent

Edward to the ground with a resounding thump. Even as the bodyguard's spine snapped against the pavement, he emptied both of his weapons into the Full Blood's chest. Teeth the size of dagger blades sunk into the Nymar's shoulder, allowing the Full Blood to toss the bodyguard into the air with a snap of its head. The creature reared up on its hind legs while its body shifted to accommodate the new stance. Canine limbs became longer and more human, bringing him up to well over seven feet tall. Its front legs extended into massive arms just in time to swat the airborne bodyguard squarely in the chest. Edward flew away from the parking structure to land in the street within a few yards of the approaching police cars.

Tires screeched against the pavement. Police shouted to each other. A few cars nearly ran into Edward, who had yet to move after his rough landing. All the while, the Full Blood watched with the closest thing to a smile that his wide, tooth-filled mouth could manage. Turning to face the parking structure, he leaned forward and let out a roar that was filled with more than enough fury to scatter the few lingering Nymar in all directions.

Paige stood her ground and tightened her grip on her weapons, knowing all too well that trying to run from a Full Blood would do her as much good as flapping her arms after stepping off the side of a cliff.

The werewolf stared at her as strings of saliva dripped from fangs that had retracted but were still longer than her fingers. Even crouched over far enough to scrape his knuckles against the ground, it was several feet taller than her. Its long ears came up a bit as sections of its coal-black fur bristled from a passing breeze. Heavy, bellowing breaths quickened into a dog's panting as the Full Blood twitched to look at a single figure that ran toward the garage instead of away from it.

Cole rushed to Paige's side, brandishing his weapon in both hands. The closer he got to her and the Full Blood, the more he cringed at the fiery sensation that shot through the wounds where the weapon's thorns had pierced his skin. "Jesus," he muttered. When he realized what he was facing, his mind lost the ability to form any other word. "Jesus!" he said more sharply.

"O Holy Night," The Full Blood mused in a voice that rumbled within its massive frame like thunder rolling over an empty prairie.

While Cole was dealing with the fact that the creature in front of him had just spoken, Paige leaned toward him and asked, "Is that the one that killed Gerald?"

"No," Cole replied with a shake of his head. "That one was brown and . . . hell, I don't even know if that helps."

"It does," Paige replied.

About a hundred yards to the north, where the park stopped and the rest of the town resumed, police cars were gathered around the Nymar that had been batted into the street. Officers went through the motions of stripping away Edward's guns while trying to figure out how the hell he'd gotten there. The bodyguard must have had a spark of life in him, because he began to put up a fight before more gunshots crackled through the air.

The Full Blood's eyes shifted in their sockets toward the commotion, but he didn't seem overly concerned by it. The mass of its frame settled in on itself and his entire body shifted into a more compact form. Once he'd taken a shape that was just over six feet tall and roughly that of a man, he focused all of his attention upon Paige and Cole. His heavily muscled body was still covered in black fur, but his snout had gotten a bit shorter and was marked with a spot of white close to his nose. With his ears pulled in tight against his scalp, the creature's face had a definite canine quality, but its eyes were those of a man.

Slowly reaching for her earpiece, Paige said, "Hold your fire, Walter."

The Full Blood nodded. "Smart call," it said in a voice that rumbled less, but still turned Cole's blood into ice water. "You did well tonight. Killing Misonyk and all these leeches proves your hearts are in the right place."

"There's more Nymar where these came from," Paige said. "They'll be out looking for all of us after a night like this."

"Spare me," the Full Blood grunted. Crouching down to

Henry, he said, "Through this one, Misonyk has been shouting his thoughts to us for months. We have always known the Nymar were weak, diseased, and pathetic. Now we also know they are fractured, confused, and just dangerous enough to warrant extermination. Perhaps the humans are as well."

"Skinners have always played their cards for everyone to see," Paige said. "You know we'll honor the old arrangement if everyone sticks to the old deals."

"There was no arrangement!" the Full Blood roared. Hearing him bellow made Cole and Paige grip their weapons tight enough for the blood to drip from their hands. The Full Blood sniffed the blood on the air and then leaned forward so he was sure to be heard over the sound of the approaching cops. "There were no deals," he said in a more reasonable voice. "Since you Skinners have done my work for me this night, we've decided to give you this warning. You cannot win a true fight with my kind, no matter how many Skinners you pool together or how many Blood Blades you dig up. As for the rest of the humans, they won't know what they're facing until they've already fallen.

"We will no longer be hunted by lesser animals," the Full Blood declared as he lifted Henry up to set him carefully upon his feet. Although the wound was still gaping open in Henry's side, it was already smaller than it had been a few moments ago. The Full Blood with the charcoal fur stepped in front of Henry, making it known that Paige or Cole would have to go through him if they wanted to finish what Brad's charmed blade had started.

"Henry comes with me and will tell us everything he's learned," the Full Blood said. "No longer will we step back and kindly let you infest our territories. We will reclaim all of our lands, even if that means cleaning out all of your cities. As a courtesy, I give you this warning to spread amongst your kind: when we arrive, you'd be wise to clear our path and find new lands to sully."

With that, the Full Blood's body exploded outward into a mass of muscled flesh and a full coat of thick black fur. Massive paws clawed at the ground and a large, wet nose stole Paige's and Cole's scent in much the same way as the creature Cole had met so many nights ago in the middle of a stark, Canadian nowhere. When the Full Blood bared its fangs, it let out a roar that melted into a howl as the creature lifted its face to the sky. Henry loped away, and the other Full Blood dashed ahead of him to blaze a trail that quickly took both werewolves out of Cole's sight.

Walter drove his van toward the parking garage. He hadn't even come to a complete stop before leaning out and saying, "We've got to get out of here. Those cops are ready for war. If this town has a SWAT team, they're probably on the way too."

Cole held onto his weapon, feeling very much like a child wielding a plastic bat. Paige cursed under her breath and jumped into the van. Once Cole was inside, she slammed the door and hung on as Walter burned through a few layers of tire rubber in his haste to get back to where the used Cavalier was parked. Paige kept quiet as Cole looked her over. The body armor was gone, but it had protected her from everything other than a whole lot of bumps and scratches.

The moment they got back to the car, Cole slid in behind the wheel and Paige dropped into the passenger seat. She had injected herself with some of the Nymar antidote before Cole even hit the gas. "You all right?" he asked as he followed Walter's van toward the highway.

She nodded.

"I don't feel that burning in my hands anymore. Does that mean those Full Bloods are gone?"

Paige chuckled. "That just means they're at least sixty or seventy yards away. Of course, they could also be halfway to Chicago by now."

Once the park was behind them, Cole could see several sets of flashing lights clustered near the area where all the bodies had been left behind. There were plenty of cops on the street as well, but they were more concerned with the newly discovered carnage to worry about chasing down every set of taillights moving through the opposite end of town. Walter navigated the Janesville streets and led the way onto southbound I–90. After they'd made it to the open road, Paige's phone rang. She flipped it open and held it up so they could both listen through the speaker.

"You all right, Paige?" Walter asked.

"I'll be sore for a year or two, but I'll live."

"Good to hear. The police band is jumping," Walter announced. "They're saying armed men with matching black tattoos were posted on the streets to shoot at anyone who came too close to the park."

"Misonyk's idea of crowd control," Paige said in a weary voice. "I'm glad you guys killed that asshole. Are the cops looking for us or our vehicles?"

"Not from what I've been hearing. From the sound of it, they're so busy with the mess we left them that we should be able to get out of here without a problem. I know a good route to Chicago using back roads that should get us there in plenty of time for a late night snack."

"Good. That means we can find a nice spot to stop and do some digging. There's a Half Breed I've got to bury."

"What? We made it out of there fairly easily, but we don't need to push our luck!" Walter snapped.

"I'd be dead if it wasn't for that Half Breed," Paige replied with even more of an edge in her voice. "The least we can do is put it to rest. You can go on without us if you want."

After a brief pause, Walter said, "The job'll go quicker if more of us are digging, but let's at least wait until we're farther away from here."

"Agreed." With that, Paige snapped the phone shut and smiled. "I knew he'd come around."

But Cole didn't have it in him to smile. Every inch of his body hurt. His hands were torn open. Another monster had his scent. Come to think of it, he didn't think he'd be able to smile for the rest of his life. Then Paige leaned over and placed her mouth so close to his ear that he could feel the warmth of her breath as she spoke.

"You did great, Cole," she told him. "I owe you, big-time."

And then, somehow, he smiled.

Epilogue

The bar was a bright, popular place on Michigan Avenue that was filled with televisions, video trivia games, and, on Tuesdays and Thursdays, karaoke machines. The beer came from microbreweries that spiked perfectly good bottles with flavors like pumpkin spice and strawberry. It was crowded almost any time after business hours, which made it the perfect place to speak without truly being heard.

One of the few televisions bolted to the walls that wasn't showing a sporting event of some kind displayed the headline that had been splashed across TVs and newspapers for the last few days: MASSACRE IN JANESVILLE. Cole didn't need to hear what the newscaster was saying. It was probably the same as what had been printed in the papers and displayed on the Internet, which was just a longer version of the report Walter had given on their way out of Janesville: police had stumbled across a bunch of armed men that had similar black marks on their necks and wrists. Shots were fired. A chase ensued and a whole lot of bodies were found near an old parking garage in Palmer Park.

"I got a message from Prophet," Paige said as she sipped her Amber Winter Brew.

Cole chuckled and swallowed some of the Jack's Pumpkin Ale he'd been talked into ordering. As he lifted the bottle to his mouth, he couldn't help but notice the light dusting of scar tissue upon his palm. The wounds had healed quickly, but still itched whenever he drove through certain parts of town. "Another dream?" he asked.

"Just a message." Paige held up her cell phone to show him the glowing, three-word text message: TOLD YOU SO.

"Not one for grace in victory, is he?"

Paige shook her head and put her phone away. "Who would expect that from a guy who lives in strip bars? Have you heard the latest about Janesville?"

"No. Is there anything new?"

"The police are blaming it all on the poor bastard who was knocked out of that park like a foul ball. He was the one carrying the most guns, so they figure he was the one who planned the whole thing and then 'killed himself by running into traffic.'" She framed the last part in finger quotes. "Oh, and those are sprouting up too."

Glancing at the television Paige was looking at, Cole saw shaky footage of the dried husks that were the remains of dead Nymar, bordered by the words, CULT SUSPECTED IN JANESVILLE SLAYINGS.

He couldn't help but flinch when he saw a police cruiser drive down the street outside the bar's front window. Lowering his voice, he asked, "Shouldn't we be—"

"What?" Paige asked in a booming voice that completely destroyed the privacy Cole had been trying to maintain.

"Shouldn't we be worried?" Cole shouted over the noise in the bar.

She shrugged and took another sip of beer. "If the cops can find us when we're doing good enough to keep away from Nymar and Full Bloods and everything else out there," she said as she raised her glass, "then here's to the cops."

Seeing no reason to argue with that point, he said, "So, I'm treating myself to a few nights in the Fairmont with my cut of that bounty money. Care to join me?"

"You'd better hit a bank first," Paige replied. "That's a real fancy hotel, and I get the feeling Ace and Stephanie will try to steal that money back even before Prophet comes along to collect his share."

"You said you owe me. I was thinking . . . maybe we could continue what we started when you showed me how to polish my stick."

Paige finished her beer and got up from the little round table that was pressed up against a wall covered with framed pictures of celebrities who'd supposedly visited the bar. She slipped her hand beneath Cole's chin, kissed him on the cheek and said, "We could have both died that night. The blood was racing. Don't get yourself all worked up." A cute yet naughty smile drifted onto her face as she parted her lips to say something else. Before she could let any of those words fly, however, she straightened up and looked at another one of the televisions.

The screen was filled with a commercial for a local interest segment hosted by a boyish news anchor in a dark suit. Although his voice was lost amid all the chatter and music in the bar, the hazy picture on the screen behind him was impossible to miss. Two animals that could easily be mistaken for two large dogs were running down an alley The black dog had bright, glittering eyes, and the tan dog held its head down at an awkward angle so it lolled back and forth as he ran. The tagline beneath the video read: WOLVES IN THE WINDY CITY?

Shrugging, Paige said, "I guess I'll have to take a pass on tonight, Cole. There's a lot to do. Call me tomorrow and get plenty of rest. You're going to need it."

He would have liked to think she was referring to a certain kind of strenuous activity that would put smiles on both their faces, but he knew she was probably alluding to another round of training. After using some of her cut of Ace and Steph's money to pay the tab, Paige waved to him and left. No matter what he'd been through or what kind of hell was starting to trickle down upon the world, he still took the time to admire the motion of her rounded hips and firm backside as she walked away.

Cheap thrills. That was the secret to a happy life, after all.

Rather than go to his hotel right away after finishing his beer, Cole stopped at a liquor store so he could get some snacks and check on the lottery ticket he'd bought. Things were looking up. A fresh batch of beef jerky had just been put on the shelves, and a few of Prophet's numbers hit.

It was the easiest $23.75 he had ever made.

Don't miss
Skinners, Book Two

HOWLING LEGION

Available 2009

Cole had never felt so scared and so stupid at the same time. The concoction that Cole had put together at the hotel had been split into three different containers, all of which were basically mustard or ketchup squeeze bottles. Each held a mixture that ranged from weak to strong on whatever scale was used to measure bait for Half Breeds. Paige drove him around to the spots where they'd already found werewolf dens and Cole hopped out to squirt some of the gunk onto a sign or post where it could get the most air. The most diluted stuff had the consistency of jelly and hardened into a crust in a matter of seconds.

Having started at the tail end of rush hour, Paige and Cole managed to get from point to point without getting snarled up in too much Kansas City traffic. Every so often, Cole would dash from the car, look around for cops or the occasional concerned citizen and then deface a public spot with foul smelling pheromone paste. He got plenty of surprised looks and a few harsh words from people who saw him at work, but nothing bad enough to slow their progress. As they worked their way east, he switched to the next potent mixture. That stuff took some getting used to, but Cole was at least getting some fresh air every few minutes. When the thicker, pastier mixture splattered against whatever he'd chosen as his target and hardened into a brown shell, he felt as if he was defacing the air along with whatever property had caught his eye.

The stronger stuff didn't go unnoticed. Per his instructions, Cole had squirted the stuff up high and it hardened into a permanent fixture before Paige drove him away. People gathered to look up at a lot of those spots but were driven away by the smell before they figured out a way to clean it off. Just to be safe, Paige and Cole hit several spots along the way to Highway 24 over the next hour or two.

Outside of the city's limits, Cole switched to the heavy duty stuff. The instant he removed the stopper of the last squirt bottle, the car was filled with a sweaty, bitter odor that stuck to the back of his throat like the nauseating jelly from the other two bottles had stuck to any available surface around the city.

"I kind of feel bad about this," Cole said after hanging his head out the window. "KC seems like a pretty nice place and we're spraying this crap all over it."

"The Half Breeds will be coming out . . ." She paused to stretch her neck toward the windshield and get a look at the sky. The moon was full enough to be seen through the fading sunlight. "Should be any time now. If my timeline is correct, we lucked out."

"How do you figure?"

"I think Officer Stanze killed one of the first Half Breeds made around here."

"You mean the one in the cooler?" Cole asked. "Or, the bits that are in that cooler?"

"Yep. It's got the muscle that would have grown onto a Half Breed after a week or two and that's about how long ago that Bob Rothbard guy was declared missing after his car was found along I–70. Plus, the tattoo I showed you is a fraternity symbol. According to the fliers and some other missing person reports I dug up on the net, it's the same fraternity that 'ol Bob had belonged to."

"I suppose it could be him."

"Let's hope it is. That means the other ones we found shouldn't be hungry enough to come out until it's good and dark. They'll also be more willing to follow the scent we've left for them. The younger ones are easier to bait. Once they get to be even a few weeks older, they develop their own habits and preferences."

"You're so smart," Cole chided with an exaggerated twang. "And purdy too."

She slammed on the brakes and pulled onto the side of a stretch of rough road that didn't look to be in the best part of town. "Cut the shit and do your job."

Cole opened his door and made a mad dash to a light pole before getting run over by a convoy of pickup trucks and SUVs. For a second, he was worried that the stuff in his squeeze bottle had completely solidified. After rolling the bottle between his hands and removing the top, he worked enough of the gunk out to fling it up high onto the metal pole. It had the consistency of cookie dough, but smelled as far from that heavenly of all substances as another substance could get. It plopped against the steel, slid down less than an inch and turned into a rust-colored lump.

Slamming his door shut after hopping into the car, Cole tried not to look at the old man yelling at him from the other side of the street. "I just thought of something. Are we coming back to clean this stuff off?"

"No, why?"

"First of all, it's gross. Second, it'll just keep attracting Half Breeds, won't it?"

"Nah," Paige replied. "It stops smelling in about twelve hours. By tomorrow, it'll have dried up and blown away like any other glob of snot."

Cole held the bottle up next to his face. "Eco friendly and full of fiber. Operators standing by."

Just as Paige allowed herself to let her shoulders down from where they'd been hunched around her ears, her phone rang. She dug it out of her pocket, looked at the screen and then flipped it open. "Yeah? How far away is he?" She listened for a second and furrowed her brow. "What's his name? Never heard of him."

"Who is it?" Cole asked.

Paige looked over and mouthed the word, "MEG". Then, she snapped into the phone, "I don't care. I've never heard of him, so I don't want to work with him. Especially not right now."

Sensing the fast approach of a hang-up, Cole asked, "What's going on?"

"Here, talk to Cole. I'm driving." With that, Paige slapped the phone against Cole's chest.

He took it from her and said, "Hello?"

"I knew I should've just called you in the first place," a familiar voice said frantically.

"What's going on, Stu?"

"I got a call from another . . . well . . . another one of you guys. He says he's close to your position and that he can help."

"Who is he?"

"Nathan Jewel something. I don't know how the last name is spelled, but the first name is Nathan. There aren't exactly a ton of you guys on our list, so I thought you might have heard of him."

"Did he have an ID number?" Cole asked.

"Sure, he did. We haven't heard from him in a long time and thought he was . . ." Stopping himself there, Stu said, "We just didn't think we were gonna hear from him. He says he's in the area and can lend a hand with the KC problem. I figured you could use all the help you could get."

Cole felt the need to make an executive decision. Since Paige had handed him the phone, he thought maybe she was putting that decision into his hands. Just to be sure, he looked over to Paige and asked, "Why don't you want any help from this guy?"

"I don't know him," she replied simply. "When things get moving and the fur starts to fly, you need to know which way your partner is going to move. We start bumping into each other or make one dumb mistake and none of us come back."

"So what do you want me to say to Stu?"

Paige pulled in a deep breath and let it out with a hiss. Having just turned onto a dumpy two-lane road headed north, she pulled over next to a gas station that looked like it had nothing but dust in the cashier's booth and rainwater in the pumps. "Give me the phone," she said. After Cole handed it over, she told him, "Now slap some bait on the side of that building. Use a lot. We want the scent to carry."

"The scent from this crap could carry this whole freaking car into Kansas."

"Just go."

Having already squeezed some of the disgusting paste to the top of the bottle, Cole stepped outside, flung the stuff toward the roof and heard the slap of the clump hitting the wall. Practice makes perfect. Paige barely waited for his butt to hit the seat before pulling away and heading north.

"What did this guy tell you?" she asked.

Before Cole could fumble through an answer to that question, Stu's voice came through the speaker of the phone in her hand. "He just called and gave his ID number, said he was in KC and wanted me to put him in touch with you two."

"Did he mention us by name?"

"No," Stu replied. "He said he'd never met you but that he knew two other Skinners were in KC."

Cole grinned at the sound of that. After all the beatings he'd taken during his training so far, it was nice to hear something so official applied to him.

The more Stu spoke, the more flustered he sounded. "He asked for a number to get in touch with you guys, but I didn't give him one. He insisted on speaking to you, but I told him no. I swear I didn't tell him anything!"

"Ok, that's great. Way to hold up under questioning."

Stu let out a sigh, obviously missing the sarcastic tone in Paige's voice. "Good. I didn't want to piss you off."

"Do you have a number to reach Nathan Jewel or who-ever?" Cole asked.

"Yes, but it's a land line so he may or not be there. He insisted on calling me back."

When he looked over to Paige, all Cole got for his trouble was a stern glare and a few shakes of her head. "Give me the number," he said.

Stu rattled off a phone number, which Cole tapped into his

own phone's memory. Then, Stu asked, "What should I tell him when he calls back?"

"Tell him to either wait by his phone wherever he is," Paige said, "or he can call back some other time. Right now, we're busy." With that, she picked up the phone and slapped it shut. Although she looked like she was about to toss the phone out the window, she stuck it into her pocket instead.

"If that guy's another Skinner, whether he's new or not, he can help," Cole pointed out. "Don't you think we could use some more backup for something like this?"

"I've done jobs like this by myself. You're all the backup I need."

"But we know there's at least one Full Blood around here. If Henry's still nearby, that makes two. I know I've been kicking ass in our sparring matches, but I don't think we're each ready to take one of those things."

Paige glanced back and forth between Cole and the road. It was getting close to eight o'clock, which meant there wasn't a lot of traffic for her to contend with on the back roads she was taking. There also weren't a lot of cops along that route, which was a blessing because she'd been making up for time spent painting the town by introducing the gas pedal to the floor of the Cav. "We need to clear out as many of these Half Breeds as we can tonight," she said. "The damage they've already done only amounts to a dozen or so deaths. Maybe a little more, maybe a little less. As the rest of those things get strong enough to come out of their dens and hunt, they'll shred through entire neighborhoods before they get put down. Plus, there's the panic that will cause. Enough people are already carrying guns around here. What's going to happen once they have a reason to twitch at a strange shadow?"

As much as he hated to admit it, Cole said, "That's true. I just thought Skinners would work together more."

"We can, but this guy could be a crank caller. He could also be some asshole who'd just get one or both of us killed. Once we take care of the Half Breeds that are strong enough to come to us tonight, we'll see who this Nathan guy is. If it makes you feel any better, I've never seen Full Bloods and Half Breeds fight together. Half Breeds are too wild to follow a leader, so that should be all we get."

Cole let out some of the breath he'd been holding and looked out the window. The houses, gas stations and fast food restaurants that had dotted the road so far had given way to open spaces and low hills that stretched out for miles under a blanket of grass that had been scorched throughout the summer. "So, you've been able to survive a night like this on your own?"

"Yep," Paige said with a nod.

"You baited a bunch of Half Breeds and wiped them all out?"

"Sure did."

"How many were there?"

She crinkled her forehead and twisted her mouth into a thoughtful, crooked line before replying, "Three."

Cole felt as if someone had found the release valve in his chest. "You think that's all that'll be coming?"

"Oh no," Paige laughed. "Considering all those dens we found, there'll be a lot more than that. And with all the bait we put out, we may even attract some from the neighboring county."

Cole's mouth hung open, but he forced it shut before he asked another question. Any more encouragement from Paige and he might just throw up.

The nature preserve outside of Kansas City was a strip of open land about two miles long. There were a few campers set up here and there, but Paige drove until she spotted a place that suited her needs. It was flat, away from the road and had a minimum of trees on the side that faced the city.

A pair of campers were set up a bit too close for comfort and Cole wondered what Paige would do about them. Instead of any fast talking or threats, she took the easy route and peeled off enough money to pay for hotels all around plus a little more to speed them on their way. It was a hot enough night that the campers gladly took the bribe and agreed to eat their s'mores under the stars some other night.

As the campers were packing up, Paige scooped out some

spots in the dirt to set up a little camp of her own. She removed a few things from her trunk and buried them under a shallow layer of dirt. "Watch out for these spots here," she told him.

Sitting hunched over a metal bowl and mixing up another batch of the bait using a powdered mixture that didn't quite smell as bad as the fresh stuff they'd spread all over town, Cole looked up and asked, "Why?"

"Bear traps. Hopefully, we can hobble a few of the Half Breeds before they get close to us."

"Can you mark them with little flags or sticks or something?"

"Can't you remember three spots to avoid?"

"I've got a lot on my mind here," Cole snapped. "Just put some damn sticks in the ground. It's not like some wild animals are going to scope the place out and sidestep the suspicious areas."

Paige was already driving twigs into the spots by the time Cole stopped grousing. He used one of the campfires that had just been abandoned to heat the mixture to create a wispy cloud of putrid steam.

After that, the only thing remaining was for them to gather up all the ammunition, divvy up as much as their pockets could hold and plant the rest in strategic locations that were marked with bigger sticks. Cole took the shotgun and Paige took the revolver. Even though he wound up with his preferred weapon for most of the games he'd created, Cole wasn't feeling any better. Not even the metallic clack of the shotgun's pump could light a fire in him.

The sun lingered like an oblivious houseguest before finally dipping out of sight. He and Paige sat just outside of the campfire's glow. Her pistol was tucked away and his shotgun was strapped across his back. The thorns of Cole's weapon pressed against his palm without breaking the skin. In the relatively short amount of time he'd been practicing with the spear, it already felt comforting and familiar. Paige had her knees bent and pulled in close to her chest. One baton was propped against the toe of her boot, and she tossed the other casually in the air to catch it on the end without the thorns.

The fire crackled.

A slow wind blew.

Every so often, a car or truck engine rumbled in the distance.

Cole craned his neck to look at the stars directly over him. "It's nice out here," he said, doing his best to avoid looking at the nearly full moon.

She didn't take her eyes off the urban glow illuminating the sky to the west. Tossing her baton into the air created a subtle whooshing sound as the weapon turned end over end. The varnished wood slapped against her palm and she tossed it up again.

"I never camped much," Cole continued. "It seemed fun, but I didn't want to go through all the trouble. You know . . . bugs. Rain."

"No outlets," Paige added.

"Yeah," Cole said. "That too." He sighed and tried to pick out a few constellations, but was inevitably drawn to the moon. That pale glow led his eyes to the more yellowed glow being sent up by Kansas City. No stars could be seen over the city thanks to all that electric light. The whiff of brewing bait Cole pulled in with his next breath smelled like exhaust and garbage.

"I think we're downwind of that stuff," he said.

Paige slowly shook her head and caught her baton with another loud slap. "That won't matter. Half Breeds aren't dogs. They can smell it just fine no matter which way the wind blows."

"And you think they'll follow it here all the way from the middle of KC?"

Slap. "Yep."

When he thought about the Half Breeds he'd seen, Cole swore the weapon he was supposed to use against them felt a lot lighter than it had a few seconds ago. He swung the pointed end down to draw a few shapes in the dirt near his feet. "What did you want to be when you were a kid?"

"What?"

"You know. When you were growing up? I wanted to be a pilot. Then I wanted to be in the Navy. Then I wanted to be a Navy pilot. When I got to be recruiting age, I realized I'd just watched too many movies and didn't seriously want to go through all of that."

Slap. "This is why I don't like camping. Everyone feels like they need to tell stories. They sell the trip with a lot of promises of peace and quiet, but then they either bring a freaking CD player or they won't stop talking about hopes and dreams."

"All right, then. Let me guess. You wanted to be a short order cook. That's why you live in a restaurant." Cole snapped his fingers and said, "No, wait. A veterinarian! That's why you're so good with animals."

Slap

"Are you even listening to me anymore?"

After another *slap*, Paige said, "I was a veterinarian."

"Seriously?"

"Yep. That was before, though."

"Before," Cole muttered. That word reminded him of days spent at a keyboard when his biggest worry was hitting deadlines for new game concepts or level ideas. His nights might not have been full of parties and wild sex, but he hadn't spent them crouched on a patch of dirt surrounded by bear traps and spare shotgun shells. Suddenly, he started to laugh. "You know what? Maybe this isn't too far off from how it was before. Instead of watching a guy in a game hide somewhere in the dark with boxes of bullets laying around all over the place, I'm actually living it."

Paige tossed her baton one more time and caught it. From there, she stood up and said, "Come here."

Cole went to her and couldn't help but notice how the moonlight caressed the curves of her body as she reached back with one hand to gather her hair and clip it behind her head. The pale glow coming from above worked nicely to make the lines of her neck stand out. Even the crooked shape of her broken nose looked cute when bathed in that light.

"Close your eyes," she whispered.

Cole did as he was told.

"Hear that?"

He listened for a few seconds but couldn't pick up on any sounds that hadn't been there before. Finally, he asked, "Hear what?"

Just as he was losing hope, Cole felt her hand press firmly against his chest. Despite the roughness of her palm and the fact that her fingers felt like iron bars wrapped in a thin glove, Paige's touch felt soothing as she slid her hand along his chest and to his side. Once there, she turned him a bit in one direction and said, "There. Just listen."

The sappy, expectant grin that Cole couldn't hold back froze in place when he heard the rush that flowed beneath the malodorous breeze that carried the campfire smoke. The other sound churned with a power of its own. It wasn't anything close to thunder, but more of a current that was being pumped through a nearby pipe.

After another second or two, Cole could hear panting snarls being forced from several sets of unnaturally powerful lungs.

A few cars honked in the distance as tires screeched against pavement.

Something heavy was knocked over.

By the time he picked up on the snapping of twigs and low hanging branches, Cole could also hear the dry creak of Paige's batons stretching into curved sickle blades. Cole's hands wrapped around the thorny grip of his spear and tightened until the sharp little spikes punched through his palms.

"How many do you think there are?" Cole whispered.

After a pause that was just a little too long, Paige replied, "More than I expected."

"Should we still do this?"

She stood beside him so the side of her foot brushed against his shoe. "Just tear them up as much as you can and don't ever let go of your weapon. Those Half Breeds are hungry and riled up, which means they'll be tripping all over themselves to get to us."

The snarling breaths and scrambling paws rushed toward the last marker in the bait trail the Skinners had put down.

Cole blinked away a bead of sweat, which allowed him to make out the shapes of lean animals racing at him from the surrounding dark. Wide eyes glinted in the moonlight and the panting became intermingled with a series of frenzied barks.

"Paige, I—"

"Save it, Cole. Here they come."